J.G. BALLARD Conversations

NOVELS & COLLECTIONS BY J.G. BALLARD

The Wind from Nowhere 1962
The Drowned World 1962
The Drought 1965
The Crystal World 1966
The Atrocity Exhibition 1970
Crash 1973
Concrete Island 1973
High-Rise 1975
Unlimited Dream Company 1979
Hello America 1981
Empire of the Sun 1984
The Day of Creation 1987
Running Wild 1988
The Kindness of Women 1991
Rushing to Paradise 1994
A User's Guide to the Millennium
  (Nonfiction) 1996
Cocaine Nights 1996
Super-Cannes 2000
The Complete Short Stories 2001
Millennium People 2003

This book dedicated to Catherine
Reuther, RE/Search Assistant
Editor 1-20-57 to 8-2-04, R.I.P.

RE/SEARCH PUBLICATIONS

Editors/Publishers: V. Vale, Marian Wallace
Transcriptions/Proofreading: M.H. Beebe,
  Sandra Derian, Joe Donohoe, Toby Levin,
  Keith Eyrich, Virginia White, M. Ricci
Photographers/Artists: Ana Barrado, SM
  Gray, Charles Gatewood, Tim Chapman
Design: Brian MacKenzie, Seth Robson,
  Marian Wallace, Eric Nordhauser
Lawyers: David S. Kahn, Lizbeth Hasse
Design Advisors: Judy Sitz, Catherine
  Wallace, Scott Alexander, Peter M.
Research Staff: Gary Chong, Marian
  Wilde, Adrienne Cardwell, Alan Coe,
  Mark Pauline, Scott Beale, John Law,
  John Sulak, Christopher Trela (NYC),
  Vermilion Sands, Karlo Pastella, Ted
Interns: Yoshi Yubai, Kiowa Hammons, A.
  Colhoun, Leslie Hodgkins, Anne Kaplan
Founding Benefactors: Allen Ginsberg,
  Lawrence Ferlinghetti, D. & C. Hamby,
  Kathy Acker, Geoff Travis, Betty
  Thomas, Scott Summerville
THANKS TO ALL J.G. BALLARD INTERNET
LISTEES who helped! Also Valerie Kunz
and Robert Collison.
Inside cover photos (pp. 1 & 360) and
  back cover photo: Ana Barrado
Cover design: Brian MacKenzie & Marian
  Wallace
Cover photo ©2005 Ana Barrado with
  Planet Venus color photos courtesy
  NSSDC/NASA
Photographs © Individual photographers

ISBN: 1-889307-13-0 (paperback)

© 2005 RE/Search Publications
RE/Search Publications 20 Romolo #B San Francisco CA 94133
TEL (415) 362-1465
www.researchpubs.com   email: info@researchpubs.com
Distributed by Publishers Group West TEL (510) 528-1444
Printed in China by Prolong Press, Limited

2   4   6   8   10   9   7   5   3   1

TABLE OF CONTENTS

A View from a Cab

AS a boy, J.G. Ballard saw the light of an atomic blast over Japan from the Japanese World War II prison camp at Lunghua, China. During his three-year internment, death and violence became almost banal. He realized that the future existence of the human race had become purely arbitrary. In his world view the Age of Reason, that period which began with Galileo and Copernicus, had ended with Hitler. Early on, Ballard's goal became "picturing the psychology of the future."

I drive a taxicab in San Francisco for a living and yes, it can get pretty crazy. Every night at work, I see everything this historically-experimental city has to offer: violent youth gangs fighting for control

Photo of Joe Donohoe: Marian Wallace

of drug blocks, police actions, manic street preachers, weird performances of every stripe. I've observed a range of genders—not just "straight" and "gay." I saw a bumper sticker declaring, "In case of Rapture, this car is yours!" referring to the fundamentalist belief that when the world ends, all Christians will be teleported to heaven. Another sticker read: "We asked God why is there so much violence in our schools and God said, 'You don't allow me in your schools.' " Hanging from the rearview mirror was a Pagan Native-American dream-catcher that ostensibly traps evil spirits. Perhaps the driver didn't realize this dream-catcher might function as a Rapture-preventative, although if anyone had enlightened him, he'd probably burn it, the way kids in Christian high schools burn Heavy Metal records.

If the world's turning psychopathic, J.G. Ballard is its forensic pathologist. For over forty years, in novels ranging from *The Drowned World* to *Millennium People,* he has predicted a world whose sexuality, human relations, economy, communications and technology are going haywire. To truthfully describe madness, one must be sane. It takes a doctor to diagnose a pathological body, and J.G. Ballard trained as a physician/psychoanalyst before becoming a full-time, speculative-fiction writer.

My job makes me disconcertingly aware of how accurate Ballard's vision has become. In my taxicab I've had passengers go into drug-induced breakdowns, get into highly emotional arguments with one another, and even pull an icepick on me. One night an employee of a dye factory in a Bay Area suburb jumped out of my cab and ran down Market Street barking like a dog. His companion explained that under the influence of alcohol his friend, although normally a Christian, occasionally metamorphosed into a Pagan Finnish god. At the end of some nights, I feel like I've lived a quarter of a lifetime. My head will be feverish with the mad cinematic spectacle that J.G. Ballard perceives as having replaced "reality." Ballard has described the relentlessly expanding colonization of daily life by psychopathology, and the occupation of cab driver allows one to directly experience this. And yes, things seem to be getting worse.

After the United States' invasion of Iraq, Ballard declared that "reason has failed." The scientific project to understand the universe in lucid terms is rapidly being replaced by irrational, recidivist "beliefs" that in the past have led to disastrous results. Thus there is a President of the United States who has told the journalist Bob Woodward that Jesus Christ told him to declare pre-emptive war on Saddam Hussein. *CNN* tells Americans that countries believing in the literal existence of "Hell" do better economically. Some Islamics believe that "God" has told them to kill Americans. Are the lunatics taking over the asylum?

More than any other living writer, Ballard has exposed the toxic fantasies and assumptions which have replaced direct, unmediated perception and judgment. We now live in a Ballardian world, whether most people realize it or not. And now our most prophetic (and poetic) pathologist may also be our most trustworthy survival guide, always urging us to reject authoritarianism, trust our obsessions, and exalt our imagination: "Today, nothing is real and nothing is unreal. Nothing is true; nothing is untrue. A person's obsessions are as close to reality as you can get." How to cope? "The most prudent and effective method of dealing with the world around us is to assume that it is a complete fiction." Yet, "Often, behind the most trivial things, lie enormous mysteries." Ballard's definition of happiness? "To find yourself and be who you are. I believe in the power of the imagination to remake the world, to release the truth within us, to hold back the night . . ."

—Joe Donohoe, San Francisco taxicab driver, badge #51374

This volume presents all the previously untranscribed recordings made by V. Vale of J.G. Ballard in conversation from 1983 to the present. There is by necessity some repetitiveness, but the discerning reader may delight in the variety of phrasing revealed, much as a jazz aficionado prizes the three consecutive "takes" of "Night in Tunisia" on the classic *Diz 'n' Bird* LP, featuring Charlie Parker and Dizzy Gillespie. Ballard never repeats himself exactly, and neither should we—a true conversationalist is a constant improviser. In this book you are *there* as Ballard illuminates, with verve and imagination, the human condition.

—V. Vale, founder of RE/Search in San Francisco, 1977

J.G. Ballard Conversations

Photo: Ana Barrado

his head up out of the nearest ditch is going to get it shot off.
That way they're *safe*. But it may be a *passing phase . . .*

♦ *V: I don't think so. It's rather optimistic of you to put it that way—*

♦ **JGB:** I don't actually *think* that. **I think things are going to get worse**, actually, from our point of view. **I think a crisis will arise that will seed the neo-con mentality**, and what at present seems a rather strange aberration on the part of America's ruling elite, will come to seem completely acceptable in a surprisingly short space of time . . .

♦ *V: I completely agree. There was an old woman in line at the Post Office recently who said, "I don't mind if the government finds out everything I do and reads my email and correspondence, if it makes us safer, because I haven't done anything." And I said to her, "The thing is, there's immense potential for error. There have already been millions of identity thefts. And you just don't hear the stories of people who were mistaken for somebody else and thrown in jail—they aren't reported."*

♦ **JGB:** Yes. The accounts of errors by this "New American Security State" are rather unsettling. I was reading today a report in the newspaper that American Universities are slightly feeling the pinch because foreign students who provide quite a lucrative source of income are no longer finding it easy to get into the U.S., particularly if you come from a Third World country or a Middle East country. The idea that the free traffic of educated people should be interrupted is a worrying development, because it will help to compound the whole "Fortress America" mentality.

I think that a lot of latent strands in the American psychology are being made manifest. Anti-American acts like the 9-11 tragedy will only feed this vicious circle.

♦ *V: I was pretty disturbed to read about that Amsterdam filmmaker, Theo Van Gogh, being assassinated by a fanatical Muslim—*

♦ **JGB:** That was a nasty piece of work; a nasty bit. I mean, the filmmaker wasn't a very nice guy, putting it mildly. He had a vicious anti-Muslim line [in his film, *Submission*], a quite provocatively anti-Islamic remark. But it's far better to rely on the criminal law to deal with people like that than stab them dead in the street. The Muslim population of Western Europe is enormous, in the millions. There are six million in France, a couple of million here [U.K.], and the potential for social tragedy is enormous. One hopes it all goes away—one almost hopes for some huge distraction—god knows what.

It's not that I'm particularly sympathetic to the Muslim faith. Without trying to be provocative, **I don't find *any* religion attractive, but I must say the Muslim faith is one of the least attractive in its treatment of women.** It seems to be retrograde in every conceivable way. But, here we are . . .

♦ **V:** *Right. Well, I did my* Modern Pagans *book as an attack on the three major monotheisms, the "religions of the book," because they all help perpetuate this notion of the Pyramid Society with "God" at the top and the American President at His right hand, and everyone else is an underling following orders, with slaves, women and children at the bottom. And "This is the One True God; every word in His Book is true"—obviously, they can't* all *be right. These "sacred books" and beliefs of the three major religions seem crazy to me. I was hoping there would be an end to religion, or an end to these three major monotheisms, at least.*

♦ **JGB:** I wish it would happen but I don't think it's going to. The roots of these great religions lie deep in the human past and were probably spun into existence around the time human beings founded the first cities in Mesopotamia (or wherever it was)—roughly speaking, where the war in Iraq is now being fought. But, you know, they represent the *taming of human pathology.* As you say, the sort of social structures, the power structures of the first societies, played on deep fears about mortality, guilt, dreams of everlasting life attainment—all conflated into this *social/religious survival kit.* Those structures, those mental structures, still exist inside all our brains! One almost feels that in times of crisis people feel a need for some sort of almost psychopathic response to the crisis, which itself then justifies a religious interpretation of it.

Today, it's probably only through psychopathology that people can find God. After 200 or 300 years of the beginnings of the Age of

There are people who think that Hitler was, in effect, a religious leader. The German people became his congregation. They worshipped him as you would worship a religious leader—faith alone was enough! Even as the walls came tumbling down and disaster was on all sides in 1945, they still believed . . . because *belief* was what had sustained them from the beginning—not reason.

One almost sees George Bush as a kind of religious leader. Maybe he's making his appeal to the [alleged] 52% of the American electorate who voted him in on barely concealed religious grounds, with all his talk of "God."

I think Stalin's position was slightly different. There, I think, was a sort of masochistic submission to the "Great Leader," which has long been part of Russian history. Tremendous facility: Peter the Great and all the rest of it. I said in one of my books which you quoted, I'm glad to say, in *Quotes:* "I see the future as a sort of Darwinian struggle between competing psychopathologies." This is not something that lies in the future; it already began in the 1920s and 1930s. But perhaps it re-emerged, to some extent, with both the attack on the World Trade Center, and then the unrelated (I don't know what the justification was, even to this day) attack by the British and America on Iraq.

I feel that *realpolitik,* in the sense of a cold-eyed look at political advantage for one's own nation, doesn't apply. *We're now in the realm of purely emotional justifications.* The clearest example of that is the British Prime Minister, Tony Blair, who is not an important figure remotely in the same class as George Bush, but he happens to be *our* Prime Minister. And to give the British people credit, the majority of them are thoroughly skeptical about him. But you can see that he took us to war on the grounds of his conviction that there were weapons of mass destruction that could not be found. But he *still* believes they're there somewhere, and many people have noticed that his appeals to the British public are couched in emotional terms. He doesn't appeal to reason; he appeals to feelings. **He's also a devout Christian—a very sinister thing.**

I think these are dangerous times!

♦ *V: You've given us the notion of "religion = psychopathology."*

World Trade Center with church. Photo: Charles Gatewood

I'm not sure that's a widespread understanding yet!

♦ **JGB:** Well, I think Freud had more or less the same idea. It's been a long time since I've read *Moses and Monotheism,* but I think he was arguing for something along those lines. I think tact forbade him; **open attacks on religion can be dangerous!** Not too dangerous in contemporary England, but I daresay that in large areas in the American Midwest, you'd have to be very careful before you announce, "The Good Book is a textbook of psychopathology!" You could try it, Vale—

♦ *V: We will, don't worry! It seems nobody has any courage to say anything.*

I've been reading about a very interesting concept called "framing." A professor of cognitive science and linguistics at U.C. Berkeley, George Lakoff, wrote a book titled Don't Think of an Elephant! *He said that **the right-wing christian-conservative conspiracy has over the past 35 years spent \$3 billion funding 43 think-tanks to try to figure out how to take over America**. They produced the infamous "Willie Horton" ad which, in the minds of viewers, indelibly equated George Bush Sr.'s presidential opponent, Dukakis, with a huge black rapist-murderer.*

Lakoff also revealed Newt Gingrich's plan to have all Democrats defined by words like "decay, failure, collapse, crisis, destructive, destroy, sick, pathetic, lie, liberal, traitors, sensationalists, endanger, hypocrisy, incompetent"—words like that.

♦ **JGB:** Of course!

♦ *V: These "fascists"—which is how I think of these rightwing-christian Republicans—are always going to be better organized and unified than people like myself who just want to mind their own business, and don't want to force others to think as they do—*

♦ **JGB:** Those who rely on "reason," like you and I, are always going to come off second-best, in a *crisis,* to those who rely on "emotion," because there's something *visceral* about an emotional response. Like, "This six-year-old girl's body has been found by a riverbank." Anger rises in the community; they've got to find a scapegoat. A calmer voice that says, "Wait a minute—just because you don't like somebody's face doesn't mean that he killed this little girl," is ignored. One can see a similar sort of simple psychology of emotional recourse at work today in the election of Bush, and outside America, too, in political elections in Western Europe.

It's obviously unsettling, to put it mildly, because, of course most rational and literate and educated people are left out of the equation. They no longer "intercede" as members of the professions (lawyers, doctors, schoolteachers, intellectuals) between the political leadership of a society and the bored mass of people. The political leadership now leaps *over* them and directly plugs into the deep limbic system of the mass psyche where emotions alone rule, and where fear can be stimulated with pinpoint accuracy. You sense the human race's brain is now exposed, and all kinds of nasty little electrodes are being inserted into its depths.

♦ *V: That's exactly what has happened.* **Scientists' discoveries as to how the brain works are being used** *against* **people now**, *to control and* manipulate them.

I still like Paul MacLean's three-brain theory: the reptile brain, the mammalian brain that evolved over it, and then the human "universalizing" brain overlaid on top—

♦ **JGB:** Well, there's probably a lot of truth in it—

♦ *V: And we're being thrust back, as much as possible by the media, into the reptilian brain where fear rules—*

♦ **JGB**: Absolutely. It's all "fight or flight"; everything is emotionally driven. And of course **the entertainment culture and the entire global marketplace—capitalism itself—is being driven not by rational choice, but by *emotional choice.*** This has been going on since the first "branded" product was produced back in the 18th and 19th centuries. But modern advertising, for a century now, like the popular tabloid press and like advertising and film, plays on the emotional realm; on emotional needs. People aren't going to buy a new Buick because it's a beautiful piece of engineering; they buy it because it satisfies some kind of aggressive response: speed, power . . . it'll make you more attractive to the opposite sex, or impress your neighbors, or whatever. There are very few things that we're constantly cajoled into buying that *don't* carry some sort of emotional charge. You know: "Use this detergent and your children's clothes will be whiter than the other children's at school."

I sometimes think that in a sense we're entering a New Dark Age. The lights are full on, but there's an *inner darkness* . . . because we're retreating into a sort of [mind-set] of our pre-rational forebears who lived in a kind of animist world where everything had a spirit— every twig, every stone in a stream . . . where questions of guilt and anxiety and fear and aggression ruled our reflexes.

Reason is evaporating. It may well be that a Dark Age is slowly advancing over us. It's difficult to see how we're going to get out of it.

Now when we look around, society as a whole seems to be a structure organized by reason. The trams in San Francisco, the buses in London, the airplanes that land and take off from London Airport near me, all seem to be obeying the laws of mechanics and hydraulics and aeronautics and whatever else. But of course, **highly advanced scientific societies can co-exist with the most absolute un-reason.**

Nazi Germany is a fair example of that: highly advanced technology; in chemistry, with the synthesis of gasoline from coal which took place during the war; the continuous synthesis of ammonia which produced the vast German munitions industry; German invention: the V-1 and V-2 missiles, etc. Some of the most advanced aircraft and jet fighters co-existed with this ranting maniac who was only interested in killing as many people as he could!

So, the apparent "sanity" of the world that prevails over our neighborhoods isn't necessarily *reassuring,* because it can exist in a completely separate compartment . . . and *does.*

♦ *V: Right. You have this christian Bush who was trying to re-activate the Space Program for 15 seconds—the most advanced technology you can imagine. And he apparently still believes in a white-bearded God in some heaven up above some hell down below—*

♦ **JGB:** Well, he probably does! He *needs* to. He uses phrases like "I'm *real mad* at Osama bin Laden." Well, madness is the key, of course. He *needs* to get mad—not in the "angry" sense; he doesn't realize that, of course. When he says "angry," what he really means is "insane." Only by being *insane* and by getting everyone else around him to think like madmen can he justify the extreme actions that he would like to take, and has started to take, to some extent, in Iraq.

The same applies to Blair, by the way. Blair, fortunately, doesn't have a tenth of Bush's power. But the same mechanism is at work here. **A world entirely created in terms of emotions will be a pretty scary place.** You know, it's going to be like one of those big paranoid Hollywood thrillers.

♦ *V: It's coming true. This huge corporation called Wal-Mart, which is driving every small store out of business wherever it encroaches, has this amazing computer system which they're using in a predictive way now. By predicting the path of a hurricane, they can rush hurricane supplies to the stores where they'll be needed, and make 20 times the profit they used to make.*

♦ **JGB:** Scary!

♦ *V: You could see this as benign, but all these technologies seem to have a way of being turned against the best interests of humans.*

♦ **JGB:** Over here the big supermarket chains (they probably do this in America too; the idea probably *came* from there) issue so-called "store cards" which are credit cards with which a housewife can pay for her purchases. They've introduced "smart" store cards which can store a whole profile of a particular purchaser's spending habits, but can also store data from credit-card companies, banks, building societies—all of which operate like banks, charging extortionate rates of interest. Plus medical and criminal records. This card you carry around, with which you buy your cans of soup, will actually contain a complete profile of your identity in the most intimate way. This is *so* open to abuse. But people are very passive.

In London now, for about a year, we've had something called a "Congestion Zone." This is basically the West End of London, which includes Central London plus the Houses of Parliament and the main Ministries of State, Buckingham Palace, and the main shopping thoroughfares like Oxford Street, Piccadilly and the like, and the entertainment areas with cinemas, theatres and restaurants.

Because traffic was slowing to a walking pace, the left-wing mayor decided to mark out this large "Congestion Zone" and charge motorists who wanted to enter the Zone five pounds a day. In order to check up on which motorists were going in and which were not, it set up this huge network of cameras linked to a central body of computers which read the license plate numbers and check to see whether the driver has paid his five pounds. This system is up and running and Draconian powers of enforcement have been granted by this left-wing mayor. If you don't pay your five pounds, you can be fined eighty pounds. Then, if you refuse to pay that, they can seize your car and crush it in one of these great hydraulic ram systems! And this would apply to anybody anywhere in England.

Of course, **computer optical recognition systems make errors.** So the wrong cars have been seized from people who've never been to London in their lives! But what's so incredible is: the response has been deeply passive. **This Orwellian system of surveillance has not really prompted any protest. It's as if there's a deeply masochistic strain in the population-at-large: that we *want* to be watched by closed-circuit television cameras.** It's an extension of that whole web-cam thing: we *want* to be observed.

There's a very popular television program running here called *Big Brother.* I think it started in Holland. Anyway, it's cloned a whole series of programs that have been running for several years all over Western Europe. About fifteen young people of both sexes live for two or three weeks in a house which is sealed off from the outside world. They are watched by a huge battery of hidden cameras—even in the lavatories, and certainly in the bedrooms. The program makers are constantly denying they are trying to encourage the participants to have penetrative sex in the dimly-lit bedrooms, but they seem to have at last achieved it in the series that ended a few months ago. And I think on the continent of Europe, the French have regularly shown full penetrative sex.

Now, what is extraordinary is: the people in them who take part, *thrive.* They're the sort of people you would run a mile from if they shared the holiday villa next to you but they thrive on the attentions of the camera. Even though the camera is watching them doing something

Photo: Charles Gatewood

embarrassing, like being sick (because they're allowed unlimited alcohol), they *thrive* under the gaze of the camera. And I think this is true of the British people at large; we have more CCTV cameras over our motorways and on High Street—everywhere you go there are these cameras now. They are put there ostensibly as a security aid. And no doubt they have helped to solve a lot of crimes. But I don't think that is the reason why people tolerate them.

We *like* exposing ourselves to the merciless all-knowing gaze of these cameras. We *want* to be watched. This is Orwell's "Big Brother" nightmare come true, but in an unexpected way—far from *fearing* Big Brother, we *revel* in that sort of exposure. And that's why nobody has protested at this Congestion Zone.

This mayor who set it up is now trying to extend it. The plan is that the whole of Greater London, one day, will be a vast Congestion Zone with cameras. There will need to be thousands of them—literally thousands—because he employs about two hundred at present. Obviously this taps some deep need in the British psyche to be watched, as if we were children reverting to a kind of docile state of existence under the all-seeing gaze of a stern nanny! It's very, very peculiar.

♦ *V: Well, you predicted increasing infantilism—*

♦ **JGB**: Yes, it's part of that. Of course, **people enjoy being infantilized—it's less effort!** Like a big wallow in a sort of emotional bath. One can play with one's feces, and generally revert to the age of six months, and thoroughly enjoy it!

Human beings, I fear, want to be told what to do.

♦ *V: That's so scary. Also, I do think there is a conspiracy against "interiority." It seems that the kind of reading for reflection and musing and meditation seems to have severely declined, along with the proliferation of all these communications devices you've predicted. Everywhere you go, people are wearing these iPods. There are so many colorful, exciting electronic distractions that something like reading and writing in a paper journal seems—*

♦ **JGB:** —like *hard work,* doesn't it?

Over here, the British press is remarkable in the number of mass-circulation papers we have. In New York, apart from the *Wall Street Journal*, there's just one newspaper: the *New York Times*—one serious newspaper. In London you've got about *five* serious newspapers, and then another six or seven tabloid newspapers, all extremely well-financed. And their circulations are constantly declining, and have been.

The younger generation doesn't read books anymore. The curious thing is that the Internet, of course, is a verbal medium, isn't it? And you would think that it might have rekindled an interest in reading journals, newspapers, magazines, books. This hasn't happened over here, I think, because people prefer to be passive. They don't like the active phase—to have to think critically about what they're reading. They like to be *told* what to think, and they like—well, listening to the radio is very, very popular. They have all these disc jockeys and the like. It's one-way communication; people seem to prefer that. But all this is very negative. I feel that for your purposes I should say optimistic things!

♦ *V: I agree. I did a public interview with a filmmaker, Sam Green, who did a documentary on the Weather Underground. At the Question-and-Answer session afterwards, a young person stood up and said,* **"Look, why can't you tell us** *positive* **things that could inspire us and give us hope?"** *I said, "Yes, you're right."*

♦ **JGB:** I agree; I'm very aware of that. I think **I could say, as a rallying cry, "Think on your feet! Criticize! Be skeptical!"** But I fear these are not messages that mean very much today. Maybe one should infiltrate the power structure—go to work for the Disney corporation, go to work for some big advertising agency, work for a Hollywood studio, get into the citadel and then see if you can subvert it from within. Sadly, I don't think that could work, either.

♦ *V: These people were seeking some philosophically unifying rallying cry, an emotional engine—*

♦ **JGB:** Absolutely. Just look at the New Age section of your local bookstore. If it's anything like the ones in British bookstores, there's something deeply submissive going on.

♦ **V:** *Right: "We want all of you to just meditate by yourselves in your room." There's a crazy movement here to promulgate "Buddhism for Punks."*

♦ **JGB:** I've got a feeling there's something more dramatic needed—a real "Fight Back!" **Everyone of us should carry out One Meaningless Act A Day . . . especially in the public domain.** I don't mean anything criminal—with all these surveillance cameras around, you wouldn't get very far here.

In my little town, a little quiet place, it has surveillance cameras on its High Street. Not only that, it has several signs warning there are surveillance cameras keeping everyone under observation. *The assumption is: nobody's going to protest.* It's bizarre; it's sort of *Brave New World*, where everybody goes along with it. But yes, I think everyone has to carry out a meaningless act—paint up a portion of the sidewalk, or invent an imaginary flag and fly it from one of the telegraph poles—anything! Announce meetings that will never take place, rediscover the old Surrealist attempts to undermine bourgeois society. Because **there is a sort of soft tyranny at present.** My old fear, "The totalitarian systems of the future will be subservient and ingratiating, like a sort of headwaiter at an over-friendly hotel" . . . that's come to pass.

♦ **V:** *One of your predictions for the future said, "Maybe a new Surrealism will be born." In this day of pseudo-logical but really all-emotional control going on, Surrealism is something that they can't just pin a "criminal act" on you for doing . . .*

♦ **JGB:** Right. I've got a feeling we're going to find what I would call a kind of Quiet Zone—not quite the trough of a historical wave—well, maybe we are in the trough of a historical wave, but **many things have got to get worse before they'll get better.**

There's no doubt that over here there are terrific signs of social disaffection. The levels of public drunkenness here are incredibly high, to the point where local police chiefs are appealing to the Home Secretary (a very senior member of the cabinet) to do something about it. There are enormous signs of social unrest of one kind or another: very high levels of crime, interracial disharmony—the streets are getting really dangerous to walk at night, and so on.

Also, the gap between the rich and the poor is widening all the time. Middle-class people are feeling the pinch here. The kind of differential that allowed doctors and lawyers and bank managers and the like to enjoy some state of certain social privileges, like educating their children privately, or employing a domestic servant—all those now belong to the past.

And there's a new class of super-rich. Based on our City of London, which is our equivalent of Wall Street, there are gigantic salaries by English standards being paid. A whole new class of super-rich have come into existence. They're distorting the demographics of Inner London to the point where public services like hospitals, the bus services and the like are finding it impossible to recruit staff, because the staff can't afford to *live* in London. **Huge numbers of these super-rich are actually opting out of society. They live in gated enclaves, they travel in private planes, they go to private hospitals and the like. Their children go to private schools**; they have very little to do with the population at large. They have very little to do with the old middle-class population. It may be that this will lead to social divisions that will reach a crisis point. Maybe then the pendulum will swing the other way. Hard to tell . . .

♦ *V: I wonder about America: Was it a brave experiment in democracy that's just about to be over with?*

♦ **JGB:** I think you're probably right.

♦ *V: What with the perfection of control over the population, even in areas where people have incredibly high levels of unemployment because Bush allowed all the jobs to be exported overseas, people still support him, because all they do is watch TV—they don't read. They don't even surf the Net for sites that might post some dissent, some* real *content. They just believe images. Like you pointed out about Reagan so long ago: he had such reassuring mannerisms while saying the most vicious right-wing drivel—messages completely inimical to the interests of the working-class viewers watching him.*

♦ **JGB:** Yes. I think you're right.

♦ *V: Well, with this interview we're now more up-to-date. The first major event that happened in this century was 9-11, which you called a "revolution." The second major event (for me) has been the re-election of this Bush person, who has brought everything down in this country: he's launched two wars for fraudulent reasons, and is getting rid of all the jobs, social welfare, and now social security—*

♦ **JGB:** Yes, I've read all about that. It's very worrying, isn't it? **The whole notion of a *generous society* seems to be disappearing.** We're going back to a kind of Wild West—

♦ *V: Right, the number of homeless on the streets has greatly increased. Back when Ronald Reagan shut down all the mental hospitals and put all the inmates on the street, for about three months on every street corner in San Francisco you'd hear crazy people screaming. But after about three months that ceased; they'd all died. And this is not the kind of thing that receives newspaper coverage—*

♦ **JGB:** And that's the trouble. The idea of a sort of generous and tolerant society which many Americans and enlightened political leaders over the centuries have worked for, seems to be going. And it's going over here, too.

We're getting a kind of *Security State* where the state is sort of protecting itself from its own population! Other people are dangerous; you've got to be protected from them. Ban [all thinking]; invent new vices—this is the subtext one feels: a weird sort of self-righteousness, as if **we're living in a kind of huge institution where nobody must run in the corridors—very strange.**

♦ *V: And even worse, it's a religious institution, where the "God" up there can tell if you even think a nasty thought—*

♦ **JGB:** Yes.

♦ *V: That reminds me—I completely forgot: I was going to ask you about what "Ballardian ethics" might be. Personally, some of my ethics come from William Burroughs: "Mind your own business." But if you're a Johnson—i.e., a decent person, then "A Johnson will always give a helping hand if it's needed. If somebody falls down in the street, you don't just walk by, you see if they need your help." Things like that. And yet you mind your own business; you're not peeping into your neighbor's bedroom. And I pretty much go along with* Thou Shalt Not Kill *and* Thou Shalt Not Steal, *but obviously these are complex questions. If someone's breaking into my house and attacking my family, I'm going to try to stop them—I'm not going to be passive. And you could argue that if a corporation is stealing from YOU, then maybe you have the right to steal back. Morality is very complex—*

♦ **JGB:** Absolutely.

♦*V: And then there's* Thou Shalt Not Lie *. . . I do think it's bad to lie one-on-one to somebody's face, but the corporations do that to you all the time—we're surrounded by lies from advertising, marketing and branding—*

♦ **JGB:** Absolutely.

♦ *V: It's a different morality now.*

♦ **JGB:** I agree!

♦ *V: I love your statement from a few years ago: "Nothing is true. Nothing is untrue." Part of our fight is against what Burroughs called the "Either/Or" syllogism, which George W. Bush employs a lot: "You're either with us, or you support the terrorists." That's a total shutting down of the mental process—*

♦ **JGB:** I agree with you. It's difficult, because so many of the ethical and moral decisions that my grandparents and your great-grandparents made, have been taken away from us. How we look after our children, how we educate them, how we treat our wives—there's a huge range of daily decisions that used to have a strong basis, that are no longer made by us. They're enforced by an "enlightened society" that wills us to behave in what it sees as a moral and ethical way.

But as you say, there's a danger that we've become excessively passive. And then our moral sensibility tends to dull and atrophy, so when we're faced with a *real* challenge—for example, *George Bush*, or Tony Blair over here—**we're too restrained, too blunted. Our moral sensibilities are too blunted to react critically.**

Also, the great institutions of the past (over here, the monarchy, parliament, the church, and even the civil service) have lost their authority. And I think it's up to everyone to create their own *moral micro-climate*. It's as if there's a storm—and there *IS* a storm today—and we each put up an umbrella and that's our little micro-climate. We are drier than we would be if we didn't put up an umbrella.

I think each of us have got to put up a moral umbrella and actually work things out for ourselves. **We can't take our moral systems and our ethical systems wholesale from some central supplier—the church, the education system**, whatever. We have to do it on a piece-meal basis. **Each of us is a kind of ethical Robinson Crusoe building a replica of civilized society from the sort of debris washed up on the beach—on our own beach.**

And I think to build up children you need to inculcate them into this: "Don't be passive. You must decide for yourself whether it's good or bad, right or wrong." That's what I tried to do with my children. You do it more by example than by exhortation.

Anyway, that's another story! **I think the obligation is much more to think for ourselves, and to think ethically for ourselves. Because no one else is going to do it for us.**

♦ *V: Not even Michael Moore—*

♦ **JGB:** He has a big reputation in this country over here, too.

♦ *V: Good. I think he deserves it.*

♦ **JGB**: I haven't seen [*Fahrenheit 9/11*], but they say it's great.

♦ *V: It's just pure documentary footage. All the articles that smear and denigrate him never mention that it's virtually all just documentary footage: of things that really happened—Bush consorting with the Saudis; protestors pelting the Bush limo with rotten eggs, things that are censored by corporate TV. Actually, you do the same thing as Michael Moore: you get your insights across with a kind of deep humor, too—*

♦ **JGB:** He's very, very witty; he's a remarkable character. There have been a lot of interviews over here. Claire's always pulling off the Internet articles written by what appears to be an enormous number of skeptical voices in America. I mean, she sends me articles from the *New York Times*, which is quite an establishment paper, but that ex-theater critic called **Frank Rich** has written wonderful stuff on the Bush election. I

he loves me,
he loves me not.
who cares?

Photo: SM Gray

think he's a regular columnist—remarkably waspish and critical. There are many, many others who sound a skeptical voice, but the U.S. is so huge that they're drowned out . . .

♦ **V:** *The future seems very uncertain now; everyone wonders what they can do. I love the idea that it's time for a New Surrealism to be born. If only people could discover that they have their own imaginations and dreams and creativity. In the one-way communications tyranny that's going on, people seem to forget that—*

♦ **JGB**: I think so, because you don't *need* more. To survive today, you don't need to have more than a sort of reasonable standard of living, particularly in the welfare-state social democracies of Western Europe—this would apply equally to Japan, Australia, Canada. It's quite possible to survive comfortably without being too engaged with society as a whole. If you're lucky enough to be employed, you probably don't have to work that hard—you just have to *show up* at the office or factory or whatever it might be. And if you accept the mores of the society in which you live—that is, you go to the shopping mall, you see the movies, you watch the TV . . . *uncomplainingly,* you can get by, mentally. If now and then you buy a fresh tomato, your health will be adequate. And I think most people have opted for this; they're satisfied with this sort of existence; they're satisfied to lie on the feather bed which consumer capitalism has laid out for them.

If you look at the novels of Dickens, say, or the novels of Zola, there were absolutely fierce attempts by everybody who could, to *better themselves.* Everybody was fiercely ambitious. Survival was difficult, but Victorian society was driven by a need for social improvement of all kinds: education, a better standard of living, higher income, better housing. These are ambitions that are *gone* now. Most people have adequate housing, adequate schooling—at least adequate to make them passive consumers. How well do you need to be educated to go to a Wal-Mart?! Not very.

As long as you do what you're told—it's like driving around today. You have to obey the speed limit: stop where there's a red light, or you'll probably get killed. I think even the very passive are satisfied to be passive. They're not critical and they're not ambitious in that driven way

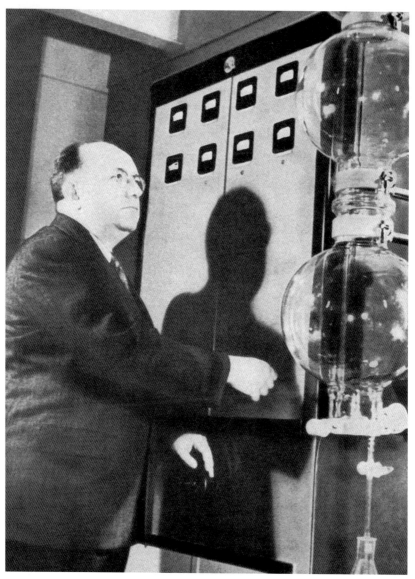

of 150 years ago.

That may change, of course. **Everything could change if there were a genuine oil crisis. If the economies of the West went into severe recession, then things would change radically.** It's just that the consumer societies that we've created in the West don't encourage a critical frame of mind. To survive today, it's best to be uncritical, it's best to be passive. Don't think for yourself too much. Don't question. It's your social duty to buy a new Chevrolet every three years (or whatever). Or a new Renault, or a new Mercedes. It's your social duty, in effect, to watch six hours of television a day!

It's your social duty to collaborate in the economic well-being of society by a certain level of consumer spending. We all know this; some of us go along with it. We obey not only a small number of the traffic lights that govern our lives that are actually in the street outside; most of them are *inside our heads,* and we tend to obey them. This is a *collaborative soft tyranny* which most people are happy with. Others, like me, would call it a New Dark Age!

♦ *V: Yes. And I'm afraid that many of my favorite books by obscure Surrealist authors will be totally forgotten in twenty or thirty years. Things you've found inspiration in, like* The Secret Life of Salvador Dali—

♦ **JGB:** Yes, that's a problem, isn't it, of marketing. People don't use libraries as much as they used to. One thing I miss terribly—I don't know if the same thing applied in America, but over here, in the Forties and Fifties **when I first came to England, what I loved were the second-hand bookshops.** Every small town had a second-hand bookshop which was constantly being stocked up . . . when someone died, the family took their books to the second-hand bookshop and got sixpence each for them. There were a lot of unserious materials, popular novels and the like . . . but there were a lot of very serious books. You know, one serious collector in a lifetime could produce enough books to keep a second-hand bookshop going for a *year.*

I did most of my reading in second-hand bookshops. I remember when I was living in London somewhere I used a local one. Also, *serendipity* came into it, because you looked around the stacks of all these books—mostly hardcovers, not paperbacks—you looked at these books and you said, "Oh, Robert Graves—I very much enjoyed something by him, but what's this? *Goodbye to All That*—a biography of his first World War experiences?"—a brilliant book! You made accidental discoveries all the time. And this sort of refreshed one. You were constantly being surprised, constantly making discoveries. All this is gone now, of course. There can't be more than half a dozen used bookshops in the whole of West London, if any.

What we've got now is a new kind of literacy. We've got people who are expert at reading the labels on products, expert at reading instructional manuals that come with a new kind of vacuum cleaner, or a computer or what have you. They're expert at *that* kind of reading, but not at anything else. Not with a more traditional book.

I don't know if the Internet has affected that. I have very high hopes for the Internet, which I think could be the sort of—**if we're entering a New Dark Age, the Internet could help to keep the lights on!**

♦ *V: Well, there are aspects of the Internet I like, for example Brewster Kahle's Project Gutenberg, which aspires to put all out-of-print, copyright-free books on the Internet for free, so anyone could get access to them and just download them. That's one way to gain access to lesser-publicized material, like an obscure Dickens novel. Since we live in the age of marketing and branding overload promoting the newest consumer products, this seems quaintly contravening.*

♦ **JGB:** The Internet is in its early days, and you want to look ahead. I wouldn't say it's in its Wild West period, because I don't think that's the right analogy, but it's certainly in its early expansionist phase, like the early days of film—or the printed word, for that matter. The early days of radio . . . or the early days of the telephone.

I think the Internet is a positive thing and I'm glad that censorship is very difficult, and that it's still a free medium, isn't it? Access to it is not restricted to—if you look at the film world or the television world, access to the creative end is restricted to a small handful of giant corporations like the BBC here, or commercial corporations. It's true that anybody can buy a cine camera and make a movie, but you're not going to get it shown anywhere—unless you work for Paramount Pictures. Or in television, unless you work for NBC or ABC or whatever. But the Internet is open, isn't it?

♦ *V: There are Internet sites that provide underground films which you can download for a small amount of money. However, there are thousands of sites which no longer exist, although some of them can be accessed through the "wayback machine" site. I do see some kind of hope there for making the potential possible, at low cost, to access neglected films, books, music and what have you, or images with more provocative potential for the imagination—*

♦ **JGB**: There are some—I don't have a PC actually, but my girlfriend is a keen PC user, a great surfer of the Internet. It's very important to her; it's a social tool because she has made friends and found people with similar interests. Amazingly, when she meets these people, there's none

of that "Ohmigod, how did I ever get into meeting *him?*" that you used to get—

♦ *V: With the old Lonely Hearts Clubs—*

♦ **JGB:** Right. And some of these sites she's dug up contain accidental poetry that is quite moving. I remember when she first got a PC about six or seven years ago, there were these "telephone booths in the Mojave desert" sites. I can't remember the theory of it, but there was some strangely poetic business about this telephone booth which was still functioning. I can't remember what the exact point of it was, but it became a kind of talismanic object. There are other websites I've mentioned in earlier conversations.

There was one she found about a year ago: an aerial survey of the California coast—

♦ *V: Right; Barbra Streisand sued to have her house removed from that site—*

♦ **JGB:** That's right! Actually, Claire, my girlfriend, communicated with the people who did it. She sent them an email telling them how wonderful the site was. We've looked at Barbra Streisand's house completely surrounded with its high fence. And unless she goes up to the top floor, she looks at the Pacific through this high, chain-link fence. I can't imagine looking out at the sea through your own living room window in the morning, and all you see is this wire fence!

But that site is a wonderful idea—genuinely poetic and life-enhancing: this endless coastal trek. I've more or less done the whole trip. And I thought, "This is wonderful." I don't know who these people are; they must have a lot of money to be able to afford to fly all these trips in a helicopter or whatever it was, but I thought, "You know, **if everybody began to realize the potential or the resources of their own imagination, and could post the results on the Internet, that would immensely enrich the *human sensorium*. And maybe that will happen—who knows?**

But on the other hand, nothing is worse than a bad amateur poet! So, Vale, I think we're coming to an end—

♦ *V: I think that's a wonderful ending .*♦ ♦ ♦

Photo: Ana Barrado

J.G. Ballard and Graeme Revell

Born in New Zealand, Graeme Revell founded the pioneering "Industrial" music group SPK in the Seventies (see *RE/Search #6/7*). In 1989 he composed the groundbreaking, genre-crossing soundtrack for *Dead Calm*. Since then he has composed over sixty soundtracks to date, besides working on projects such as television's *C.S.I. Miami*.

Graeme interviewed J.G. Ballard by phone on Nov. 7, 2003—20 years after he interviewed Ballard in Shepperton, England for *RE/Search #8/9*. Topics ranged from the death of cinema, the colonizing of our existence, the end of the Age of Reason, the infantilizing of America, the Internet, and the ascendance of "machine morality." What follows is a largely unedited transcript.

♦ ***GRAEME REVELL:*** *I've read almost everything you've written; you observe almost from the outside all these different kinds of communities and lifestyles. For some reason I've ended up practically living within them all! So in a way my questions were, "Well, James has taught me how to live—"*

♦ **J.G. BALLARD:** —reality from the *inside!*

♦ *GR: You've certainly taught me how my life was going to go for the last twenty years; I desperately wanted you to tell me how it was going to be for the next twenty—*

♦ **JGB:** I think I'll pass on that. America is quite a difficult place to "read" now.

♦ *GR: Oh, very.*

♦ **JGB:** I felt I sort of had a handle on it back in the Sixties, but now— I haven't been there for twelve years or something.

♦ *GR: Well, I'm actually calling you from Las Vegas this morning—*

♦ **JGB:** Ohmigod!

♦ *GR: —which is definitely the heart of the beast, isn't it?*

♦ **JGB:** From what I hear that's sort of "Phase Three." Vegas is now a family resort; the gangsters have gone.

♦ *GR: The gangsters are very much gone. But they also gave up on the "family" demographic about three years ago when they found that—*

♦ **JGB:** —they weren't spending any money!

♦ *GR: Right. They had what they called a "Demographic Split" in the marketing—they worked very hard to target the parents* and *the children at the same time. Then they gave up on that and now it's just the "young people" demographic they're after. You find that everywhere in the culture. There isn't a single adult movie that can even compete against the* Kill Bills *of Quentin Tarantino and the remakes of* Texas Chainsaw Massacre *and so on—all those films aimed at eighteen-year-olds.*

♦ **JGB:** It's a shame, in a way, that your rise to domination in the film music business coincided with—I hate to say it; maybe I'm showing my age—but a real *decline* in movie making—

♦ *GR: Oh, it's extraordinary. You're not showing your age at all; it really is in decline.*

♦ **JGB: There's almost a sense that cinema is** *over.* What we have is a kind of *afterlife* expressed through entertainment movies. They're just *cash tills* in an amusement park urging you to jam your coins in, awarding you with a lot of bright lights and god knows what. There aren't *that* many interesting films around . . . but there we are.

♦ *GR: Well, the extraordinary thing with the medium, having experienced it from the inside, is: there's almost nobody who understands, or cares at least, about the* function *of cinema. They have an extreme inability to analyze what it is that they're* doing—*let alone all the broader social implications of becoming a cultural hegemony for the entire world. There are no Godards, or anybody even a millionth as close as him, who understand what they're doing—it's just a* job. *It's the big billboard, the big signpost of culture in general.*

♦ **JGB:** I think so, absolutely. It's difficult. As long as you're targeting not just American teenagers but European and Asian teenagers; as long as you keep the *dialogue* down so you don't have comprehension difficulties when the movie is screened in Manila, you're never going to be able to escape from the *cinema of pure spectacle.* You're not going to get something like Billy Wilder's *Sunset Boulevard* or Godard's *Pierrot le Fou* occurring. We'll see. Maybe *you'll* lead a renaissance!

♦ *GR: I have some films in mind, but it's very difficult to make a film at all, especially something that's not one of those ones you just referred to.*

♦ **JGB:** One of the interesting little films I saw recently was called *Ivans xtc.* I don't know if you've ever heard of it. It was made by a British director in America, Bernard Rose. He did—oh god, I can't remember the other films he made. But *Ivans xtc* had Danny Huston in the lead and was about an L.A. agent and his world. It was an interesting film. Anyway—

♦ *GR: I was re-reading the BBC Radio 3 interview you did in 1998. It was very interesting to me because you used phrases like "the colonizing of existence." You said, "I think people are beginning to wonder what* does *life really offer us in terms of its possibilities?" And you don't think that they touch the truth.*

One of the things about your writing that really interests me is that in the background there is, in the way that we're talking now, a sense of disappointment that there isn't a truth there somewhere, or that there ought to be. Do you still think that? So much of your writing could indicate that maybe it doesn't matter, maybe it's all over, maybe there isn't any. I'm not sure which way you come down on that—

♦ **JGB:** I can't remember the context in which I said that, to be honest. It might have been in connection with a novel called *Super-Cannes,* or maybe the previous one, *Cocaine Nights.*

♦ *GR: I think* Cocaine Nights—*right.*

♦ **JGB:** I do think we're living in very uncertain times; there's no doubt about that. In some ways this is good to see, because the main *pillars* that used to prop up society (in this country, anyway)—the monarchy, religion and politics—have all been knocked aside.

I don't know about America, but here **the era of television is over.** Television created the British national consciousness in the '70s and '80s. It defined people's sense of civic responsibility: what you should do about single mothers and the poor and all the rest of it. TV doesn't do that anymore. All people have got left now is the consumer culture: buying things. Going around to big shopping malls here is quite a depressing experience.

◆ *GR: You mean "entertainment resorts"—they're redefining the name now!*

◆ **JGB:** Yeah. One sees a terrible boredom coming in. There's a limit as to how much time you can worry about what sort of trainers you should buy, or how you're going to redecorate your kitchen for the tenth time. Out of boredom comes a need for change. The *status quo* now, thanks to the vast consumerist culture, is very difficult to shift. It takes real *violence* of 9-11 proportions, practically, to shift the status quo.

I see a future of deepening boredom interspersed with random acts of violence. I think, going back to what you're saying: people *do* feel that there's some sort of *core identity* which they haven't quite been able to get hold of. That's common to everybody in all the eras, but now there's so little to get hold of. As I was saying to Vale a few months ago, **we're living in an era when nothing is true and nothing is untrue.**

I think the Gulf War, whose end George Bush proclaimed in his "Top Gun" gear on the aircraft carrier (proclaimed "over," but it's still running) . . . I think the Gulf War slipped through the normal cordons that we erect to protect us from our politicians, to restrain them from doing anything too dangerous. It was almost a sort of *virtual war.* I don't mean in the Baudrillard sense of it not taking place at all, as I think he said of the first Gulf War—because we simply weren't given enough information about it—but because it was a virtual war that, thanks to the brilliance of the American military machine, was over in no time at all, militarily.

The virtual war was . . . *confused* by all the PR and *mob-speak* poured out, and the very confused psychology of Bush and Blair. They needed a war for *evangelical* reasons, so they created a war with their huge military toy. But nobody feels that it was fully *real* . . . it was a kind of *imagined war* to satisfy the needs of Bush and Blair. That's shorthand, but do you know what I mean?

◆ *GR: Oh I do know, and I agree entirely. The term I came up with watching Fox News—which is also called "Watching the Beast"—I called it the* Subjunctive War. *It was the absolute* **Triumph of the Subjunctive.** *At* *every point it was: "A canister was found today which* might be *weapons of mass destruction." The "might be" passes as news because by the time anybody apprehends what it is, apart from the immediate psychological impact of "weapons of mass destruction," the line item has gone and it's never recanted. It's just a* suggestion *that's put into people's minds over and over and over again.*

♦ **JGB:** They say here in the newspapers that Bush and the Pentagon are *playing down* the casualties: the dead American servicemen who are being bumped off at the rate of about ten a week are flown into some air base near Washington under cover of darkness. There are no photographers allowed. I don't know if this is true or not.

♦ *GR: It's very true.*

♦ **JGB: There are hints of Orwell's *1984* in this sort of manipulation of language, manipulation of the truth**, to the point where nobody can *define* what the truth is. The whole thing, the whole Gulf War, is a projection of Bush's and Blair's political evangelism on the one hand, and the kind of strange virtual plan for global domination which the *neo-cons* in Washington have been dreaming up with their menu that goes beyond Iraq into Iran, Syria, North Korea—you name it: "The Project for the New American Century." The whole thing reads like a scenario for, on the one hand, a sort of new movie (*Armageddon II?*) . . . and also **a new blueprint for a kind of militaristic religion—**

♦ *GR: —which needs to be scripted* a priori; *they have to know what the blueprint is.*

♦ **JGB:** Of course England is a minor player, but we did have something like 40,000 troops in Iraq a few months ago, and have quite a number there now. **Blair has come up against constant criticism for the failure to find these weapons of mass destruction, which over here was the main reason for going to war.** I don't think that's true in America.

♦ *GR: It initially was here, but they shifted rather quickly to it being a "humanitarian mission."*

♦ **JGB:** Here it's still clung to as the main reason for going to war. You'd think that Blair would have been put out—slightly *fazed* by this failure to find these weapons. But some cranky evangelist who predicted the world was going to end on December 17th isn't the least put out when Armageddon fails to materialize! In fact, his faith is only strengthened. Prophets throughout the ages who have claimed that the world was about to end on a specific date but are then proved wrong—far from disappointing their congregations, they proclaim, "We didn't believe *enough* . . . so God withheld his lightning bolt until we *do* believe enough." Blair takes that same sort of view.

It's clear that some pretty strange political leaders are now emerging in the West: Bush, Blair, Berlusconi in Italy, one or two really hard right-wingers on mainland Europe. I think that people are withdrawing from politics. Turnout at the last British general election, high by U.S. standards, was very low. The Labor Party won a vast landslide here—they have something like 450 seats in the House of Commons. But they did so on something like 25 percent of the potential vote, because huge numbers of people just didn't turn up at the Ballot Box.

You sense people withdrawing from politics in a way they probably started to do years ago in America. I don't know the American psyche well enough, but something like the election of Schwarzenegger is such a strange thing to do. It's happened before . . . when Reagan was elected.

♦ *GR: Your observations in* The Atrocity Exhibition *were wonderful, and I'm sure you've got some things to say about Arnold—*

♦ **JGB:** I'm not sure I do, actually.

♦ *GR: Really? It's almost completely predictable in the sense of it being totally expected.*

♦ **JGB:** It's slightly baffling in that **Reagan was a very cunning manipulator of the popular psychology of his TV and radio audiences.** I remember watching his TV commercials in 1965, which inspired my piece on him when he was running for Governor of California. He was a very astute and much tougher man than he was when he reached the White House. He had a sneering tone that he had completely lost by the time he was elected President. But he was very skillful at manipulating the psychology, the moods and emotions of his audience—probably something he learned to do when he was a sports commentator. Schwarzenegger doesn't have *any* of those manipulative skills. He's as blank as the *Terminator.*

♦ *GR: Most of his rhetoric is just repeated lines, in the same way that Reagan quoted* Star Wars *when talking about the "evil empire."*

♦ **JGB:** I wonder if the election of Schwarzenegger wasn't an unconscious rebellion by the California electorate against the whole democratic process. They'd elected Schwarzenegger's predecessor—

♦ *GR: Gray Davis.*

♦ **JGB:** —who was a machine politician, by all accounts, and who apparently did a very bad job. They simply wanted to hold up a middle finger to the whole notion of electing a sane politician to fill the role. In the same way Jean Le Pen [extreme right candidate] a few years ago, when he ran against Chirac for the presidency of France, on the first ballot got a stupendous 30 percent of the vote. The same way Berlusconi was elected.

People have literally *assigned* the political process to the wastebasket—they'd elect Mickey Mouse if given a chance! It may be the civil service in California, like the civil service here and in most European countries, is strong enough to run the state . . . we'll see. But **giant deficits don't just *go away!***

♦ *GR: Something very symptomatic happened in California. Briefly, there was an energy crisis which was essentially manipulated by a free-market company called Enron. The Federal Government ignored what they were doing because they were quite happy to see a Democratic government in California get into big trouble—*

♦ **JGB:** Right.

♦ *GR: Apart from all the ins and outs of this, the public's ability to understand how that happened has dissipated. It's much too complicated a soundbite for anybody to apprehend. When you're down to the McLuhan world of the one-and-a-half-second soundbites of Arnold saying, "I'm going to terminate [something]"—that's about the level of understanding. There's no other way to understand this except: it looks like a mess, and they must be to blame—it's an extraordinary manipulation by the Bush government. I think just yesterday two other states went Republican. It really is quite a little conspiracy that's going on.*

♦ **JGB:** How far do you think 9-11 has cast a shadow over local politics in America, at the governor level, senators' level, and so on?

♦ *GR: It's become all-pervasive. I'm quite surprised that the Democratic runners are even attacking the government being at war, because it's such a dangerous thing to do, what with this ubiquitous "War on Terror." Whenever you turn on the TV news, that's the headline that's behind the fool reading whatever they're told to read. You cannot move without this reminder that somewhere there's an Arab about to attack you in your bed. Quite extraordinary . . .*

♦ **JGB:** The curious thing is, as people have been pointing out for quite some time: **there's no obvious connection between Saddam and the Iraqi regime . . . and the Al Qaeda, Arab, Islamic terrorism against the West.**

♦ *GR: Quite the contrary.*

♦ **JGB:** Saddam's secular, Baathist regime, is hated by bin Laden, apparently—I've seen quotes or statements made by him years ago. I don't think anyone over here believes that Blair's war, as it were, was in any way a kind of pre-emptive strike against Bin Laden activities in the West. But I get the impression, sometimes, that Americans *do* think this.

♦ *GR: Fifty percent or more of Americans still believe it. You still find generals and talking heads every day suggesting it: "Oh yes, there were connections." They make very vague statements, so they can't be held up to scrutiny, but the suggestion is always there.*

What's extraordinary is: I get the sense that in England, with the size of the demonstrations and so on, most of the population is quite sure that Tony Blair has been caught in a lie—a big lie, that in the past would have qualified as treason: "You're killing your citizens for an extraordinary lie, a manipulation of the truth" . . . but it's not sufficient to bring him down anymore.

♦ **JGB:** No, and that's a very worrying development. There's something very unsettling about that. Particularly as just before the war began here, there was a vast peaceful march by a million-plus people through the streets of London protesting against the war which everyone felt was about to open. Opinion polls show that something like a scant majority of the people approve of packing up our troops and bringing them back home. You'd expect that, once the first bullet has been fired . . .

Most (how should one put it?) *reflective* people—readers of broadsheet rather than tabloid newspapers—realize that we were taken to war on a false perspective. And yet it seems to make no difference. It's as if people have unconsciously *written off* the political process as belonging to a world which they can't influence in any way. That's worrying, because it leaves people sort of falling back on a very different set of resources.

It's difficult to envisage what the reactions of the British public, or the American public for that matter, would be to another 9-11—a gas attack or dirty nuclear device or something similar. Because people have *uncoupled* their belief in a sane world that they can influence through the political realm. That's a very dangerous state of affairs. It turns Western Europe and the States into a sort of unstable *Weimar*-like era where: **if reason sleeps, monsters are born.** One prays there *isn't* another 9-11.

♦ *GR: I can agree with you. This war was quite a* paradigm shift *because in the past I've read "they" used the same kind of justification when they invaded the Philippines, or when the British were invading various parts of Africa. The language hasn't changed all that much.*

I think what has *changed is that in those days you could say, "Well, people back then weren't very well-informed or very well-educated; that's not surprising." Now I think (even though that's still very much the case)* **there's almost a deliberate program, especially in America, to keep the population under-educated.**

There are many, many people who do *have the information, who know that this is not the truth. But I feel that basically even though we still have the* language *of the Enlightenment and Truth and so on,* **the**

"Enlightenment Project" is absolutely dead. *Because now we* know, *but we still don't do anything about it, or we don't* care *enough to. Do you know what I mean?*

♦ **JGB:** Absolutely—I agree with you one hundred percent.

♦ *GR: In that sense the 21st century is already becoming a different mind-set from the 20th century—*

♦ **JGB:** Absolutely. At the time, shortly after 9-11, like practically everybody else, I was rung up by newspapers to ask for my thoughts—but I really didn't *have* any thoughts! I said, "You know, 9-11 was an attack on the Enlightenment and everything it stood for." Sadly the Enlightenment has nothing to offer in return—in a way **we're coming to the end of the Age of Reason.**

We ran from Voltaire to Freud. Freud ended his life on a very pessimistic note. If you read the grimly wonderful last paragraph of *Civilization and Its Discontents* which was one of his last books, written when he managed to get out of Austria and make it to Hampstead in North London for the last year or two of his life, he was more or less saying that human beings now have the power to destroy themselves utterly if they wanted to.

The death instinct seems to be in the ascendant. If you think of the Enlightenment (roughly speaking) as running from the birth of modern science up to 1933 and the arrival of Hitler, obviously its influence continued on through the Second World War and beyond that. One senses that the Age of Reason has now begun to *fade.* Because most of the *appeal* by politicians, church leaders and the like when they address their congregations, is not to appeal to reason anymore, but rather to emotion or evangelical ideas about a "better world."

The flight of reason leaves people with these partly-conscious notions that perhaps they can rely on the *irrational.* Psychopathology offers a better guarantor of their own freedom from the cant and bullshit and sales commercials that fill the ether every moment of the day. *That's* the real danger. One saw it in absolute peak form during the Nazi period, but already there are hints that the *appeals to the irrational*

Photo: Ana Barrado

are becoming more and more to the fore. It's present in the entertainment culture, but now you see it in politics, you see it in the evangelical churches. One good thing I could say about this country is that most people still don't go to church, but in America, of course, it's incredible—you see figures like "Ninety percent of Americans believe in God." Fair enough . . . but do something like 50 percent of Americans go to church on Sunday? Do you think that's true?

♦ *GR: Oh, it's very true. There was this wonderful poll the other day: 78 percent of Americans not only believe in Heaven but are sure they're going to go there. But oddly enough, only 71 percent believed in Hell!*

♦ **JGB:** That's funny. [laughs]

♦ *GR: Wonderfully optimistic. I'm blown away by that statistic—*

♦ **JGB:** It's extraordinary. **This "New Religiosity" is a *retreat from reason*. People are not putting their faith in reason but in a huge irrational system built around various supernatural beliefs.** And this retreat from reason is taking place at the same time that the United States has developed these *super-technologies* that are really changing our lives. **It's an extraordinary development that someone working on the forefront of advanced science and technology should on Sunday put on a different hat, go off and listen to fables spun about a Palestinian resurrection cult 2000 years ago.** It's bizarre, in a way.

I'm reading your great countryman Robert Hughes's book on *Goya* at the moment . . . he seems to have broken off relations with Australia; I don't know why, but there we are . . . Goya's Spain around the last quarter of the 1700's—1780 and the like—was still dominated by the Catholic Church. The Inquisition was still active, even though modern France had emerged and was beginning to transform everything. It's a very peculiar coincidence which makes me . . . if the British population started going to church again, I would be really *worried*. People have always gone to church for *social* reasons: to establish themselves in their communities and all the rest of it; as a *status* thing. But **I get the impression that a lot of American churchgoing is utterly sincere . . . that it is an expression of the *devout*.**

That is *genuinely* scary!

♦ **GR:** *It's very strange. And also, the other salient point is that even though these people consider themselves fundamentalists (and they are in most ways), many of them also believe in "karma" and a whole lot of New Agey notions that are completely extraneous to fundamentalism. It made me think of your idea that they were just embracing whatever mythology came along, and making this wonderful* mélange *of the whole thing; and it doesn't really worry them that something wasn't in the Bible at all. They somehow imagined that it was.*

♦ **JGB:** Is that what is happening, in effect? A whole goulash of New Age and Christian fundamentalist notions—

♦ **GR:** That's *what I think is happening. I was musing on the whole Enlightenment Project . . . that it wasn't very long after Newtonian physics that the Enlightenment was formed, especially the American experiments—Jefferson and so on. It must have taken about 100 years, from 1687 to 1770 or so. It was a fairly easy set of precepts to organize into a social organization, whereas many of the things that you've been interested in, like Surrealism and Quantum Mechanics—it's very difficult stuff for people to formulate: "What does that* mean *for life? What does the universe actually* look *like?" So you get this trend away from sense itself. Suicide pathology is one expression of this.*

*At the same time I think it's fairly natural that people will then turn to archaic mythologies in an attempt to make some structure, some sense of it. We're finding about 100 years later that society actually does seem to look like a contemporary paradigm of the universe. Unfortunately, it's a rather desperate and very unhappy embracing of **what the "new universe" looks like: just a bunch of probabilities.** Whereas in the past, people's idea about "the universe" seemed much more certain; it was an easier paradigm for people to embrace and to live with.*

♦ **JGB:** Right. What bothers me is that something is happening that you could almost call the "Normalizing of the Psychopathic"—the greater and greater *areas* of what used to be regarded as the psychopathic by, say, my parents. They were born at the turn of the previous century, and they would have regarded certain behaviors as psychopathic sexual behavior. For example, almost any form of criminal behavior, like shoplifting, they would have regarded as a sign of real mental deviancy—things that are now *accepted.*

Sexual perversions that would have horrified them are almost dinner party conversation now. **Nobody feels guilty about any deviant sexual behavior of the Krafft-Ebing type.** Likewise, when you hear that a friend or a neighbor has been arrested for shoplifting, there's no question of social exclusion as would have happened in the 1920s, 1930s, 1940s or even 1950s here. One just feels sorry: "Oh, poor woman, you know—her husband left her. She's been under a lot of stress." More and more areas of once-serious psychopathic behavior are now admitted into what is loosely called the "normal."

There was a case here about four or five years ago. A group of sado-masochistic homosexuals met at a little club of their own making and performed a lot of very violent sexual acts involving hammers and nails and planks of wood. I won't try to describe what they were doing—you can imagine: having your scrotum nailed to a plank . . . not my idea of fun, but each to their own taste.

♦ *GR: I saw that show with Vale—he drags me along to those sorts of things.*

♦ **JGB:** For some reason the police got wind of this particular club's activities, and arrested the half-dozen men involved—all of whom were willing participants, incidentally. They were prosecuted. I think they were fined, and one or two were given suspended sentences. They went to appeal and all the newspapers discussed this at great length.

The overall sentiment by columnists and the like, even among quite right-wing newspapers here, was that these men had been wrongly prosecuted. What they got up to was their own business and they should not have been . . . I think their appeals were denied, but the general consensus of intelligent opinion was that they shouldn't have been prosecuted. I thought, *"That's* a change." Here is what my parents would have regarded as absolute, out-and-out psychopathic behavior that deserved the men in white coats coming around immediately, and long-term incarceration. That's changed.

On the one hand it's good to see tolerance. On the other hand, one senses that almost a kind of *elective* psychopathology is now in the air. **One can almost choose to indulge in a mode of psychopathic behavior without any sort of moral inhibition at all.** In fact, given the suffocating effect of the entertainment landscape, the sort of *smothering flow* of manufactured television programs and advertisements and all the rest of it . . . the only kind of fall-back position that any of us has, lies with the human potential for madness.

We're being driven by some kind of compulsive need to cut the pigtails off a six-year-old girl sitting on the bus in front of you, or steal underwear from a neighbor's wash line—far from being driven, you choose, you *elect* to pursue some odd impulse. I suspect that a lot of the people who have been charged by the police, including Pete Townshend who was one of the prominent members of The Who—I don't know if you heard about this—

♦ *GR: Yes, I did. The pedophile thing—*

♦ **JGB:** I think he was let off with a caution, in fact. He was charged with downloading a huge amount of pedophile material. The FBI carried out a big investigation of one or two major suppliers of pedophile material on the Internet—arrested them and found thousands of addresses—I'm not sure if it was e-mail addresses, or what.

♦ *GR: To me that was a kind of critical question. Because I wasn't sure if it was the e-mail address, or just—*

♦ **JGB:** —passive downloading.

♦ *GR: Yes. I spend most of my day on the Internet. It has become my research tool for all sorts of things. Of course, I admit that I look at pornography occasionally—it's very difficult, with the way people organize their enterprises, to avoid those things popping up. If you're in that arena, pornographic sites will pop up, and I don't know to what extent you can be accused of "downloading." I've never downloaded in the sense of printing anything out; I try to get out very quickly.*

♦ **JGB:** These are paid sites. You actually have to give your credit card number, and that's where all these people like Townshend were tracked down. A large number of police officers were among the paying customers—even one or two magistrates as well—the usual suspects, in other words!

As you say, **there's a huge amount of sexually deviant material on the Internet.** Recently my girlfriend said, "Migod, I've just been watching a lot of defecating women on some bizarre site." I didn't offer to look over her shoulder. She was, as you say, a *passive spectator,* but I suspect that even among those over here who have been charged by the police as paying customers for pedophile material— they may not be pedophiles at all, or have any kind of pedophile interest. **What they are looking for is some sort of *dramatic stimulus* that will penetrate the kind of *bland manufactured pap* that makes up most of the media landscape today.**

It's like watching films of public executions. Someone sent me some strange compilation cassettes a couple of years ago, under the assumption that they were to my taste. They were all semi-commercial—no, they were out-and-out commercially-released videos of executions from the Third World—god knows where—Vietnam, Biafra, the civil war in the Congo, and so on. Much of this had been shown on TV and in newsreels, or got into the public domain. Some things went back quite a long way—twenty or thirty years.

There's something deadening, and at the same time very shocking—it's a jolt to the central nervous system—to see a close-up, from an apparent distance of about three feet, of a man tied to a pole being machine-gunned to death. I suspect that a lot of people accessing this kind of material on the Internet—particularly the sexual material— are just driven by a need for something that seems *authentic.*

♦ *GR: I had an experience three nights ago. I was catching up with a friend of mine in a bar. I don't go out very much anymore, because I don't even want to* look *at the outside world—*

♦ **JGB:** You stay in your gated community—

♦ *GR: Yes, and you know what—I draw the curtains now . . . even in the gated community. It's out towards Santa Barbara in an equestrian kind of setting. It's rather nice, but once again, you sort of* retreat *from the*

world and then you live in a universe of one, really. Anyway, I was in the
bar catching up with a friend and there were two other people in the bar: a
chap he knew who was a small-time TV actor, with his girlfriend (I
assumed). My friend was talking to the guy so I started talking to the girl;
she was sweet and perhaps Asian, I think, very demure, wearing a
pullover—nothing special—

♦ **JGB:** Right.

♦ *GR: She said, "Oh, I need to go soon—I have to get up at 3:45—I've got*
to have my enemas for my work. I'm on set at 5 o'clock."

I thought, "Ohmigosh"—I felt like your parents, or my grandparents,
would have felt. Was my leg being pulled halfway out the door here, or is
this girl just speaking about her job in a certain industry as if it were the
most normal thing in the world—

♦ **JGB:** You mean she was being forward about her porno films?

♦ *GR: Yes; she had been in "Asian Debutante" I, II and III.*

♦ **JGB: Asian babe enema films?**

♦ *GR: Yes, I think so.*

♦ **JGB:** How bizarre.

♦ *GR: Of course, the fact that those type of films exist doesn't surprise me*
in the slightest, but the fact that this girl, as a part of a perfectly normal
conversation, should tell a stranger this, while smiling—

♦ **JGB:** This is *the normalizing of sexual pathology.* It's bizarre. I don't
want to make an "apocalyptic prophecy"—I hardly ever do anything *but*
make apocalyptic prophecies [!]—but I see elective psychopathy as *the*
coming thing.

♦ *GR: What worries me, though, is: I think it's a fairly finite universe. We*
only have so many orifices and we only have so much blood to let.

It seems that what you're saying, about people in this world being into
pedophilia who aren't really pedophiles, is symptomatic of this need:
"Well, I'm bored with Asian enemas now; I need to move on!"

♦ **JGB:** Exactly.

♦ *GR: How extreme does it get before—?*

♦ **JGB:** Well, that's what's worrying, exactly.

♦ *GR: That prurient fascination can only last for a few days or maybe a*

Photo: SM Gray

week at the most.

♦ JGB: A trial has just started here, of a young man who worked as a caretaker at a school in a small town in the Midlands. It's a very big case here, in a place called Fulham. I think his name is Huntley and he's charged with the murder of two ten-year-old girls who went out for a walk about a year ago one evening. They seem to have been invited into this man's house; as the local school caretaker he knew them well. They died within a very short time and he buried their bodies about twenty miles away. He and his girlfriend, who helped him in the cover-up (although she didn't take part in the murders) have just gone on trial in the Old Bailey. The trial is in its second day . . .

The bodies weren't found for several weeks. There was a huge manhunt in this country; it wasn't known who had killed them. Their bodies were only discovered in shallow graves by *chance.* The small village, where everybody knew everybody else, was absolutely devastated. The four parents were totally shattered, and the police, sensibly, appointed a male police officer to look after them—to steer them away from the prying press and help them get over these deaths. An amazing thing happened: the particular officer who had been assigned to look after the parents was charged with downloading pedophile material from the Internet; he was prosecuted, had to leave the police, and may have been imprisoned.

Everybody was just amazed that this kindly and enlightened attempt to help the parents of two murdered girls, had been handed to a man who was a closet pedophile! But obviously, isn't there some kind of bizarre connection? The media *feast* of salacious fantasies about what had actually *happened* to these two girls at the hands of this young man, had probably *infected* this policeman—he wasn't necessarily a hardcore pedophile at all! He may have been a case of "innocence being corrupted." I'm probably putting it a little too strongly, but these strange paradoxical crossovers sort of *standing logic on its head* seem to be going on all the time. It's absolutely baffling.

♦ GR: *That's interesting. In the past there was the sense that you had "the centered self" and that psychopathology was where you had multiple personas, or something like that. It sounds like what you're saying is: in the* *past you might have had your favorite psychopathology, so you might be a pedophile and that would be your psychopathology.* **Now it seems there's an idea that there are** multiple psychopathologies. *You're a pedophile for two weeks, and then you move on—*

♦ **JGB:** —then you move on down the menu! Right, and this is sort of *elective.* I'm a great supporter of the Internet, but what you find is: people are developing *distributed personalities*, in a way. My girlfriend is taking an Internet university course and has built up quite a large collection of Internet friends over the last few years, depending on the various courses she's doing. Some of these have led to her joining certain Internet societies; she's interested in the fine arts. I talked this over with her and she agrees that she has a wide-ranging personality spread, depending on which of these Internet contacts she's making. *That* you would expect.

But what is interesting is: when she started meeting these people face-to-face, to go to an art gallery together, or whatever it might be— seminars they have to attend—she got on well with people whom she had only known as glorified pen-pals. That's very unusual. Usually you go, "*Ohmigod*—how did I ever share so many letters with this strange person?" That hasn't happened. It's almost as if there's something about the Internet which is filtering out people who are *not* going to get along well with you. It's most peculiar.

Actually, I'm wondering if it isn't so much *that,* as the fact that given a sort of "distributed personality" across the whole range of Internet contacts, when you *meet* the actual person, you are only bringing to bear a small portion of your *actual* personality, and you're quite satisfied. Whereas in the old days, when you met a pen-pal and you were pulled up short and thought, "Oh god, how are we going to get through this strange meal together?" because you were expecting a complete meeting of minds, *now* you only meet that small portion of the mind that's being offered across the Internet bridge.

I observe the Internet over my girlfriend's shoulder; I don't want to get too close because it might *suck me in.*

♦ *GR: Yes, it does.*

♦ **JGB:** I can see that. I imagine that one could develop a kind of *broadband personality* that can range across a much wider moral and imaginative human spectrum than appears when we meet people in an office or factory space or wherever it may be. I think the Net is an absolutely extraordinary development. **Maybe the Internet will save the human race!**

♦ *GR: I think so. On a positive note, that's very interesting. The third installment of* The Matrix *came out today and some people find that quite fascinating—*

♦ **JGB:** It's seen as an art film—very interesting.

♦ *GR: It's interesting, but **for me it's rather a sci-fi chestnut: "Man against the machine, and the machines are dominating,"** and then they go off into the "philosophy" which is by-and-large just mumbo-jumbo. The film is "saved" by the wonderful special effects. There is an interesting mix of things, but very much there's still this science-fiction notion that "machines are the enemy."*

Whereas in a way, I think machines may be what is going to save us, because psychopathology seems to me to have a fairly finite application. I can't see the period of experimentation lasting all that long. Certainly the machine interface is going to make it a lot more exciting, or at least lead into many different areas.

Recently I was reading a book by Ray Kurzweil, The Age of Spiritual Machines, *which speculated that **within 50 years we would all be running around with a chip in our head which would be a direct link to the entire store of human knowledge.** He was taking a very positive, optimistic view of things. Of course, it's also a direct link to the entire darkness of the human race—you must get one with the other. What we make of that will be very interesting.*

♦ **JGB:** I agree.

♦ *GR: He was also saying that the chip itself would eventually take on a personality of its own, because it would in fact be* our *personality that would be stored there—in a sense, a window to immortality. I don't think it's very far off. There's an extraordinary doubling of chip memory these days; it doubles every year now, I think.*

♦ **JGB:** I agree with you. The difficulty with watching movies like *The Matrix* and many, many similar movies of that kind, is that they extrapolate from a few possibilities into a completely self-sustaining vision of the future which has lost touch utterly with the world you and I inhabit. Progress tends to advance in a more *bleak* way, if you know what I mean—

♦ *GR: Oh, absolutely.*

♦ **JGB:** People still go on gossiping over the garden fence. We go on worrying about where the hell we're going to park our cars! We suffer from indigestion and god knows what else, *but* life in the universe is pretty much as it's always been. But, at the same time, Bush and Blair are running a mysterious and largely inexplicable war on the other side of the world, where some of our fellow citizens are getting killed and others bereaved. It's an inexplicable war—

♦ *GR: It's irrelevant; why are they worrying—trying to manipulate the "real world" like that?*

♦ **JGB:** Well, I think it's a case of thwarted progress based on a paranoid vision. I think of films like *Blade Runner* and *The Matrix* which are deeply paranoid in many ways. A huge number of American entertainment movies have this strain of paranoia—very curious. The sort of *vast conspiracy:* some super-Enron-style corporation which, when Denzel Washington breaks away from his captors and starts running across some Washington suburb, can put twenty black helicopters into the sky at five minutes notice—

♦ *GR:* The Siege—*yes, I worked on that one.*

♦ **JGB:** Oh, did you?

♦ *GR: Yes . . . a very predictive film.*

♦ **JGB:** I wish I could say I remembered the music, but it must have been good.

♦ *GR: Oh, it was, yeah! [laughs]*

♦ **JGB:** There's a huge strain of paranoia in a lot of these future visions. But I don't feel that *1984* is going to arrive at the front door— or *Brave New World* for that matter, or the updated versions with a complete *mise en scène.* I think it's more oblique—you know, the discovery that some big corporation is covering up contamination of our water supply (or something), and doing it in collusion with the government. It's much more oblique, and anyway much more threatening for being oblique. It's sort of *damaged* (that would be true in the case of Blair) and *inadequate* (that would be true of Bush) *men* that lead our nations!

♦ *GR: Do you think that is because we by-and-large feel that what they do has nothing to do with the world that we really inhabit now? They still live in this unreal world—*

♦ **JGB:** The world of Bush and Blair?

♦ *GR: Yes. In a way I feel that the reason that* way *less than 30 percent of young Americans under 25 bother to vote at all is an indication of that. They don't really get it, they don't care; they go, "Why are these people doing* this stuff?*"*

♦ **JGB:** The young people have abandoned politics. They've abandoned rational choice. They'd rather make the irrational choice, because the irrational choice offers more *freedom.* **If you're going to enlarge your sense of personal freedom, your personality and the range of your responses to life: your ambitions, hopes, dreams, and all the rest of it, it's probably better to rely on *irrational* choices than a rational choice!**

♦ *GR: Absolutely.*

♦ **JGB:** The Age of Reason is probably petering out slowly. Only our machines will be reasonable, because they make sense. We can *rely* on our computers to be moral beings. **A machine, in a sense, is a moral structure—like a thermostat.** If the room is too hot it will bring the temperature down. A satellite positioning system will tell you exactly where you are; it won't fake it. And that passes for morality, practically, now.

♦ *GR: [laughs]*

♦ **JGB:** The various computers that are installed in, say, the US Treasury Department or the British Treasury or the French Treasury, that try to work out whether taxes should go up or down next year—

these computers are highly moralistic. They're not swayed by short-term political advantage; they tell you the truth.

I think we are subcontracting our moral universe to that of the machines—in principle, the computers. **Maybe the Internet itself is a kind of vast machine.** We are subcontracting the moral dimensions in our lives to the machine world. This will allow us to play—like some millionaire's kids in a highly advanced nursery—to play with our elaborate toys, which are our various deviant psychological impulses . . . *without hurting ourselves.* That's the hope.

The trouble is, you know, elective psychopathology has been tried many times. It was certainly tried during the Nazi era, by a complete nation. It was tried by half of Europe, and led to madness. Of course, it was all *intended* to lead to madness; it wasn't an accident.

One worries . . . I worry for my grandchildren growing up in a world where a damaged leader like Tony Blair can actually take his country to *war.* It's a bizarre state of affairs; **we're going back to the era of the more eccentric Roman Emperors!** You read about Bush and the neo-cons Powell and Cheney and . . . they've got their own *think tank*—is it called the Heritage Institute?

♦ **GR:** *That's one of them, yes.*

♦ **JGB:** This man, Paul Wolfowitz?

♦ **GR:** *Wolfowitz. Karl Rove is the very dangerous one.*

♦ **JGB:** These people are *maniacal,* actually. During the Clinton years they came up with this "Project for a New American Century." They've now got control of all the levers and triggers run from the White House. Rumsfeld runs the Defense Department. They are police strategists with delusional fantasies of omnipotence. **They've got this "omnipotence" dream which they want to impose on the rest of the world**, and they've started—there's no doubt about it. They have this super weapons technology that is capable, practically, of erasing human life on the planet.

I thought it was very interesting when Wolfowitz was in Baghdad, staying in a hotel in a big U.S. compound. Some guerrillas—pro-Saddam guerrillas, one assumes—fired several rockets at the hotel and one narrowly missed Wolfowitz. He was shown, visibly shaken, at a press conference. Then they took him out and found the multiple rocket launcher that had been abandoned—

♦ **GR:** *—in the truck, yes.*

♦ **JGB:** —by the guerrillas. You saw him staring at it. This was a man sort of *changed,* who had *briefly* glimpsed reality.

♦ **GR:** *I loved the line in* Super-Cannes*: "I'm not worried about any alternative ideology—there isn't one. Reality is what we have to worry about." I think the next day Bush came on TV and said the most wonderful spin I've heard in a long time: "This shows that we are winning . . . that they have to stoop to tactics like this." [laughs]*

♦ **JGB:** It's wonderful, absolutely. To an outsider like myself who has always been interested in America, one wonders whether something hasn't gone wrong! . . . it's the *infantilizing of America,* which isn't actually confined to America—it's happening here, too. But **the infantilizing of America has reached a dangerous point.** We've moved down. Back in the Sixties and Seventies, the middle-aged 30- and 40-year-old Americans that had fought the Second World War went on to fight the Korean War, and then something happened: *Vietnam.*

The *mental age of America,* as it were, fell down—lowered itself—to the college era; college-era kids dominated the American psyche. Everything from Haight-Ashbury to Kent State where those kids—students—got shot, and all the marches and the youth explosion scene—the anti-Nixon movement. America became "a sensitive, caring college youth." Since then, one senses, the infantilizing process has reduced the . . . this sounds terribly glib and British; I don't mean it to be, but it's shorthand—

♦ **GR:** *Yes.*

♦ **JGB:** **—we now have an adolescent America with enough intelligence to run a war and run a vast economy. It's beginning to swallow its own myth.** I worry for the future when the infantilizing process takes America and parts of Western Europe (including us) down with it, to be ten years old, or even younger. What happens when we get down to the nursery, and find we can't change our own diapers?

Photo: Ana Barrado

♦ *GR: I think that's where we are now. I notice it very much in the entertainment industry and I think it's very symptomatic of society as a whole. At this point the stories we're telling are definitely aimed at the 13-year-old, it's getting lower every year—*

♦ **JGB:** That's what I think—

♦ *GR: Yet the people who work on the stories, by and large, are fairly intelligent people. What they're doing is just telling stories—fairy tales, unfortunately—in a very, very traditional way. You have to have your first act end at page 28 or you're not going to make it—*

♦ **JGB:** Yes; one act every four frames—the old comic strip rule.

♦ *GR: Exactly, and there's very little experimentation with that. My point is, there's a complete divorce between the* telling *of the story and the* why *are we telling the story. "We're just telling the story because it's purely a marketing thing: we're going to make money; we have a job."*

♦ **JGB:** It's a *product*, like Parker pens or Twinkies or something.

♦ *GR: Absolutely. The problem is, I don't think that any of them really realize that it then becomes the predominant story, style—the outcome is always the same, and everything happens at the same time . . . for the* entire world!

♦ **JGB:** It becomes the *climate*. **That's the danger: when an entertainment system becomes a mental climate** . . . and we now have a mental climate where the whole planet inhabits a kind of *Con Air-Armageddon-Independence Day* world of super-paranoid visions, with all that they summon up in the minds of the spectator. Hollywood's audiences have always been passive—the movies aren't interactive. I think one saving grace of the Internet is that it *is* basically an interactive system in large part, from the ordinary user's point of view.

Talking about your gated community—they're starting to spring up over here. In fact, my little back street in Shepperton basically has its own little gated community. They found a plot of land only about 100 yards from where I live, some former stables. Of course, they razed the stables and built six "executive houses"—detached houses with two bathrooms (that's a sign that you've "arrived" in this country) . . . *and* they've got a gate. It's its own little gated community. Of course, there are much larger ones around.

♦ **GR:** *Do you think the impetus for that is really "security," or do you just think it's sort of a vague excuse for "the thing to do"?*

♦ **JGB:** It's probably security—I mean, they've existed in America for doubtless years.

♦ **GR:** *Oddly enough, though, they're not in dangerous areas—they're in exactly the opposite. The idea of the "dreaded black man" driving 30 miles from downtown L.A. to steal something from my house is ludicrous!*

♦ **JGB:** Well, it's an interesting move. It's almost as if a sort of *re-tribalizing* is taking place, where we've lost faith in society as a whole, in the sort of very large aggregations of populations which we have been brought up to think of as "the norm" . . . in the case of Britain our complete nation, or the Welsh people, or the Scottish people, or California, or the South, or whatever. I don't know how strong "state consciousness" is in America.

But anyway . . . **it's as if we've lost faith in these sort of larger aggregations, and are re-tribalizing ourselves—not on the basis of *blood* kinship, but on the basis of *professional* kinship.** So all the dentists get together in gated communities. They tend to be professional middle-class people of certain income groups, and therefore of rather similar professions (or of rather similar professional *status),* as far as I can make out.

It may be that this re-tribalizing is a kind of deep-layered response to a feeling that *stormy weather* is approaching. Perhaps not, but I *wonder* about this.

I've been reading Mike Davis's latest book. You know—the *City of Quartz* man?

♦ **GR:** *Yes.*

♦ **JGB:** Brilliant writer in his way. His latest book is *Dead Cities;* I reviewed it for *The Guardian* newspaper. He's absolutely steeped in the social history of California, but he hates big corporations—he feels they've destroyed L.A. and large areas of California.

♦ **GR:** *I'm not sure what there* was *to destroy in L.A.!*

♦ **JGB:** Yes, I agree with you, but . . . essentially, he devotes a wonderful chapter to Las Vegas. If you know Las Vegas well, it's worth digging the book out.

♦ *GR: I will, yes. There are some stories here—*

♦ **JGB:** I'll bet! . . . He sees the old "Casino Las Vegas" as only a tired little corner of the "*New* Las Vegas" which is a vast network of retirement homes, executive housing, and gated communities. He actually lavishes a lot of space on what I called, in my review, "the innermost circle of hell." I have a nightmare vision of a gated community of extremely expensive houses inside a *larger* gated community. It's bizarre.

♦ *GR: [laughs] Even within our gated community in California, there's the "old side" and the "new side"—and never the twain shall meet!*

♦ **JGB:** Yes; they're *all* insecure these days—middle-class professionals are some of *the* most insecure people—

♦ *GR: I had an incident recently with this young chap down the road who likes cars, and I drive quite a nice car. He's a little kid who's in school, and he lives just outside the gate—I talk to him frequently. Apparently he was arrested the other day because he was playing a modern version of "Cowboys and Indians" (whatever that is) and had a little plastic gun. The armed guard at the gate said one of the residents coming in was terrified that this twelve-year-old child might be a danger to the community—*

♦ **JGB:** Amazing.

♦ *GR: So, we're surrounded by armed guards that we don't know from Adam; any one of them could be a psychopath that could run amok at any time. But because they put a uniform on, they're okay!*

♦ **JGB:** That kid needs to do hundreds of hours of community service! His parents will be hauled in front of the local judge and given a stern warning.

♦ *GR: [laughs] There's a wonderful writer in Los Angeles I like—a member of one of the few independent think tanks in L.A.—named Jeremy Rifkin. He's written a fabulous book on genetic research, one on the Internet, and one on the hydrogen economy. I love his books; he's a very smart man.*

In his latest book on the coming of the hydrogen economy, he gives the

idea that this might be the end of the immense centralization and hierar-
chal organization that we suffered through the petroleum years. He said
that perhaps the gated community, or small independent communities,
may be the end of this idea, and that we'll all be organizing ourselves and
becoming self-sufficient with this new resource. I was wondering what you
thought about that—

♦ **JGB:** I read a little bit here and there about the hydrogen economy, but **it's difficult to visualize self-sufficiency operating on a very local level.** I mean, we're enormously dependent—too dependent—on a vast range of products and services; we seem to need big corporations to develop them and supply them. I think we're *stuck* with Dupont and ICI and Bayer and so on, for quite a while.

♦ *GR: We* are *so infantilized; we've almost handed off all those grown-up responsibilities to the corporations to take care of, haven't we?*

♦ **JGB:** Absolutely.

♦ *GR: It would be far too much work to have to change our own battery, or something—*

♦ **JGB:** Going back to what we were talking about earlier: **we seem to have subcontracted out the moral dimensions to our lives. We rely on someone else to make moral decisions for us.** We're happy to be told what a successful stock market portfolio is; we don't want to have to do the thinking ourselves. We're happy to be told what the best way to educate our children is; **the fewer moral decisions we make, the better** . . . as far as most people are concerned.

You know, we want to move through life as if it were an elaborate-ly-signaled highway with red, amber, green, filter left, filter right, and the speed limits clearly marked. Just like children much prefer the moral decisions to be made by their parents, while they get on with the business of unwrapping the latest piece of candy.

♦ *GR: [laughs] It's a shame, isn't it? Just at the moment that technology has almost allowed "the great utopia" to take place, with a sort of "informed society" and all this kind of thing, the* desire *to go there has completely evaporated—*

♦ **JGB:** Exactly. People begin to feel that a *dystopia* might be more fun! It might appeal to masochistic impulses. Many twentieth-century societies clearly displayed huge levels of latent masochism; you could say that the Soviet Union for more than fifty years was a masochistic dystopia which was partly willed by its population. Likewise, the German population under Hitler—yet another masochistic dystopia.

♦ *GR: I think America is, too.*

♦ **JGB:** People are mystified: why did the Germans go on fighting to the end? The obvious answer is: they *liked* having the shit bombed out of them! I'm not trying to be flippant; **there was a deep need for punishment—their *own* punishment**—and there may be strains of that in the ordinary Soviet citizenry.

Likewise I think that, having lived through the post-war austerity years in England, there was a deep masochistic strain in the English population of the late Forties and Fifties which was only thrown off in the Sixties. I mean, for twenty years the British *wanted* to be rationed. We *needed* to be rationed; we *needed* to be short of clothes, fresh food, possibility . . . we *needed* to feel guilty because we'd lost the war, we'd lost the empire, and ceded the running of the world to the Americans. We felt we needed to be punished for all that. And we *embraced* austerity. Populations have these deep-rooted needs.

I'm frightened that the possibilities of a genuine dystopia may be much more appealing than any utopian project that people can come up with—

♦ *GR: I think you're right. Have you seen Michael Moore's documentary,* Bowling for Columbine? *Essentially he's asking, "Why on earth do Americans need to be armed to the teeth? Why are they so paranoid?" He doesn't get to what you just explained—there's a line from* Super-Cannes: **"People no longer need enemies; their great dream is to be victims."** *I think this is universal; it's not a national trait at all. This in fact is what America is going through: this "wonderful" feeling that they're a victim. It can only be described as some kind of primitive masochism—*

♦ **JGB:** I think so. That seemed to be the personal reaction in and around New York. Granted, a horrific event had taken place [9-11]. It was interesting how the character of the city seemed to change.

♦ *GR: You could get lynched in America if you publicly stated that—*

♦ **JGB:** Tell Vale to press the "delete" button! Graeme, listen, have we touched all the bases? My brain's getting tired, and your phone bill must be astronomical—

♦ *GR: It was wonderful to catch up with you.*

♦ **JGB:** Good. Good luck. What about your group [SPK], the heavy-metal group you ran a thousand years ago?

♦ *GR: Yes. There's a very funny story about that. I did a small film treatment based on it and took it to Disney, because I have this rather warped sense of humor. Here's how the meeting went: the President of Disney said, "Well, tell me about your movie?" I started to, and was about a sentence-and-a-half into it when he went, "Don't mean to insult you, but composers aren't the most interesting people in the world." [laughs] I'd hate to hear how he would have* really *insulted me! I was nailed to my chair. Then he said, "This movie is like when Dumbo finds a feather and thinks he can fly."*

♦ **JGB:** Weird.

♦ *GR: I said, "It* is?*" And everybody who was in the room leapt to their feet and said, "Yes, that's* exactly *what it is—we're buying it!"*

♦ **JGB:** I believe you. When we talked before about the infantilizing of America, one has to bear in mind that it literally is taking place. If the future is a marriage—and I think it probably *is* a marriage between the Disney corporation and Microsoft . . . you know, **you're going to have these infantilizing Disney fantasies brought into the deeper levels of your brain by the super-technologies engineered by Microsoft.** There's going to be nothing else—

♦ *GR: Yes, even if we do have these wonderful technologies connecting to our heads, they'll just bring us the worst imaginable rubbish—*

♦ **JGB:** TV babble.

♦ *GR: We need good filters in our heads—*

♦ **JGB:** Yes. Great talking to you—

♦ *GR: And keep up the wonderful work. Thank you so much—*

♦ **JGB:** Bye bye. ♦ ♦ ♦

Photo from archive

J.G. Ballard and V. Vale

J.G. Ballard was interviewed by V. Vale in four separate phone conversations throughout 2003. Topics included computers, the Internet, terrorism, surveillance, home videos, Reality TV, SUVs, conspiracy theory, the Arab bogeyman, sex, drugs, NASA, elective psychopathologies, corporate and governmental crime, music, art, and Pranks!

♦ **J.G. BALLARD:** Hello? It's very early in the morning where you are—

♦ *VALE: Yes. But through some technological miracle that I really don't understand, we can talk—*

♦ **JGB:** I know; it's amazing. It's great to hear from you after all these years, and great to know you're still in business. You have a nice family now, and all sounds as well as can be—

♦ *V: Perhaps! And now you have four grandchildren—the last time I talked to you, your first grandchild had just been born. I can't even fathom what that must feel like—*

♦ **JGB:** It feels good, take my word for it. It does. I don't want to sound macabre, but *it takes away the fear of death.* There's no doubt about that. One has done one's biological duty, and that's very meaningful. Anyway, I'm thrilled about the *Quotations* project.

♦ *V: Incidentally, this is the first book I've expressly aimed at the "commuter." But everybody has to work full-time to pay the rent, these days—*

♦ **JGB:** I like that. You'll be remembered as "Vale, the publisher of in-flight books." *[laughs]*

♦ *V: A book of quotations seems ideally geared for the interruptions and stops and starts that commuters experience. But I also want to do a series of hour-long interviews with you.*

♦ **JGB:** Well, don't bankrupt yourself!

♦ *V: Actually, it's strange how much cheaper it's gotten to make international calls—*

♦ **JGB:** Yes. This young American who made a film of *The Atrocity Exhibition* spends a lot of time in New York and Pennsylvania. He was talking to me, going on and on, and I said to him, "Hey—this is going to cost you a fortune." He said, "Oh, no—international calls are cheaper than local toll calls. It's cheaper to ring you across the Atlantic than it is to ring my girlfriend across town."

♦ *V: It's crazy, but he might be right.*

♦ **JGB:** And the Internet is pretty cheap, isn't it? I mean, what does it cost to send an email? It costs less than an airmail letter. The transmission charge is almost nothing.

♦ *V: Right; if you pay your monthly charge, you can send almost as many emails as you want. In fact, let's discuss the futuristic implications of the Internet—how it is changing society. You've always been so prescient at extrapolating the larger implications of new technology—the social changes that technology brings about—*

♦ **JGB:** I think I'm being left behind, you know. I'm not sure I *am* a good guide anymore, but I'll do my best. My girlfriend Claire Churchill *lives* on the Internet, and when I visit her I'm looking over her shoulder.

♦ *V: This is a drastic change of "lifestyle," isn't it? She wasn't doing this ten years ago—*

♦ **JGB:** Well, she's ten years younger than me, and got her computer about five years ago. And she's a highly intelligent woman with no technical background of any kind—I mean, she's not particularly good with camcorders or any kind of advanced domestic appliances; she's all fingers and thumbs. But when she got her computer she took to it, really, like a duck to water. It was quite amazing.

Every day she faxes me great masses of material that she's taken off the Net. So I'm reading editorials from the *New York Times* or the *Wall Street Journal* before the people in New York read them! I'm not exaggerating, because of the time difference. She's a wonderful surfer of the Net, often coming up with some marvelously poetic material that's quite extraordinary. The Internet is an amazing development.

♦ *V: My friends and I have been combing the Internet looking for*

"Ballardiana"—

♦ **JGB:** There isn't much, is there?

♦ *V: People used to say, "You can find anything on the Internet!" But it's simply not true, and what's there is—*

♦ **JGB:** —inaccurate, too. On any topic, you get these "digests" of topics that are full of holes of various kinds. You've got to be careful, particularly on medical sites—some of the material is downright misleading, and you can't rely on it.

If you go to a website like the *Encyclopedia Britannica,* the information on the whole is fairly reliable. If you want to know the population of Venice, you can rely on the *Britannica* to give you a fairly (or approximately) accurate answer. **But you can't rely on the Net** . . . at least, that's *my* experience.

♦ *V: I couldn't agree more.*

♦ **JGB:** Since Claire lives on the Net, whenever I'm with her at her home, she's very keen that I become a kind of "Net person," too. I'm resisting this to some extent—I mean, you're talking to a man who writes his novels in *longhand!* Still, you can't help but be amazed by the sort of *transaction speed*—the Internet is like that "Democracy Wall" in Peking ten years ago, where anybody can post up anything. It's quite extraordinary.

♦ *V: Unfortunately, there's almost no one to challenge the accuracy and veracity of the information posted.*

♦ **JGB:** Yes. But so far it's supposedly uncensored—

♦ *V: Although I'm not sure that's true. I put out an occasional e-newsletter, and recently it has been rejected as "spam" (even though the people on my list subscribe to it). And because the word "sex" or "sexy" may have been mentioned, some servers reject it as "obscene"!*

♦ **JGB:** You'd better be careful there, because I think **they've got computers scanning all this email traffic.** Certain key words are supposed to detect people with pedophile interests, and Al Qaeda terrorists trying to communicate with each other. So don't refer to "home-made bombs" or the weaknesses of large engineering structures like skyscrapers—don't make *any* reference to that sort of thing! Or you'll find some guy in a raincoat with a radio mic in his ear knocking on your door. I mean, this is understandable in America because "September 11" was such a shocking event . . .

[At this point, possibly because of the words "terrorists" and "Al Qaeda," our telephone conversation became intermittent. It was necessary to redial and get a fresh connection.]

♦ *V: Let's have your thoughts on "9-11"—did it really change the world?*

♦ **JGB:** Well, it certainly changed America.

♦ *V: Yes, it gave George W. Bush practically free license to do whatever he wants.*

♦ **JGB:** Absolutely. As always with these things, it's the sort of *secondary effects* that often turn out to be the most worrying. It's the effects on free speech, on tolerance—**what's going on now is like the McCarthy era after WWII, during the Cold War in the 1950s.** All these academics were being hounded out of their jobs because once during the war they had gone to some pro-Russian fund-raising event in 1942 or something.

♦ *V: Right, or attended a Communist Party meeting just to "find out what it's all about"—*

♦ **JGB:** Exactly. If you read accounts of the secondary effects of the McCarthy era during Eisenhower's presidency, amazingly thousands of "innocent" Americans lost their jobs and had their careers destroyed. The whole climate of intolerance and conservative reaction came into existence very rapidly. It wasn't just the "Hollywood Ten" [those singled out for high-profile persecution/prosecution] who suffered; the knock-on effects were enormous. And there's a danger of that happening now—over here in England as well.

Our British tabloid press is in a perpetual frenzy over what we call "asylum seekers." These are refugees from Eastern Europe, the former Yugoslavia, from Iraq even, who are trying to get in here. Not only is the tabloid press going mad, there are unattractive signs of right-wing fanatics making the most of it, as you'd expect. The so-called British National Party, which is our Hitler-right/fringe group, have started winning council seats, which is more significant than it sounds, because local councils here have quite a lot of power. So it's that secondary knock-on effect that's worrying. But we'll see.

In America, you've got a "climate of conformity" coming in, don't you?

♦ *V: Yes, enforced by surveillance cameras absolutely everywhere. Also, everybody seems to have a videocamera these days—*

♦ **JGB: Now everybody can document themselves in a way that was inconceivable 30, 40, 50 years ago.** I remember my parents in the 1930s had a cine camera.

♦ *V: Oh—was it Super-8 or 16mm?*

♦ **JGB:** I don't know what it was, but people rarely used it; it was too much trouble. You bought a roll of film that was probably about three minutes long. You couldn't edit it, and the picture quality was . . . People just ended up photographing their children running across the lawn. And if you pointed the camera at the sun, it was a complete waste. Then, after you'd had the film developed (at great expense), you had to get an old-fashioned projector and set the whole thing up. It was too much bother! Now, *everybody* has a camcorder which you can play through a laptop. Absolutely amazing.

♦ *V: You can show your videos on an ordinary television set anywhere.*

♦ **JGB:** Yes; *I* have a camcorder. I've taken a lot of footage of my grandchildren as an investment for my daughters. My son doesn't have any children—he isn't married, but I know that my daughters, as mothers with two young children, are run off their feet most of the time. They never get around to taking any photographs. So I'm taking this for *them.* Periodically I give them these cassettes and say, "Keep this for ten years—you may find it interesting . . ."

♦ *V: I'd love to see* **Home Movies by J.G. Ballard.** *That would be amazing—*

♦ **JGB:** It *is* quite interesting. Three or four years ago I photographed a big Christmas gathering at my sister's house with her children and grandchildren—a big crowd of people. This particular camcorder I have has a very sensitive microphone that can pick up conversation miles away, and it sounded and looked like a Woody Allen movie—you know, the jabber of voices. Everybody seemed sort of over-confident and self-critical in that Woody Allen way—it was fascinating. I haven't yet moved into the *Last Year at Marienbad* phase . . .

♦ *V: I wish someone would make a film explaining everything in your house! Your interview on the Internet has a kind of herky-jerky movement. The audio is continuous but the video is puppet-like—*

♦ **JGB:** Yes, it all comes through a phone line, and I gather that the phone lines can't carry enough units of information yet. But they're working on it!

♦ *V: Three hundred years ago, Gracian demystified a lot of the workings of power and power interactions between people. You yourself are good at deciphering the "real" workings of what Burroughs called "The Control*

Photo: SM Gray

Process." There are people who seem to be addicted to control, working at controlling others, and then there are a few people like Burroughs who are fighting it—trying to demystify what's really going on behind the "reality theater" show we're subjected to, especially by the corporate media.

*I read that **thanks to pervasive television and movies everywhere, humans have never been exposed to so much** theater **in their lives. Even the thirty-second commercial is a mini-play with a plot arc.** So people are inundated, exposed to every possible situation life brings about, and are shown how to respond to it. I saw a quotation, "The best things in life are not rehearsed." Yet thanks to this inundation of media, it seems that young people who were raised on television communicate mainly in pre-rehearsed responses, not original verbal formulations. There's dozens of phrases that can fit any number of situations (like the phrase, "Whatever") and I suppose the mind uses them because they're so accessible.*

♦ **JGB:** People use mental formulas that they've learned from TV. Even in ordinary conversation, if you're talking to the mechanic at the garage about whether you need new tires for your car, you and he probably talk in a way that his equivalent thirty years ago would never have done. You use—not catch phrases, but verbal formulas. Suddenly you realize you're hearing echoes of some public-information, accident-prevention commercial. It's uncanny.

Here and in Europe **there's been a huge surge in popularity of so-called** *Reality TV* **shows. In England there's a famous one, that's now in its third or fourth season, called** *Big Brother.* The producers take a collection of mostly young people, 5-6 women and 5-6 men, and stick them in an environment for months. There are cameras everywhere, even in the bathrooms, watching them 24 hours a day; there's no escape from these cameras. I've seen half-hour programs of highlights.

Now what is interesting is that almost nothing *happens.* There's a certain amount of bitching and gossip and sitting around the supper table talking in a sort of half-hearted way, but there's no drama. Nonetheless, the audiences are *riveted.* And they're riveted by very similar programs where TV producers put people on desert islands and see how they survive; a series called *Survivor* did just that. I think this reflects a tremendous hunger among people for "reality"—for ordinary reality. It's very difficult to find the "real," because the environment is totally manufactured.

Even **one's own home is a kind of anthology of advertisers, manufacturers, motifs and presentation techniques. There's nothing "natural" about one's home these days.** The furnishings, the fabrics, the furniture, the appliances, the TV, and all the electronic equipment—**we're living *inside* commercials. I think people realize this, and they're *desperate for reality*,** which partly explains the surge in popularity of "adventure" holidays. People think that by living on some mountainside in a tent and being frozen to death by freezing rain, they're somehow discovering reality, but of course that's just another fiction dreamed up by a TV producer. And there's no escape.

◆ *V: There is definitely a search for "authenticity"; for something "really real." People want something that isn't contrived and prepackaged.*

◆ **JGB:** I think people buy these SUVs, these Sports Utility Vehicles, under the impression that somehow *because* you've got a vehicle that will climb a mountainside, you're suddenly getting closer to "reality." I live in a quiet suburb where there's no mountain for about 200 miles. Yet half the housewives are driving Cherokees, Land Cruisers, and Range Rovers—these vehicles equipped with huge tires. They're almost *military* vehicles, which they're using to go shopping in this peaceful suburb. It's all part of this quest for reality, or (as you say) for authenticity. Hilarious, really.

◆ *V: You wonder if they know that. They must, on some level, realize that it is a fiction, a fantasy.*

◆ **JGB:** I must start conducting some interviews. My impression, talking to people over the years, is that they don't regard these matters with any sense of irony. They take it seriously.

◆ *V: Here in the Bay Area, there were hugely-attended protests against Bush's war with Iraq, which were only marginally covered by corporate media. People attending these remark that at least they're doing something "real."*

♦ **JGB:** I think the environmental movements of the past thirty years have been a search for authenticity and reality, haven't they?

♦ *V: Well, they're also motivated by the emotion of* horror . . . *at how quickly all the other species are being exterminated. There's been an escalating increase in pollution and the cutting down of rain forest trees, etc.*

♦ **JGB:** There's a very powerful writer, Mike Davis, who wrote *City of Quartz.* I'm reviewing his book *Dead Cities,* a collection of essays in which he surveys the whole United States West of the Rockies. **Nevada is one huge atom bomb graveyard; Las Vegas and Los Angeles are sucking all the water out of the land so that people can sprinkle their lawns.** "Crack housing" is spreading at an enormous rate, and gated communities are a disease across the landscape. He gives quite an impression of *The End of the World.*

I don't know how "right" he is. Sometimes I think he goes too far—putting it mildly. The funny thing is, the people in those gated communities are probably having a good time. Or are they? I don't know.

♦ *V: Maybe they're caught up in re-enacting all those pre-rehearsed parties and tennis games. It seems like there's a great deal of pre-rehearsed social scenarios going on, being re-enacted over and over.*

♦ **JGB:** I agree.

♦ *V: You know, in your writing you remind us of archetypal events, like the shooting of JFK—*

♦ **JGB:** Actually, I get the impression that that has been *forgotten.* Up to about ten years ago, there was a torrent of books rolling off the presses with the latest conspiracy theories, but that seems to have dried up—possibly because anyone who was alive at the time is now too old, and the younger generation couldn't care less. Have Americans forgotten Kennedy?

♦ *V: Actually, JFK is not mentioned much anymore.*

♦ **JGB:** Today all politics has been given the "Kennedy treatment"—spin doctors and public relations experts routinely reshape politicians' images. Part of the novelty of Kennedy was that he seemed largely a media creation, and when he was struck down by Lee Harvey Oswald, you felt the blow was aimed at the mass media—i.e., the world as created through the mass media. The whole system of a kind of *artificial existence created by television and the press* was itself threatened.

Now, politicians have about the lowest ratings in public estimation that they've ever had.

♦ *V: Well, there may have been a slight increase in awareness about the lives of CEO power figures behind all this global corporatization. Thanks to a tell-all divorce case, Jack Welch, the head of General Electric for thirty years, was revealed to possess a kind of kingly, stupendous wealth—the company bought him things like a $17,000 18th-century French umbrella stand.*

♦ **JGB:** In England, we're getting unprecedented disparities of wealth. The people who run our biggest corporations have begun to affect life in London primarily by buying up property, and the old middle class (doctors, civil servants, teachers, salaried professionals) can no longer afford to live in central London. Now there are whole areas of central London given over to the rich. I've often thought that in due course all these very rich financiers are going to leave very large sums of money to their children. Then you'll get a sort of *New Leisure Class* who never work, but have huge spending power—like the *ancien regime* in France. Supposedly the same thing is happening in Manhattan: the middle class has been forced out—

♦ *V: —and in San Francisco as well; New York and San Francisco are the most expensive cities in America. Realtors say it's because there's only a limited amount of real estate available.*

♦ **JGB:** It's quite extraordinary to see Enron and other U.S. corporate scandals being well-reported. Britain has had a few scandals of our own—some of the financial benefits in share options and pension schemes these people have awarded to themselves are almost unbelievable. In due course this sort of thing will prompt *revolutionary thoughts*—once again.

♦ *V: One hopes so. Globally, there have been some huge protest marches against the War on Iraq. More people are realizing that this is basically a* *war to enrich the Bush team's oil holdings; Saddam Hussein is virtually no threat. **We'll see who ends up owning Iraq oil after this war is over.** I read that **the real reason the war was launched was because Iraq said it would stop taking American dollars, and only accept the Euro.***

♦ **JGB:** My impression is that Saddam Hussein is probably a dangerous man and has been for quite a few years. He is a *substitute* for Osama bin Laden. Americans understandably wanted to destroy the Al Qaeda operation, but they haven't had much success—and this is surprising. I assume thousands of CIA men with large suitcases full of dollar bills are prowling around the Middle East buying information. You'd think that by now the people backing the September 11th terrorists would have all been revealed.

Also, there doesn't seem to be any connection between Al Qaeda and the Saddam regime. So what we have is a sort of *substitute* phenomenon. Saddam is a substitute target, and attacking him does have certain benefits from the Bush point of view: mainly, oil.

Americans will have to occupy Iraq for years to come. Paradoxically, Saddam Hussein may have been a *stabilizing* influence in the Middle East—like the bully in the school playground, or the boisterous drunk in the airliner . . . all the other passengers or boys on the playground start cooperating to keep an eye on him. With Saddam removed, the whole pack of cards could collapse. And as we depend so much on oil to drive the world's economy, this instability could be very dangerous—Bush may bite off more than he can chew. I hope not—

♦ ***V:*** *What do you mean? Everyone I know wants to get Bush out of the White House. There are "Impeach Bush" stickers pasted all over the place. Remember, he stole the 2000 U.S. election, literally—*

♦ **JGB:** But you're stuck with him, aren't you? As far as I can tell, the only Democrat who has a chance to beat him is Hillary Clinton, and she's probably too astute to run; she realizes that two years from now she could lose. Incumbent American presidents tend to win—

♦ ***V:*** *Although Bush's father only lasted one term.*

♦ **JGB:** The economy was wobbly. And Bush lacked authority—

♦ *V: He was perceived as "the Wimp President"—*

♦ **JGB:** —unfairly, because he was a genuine combat flyer during the Second World War. But he didn't have the right image—and that's all-important these days. You're stuck with his son probably for the next six years, and then you will have Hillary Clinton. Her husband will be back in the White House with nothing to do except chat up the next generation of Monica Lewinskys. I'm sure they'll set aside a suite of rooms in the White House where Bill will be able to pursue his *amours*, uninterrupted. It should be fun!

♦ *V: When Bill Clinton first emerged, he was reminiscent of JFK: handsome, charming, youthful and dashing—*

♦ **JGB:** I can't really remember his early period. In England, perception is slightly different—he seemed embroiled in that Whitewater scandal from the earliest days. From this side of the Atlantic, American presidents are a pretty baffling lot—particularly to someone of my age.

I can remember listening to Roosevelt's speeches on the shortwave radio in Shanghai, and after him came Truman and then Eisenhower. This was a different generation. Then came Kennedy, who was a media creation. After that the *reductio ad absurdum* was Ronald Reagan, who really baffled us over here. But Americans seemed to like him. He obviously had a special charm, but there we are.

♦ *V: Well, he was just a B-movie* actor, *for chrissakes, as well as a media creation. He had no background in international politics, history, economics, and whatever else a President is supposed to know. There was a book about how he was groomed to be President. His spinmeisters even changed the pronunciation of his name—when he was host of the Fifties show* General Electric Theater *his name was pronounced Ronald REE-gun—like one of the evil sisters in Shakespeare's—*

♦ **JGB:** *King Lear.* He really was a baffling figure to us. There are many American medical specialists who saw traces of his Alzheimer's before the end of his first term! This condition was obviously well established by his second term, but that doesn't matter because the American President is very much a figurehead, like a chairman of the board. He's not a Prime Minister who directs the country like a captain sailing a ship. Actually, the American presidency is a collective leadership—

♦ *V: That's why Bush's critics call it "Team Bush."*

♦ **JGB:** And they're quite an unusual crowd . . . oil company executives who've discovered their own emotions for the first time. Politics is where they can express their emotions. They've had to bottle up their anger during thirty years of corporate life—their hatred of the people above them in the company hierarchy, and their contempt for the people below them. Then they get into politics—in particular, into the White House—and discover that all these emotions can come pouring out. They're having a good time—they can declare war, they can do *anything.* It must be quite exhilarating! But . . . you're safe in San Francisco?

♦ *V: I don't know if one is ever safe these days—that's what 9/11 showed, although that was a very urban phenomenon. That's why people move to the country—no one's going to send a cruise missile where there's nothing but cows.*

♦ **JGB:** But there are other targets . . . if Al Qaeda wanted to release some nerve gas, they'd do it in New York or Washington. But San Francisco—there's nothing Al Qaeda can do that can match what the San Andreas fault can come up with at any moment.

♦ *V: You reminded me of Clinton and Monica Lewinsky. The American author Philip Roth wrote a very funny piece about how Clinton should have f— her in the ass—she wouldn't have talked about* that *with Linda Tripp. Clinton never had penetrative, penile/vaginal sex with Monica Lewinsky—*

♦ **JGB:** I imagine Clinton as a great fondler of women . . . any woman within arm's reach—particularly when he was President—got fondled. And he probably didn't really regard that as "sexual"—it was his *right* as the tribal chief—like some African chief running his hands over the bottoms of all the teenaged girls. From his point of view he was probably telling the truth: "I did not have sex with that woman."

Of course, the time is going to come when no young woman will regard penetrative, penis-and-vagina sex as real sex, because it isn't deviant enough to be considered "real sex." These days, magazines for teenagers sold openly on newsstands have headlines like, "Interested in S&M sex? *Junior Cosmo* explains all you need to know." And this is a magazine that's going to be bought and read by 14-year-olds. The period of conventional, penetrative, penis/vagina sex will be over by the time you're about 15, and then you'll move into the area of conceptualized sex, S&M, and *whatever*—that's what will be regarded as *real* sex. To me, this seems like a daunting thought.

♦ *V: I remember a young man who attributed his success with women— and he seemed to be* very *successful—to the fact that he apparently was the first to introduce his dates to anal sex. His little groundbreaking act, so to speak, seemed to really impress the young ladies—*

♦ **JGB:** Well, the young want to embrace as much of experience—as many of life's possibilities—as soon as they can. And this is facilitated by the Internet. We've had one or two unhappy murder cases of schoolchildren recently—schoolgirls, that is. They all turn out to have these complete, private lives on the Internet. Many of these 13-year-olds are having passionate Internet romances with what they think of as 14- or 15-year-old boys who often turn out to be 40-year-old men. I suspect that in many cases they *know* this—but that only adds to the thrill.

It all confirms my belief that as a society we're beginning to exhibit the first signs of profound boredom. In that state of mind we're prepared to tolerate anything that *distracts us* from that boredom: terrorist violence, wars—you name it. *Anything* to break the deadly dread of . . . seeing oneself in the mirror. I often wonder—I won't be around to see it—what sort of lives my grandchildren will have, or rather what sort of world they'll emerge into. I can only guess.

♦ *V: I recently had what I consider to be a "Ballardian" experience. Last month we reprinted* The Atrocity Exhibition, *which is printed in Hong Kong. We used to hire customs agents to clear our shipment through customs, and then a professional trucker would pick up the books from the port of Oakland and deliver them to us. But in these days of tight money we realized we could save about $1,500 by doing this ourselves, so we learned how to clear customs ourselves (it's a bit complicated), and began renting a*

$19.95-a-day truck (it ends up costing about $110 after you pay all the extra charges buried in the fine print).

Anyway, we went to the truck rental office, which is in the worst part of town, and there were three young men in the office all sitting at computers. One of them had his computer monitor positioned so that I could see it. The whole time we were there doing the paperwork—about 25 minutes—this young man was calling up a succession of "free" sexual images, like enormous close-ups of blow jobs, one after another. There must be millions of young men like this who are getting paid to literally call up one blow job after another—

♦ **JGB:** Amazing, really. **You wonder: is the human sexual instinct strong enough to overcome this *deadening* effect of massive overexposure to sexual imagery?** What will this fellow be like, say, ten years from now, or twenty years from now?

♦ *V: Then he'll be forty-five, I guess.*

Photo: SM Gray

♦ **JGB:** Assuming he's spent thousands of hours or days immersed in a continuous stream of pornographic imagery, beyond the dreams of the Marquis de Sade—how is he going to cope with any kind of skin-to-skin sexual experience? It's hard to imagine. But I've read that **60% of all Internet activity involves porn sites.** That's a large part of the Internet's appeal. It'll be interesting to see! *[laughs]*

It's rather like the creeping legalization of drugs that's occurring in England. The seriousness of offenses involving cannabis has been downgraded, and there are strong moves afoot to reduce the penalties for cocaine and heroin possession. Ecstasy is huge—it's the most popular drug of all, thanks to all the kids going to their clubs. Millions of teenagers—virtually, most of the teenage population—are taking Ecstasy when they go out. And the police no longer do anything about this, as far as one can make out.

There are calls for the eventual legalization of heroin on the grounds that a very large proportion—something like 50%—of all burglaries and thefts from cars are carried out by addicts who need money for their next fix. Consequently, a huge amount of police time is consumed uselessly, which could be better spent if heroin addicts could simply *buy* the stuff. **There have been serious calls here for heroin to be medical-ized, as it was until the 1960s. It would be purer, there would be fewer deaths through overdoses**, and so on.

Eventually, I'm sure, hard drugs will effectively be legalized as they have been in parts of Europe like Holland. In certain Swiss cities like Zurich, heroin is available by medical prescription; city authorities give addicts clean needles.

The intention is to eliminate crime. Whether you eliminate the desperation, I don't know. Personally, I missed out on hard drugs. I was too late for the 1930s morphine craze, and too old (family responsibilities and all that) for the '60s and '70s. Now I'm much too old, so I'm stuck with alcohol.

♦ *V: Alcohol seems to have served you well; at least it's legal. Actually, for awhile it wasn't legal in America, during Prohibition in the '20s.*

♦ **JGB:** We never had Prohibition here; I think British society couldn't cope with it. The British need alcohol. There's something missing in the British character that alcohol supplies.

♦ *V: Well, alcohol is a de-inhibitor. And the British and the Germans seem to be much more formal in their social interactions—*

♦ **JGB:** I think that's true. All over Europe, the British are known as very heavy drinkers who feel no shame about being drunk in the street—which is something you never see in Spain. You see drunken Brits there, but you don't see young Spaniards drunk in the street—the same is true of France, too. I've been traveling all over Europe for more than fifty years and it's almost unheard of to come across young Europeans getting drunk in the street. Whereas in England, this is commonplace.

There must be something missing in the British make-up—it's probably genetic . . . maybe we've *evolved* this way. For example, the British Navy has never been "dry" like the American Navy—until quite recently there was a daily rum ration on British ships, and it was a *large* ration—something like half a pint! How they managed to fire their guns in the right direction, I have no idea. Still, it served the Royal Navy well for several centuries.

♦ *V: Yes. They ruled the world with that navy.*

♦ **JGB:** No thanks to the rum ration! How is everyone coping with the space shuttle disaster?

♦ *V: Well, it certainly reminded me of your writing. I recall that Roberto Matta quotation in the notes to* The Atrocity Exhibition: *"Why must we await and fear disaster in space in order to understand our own times?"*

♦ **JGB:** That was remarkably prophetic; it says everything. It was a terrible tragedy. The paradox is that NASA is now a huge *obstacle* in the way of space exploration. It originally got off to a tremendous start landing men on the moon, but now it's become a kind of public-relations-driven corporation that needs manned space flights in order to justify its huge funds.

But as long as we have manned space flight dominating the show, we're not going to get any real advances in space exploration, because the job of leaving this planet is prohibitively expensive. If they dissolved NASA and replaced it with some successor organization committed to *unmanned* space flight, there'd be an enormous expansion of interplanetary activity of all kinds. Dozens of probes would be going off to the planets; the Space Age would *really* begin. But it won't happen, of course, because NASA is deliberately, willingly, and willfully trapped in this Buck Rogers dream that it's constructed around itself.

Also, NASA is using very out-of-date technology. The space shuttles were all designed back in the '70s, or even before that, I think. They don't use the latest high-tech communications gear. They rely on these huge brute-force rockets to get them up in the air. The shuttles are like a high jumper who's got a ball-and-chain attached to one leg—he'll never get over the bar!

It's a curious state of affairs, because a kind of very old-fashioned, 1940s and 1950s dream of space travel (first created by the Science-Fiction magazines of the time) is now frustrating any sort of future evolution. It's very, very odd. But that's because of the need to include the "heroic human dimension." My girlfriend sends me editorials from *Time* magazine, and its latest issue attacks NASA. You probably don't read *Time,* nor do I, but it's interesting that *Time* magazine (which is a huge myth-making organization in its own right) should attack NASA—it's like McDonalds launching a fierce attack on Disney; you don't expect it. These big corporations are difficult to shift.

♦ *V: And these big corporations exported all manufacturing overseas, so now*—surprise!—*many people can't find a job anymore.*

♦ **JGB:** This is a problem that has beset England for a very long time: the decline of manufacturing. Ninety percent of new jobs are in the service sector. The requirement that everybody has a job isn't built into modern societies, and it's difficult to see any way around that. We don't have huge standing armies anymore to mop up a large part of the idle work force. Europeans take very long holidays, something that I gather doesn't happen in America. By statute the average German worker gets five or six weeks' holiday—the same in most European countries. In England it's four weeks.

♦ *V: And in the U.S. it's one week, or maybe two.*

♦ **JGB:** So I've read. I think long holidays are a kind of *virtual unemployment,* a sort of work/share, in effect, because a large part of your workforce is perpetually on holiday. If one in twelve of your workforce is on holiday, which would be the case in most businesses here, you need to hire a few more people. Eventually you'll be given three months' holiday . . . six months' paid holiday, so that the leisure society can be introduced by the back door.

Machines are so much more efficient at making things than we are, so a lot of old mechanical skills have been lost by workers in this country. We can't really make a decent car—that's why all our cars are made in Europe or Japan. We don't make TV sets anymore. If you want a camcorder, it's going to be made in Japan, and so on.

♦ *V: Right, and how can this continue? During the '30s Great Depression, Roosevelt instituted the WPA which hired millions of people to make wonderful murals on public buildings, and build dams and highways—*

♦ **JGB:** Well, military spending is one way . . . We think of the United States as the home of free-market capitalism, the absolute opposite of the old Soviet Union, when in fact in the middle of the American free-market system, there is this "command economy" run from Washington and the Pentagon, with its huge military spending. It's just like the command economies of Russia and Eastern Europe. And this helped direct lucrative contracts around the country to areas of need. From what I've read, **that's the main job of American senators and congressmen: lobbying central government for defense or government contracts.** If you've got high unemployment in Texas, that's where you build your new stealth bomber. Supposedly, everybody gets a piece of the cake.

♦ *V: I like this quotation from* The Atrocity Exhibition: *"Earthquakes, plane and car crashes seem to reveal for a brief moment the secret formulas of the world around us . . . But a disaster in space rewrites the rules of the continuum itself."*

♦ **JGB:** Difficult to enlarge on that!

♦ *V: I liked your essay on the similarities between the WWII Japanese soldiers you met as a boy, and the terrorists of Al Qaeda—*

♦ **JGB:** Right. I didn't mean that too literally. **The reasons for Japan's attack on America have been rather obscured over the years.** In fact, **the Japanese were faced with an oil boycott by the United States and were desperate to do something about it.**

♦ *V: Again, maybe we shouldn't use the words "terrorist" and "Al Qaeda" over the phone—this might make the CIA, or whoever, monitor our conversation—*

♦ **JGB:** You never know. They've got these computers, supposedly, that scan all telephone communications for certain key words. We probably use those key words all the time. Then, you'll have suspicious-looking vans parked outside your house, and god knows what—

♦ *V: Yes. You were talking about an oil boycott by the U.S.—*

♦ **JGB:** In retrospect, Japan's attack on Pearl Harbor and its war with America seemed doomed from the outset. You wonder how this intelligent race could put everything at risk, because they knew America's strength and industrial power. I think most historians now accept that they were driven into a corner. The American oil boycott threatened to destroy Japan as an industrial entity.

Now, one doesn't want to push it too far, but there are faint echoes with the reactions of the terrorist fringe of the Arab world to the American power today. This doesn't in any way excuse 9-11, of course. I'm a strong opponent of *all* religious belief, and among the world's religions, I must say that Islam seems one of the least attractive, in its treatment of women, its utterly medieval/primitive punishment system, its failure to cope with the modern world . . . It's an extraordinary fact that **if you look across the whole spread of Islamic countries, from Morocco on the Atlantic all the way across the Middle East to Indonesia (a huge spread), there's scarcely a country that you would regard as industrialized.**

These are all pre-industrial countries who can't industrialize because that would mean giving freedom to women. If you want to industrialize, you need a very large workforce, and you need to liberate women both as productive workers and as consumers. The Islamic countries can't do this, so they're stuck in a sort of pre-industrial twilight where they can only feel resentment at Western power. The Enlightenment, in the historical sense (the movement that started a couple of centuries ago) never touched them. There has been no Age of Reason.

So the view that the West may be in some sort of global conflict with Islam—the "Clash of Civilizations" theory—may have something going for it. There are an estimated two million Muslims in England— large numbers from Pakistan, but others from North Africa, and so on—living in enclaves in our major cities. These enclaves are hotbeds of disaffection and possibly terrorism. There are mullahs openly and literally preaching in mosques the most vicious anti-Western propaganda. However, one doesn't want to inflame the temperature by making unguarded remarks.

♦ *V: I read about a movement in England to eliminate immigration from Islamic countries—*

♦ **JGB:** Well, it's understandable because the Muslim communities have not really integrated into British society. There are large numbers of young men who (in the old days one would have said that they had a "chip on their shoulder") are very resentful, like that would-be Shoe-bomber, Richard Reid. He was a Muslim who came from some London suburb—a complete misfit who fell into the hands of one of these hyper-violent clerics. Most people agree he was probably being used by Al Qaeda operatives who financed his various trips around the world. He spent some time in Afghanistan, and almost certainly was supplied with the explosive shoes. People who know him have said he was quite incapable of building an explosive device himself.

So it's understandable that people are worried, because **fanaticism is something that's almost impossible to contain by usual law enforcement procedures—particularly if the fanatic is prepared to kill himself**, like the September 11 group. There's nothing you can do about it. People know this and, of course, it's an understandable reaction to want to cut down on the number of so-called asylum-seekers. Over the years, Britain as a country has always been enormously welcoming to people seeking asylum. But I think people realize that

Photo: Charles Gatewood

post-September 11, the world changed.

International jet travel means that some would-be assassin in a suburb of Karachi can get on a plane and be in London or New York virtually the same day. That's something that wasn't true in the world until thirty years ago. There used to be a huge time delay built into travel. When my parents first set sail for China in 1929 on a P&O steamer, it took them five weeks to get there. I remember very long voyages around the end of the Thirties and just after WWII. Now travel is damn near instantaneous.

Also, **there's a secondary effect to Islamic terrorism: violent acts are extremely suggestive.** It's long been known that suicide runs in families; I suppose it might just be genetic. The sort of violence represented by an act of suicide is highly suggestive. If your father committed suicide, this almost sanctions a further act of suicide by yourself, and the taboo is lifted.

Copycat crimes have a particular attraction for certain kinds of disordered minds. An event like September 11, or any major terrorist act, has a kind of energizing influence on other people with mental problems or deep self-dissatisfaction. They may be incited into thinking about committing similar acts. It only needs a few of them to actually *commit* these crimes, and havoc follows.

The kinds of liberal societies we live in have almost no defense against this psychopathology—we're not equipped to cope with it. **The liberal, humane edifice that rules life in the West can't cope with the psychopathic tendencies of small disaffected minorities.** It can't cope with the very notion of psychopathology, in a way, because liberalism has consistently underestimated the latent psychopathology of all human beings.

The horrors of the Second World War and Nazi Germany, according to liberal opinion, are the responsibility of a very peculiar historical conjunction of economic conditions, plus these mad gangsters with their perverted ideology. That's the conventional explanation, but it's probably far from the truth. All the later researches show that complicity in the Nazi crimes occurred on a much larger scale. Those crimes were carried out by literally millions of Germans in the armed forces. Nazism represented a peculiar psychological cataclysm that affected a whole nation, not just a handful of psychopathic leaders.

I think that the liberal imagination just cannot understand the substratum of psychopathic possibility that exists below the surface of the everyday rational mind. Even today, we think of serial killers as bizarre freaks, and they may be, but maybe they're not—the same impulses are shared unconsciously by probably all of us. This explains the huge popularity of Hollywood movies about serial killers, and TV documentaries about psychopaths like Fred and Rosemary West—a nightmare English couple who killed their own children, along with a lot of other young women. The Wests went on trial here a few years ago.

What *is* worrying about September 11 is that an act like that opens a lot of trapdoors, and other demons are going to leap out and sniff the light.

There's another very peculiar, frightening phenomenon as well: the whole idea of *elective* (that is, voluntary) *psychopathy*. (Or, willingly embracing psychopathic behavior because of its *energizing* potential.) Psychopathic behavior appears to immensely increase the possibilities of life—that's how whole nations can embrace, quite voluntarily, psychopathic acts.

One could argue that both Nazi Germany and Stalin's Russia were elective psychopathies on a nationwide scale. They represent a collusion, on the unconscious level, between the populations and the leaders. Far from being victims—*if* they *were* victims—the Russian and Nazi Germany populaces were at least partly *willing* victims.

There may be profound masochistic strains running through modern industrial man, that every now and then summon forth these demons like Hitler and Stalin who then do what is expected of them. It's a frightening prospect, but I think the Age of Reason is over.

So, I think profound masochistic strains run through modern industrial societies. Because of the enormous degrees of self-discipline required to maintain a job, keep a family, get to work on time, discipline yourself for eight hours without killing the foreman or the office boss—day after day, year after year—some sort of **imposed or self-imposed**

masochism is one way of coping. You learn to *like* your captors (the old Stockholm syndrome) even if your captor is the department head or foreman or whatever.

It may be that Nazi Germany and Stalinist Russia were masochistic societies. Masochistic societies are the pattern of future societies, where because of the immense potency of psychopathic behavior, it may become the command structure that links people's unconscious minds to the governments of the day. One can see already, in the case of the war in Iraq, that people in England (and as far as I can tell, people in America) realize that to some extent they're being manipulated by governments who have agendas of their own. The British are very suspicious of Tony Blair. He's a devout Christian—always a worrying sign—and he has a strong evangelical streak; actually, it's more than just a streak. One gathers that the White House is now run by a group of devout Christians who actually start the day with a Bible class.

♦ ***V:*** *I read that Team Bush starts each day with a "prayer circle."*

♦ **JGB:** In England, church-going has fallen away to almost nothing— only two or three percent of the population goes to church on Sunday. I think the figure in the United States is much higher—it may be something like 50%. And supposedly 95% of Americans say they believe in God—that's worrying. The role of psychopathy in government is becoming more and more apparent. But let's hope I'm wrong.

♦ ***V:*** *So you've just illuminated how psychopathy sneaked in through the back door of society's "house" disguised as religion, or religious ideas—*

♦ **JGB:** Right. Religions are Trojan horses which conceal profoundly strange psychopathy strains. There's no other explanation for them. **The sheer *fear of death* has been the main engine of religions for a very long time.** The Christian religion is based on a 2,000-year-old Jewish resurrection cult, but it has become something very different.

The Roman Catholic Church—well, my girlfriend Claire was brought up as a Catholic, and went to Catholic schools—she says that indoctrination resembles a horror comic. Six-year-olds are taught the most horrific tortures that saints endured. Touring European art galleries with Claire is always a revelation, because she can say, "Oh, that's Saint Joan," or whoever—Claire knows all the tortures that led to later canonization. So, in Catholicism an entire catechism of horrific violence indoctrinates young children in a way they never forget. The persistence of religions is an extraordinary phenomenon, given how antisocial they are.

♦ **V:** *What do you mean by "antisocial"? Do you mean that religions militate against a healthy society?*

♦ **JGB:** Absolutely. **I was brought up in one of the very few societies on Earth which had no religious beliefs (and as far as I can tell, has never had any), and that is China.** There's a bit of animism and a bit of burning of incense to ancestors, but there's no belief in the supernatural—it's rather like you or I talking about the spirit of Shakespeare—we don't *literally* mean some sort of supernatural entity is floating around. When the Chinese talk about the spirits of their ancestors, they mean it as a *metaphor*—the Chinese have no religious beliefs. Confucianism is not really a religion at all, nor is Buddhism, and Taoism is not a religion in the strict sense. There's no *supernatural* element in any of those religions—which is why I like them. And the Chinese character is interesting for that reason.

It may be that the backwardness of China could be blamed on the absence of religion, because **religions (whatever their faults) are energizing by virtue of the unconscious and psychopathic strains which enter into the individual's mind and into the social mind.** That is a very curious thing—*that*. Religions, for all they are to be campaigned against (if not actively *despised*), are vehicles for energizing psychopathic behavior. So it's no coincidence that the fiercely Protestant countries of Northern Europe launched the industrial revolution and launched the United States, if you like. The Puritan fathers took that fierce Protestant work ethic with all its repressions and created the most dynamic society the world has ever seen.

So it may be that the absence of a religion in China acted as a sort of brake on that country's industrial development . . . lack of religion may have had a restraining influence, turning China into a kind of eventless world. For something like 2000 years nothing happened! You read

Chinese history, and nothing happened until 1910. There was this vast agricultural society run by a class of elite administrators who traveled around in sedan chairs . . . and nothing happened! Now and then they invented something like moveable type or gunpowder or accurate timepieces, but they lost interest in them because there was no imagination to energize these discoveries. It's very strange . . .

♦ **V:** *European explorers like Columbus and Vasco da Gama were impelled to convert the rest of the world to Christianity. Some of them brought along missionaries—*

♦ **JGB:** Yes, they did. **All the great conquistadors who colonized the New World brought the Catholic clergy with them and raised the cross over the slain bodies of the natives.** This continued through the 19th century with British missionaries spreading out over Africa and the Far East. American missionaries were enormously active in China over the past two centuries as well. So it may be that George Bush and Rumsfeld have realized unconsciously that America needs enemies to keep everybody on their toes. The only question on our minds (on this side of the Atlantic) is, "Who's going to be next?" I see Europe as next in the firing line! *[laughs.]* Maybe Tony Blair, who is being criticized as "America's poodle," is more astute than we give him credit for . . .

♦ **V:** *Yes, why is he such an adoring lapdog to Bush? What does he have to gain?*

♦ **JGB:** Oil, primarily. Back in the 1920s, Britain controlled Iraq and had huge oil investments in Iraq. Also, the British might benefit from close intelligence and commercial ties to the United States. In the case of Tony Blair, I think he's on a personal crusade. He's a very devout Christian, and I think he genuinely believes that the war against Iraq is not merely a just, moral war, but is almost a *sacred duty.* When you see him being interviewed he has a sort of evangelical certainty—he ceases being a mere politician.

Blair was interviewed last night on television. He was faced with an audience of ordinary citizens, all of whom, as far as I could see, were hostile to him and the war in Iraq. And this didn't bother him;

he rose above it, saying, "This is unpopular, but I'm going to do it." That's frightening! I think most of his fellow European leaders are just baffled by him. We'll see.

When you see Blair and Bush talking about the war in Iraq, they look like men who haven't slept for months—very tense. In the last few months Blair has aged years—he's stopped smiling. He was one of these *involuntary smilers*—that was a large part of his appeal, but now he looks very drawn. He has also lost weight. I must say that Bush looks confident—he doesn't look in the least bit worried about anything . . . which is rather a relief, since his father always looked worried.

♦ *V: That's probably because "Dubya" is barely above the level of a village idiot—incapable of feeling any consequences of his warmongering.*

♦ **JGB:** There's no doubt about it. That's probably a good explanation, because—if you think of Richard Nixon, who was a highly intelligent man (no question about it), he always looked nervous and shifty.

♦ *V: We're trying to get to deeper bedrock—almost archetypal levels—to account for these seemingly irrational and highly destructive campaigns against humans. Team Bush is a kind of criminal conspiracy. These are oil and weapons corporation executives who have actually committed criminal acts—but they're so clever that they simply change the laws! That's how Enron ripped off California. So, **there's a very strong bonding between people who share a criminal commonality**; their thievish taboo-breaking also gives them a lot of energy. Think of* Bonnie and Clyde—

♦ **JGB:** I think this is true.

The ostensible motive for war on Iraq was to protect the United States and the West from another September 11, but even Bush and Tony Blair have admitted that there's no connection between Saddam and the September 11 terrorists. And they've gone to enormous lengths to find some connection, but haven't succeeded. So the war against Iraq is a kind of *compensation activity* . . . it's really designed to assuage all that repressed anger and frustration stemming from not being able to find bin Laden and his Al Qaeda set-up. It's a sort of *surrogate* activity, a substitute activity.

You can almost imagine a scenario in which the attack on Pearl

Harbor is achieved by unknown enemies—these flyers flew in, sank all these battleships, killed all these sailors and soldiers, and then flew off. The U.S. suspects Japan, but can't be certain, so it decides to attack Australia as a way of getting rid of all this pent-up anger—I'm talking about the American leadership under Roosevelt. This is not quite the right analogy, but you know what I mean.

In other words, there's no real justification for a war on Iraq. I watched a recent speech by Secretary Colin Powell to the U.N. Security Council. He was very persuasive; he's a good speaker with a lot of personal authority. But his actual evidence of Iraqi wrongdoing was rather *thin.* Any threat that Saddam poses lies very far in the future, whereas **in North Korea this tin-pot dictator does indeed have nuclear missiles with a 4,000-mile range. But Saddam is no urgent threat to the West.** We've all been waiting for the myth-ical "smoking gun," but it's never been drawn from its holster. That's not to say that Saddam isn't a danger and a menace. But he may have been a stabilizing influence on neighboring countries who feel oblig-ed to cooperate—like I said, he's the bully on the playground or the drunk on the bus.

There's this feeling one has that **Reason alone is no longer directing the affairs of nations, just as we know that Reason alone does not direct the affairs of individual human beings, or groups of human beings.** The office has its own collective emotion-al life comprised of all the people who work in the office. Nations have an emotional life. It's all very peculiar. Meanwhile, one goes to the supermarket and the garage, watches television, and hopes that the world is running along parallel rails . . .

♦ **V:** *Do you have any other comment on Team Bush's corporate crimes—*

♦ **JGB:** Bush was on the board of directors of some Texas oil compa-ny and is supposed to have taken part in insider dealings. Of course, there's the Enron scandal. You get the impression that business cor-porations all over the world are probably run by men who've got their hands in the till, enriching themselves by any means they can.

Going back in time: Ronald Reagan was surrounded by a lot of former executives of Bechtel, a huge American construction company that operated worldwide. But I can't recall anyone ever suggesting that they were involved in any kind of semi-criminal financial dealings—

♦ **V:** *They must have been—**how can you make** any **massive profits without being a criminal?** Bechtel went all over the world, plundering natural resources from the earth.*

♦ **JGB:** I agree. It's a matter of "You're a criminal *if* you're indicted. If you're *not* indicted, you're not a criminal." Sort of a *Catch-22*. These big public corporations are enormously rich, and the senior executives are not playing with their own money, they're playing with the shareholders' money. *That* doesn't encourage fiscal responsibility.

It's very difficult for an Englishman over here to "read" the psychology of Rumsfeld, Bush, Cheney, and so on, because they're so carefully protected by their media people—

♦ **V:** *—their spin doctors, advisors and speech writers—*

♦ **JGB:** Whereas, **when I first clapped eyes on Spiro Agnew [on TV], you took one look at him and you *knew* this guy was a crook!** There's no doubt about it—all your instincts told you he was a crook. So when you read about people going into his office (when he was Vice President) with shoeboxes full of thousand-dollar bills, there was nothing surprising about it—the guy was clearly a crook. And many of Nixon's other sidekicks were obviously sailing pretty close to the wind—putting it mildly; half of them went to jail. There was nothing really surprising about that.

♦ **V:** *With Team Bush and his cronies,* ***instead of breaking the law, they simply change the laws.*** *They pay*

Photo: SM Gray

the money or arrange the behind-the-scenes machinations so that whatever they do to increase profits becomes legal. Of course, we'll never know the full so-called truth about any of this, ever. But at least let's not swallow hook, line, and sinker their propaganda. In a sense you're also among those who actively oppose their propaganda—

♦ **JGB:** Well, in England there's a lot of apathy. In Europe and in America, there seems to be an assumption that politicians (and the political system as a whole) are endemically corrupt—but the level of corruption is *tolerable.* And this apathy leads to very low turnouts at elections—which is a bad sign.

Also, you've got the *end of ideology.* After WWII, France and Italy had big Communist parties, and sometimes at the same time very big Socialist parties—this was true in England, too. So you had a very clear ideological dividing line between Left and Right (in England, between Conservative and Labor) . . . far greater than the dividing line between Republican and Democrat in America. But that dividing line has dissolved in the sand; in England there's almost no difference between the Labor and the Conservative party. Both accept the free market economy, both accept the welfare state, both accept that the power of unions to call national strikes has to be reigned in.

We recently had a firemen's strike. They've been campaigning for better pay and they put on short two-day strikes; they threatened to turn these into much longer strikes. Tony Blair's Labor government has come up with a wonderful idea on how to solve this problem: they're going to make firemen's strikes illegal!

♦ ***V:*** *That's how to solve any social "problem"—*

♦ **JGB:** Yes. If nobody can strike for more pay, then the government has more money to spend on private limousines for government ministers! **There's an End of Ideology: both Conservative and Labor completely agree about everything.** And the public realizes this—they want a suburban shopping mall society where the government is regarded as a public utility. No one's interested in the *politics* of electricity distribution, they just want to make sure that electric light flows into the house and you can work the stove when you want to cook breakfast for the kids.

In some ways people regard the government as a public utility. You've got to pay the police, you've got to pay the firemen. In England we have a national health service, so you've got to pay for the hospitals and the education system—but that's *it*—"We don't want any *Brave New World,* thank you very much."

Of course, the End of Ideology means that we get apathy. Now, people hate being bored—the central nervous system needs stimulation, otherwise we become like those polar bears in zoos who restlessly walk up and down and then start hitting themselves. So after apathy comes a hunger for *any* kind of violent act that will break the boredom. That's the really dangerous phase . . . because **whole nations can embrace madness deliberately, willingly, just to break the boredom.**

The sense is that the political class has a vested interest in artificially maintaining an ideological polarity merely to give the voters the illusion that voting *means* something. In England, at general elections, both of the leading parties make the kind of extravagant claims that politicians always make—party manifestos advocating the most radical changes to this or that, but when one or the other party gets into power, the manifestos are forgotten—they've served their purpose.

♦ *V: Nobody remembers any promises that politicians make, especially in the United States of Amnesia. Do you think that the British educational system is better than America's?*

♦ **JGB:** Well, I think the penetration of social life—particularly family life—by the Entertainment Society (or the trashier end of it) has produced kids who just spend their time in their rooms playing computer games, and hanging around in video arcades seeing junk movies and eating junk food. There's no parental discipline.

Of course, if you create the *self-devouring end* of the consumer society, you're bound to get a fall in educational standards, because **the self-discipline needed to learn to read and write is missing.** That has definitely happened in England, although it hasn't happened in countries like France, Germany, and the Scandinavian countries which are, on the whole, much more authoritarian, and in a way protected by the language difference.

Native language is still very important there, so that the trashier end of the American entertainment culture doesn't penetrate so deeply. England tends to get the worst of America: the junk movies, junk TV and so on, without the much more *positive* sides to American life. Life in England today is pretty "scuzzy"—or whatever the word would be.

♦ **V:** *In America, some of the only joy people have is derived from things like the latest Palm Pilot-cellphone, which function as a badge of eliteness. This "positive" aspect of American technological innovation keeps young people from being completely disheartened. Actually, a lot of these "advances" inevitably get bent to sex; I think of your quotation "Sex times technology equals the future." I just met someone with a host of pornographic images stored on his laptop, downloaded from the Internet.*

♦ **JGB:** There's a pedophile hunt directed at people who have downloaded huge quantities of illicit pornographic images—the Who's guitarist [Pete Townshend] was named. But there are many others. The American FBI had given the British police a list of 6,000 British subscribers to a paid pedophile website run by a couple in Texas, who have now gone to jail. In the course of prosecuting this couple, who were running an Internet pornographic warehouse of imagery that you paid to access, the FBI came across a list of subscribers which included 6,000 British. So Scotland Yard began going through this list and spotted Townshend and many others, including [reportedly] former cabinet ministers, senior judges, police, and various other people.

Scotland Yard, with its traditional thoroughness, is slowly working its way through this list. Meanwhile, our tabloid press is having a field day passing on all kinds of inflammatory rumors. It turns out that according to the law of the land, even *looking* at pedophile imagery on your PC is a criminal act. Apparently, everything you see on your computer screen is permanently recorded onto your hard drive, and this is considered to be solid evidence of your possession of child pornography. It's this law that Townshend is being held under. He claims that he was just researching a book that he was writing about child abuse. Of course, everybody laughs at this, but it seems to me that pressing the wrong button as you sit in front of your PC could be rather dangerous. But, I think the vital thing is not to pay *money* to look at any of this stuff. *That* seems to be the incriminating act: the cash transfer.

♦ **V:** *What worries me is that one of my favorite spokespeople against the war in Iraq, Scott Ritter, a former U.N. weapons inspector, has been accused of being in an Internet chatroom with someone underage—*

♦ **JGB:** Right; I think he was accused of setting up a date with a 14-year-old girl.

♦ **V:** *Of course, I'm worried that this is some kind of entrapment, or set-up.*

♦ **JGB:** Are there entrapment laws in America? In England there are. **Society as a whole is desperately in need of new vices, and there aren't enough criminal acts to go around! So we need to criminalize more human behavior.** This has been going on for years. Lewis Carroll, the author of the *Alice* books, would be in jail if he were alive today. You know, for photographing underage little girls that were half-naked—in some cases, they *were* naked.

More and more human behavior is being *criminalized.*

♦ **V:** *That's a trend!*

♦ **JGB:** You've only got to get a new invention like the motorcar, which hasn't been around that long (about a century), and a huge body of statute law now exists that covers criminal acts involving the motorcar. **It's almost impossible to drive a car in England without committing some sort of crime!** And that applies to the computer. It's a curious *need* we're dealing with; the motives are probably mixed, but maybe we need more and more of life to be criminalized!

♦ **V:** *How's your health?*

♦ **JGB:** Well, I have had one or two medical problems over the last few years, but I seem to have come through, touch wood. Healthy living, you know: lots of wine and attractive girlfriends—that's the solution to life! What about you?

♦ **V:** *I occasionally find myself trying faddish diets, especially when they're invented by Harvard medical professors like Walter C. Willet. After a certain age it seems to be a constant struggle to* not *put on weight.*

♦ **JGB:** Yes. Well, as long as you don't become grossly overweight, I don't think being plump has any effect on health. It's more important to take a certain amount of exercise—I find it clears my head. **I go for a walk every day, down by the river here, and this refreshes all those tired brain cells** that have spent too much time reading editorials in the *New York Times*. But, also, sadly, genes play a big role; some people inherit good health and some don't. Your daughter looks terrifically healthy—

♦ *V: Seems to be, knock on wood.*

♦ **JGB:** They're *too* healthy at that age. [laughs]

♦ *V: It's funny, in America people say, "Knock on wood," and in England people say, "Touch wood." Wasn't the idea that you scare away bad spirits by making a loud sound?*

♦ **JGB:** Well, that makes more sense.

♦ *V: Maybe. I often wonder where sayings like that come from . . . that we just use and take for granted.*

♦ **JGB: We're a vast living museum of the past**, aren't we? It's very strange.

♦ *V: You know, even though I've visited you several times, I had no idea there was a river there—*

♦ **JGB:** It's about half a mile away: the Thames. It's a small stream by Continental standards, but it's pretty. It's a good reason for being here. I'm torn between nostalgia for the river (and a kind of landscape of meadows) and the airport, which is also nearby—a nostalgia for airports. Shepperton is a very quiet place. Unlike you, I don't think I could live in a center of a city anymore.

♦ *V: When William S. Burroughs was about sixty, he remarked, "It can't get too quiet for me now."*

♦ **JGB:** That's so true, actually. **You *do* become sensitive to random noise as you get older. You want nothing to change. It's a way of slowing down time!** I remember when I first used to drive through the residential colonies on the south coast of England, which are populated entirely by elderly people—you know, quiet roads where nothing happens, lined with quiet gardens. And I'd think, "How *could* people live here?" Now I rather look forward to living somewhere like that! It slows time down—or that's the illusion.

By the way, it's almost twenty years since you brought out the *RE/Search #8/9* on me, and it's still in print—

♦ **V:** *Isn't that normal? I think corporate publishing is abnormal, in their emphasis on just the latest book done 15 minutes ago—*

♦ **JGB:** When I did my U.S. book tour back in 1988, in Seattle I was taken to some bookshop that was absolutely enormous by British standards—I think it was Tower Books. It had once been a supermarket, and I was very impressed by this gigantic sign in the sky, on top of a huge steel pole. This sign was about twenty feet wide, rotating slowly against the backdrop of a suburban neighborhood, and it said in huge letters: "J.G. Ballard Today." Normally this sign would have said "Ground Beef, $1.99" or "Canned Peaches"—you know, the special offers of the day.

I walked into an absolutely enormous aircraft hangar of a bookshop. I was so impressed as I wandered down what seemed like miles of shelves; the store seemed to have books on every subject. Gradually I had a curious revelation: all these books were brand-new—this season's books. For example, there were hundreds of cookbooks, and it seemed that they'd all been published within the past two or three months. **The people running the shop confirmed this; they said, "After about three months, the books get returned. There's no backlist here." That's a frightening development.**

♦ **V:** *I couldn't agree more.*

♦ **JGB:** That's why it's so impressive to see *The Atrocity Exhibition,* in particular, still ticking away.

♦ **V:** *Yes, that's a book that two previous publishers [Doubleday, Grove Press] had the nerve to remainder. They didn't know what they had. It's actually one of my best sellers.*

♦ **JGB:** Well, I'm very impressed. It's wonderful to see *that* book, of all my books, doing best in the States. Very curious.

♦ **V:** *The book is uncompromising and seems full of lasting "truth," if I dare* *use that word. Maybe it's your equivalent of Burroughs'* Naked Lunch.

♦ **JGB:** Well, I'm not sure that today's readers want "the truth." I think they're actually looking for reassurance—blandishments of one kind or another—

♦ *V: —with emphasis on the word "bland." Or things offering shock value or in-your-face, exaggerated kookiness or craziness.*

♦ **JGB:** The last thing they want is the truth, in many ways. It's like the movies today. I rent a lot of videos, and I must say the film industry is in a dire state. And it's difficult to see it pulling out. *Entertainment* rules everything, except that these films aren't that entertaining—

♦ *V: —they're annoying.* **There are only a few directors I really like: Dario Argento, David Cronenberg, David Lynch, and John Waters.** *None of them are really "Hollywood."*

♦ **JGB:** Also, **it's amazing how critical standards change—always in a downward direction, needless to say.** Our British TV is supposed to be rather "better" than anyone else's, though there's been a terrific dumbing-down of the BBC in particular. Of course, for the first time British television faces intense competition from the cable channels, which have cornered the market in things like football. And what is amazing is that two American television programs, one called *CSI,* which is a crime series set in Las Vegas, and *Law and Order*, set in New York—both are perfectly fine entertainment crime shows, but these two programs are now practically referred to as highbrow programming! They're considered to have a unique integrity, an *intellectual* integrity, that other crime shows don't have. Bizarre, but there we are.

♦ *V: I haven't seen either of those shows because I don't have a TV.*

♦ **JGB:** You don't have television?

♦ *V: We got rid of it because our child threw a tantrum one day—*

♦ **JGB:** She threw a tantrum because of some program?

♦ *V: She just really wanted to watch a program, and we said, "No, you have to do your homework first." And the tantrum was so profound that we said, "That's it—we're getting rid of this."*

♦ **JGB:** That's a pretty brave step.

♦ ***V:*** *So now we have to spend more time with her. Actually, we* enjoy *spending more time with her. Well, we'll see how long this lasts—*

♦ **JGB:** I think you'll find that she'll grow out of TV fairly quickly. I think that here there's a kind of post-TV generation—people of all generations, from teenagers onwards—who don't watch television.

Photo: SM Gray

They've had *enough*. They get on with all the other activities such as sports, going out to music clubs, hanging out wherever people hang out these days, and other leisure activities—everything from archery to learning to ski, to learning a foreign language.

People have grown out of TV—in fact, **I suspect that television is over as an imaginative and creative medium.** It goes on pumping out its sitcoms and news and documentaries, but it's dead, imaginatively. *TV IS OVER.* It's a medium which has exhausted itself. I think that to a large extent it has been replaced by the Internet, which is much more interesting in many respects.

♦ **V:** *Right—on the Internet there's a little movie of you talking—*

♦ **JGB:** That one I haven't seen; I don't know what it is. The trouble is: what's on the Net is not necessarily the best of its kind. I don't know what it is and have no idea who put it on the Net.

♦ **V:** *So the subject himself does not know!*

♦ **JGB:** Well, there are so many sites, aren't there? All the big broadcasting media have their own sites, and so do universities—

♦ **V:** *The university websites are better in general, I think—*

♦ **JGB:** Yes. **There are so many sites; there's no end to the proliferation of material on *everything*.** Claire, my girlfriend, spends a lot of time hunting down interesting new sites. There's a wonderful website which covers the entire California coastline. Some enterprising people must have paid for a helicopter; I assume it took a long time to do, as the California coast is pretty extensive. They flew all the way from San Diego down in the South, to the northern boundary of the state—a helluva long way. They photographed the coast from about three or four hundred yards above the beach—it's wonderful.

You see all these houses when you're over Los Angeles, and you can pull back to get a real bird's eye view so you see Los Angeles in the distance. Same for San Francisco, or wherever the camera may be. It's absolutely fascinating, slowly tracking along, particularly when you go to places like Malibu. The site provides a little information, like, "This particular house belongs to Barbra Streisand!" and you see a house on an imposing cliff. And it's a very large mansion, needless to say, with wonderful sea views from its terraces. The only drawback is that the whole place seems to be surrounded by a twenty-foot-high steel fence, so that she's looking out on her spectacular view through this grille that's defending her. And I daresay she needs defending!

As you move up the coast, you can see the enormous prosperity of California with its extraordinary coastline. Tracking along it, you feel like a visitor from Outer Space who's coming in over this huge continent and wondering what's going on. You feel like you're a visitor.

This site is amazing; you might actually see your own apartment in San Francisco, although you're probably too far inland.

♦ **V:** *Perhaps. That site sounds Ballardian.*

♦ **JGB:** It's wonderful, actually. **The Internet really impresses me. I think it is taking over from television. It still contains magic, which TV doesn't contain anymore.** The medium of television has died, partly because it's entirely controlled by very large corporations. The result: you get a completely homogenized, self-imitating landscape of programs where nothing new ever really appears—and that's a shame.

♦ **V:** *Once a network finds a program that magnetizes an audience, they feel compelled to repeat it until the show is long past its death.*

♦ **JGB:** Well, I think the whole medium is dead, in a way.

♦ **V:** *And most people don't realize that there are 20–25 minutes of commercials per hour now—*

♦ **JGB:** The BBC still has no ads, but that doesn't really make much difference. It's extraordinary to see a great medium that has failed to renew itself, whereas the printed word is still capable of great novelty or liveliness. After all, we have not just the tabloid press at one end, but we have RE/Search publications at the other. That certainly hasn't happened in the case of TV.

♦ **V: There's too much money at stake. The whole phony notion of "corporate culture" is just a euphemism for censorship.**

♦ **JGB:** The Net doesn't seem to be in danger of being taken over by giant corporations, although who knows?

♦ **V:** *I'm always paranoid that the worst will always happen, eventually. I've read that corporations are buying up more and more bandwidth so they can have a monopoly. Then they'll claim there's a scarcity of bandwidth and raise prices. Soon you'll have to be wealthy to have your own site!*

♦ **JGB:** That will probably happen; I can see that coming.

♦ **V:** *Artificial scarcity.*

♦ **JGB:** If you raise gasoline to a thousand dollars a gallon, then most people will stop driving their car. At present it's a golden age.

♦ **V:** *Right; it often happens that you don't know when you're having it good! [laughs] Maybe we've lived through some extraordinarily rich times,* *and now we feel great trepidation for what our children may face—*

♦ **JGB:** I look at my grandchildren who are about the age of four, five, and six and who may well live 'til the end of this century. Extraordinary changes may take place in 2130, 2150, 2170, but on the other hand they may not. Maybe we've lived through the last period of enduring change, for good or ill, and **in the future the needs of security and god-knows-what-else will turn us all into the inhabitants of some huge gated community that is watched relentlessly by surveillance cameras.** Armies of private police will be patrolling—for our own protection, needless to say. Maybe no one will be able to fly a kite—this might be a signal to some terrorist—or light a bonfire; that will violate hundreds of local bylaws. **Perhaps the ending state of the human race will resemble a well-run airport where no planes ever take off!**

On the radio today, I heard that 400 soldiers with tanks have been deployed around London airport, plus a thousand extra police, to guard against possible terrorist outrages. I don't know what these tanks will do in the event of a terrorist emergency—is Al Qaeda going to fly in a couple of parachute brigades? This is purely public morale boosting, and it certainly makes you *wonder.*

♦ **V:** *There are armed guards at both ends of the Golden Gate Bridge, ostensibly to guard against terrorists—*

♦ **JGB:** —or suicide jumpers?

♦ **V:** *I don't know; I just read the papers. I get my news through print still.*

♦ **JGB:** So do I; it's the best method these days. I find that television is not a good medium for news.

♦ **V:** *I couldn't agree more.*

♦ **JGB:** I'm a great devourer of newspapers—for me it's an out-of-date technology that delivers the goods, rather like the violin. If you were starting from scratch to invent musical instruments, you wouldn't invent the violin. What you came up with would be done electronically. There'd be a black box with a few knobs which would produce the sound. But the violin does work!

♦ **V:** *That's true. What an idea: that electronic technology itself may prevent the development of new, lower-tech musical instruments.* **Has every possible wonderful acoustic instrument been invented?** *Probably not.*

♦ **JGB:** The evolution of musical instruments more or less came to an end, I think (with one or two exceptions) about a century ago. Since then, it's been mainly electronic instruments that have been created.

♦ **V:** *Twenty-five years ago you said in a* Search & Destroy *interview, "I don't listen to music. It's a blind spot." I've always thought about that. These days, I prefer hearing music "live." There's something about being in the room with the musicians and watching them and knowing that it's transient, it's not being recorded—*

♦ **JGB:** And the given performance is *unique.* Whatever errors there may be are intrinsic to the unique occasion.

♦ **V:** *Actually, one of the main reasons I prefer live music is not for the perfection but for the mistakes—in a perverse way that can provide enjoyment.*

♦ **JGB:** Well, I'm not in any way musical, I must admit. I *am* a complete blank spot there!

♦ **V:** *So you didn't receive any musical training growing up?*

♦ **JGB:** Well, I think that in my case there's a slightly different factor at work. I think I've got a fairly visual orientation. **I'm very interested in the visual arts: painting and sculpture, from the caves of Lascaux onwards.** I'm intensely responsive to visual arts, and yet Shanghai, where I was brought up, didn't have a single museum. I came to England when I was sixteen and had only the faintest idea who Picasso was, although I might have seen a few reproductions. During the war, of course, I didn't see anything.

My mother's parents were lifelong teachers of music. Both of them taught music at home—usually the piano, and all day long there were two pianos going with various pupils practicing their scales or whatever they do. I think this completely turned my mother off to music. Consequently, I don't remember my parents *ever* playing music of any kind! It wasn't until I left home and went to college that I discovered the old 78rpm record players, which is what we had at the time. Parents can leave blank spaces in their children's minds!

♦ *V: Perhaps that very absence of musical data in your brain left more room for your visual/verbal imagination to flourish—*

♦ **JGB:** Well, I like to think that! But who knows? **The imagination—it's such a mystery as to what drives it and what role it plays. It's still totally unfathomed**, despite the huge amount of research that's been done in the neurosciences. Almost nothing is known about the "how" and "why" of the imagination. Extraordinary.

♦ *V: The imagination can manufacture words, images, and even music. These can all appear unbidden in your dreams—*

♦ **JGB:** And you write it down!

♦ *V: I always thought it was an extraordinary idea for you to have paid somebody to recreate, on canvases, those two Paul Delvaux paintings that were destroyed in a London blitz. Like, who would have thought of that?!*

♦ **JGB:** Oh, I don't know about that. The reason I did it is that Delvaux's paintings are so expensive; now they sell for upwards of a million dollars. I thought, "I haven't got a million dollars to spend, so why not recreate his lost ones?"—particularly because I *liked* the two that were lost. They are his early paintings. I got a lot of satisfaction from the idea that I'd sort of, in a way, brought them back to life!

♦ *V: Exactly, and they have real brush strokes on them; they possess three-dimensionality.*

♦ **JGB:** They're genuine oils! [laughs]

♦ *V: Duchamp said that the spectator completes the work of art, implying that the "real" art is not on the canvas but in the brain activity that's "processing" the painting (that may be a misinterpretation).*

♦ **JGB:** I'm sure, strictly speaking, that's true. Of course, it led the way to . . . I don't know whether the American art scene is as dominated by "concept art" and "installation art" as the British art scene has been over the last ten years, but here installation and concept art have driven out, more or less, all other kinds of artistic activity among younger artists. **Huge reputations here have been made by people who have never, as far as I know, painted a canvas and can**

barely draw. People famous over here include Tracey Emin, Damien Hirst, and one or two others. And there are many others who specialize in installations of one kind or another.

I half suspect that **these people are not really working in the field of "art" at all—they're working in the area of** *pure sensation.* In a curious way, it's no longer possible to shock people by purely aesthetic means, in the way that, say, the Impressionists certainly shocked their audiences in the 1870s, or Manet shortly before with his *Olympia,* and so on. Manet's handling of paint shocked his audiences. The same is true of the Post-Impressionists like Van Gogh, Gauguin and so on—they shocked their audiences by aesthetic means alone. And so did Picasso. But I don't think that's possible now; you can't shock people by aesthetic means anymore. You can only shock them by virtue of the *subject matter,* and that doesn't necessarily need oil paint or canvas or even marble or steel. Tracey Emin became enormously famous by exhibiting a sort of rumpled bed, and Hirst became famous by putting a shark in a tank of formaldehyde or whatever.

♦ *V: Didn't he cut it in half first?*

♦ **JGB:** He did that later with a cow and a calf, but the shark is a real shark that was caught (not by him) off the Australian coast and shipped back here. Sadly the beast—I've seen it—has begun to disintegrate. I wrote somewhere that it should be released back to the sea in an act of kindness, you know, like an old circus whale.

So in a way, I think it isn't possible anymore to touch people's imaginations by aesthetic means; the aesthetic aspects of art have been almost *superseded* by a climate of pure sensationalism. And this has been going on for a long time. I remember **back in the '60s there was a woman artist, at a gallery in London, who exhibited her used sanitary napkins.** And of course, many of the artist-performers in the *RE/Search* books hover on the borderline between the aesthetic and the purely sensational, partly because the naked human body and its functions is endlessly fascinating. I mean Annie Sprinkle and all those people you've covered in *Modern Primitives* . . .

♦ *V: By allowing men to peer inside her with the aid of a doctor's speculum,*

Annie Sprinkle certainly (I don't know if "enlightened" is the right word) enabled *literally tens of thousands of men to see something that they had probably never seen before in their lives.*

♦ **JGB:** Bizarre, really!

♦ *V: But, you know, she provided a flashlight, too.*

♦ **JGB:** Well, I suppose it was an education!

♦ *V: Yes, it was, indeed.*

♦ **JGB:** Most wives and girlfriends would draw a line at that kind of thing. They would suspect the man of having something slightly wrong with his curiosity.

♦ *V: But it's art! [laughs]*

♦ **JGB: Most art being created these days is sensationalism. There are very few artists, I'm afraid, who touch the imagination in any kind of real way.**

There's a young Japanese woman artist [Mariko Mori?] who had a big show here. She makes very strange five-minute and ten-minute films. One is set at the Tokyo Airport, where she wears a strange silver suit—there's something very odd about it. She produces these gigantic visual images, 25 feet by 15 feet, of strange landscapes—I don't know whether they're computer-generated, but they're rather unearthly. There are hints of Science Fiction in her work, but it's very subtly done. Her stuff was extraordinary; she's one of the few impressive artists I've seen . . . There's a terrible dearth. It may be that we've gone off experimental art.

♦ *V: Yes; maybe that's dead, too.*

♦ **JGB:** In a way, we've got enough Romantic symphonies, we've got enough great operas—we don't need anymore. Between them, Puccini, Rossini, Wagner, Mozart have done it all—there's no need for any more. That may be the case.

I'm not sure if I was having my time again I would be a writer. It may be that we've got enough novels. [laughs] It's hard to say.

♦ *V: But in my opinion there's no such thing as too much elucidation of what's really going on in this information-overloaded, nightmarish world of ours. And it seems there'll always be a need for poetry or poetic evocations—*

♦ **JGB:** The trouble is: so much of modern life is inaccessible, isn't it?

If you think of all these giant business corporations, here and in America and elsewhere, it's obvious that these play a crucial role in deciding how our society evolves. And yet most people, including myself, have absolutely no access to what is going on in the boardrooms of AOL-Time-Warner or MCI, or British Petroleum. That whole corporate world, dictating how very large numbers of people are affected lower down on the hierarchy, is closed off. We don't know any more than the peasantry in classical China knew what was going on in the court of the Emperor. **There's a sense that we're all excluded and given a *facsimile of reality* to amuse ourselves with, while real life is taking place in a corporate tower block!** Although it may not be true, I dare say, but one has the feeling that one's shut out.

The *professions* are so isolated from everyday experience. Whenever you go to a hospital for some sort of specialist check-over or what have you, I'm always amazed by the high-tech world of modern medicine. You're kind of excluded from it even when you're lying on a—

♦ *V: —gurney or X-ray table—*

♦ **JGB:** —or going through a CAT-scan machine. There's a sense of this intensely complex and advanced technology involving the operators that is shut off forever from us. And that's true of the business world, and a lot of politics. What's really going on in the White House at this moment? Or at 10 Downing Street? It's hard to believe that what we *do* see is real. It's very, very peculiar. One doesn't know where the truth lies—or if there *is* a truth.

♦ *V: Maybe that word's obsolete.*

♦ **JGB:** Well, I think it is, isn't it? It *is;* it's all relativistic now.

♦ *V: Nothing seems absolute—*

♦ **JGB: Nothing is true and nothing is untrue.**

♦ *V: Now* there's *a slogan for the future! Back in the '60s I used to quote William Burroughs' slogan, "Nothing is true; everything is permitted," from Hassan i Sabbah, but I like this one better. Yes, for today's media-sat-*

urated existence, "Nothing is true and nothing is untrue."

♦ **JGB:** It's got a nice Orwellian ring, too! Just don't think about it for more than two seconds or you'll start to get frightened . . .

♦ *V: In America—speaking of "Orwellian"—Team Bush started some agency with a title like the Ministry of Total Information Awareness. The implication seemed to be that* **with massive surveillance technology**

Photo: SM Gray

blanketing the country, these "thought police" could know every-thing all the time, including what you're thinking.

♦ **JGB:** That's probably going to come, if it hasn't already.

♦ *V: I've often wondered if these thought police could, simply by monitoring your brainwaves in some unbeknownst way, translate those waves into what you're thinking, and "read" the flow of forbidden thoughts and fantasies coursing through your brain—*

♦ **JGB:** It's scary. I may have mentioned this before, but starting on Monday, in central London, the police are introducing what they call congestion charges. They've marked out an enormous area, about 5 miles by 5 miles by 5 miles, in central London. And—this really is Orwellian—they've mounted literally hundreds of cameras at all the entry points, by side roads, into this zone.

These cameras are hooked up to a license-plate recognition system, and if you want to enter the zone in your car, you have to pay five pounds. They're already talking about doubling this to ten pounds per day. The idea is to get rid of the congestion in central London. The average traffic speeds there are falling to about three miles an hour, so it's more or less always hovering on the edge of gridlock.

Anyway, what's interesting is that *nobody* seems to have minded! **To me, this is an *outrage:* all these cameras everywhere.** When you buy a car here, your license, your personal details, and your car license number are fed into a central depository, and these computers are hooked up to this depository. So they will know if you haven't paid your five pounds, they'll know who you are and where you live. And this scheme has been in development for months. Somebody pointed out that people will tamper with and change their license plate numbers, but the reply was, "Well, they won't be able to get away with it, because our cameras will also register the faces of the drivers." Previously we hadn't been told this!

In a way this is beyond the dreams of Joseph Stalin. Now the where-abouts of everybody who drives in central London, and their identity, is going to be known to these authorities. They'll also have patrolling vans inside the zone, equipped with cameras. So hundreds of thousands of drivers and their vehicles in this huge zone will all be logged into these giant computers. It's *Alphaville*. But again, what is amazing is that nobody (or *very few*) people seem to have objected. They tolerate this because it's ostensibly *for the public good.*

The day may come when you can convince people that, to avoid getting a brain tumor, all you have to do is wear this special helmet that amplifies brain waves and can spot a small tumor . . . and people will wear it. The fact that this helmet will also detect what you're thinking about . . . whether you approve of the government of the day, or whether you approve of conflicts in the Middle East, or General Motors cars, doesn't seem to worry anybody! It's bizarre.

♦ *V: That's rather dark humor! There's another way to thwart those surveillance cameras: start a fashion movement in which everyone wears ski masks that completely cover their faces, and big hats that shade people's faces from recognition. Maybe the fear of surveillance is what's prompting so many people these days to wear caps, even in hot weather. Actually, I read that somebody caught going through a red light by a surveillance camera got off because they were wearing some huge hat, and it could not be conclusively determined that he was indeed the person driving the car.*

♦ **JGB: That might be the key to our survival: clownish behavior! To survive, people will dress up in the most outlandish outfits; everyone will become a quick-change artist.**

♦ *V: That's a word I haven't heard for a long time. I guess that used to refer to somebody who robs a bank dressed in a black jumpsuit, and then strips it off and is dressed in white . . .*

♦ **JGB:** Well, we'll see.

♦ *V: That's a perfect ending for this section. Yes, that's our future: we'll all become pranksters, clowns, and camouflage artists.*

♦ **JGB:** That may be necessary. I can see it happening.

♦ *V: Multiple identities.*

♦ **JGB: Eccentric behavior, highly imaginative eccentric behavior, may become a survival imperative. *The opposite of conformism.* ♦ ♦ ♦**

Photo: SM Gray

J.G. Ballard and Mark Pauline

A while ago Survival Research Laboratories founder Mark Pauline visited J.G. Ballard at his home in Shepperton, England. They discussed various topics including Ronald Reagan, conformism, the triumph of bourgeois society, travel, recreational drugs, nostalgia, Kathy Acker, and William S. Burroughs. What follows are excerpts from that encounter ...

♦ **J.G. BALLARD: People take you at face value. Any role that people see you in they will accept, by and large. That seems to be a rule of life.**

♦ *MARK PAULINE: They don't need too much information. Imagination takes care of the rest.*

♦ **JGB:** You've got to remember our perception of things in England is very different because it's very important, from our point of view, that America be well-led—for obvious reasons. You're defending us—it's *your* rockets that are keeping the Russkies away—

♦ *MP: Where's the closest Cruise Missile?*

♦ **JGB:** Well, it's not that far away. Greenham Common is where the Cruise Missiles are—that's where the women protestors have been camped, about thirty or forty miles southwest of here.

♦ *MP: There are two bases in England—*

♦ **JGB:** Yes, Millsworth [sic] is the other one, I think—southwest of London, about fifty or sixty miles. Most of the big American air bases are in Norfolk, about 100 miles to the northeast of London. You know, I want my *own* cruise missile at the bottom of my garden, with three technical sergeants smoking Lucky Strikes and asking where they can buy a good hamburger. Also, I would like an encampment of Greenham Common ladies living in a cardboard box out front. That strikes me as perfect!

My reaction to Libya was *three cheers*—I'm all for bombing Khadafi. [*April 15, 1986, the U.S. bombed Libya in retaliation for linkage to ter-*

rorist activity, including the bombing of a disco in Berlin which killed several U.S. servicemen and dozens of others.] But I was practically alone—Thatcher and I are the only two people who supported the action! The British reaction, on the whole, was hostile, and I thought this was deplorable and showed the country in its weakest light, frankly.

There are generations of people here—children of parents who are themselves children of parents who were brought up in the post-war welfare state. Their freedom has been guaranteed by the United States, basically, and the nuclear defenses that France and Britain have as well. These people have no perception of the realities of the world, and what it's like to live under a tyranny east of the Iron curtain. They think that consent and "appealing to reason" is going to mean something in times of international crisis. This vast army of half-baked and inexperienced people were the ones protesting the loudest, while my lonely voice was cheering vigorously.

I thought that was a remarkable feat of arms actually, to fly all that way and hit those targets in Libya.

♦ **MP:** *Well, it's not like those Libyan terrorists are really the people's terrorists. They're really just an arm of Khadafi's government. It's not like going and bombing Nicaragua, which is obviously much more complicated.*

♦ **JGB:** If you look at the East and West today, the situation is stable and has been for years and years. If you look at the Thirties when you had Hitler, Mussolini, and Stalin, it was damned unstable then. People like **Mussolini and Hitler tapped psychological forces that came straight out of the abyss.** Forces deep down in the core of the human psyche were certainly empowering Hitler, the Nazis, and Mussolini to a large extent, and, I would guess, Stalin and the Soviet regime. And Hitler and the Nazis were these huge media constructs . . .

The only wars that the United States has involved itself in the last twenty years are all rather peripheral matters, aren't they? You wouldn't even be *allowed* to have World War III—

♦ **MP:** *They'd vote it down in a referendum . . . During Vietnam, there was a lot of exciting ill will that isn't around these days—*

♦ **JGB:** In Vietnam, they stopped calling American soldiers on the ground "advisors" and started calling them "soldiers"—then things started going wrong. Around '66 I said to a friend of mine, "They should start calling those soldiers 'advisors' again—then everything would be *okay*." **As long as you call them "advisors," there's no emotional commitment, but once they're G.I.'s or soldiers or British Grenadiers or whatever, and they walk into battle carrying the flag, then you want them to win, don't you?**

♦ *MP: There's a difference between "winning" and just persuading someone nicely: "I think you'd better just* move along *now."*

♦ **JGB:** If you're only an advisor, you can step back and say: "Well, the client was a damn fool and he lost," and go off with another client.

  What about your own life, Mark—how is that?

♦ *MP: We're just moving along. Since* RE/Search #6/7 [Industrial Culture Handbook, 1983] *came out, things have changed a lot. We have a real factory now, literally. We have big lathes, milling machines, punch presses and we've been able to get people to work on making much more complicated machines that rank on a par with what university-level facilities can produce.*

  We sort of operate like corporations do: act ruthlessly and deal with other corporations in the way that businesses do. We see what they have that we want, and find ways of getting it from them without entering the sphere of legal problems. So we've been making much larger machines, and doing larger shows. Now fifty people help to work on making huge machines. For our "spring line"—

♦ **JGB:** Oh, an annual model change!

♦ *MP: Yes ... I made a walking machine that weighs about a ton. It's nine feet tall with four legs and it actually walks. It's as big as an elephant and has articulated, complex, progressive linkages in the joints. The machines are all radio-controlled now. My partner, Eric Werner, made an enormous square-wheeled car which is about 18 feet long with a 400-horsepower American V-8 in it. It has a complex Grand Prix road racing suspension system so it can take the bumps of the wheels, and it's radio-controlled.*

  We've reached the point where we are inventing machines that are truly new inventions. I invented a way to focus the blast from high explo-

sives into a shock-wave device that weighs about a ton. We found an abandoned twelve-foot-tall high-pressure cylinder. On Labor Day we cut it down and dragged it into a truck.

Nowadays people who are Professors of Mechanical Engineering at Stanford University give me advice. We developed a system whereby an explosion is focused into a donut and then collapsed and speeded up so it projects a ball of energy that can go 700-800 feet and blow something apart. In a show we made a whole town, and then blew it up.

♦ **JGB:** Sounds wonderful!

♦ ***MP:*** *My last show was titled "Failure to Discriminate: Determining the Degree to which Attractive Delusions Can Operate as a Substitute for Confirmation by Evidence." My shows are all about machines doing things and undoing them, but in these enormous panoramas. We might start a large house on fire with this V-8 engine attached to a huge grain blower, and inject gasoline into it. After it starts burning, you blow it out with a big blast from the shockwave cannon. There are machines walking drunkenly alongside the crowd, then they might turn around and destroy what's left of the whole house . . .*

I think **pretty soon you'll probably be able to go down to the auctioneers and buy yourself an old Cruise Missile.** *Let them get a couple years out of date first. You know, a used one—slightly used. . . "Pre-owned"!*

♦ **JGB:** Yes, yes. Of course, **with computers especially, obsolescence sets in very fast—it's almost built in** . . . How's San Francisco? I've never been to San Francisco, but friends of mine have. They say there used to be a lot of gay social activities—

♦ ***MP:*** *Well, things have totally gone by the way now. There's no street action. The AIDS explosion changed San Francisco completely.*

♦ **JGB:** This chap described this to me: he was in San Francisco, and he wandered into a municipal building of some kind—it could have been a large hotel foyer. There appeared to be a fashion show taking place with about 200 women in long ball gowns and wonderful hairdos bouncing up and down. He thought, "How lovely all the women are!" It took him about five minutes to realize that it was 200 *men* that were

SRL Los Angeles Show, April 2, 2005, Dangerous Curve Gallery, cur. Susan Joyce. Photo: V. Vale

prancing up and down. I take it that sort of thing isn't going on quite the way it used to?

♦ **MP:** *Not really.*

♦ **JGB:** All those gay pageants. Does that mean there's been an exodus of gays from San Francisco?

♦ **MP:** *Well, so many people are dying that someone who works for a funeral home brought a dead AIDS patient over to our shop to show us. We looked at this dead man and were like, "Hmmm . . ." There's like seventy or a hundred people a day dying.*

♦ **JGB:** I take it that a lot of the more liberal attitudes that have developed in the middle class, bourgeois, straight society in the last ten or fifteen years have slammed into reverse.

♦ **MP:** *Not really; people are very sympathetic.*

♦ **JGB:** That's good. You know, I was just reading about Ronald Reagan's oldest daughter—it appears that she's quite a raunchy lady.

♦ **MP:** *She's sort of schizophrenic—she supports the ERA [Equal Rights Amendment] and women's rights and even abortion, yet at the same time she's this staunch Republican who claims to support her father. She doesn't go along with him on many issues. It's kind of embarrassing for him on that level—she's not behind him all the way.*

♦ **JGB:** But he seems to ride out all those little storms, though, doesn't he?

As far as I can judge from over here, Reagan represents a radical breakthrough—

♦ **MP:** *He sort of defines the "star" image—*

♦ **JGB: The Presidency *is* Pure Image now—**

♦ **MP:** *Well, respect for "stars" is always tied into how much power they have. People start to hate their stars when they begin losing the power of their draw at the box office. Before he became President, people thought Reagan was just a* has-been, *but now he has more power than any star ever had. As a political person he's really just a nut, but he's a star—*

♦ **JGB: The Presidency is now a movie, and presumably will remain so from now on.**

I saw a film that was a documentary investigation into the way

Reagan confused fiction and reality. It was conducted by some university researcher, I think. The documentary showed Reagan delivering speeches referring to brave bomber pilots in the Second World War who refused to bail out because of two or three injured crew members, and went down to their deaths. Reagan even quoted their last words over the radio transmitter. Then the documentary excerpted the film clip from the 1940's which Reagan had actually quoted from—in his mind he had confused movie reality with "real" reality—the two had just merged.

I remember Reagan when he was in his fifties; I wrote my ["Why I Want to Fuck Ronald Reagan"] piece in 1966. I wrote it on the strength of his performance as Governor of California. Then he was a much tougher character, with a real latent nastiness. Well, not so latent—*manifest* nastiness, with a sneering side to his makeup which is completely absent now. His platform was: "Get government off our backs!" Well, an ideal society *is* the one with the least government—

♦ *MP: Why even have a President anymore?*

♦ **JGB:** One thing that puzzled people over here during the Watergate crisis was the way in which Americans as a whole, even the hard-bitten press, seemed genuinely shocked by this evidence of wrong-doing in high places in the White House and elsewhere. Yet every Hollywood movie made since the 1930's (and there must have been tens of thousands) always showed politicians in an unfavorable light. In all those Frank Capra movies and all those small-town melodramas, if you want a corrupt figure you don't pick the local doctor or schoolmaster or fire chief, you pick the local politician. And, if you make a movie set in Washington, the politicians are always shown to be corrupt. Yet not withstanding this, Americans seem shocked when—

♦ *MP: Well, you're not supposed to get caught.*

♦ **JGB:** Yes—it's *getting caught.*

♦ *MP: Yeah; it's fine to be crooked, it's fine to be a criminal, it's fine to be all that. But good criminals never get caught; good criminals never go to prison. And good politicians never get tripped up. Nixon just didn't know how. He had no precedent to act from . . .*

♦ **JGB:** Yes, Nixon was a *very* confused character—an internally confused character, wasn't he? Of all the post-war presidents, he was probably the most capable intellectually, in terms of being fit for the highest office—more so than Eisenhower. Yet there was this deep internal flaw that became quite evident. God knows what that flaw was, but—!

In England we have as our Prime Minister Margaret Thatcher. I've always admired her enormously. I always found her extremely mysterious and attractive at the same time. I think she exerts a powerful sexual spell, and I'm not alone. I think there are a *lot* of men who find themselves driven to distraction by the mystery of Margaret Thatcher. She's remarkable. I think she taps all sorts of extreme responses on the part of, certainly, *men* in the population at large.

♦ *MP: How do you think she fits in with the whole English historical tendency to have female rulers?*

♦ **JGB:** I think she exemplifies that. She taps very deep levels of response. There are elements of *La Belle Dame Sans Merci*—the merciless muse, in her. Also the archetype of the—

♦ *MP: Medusa.*

♦ **JGB:** Yes, **the Medusa. She taps a large number of deep responses which people express in present-day terms. She's the nanny, she's the headmistress, and she's school-marmy as well.** I think her appeal goes far *beyond* . . . it's a very ambiguous appeal. She represents all these sort of *half-stages*—half-conscious, primordial forces . . . that she certainly tapped.

There's certainly no other woman politician here who remotely approaches her in that respect. I don't know if she's aware of all this; I don't think she is. She's quite unlike Reagan in that respect, because I think Reagan is quite aware of his appeal. He is quite cunning in his way, orchestrating his image with a lot of help from his friends. Whereas I don't think Thatcher does that; I think she just plays her hunches and acts from her gut—like her response to the Falklands crisis. I don't think she realized this would be a popular move electorally at the time—she just sent the fleet down there. Yet sending the fleet down was the right thing to do—it touched the right nerve.

Photo: Ana Barrado

Thatcher is a mysterious figure. Her day is probably over because she's been in office for seven years. That's a long time—you want a new show or you'll get bored. That's a very important consideration, you know, because England is a much smaller country and there's less variety. It's more of a village here, and once you've exhausted the pool of gossip, you want something new to happen.

♦ *MP: Here in America we have Bush set up to be Reagan's replacement. But he has no character. People won't settle for him after having a Reagan.*

♦ **JGB:** You've got to have somebody in the public perception who has a possibility of media transformation. He's got to be able to be *media-malleable* . . . somebody who has media possibilities screaming out of his eyeballs.

♦ *MP: It could be a TV newscaster.*

♦ **JGB:** Somebody who has those sorts of possibilities, and it seems to me that there's a motorcar maker—

♦ *MP: Lee Iacocca?*

♦ **JGB:** I've seen him on television quite a bit over here. For all his deficiencies: the fact that he knows *nothing* about the world outside of the automobile industry—that doesn't matter! **He clearly has the possibility within himself for other people to impose their fantasies on him. *That's* the key thing.** I can imagine that other people's fantasies will stick, will accrete to him, and that's all that matters.

It's almost as if what one needs is sort of a *reverse charisma* now. Not a light that shines outwards, but the ability, like a black hole, to draw light *inwards!* You've got to be able to draw other people's fantasies to you. I agree with you: Bush doesn't have it. He's hopeless.

Most people over here, I think, are secretly sorry that Geraldine Ferraro [Walter Mondale's V.P. running mate against Reagan and George Bush in 1984] didn't get elected. Within six weeks Mondale would have fallen ill with some serious but unspecified complaint. Then we would have had the Mafia running the White House! Women are entitled to be as corrupt as men.

♦ *MP: Well, that's the thing—there's so many women getting into politics and positions of power nowadays, but as soon as they drop one pen, that's* it—*they just get fired. You see it happening all the time.*

♦ **JGB:** That's a resurgence of the old feeling that a man can be sexually promiscuous, but a woman can't—if she is, that woman is a slut. A woman must be purer than snow; we can't have anybody who is a little tarnished around the edges. Otherwise, it's like Mother Nature has VD! [laughs]

On Writing Book Reviews

♦ **JGB: I don't write many reviews; I find it very difficult. It's so time-consuming because you have to read the book!**

I used to review science fiction back in the Sixties for *The Guardian* and various other papers. I could trade on the fact that I'd already read half the stuff when it first came out in magazine form. I ended up not ever reading the books, so I stopped—I thought it was unfair to the authors.

Also, **I find writing non-fiction very difficult—it's sort of using *the wrong side of the brain.*** I feel I'm literally using the wrong neural wiring, sort of going against the current. It's like writing with the left hand if you're a right-handed person. It's *torment.*

I've slowed down my writing . . . For something like a year and a half I was caught up in heavy promotion for *Empire of the Sun.* For eighteen months I was my own publicity agent, chauffeur, media advisor, and client. I just zigzagged around, totally exhausted half the time; I even made a trip to France for promotion of the book there. A lot of Continental and American journalists came over to interview me; I was never able to have a moment alone. I lost a year and a half of my life doing that, but I knew it was worth doing—and that after that it would never happen again!

♦ *MP: You only get one biography—*

♦ **JGB:** Exactly, then I would sink back again into total obscurity, after some decent interval . . .

There's always been people keen on my stuff, and I feel my earlier books over here were quite big successes—well, *reasonable* successes—but *Empire of the Sun* was way out in a different league. I'd left the area of imaginative fiction, which isn't popular—one's got to face that fact: imaginative fiction isn't a popular form . . . into something much more in the popular bourgeois taste.

People here are in the middle of a huge nostalgia boom; they love anything connected with the Second World War. And I wrote a book that seemed to have an eye-witness account about a virtually unknown theatre of World War II, taking the lid off British behavior and all that sort of thing. If I'd planned it myself, I couldn't have hit the target more exactly. It did create a huge amount of interest which no other book of mine ever will, because I've gone back to writing imaginative fiction again.

I've always wanted to write a book about my China background, and there was only one way to write it: as a sort of fictionalized autobiography. It really isn't all that different from most of my other writing; it's just that my other fiction doesn't have *the reassurance of the familiar.* In *Empire of the Sun* you actually have planes bombing half-deserted cities, enemy troops invading, and people know where they are. But with a novel like *Crash* that deals with crashing cars—people say, "Ugh, this is weird. This is horrible."

♦ *MP: Writing* Empire of the Sun *hasn't helped you forget those horrible years in the camp?*

♦ **JGB:** But I've been writing about it all the time—I just wrote about it *in disguise.*

♦ *MP: Well, supposedly people drink to forget, and write to forget. Is that a myth?*

♦ **JGB:** I'm not sure that's true, actually. Now, they say you can "talk things out and have a good cry"—assuming you have somebody to confide in. But I'm not sure if that makes any damn difference. I think it's just a matter of letting time go by, you know?

♦ *MP: A "delaying" tactic!*

♦ **JGB:** Yes. As I was writing *Empire of the Sun* I was constantly seeing bits of my other novels coming up. It was like an assembly kit made up of bits of my other novels set not in the near-future, but in the 1940's. It has already receded into the past; I'm concentrating on turning my mind to other things.

♦ *MP: I spend much of my time reading books, finding out what I like, and then pursuing that. But it's so hard to find good books—*

♦ **JGB:** Hasn't Burroughs, who I've always thought was a genius, made a big comeback in the last five years? Hasn't he spawned a mass of—well, let's put it at its best—hasn't his *example* helped stimulate a large number of younger writers?

♦ *MP: There are no younger writers that show the same sort of honesty and courage. Burroughs has spurred derivative attempts to write, with none of the soul.*

♦ **JGB:** I was thinking that his example might . . . I mean, *there's* a man who is prepared to go all the way!

♦ *MP: People are illiterate. There's no literary community of young writers now. The important thing is to look back and find amazing authors who were passed over, who were doing really ground-breaking things. You've got to really dig to find them.*

♦ **JGB: Iain Banks wrote a book called *The Wasp Factory*—if you come across it, read it!** It's an unusual book. He's one of these very prolific writers who had written six novels before he got his first one published. Sure enough, he's published about three novels since *The Wasp Factory*, and they aren't even remotely in the same class. There's problems . . . there *isn't* that much around.

Kathy Acker enjoyed quite a vogue over here about two years ago. Everybody was talking about Kathy Acker, and magazines like *Time Out*, which is devoted to the word "new" in the arts, printed extracts from one or two of her things. There was a real hint of Burroughs in some of her stuff. I thought, "Migod, this is the new young talent, come on . . . more!" I think I was sent a copy of *Blood and Guts in High School*. But . . . I wish it could have been better than what it was! I met her at a party and expected a real sort of freak with a needle hanging out of her arm, but in fact there was this extremely pleasant, sensible, good-natured, likeable soul.

♦ *MP: I was pretty good friends with her when she lived in San Francisco.*

♦ **JGB:** Well, my feeling is: she's not as wild and original as the form suggests she should be. **There ought to be *real madness* there, but there isn't, actually.** But I liked her a lot, and gave her my very best wishes. Somebody sent me her book *Don Quixote,* but I didn't think that was up to much. At least she's better than William Styron. Anyway, if you happen to see her, give my regards to Kathy Acker. Sweet lass.

♦ *MP: I think a woman writing about that kind of stuff is automatically treated as a novelty.*

♦ **JGB:** If there were any new young Burroughs around, you would have heard of them by now, wouldn't you?

♦ *MP: We would have heard about them.*

♦ **JGB:** Maybe the young writers are going into things like movies, and non-commercial movies?

♦ *MP: **People that are the most rebellious often have the least capabilities, or they're sort of unable to focus themselves.** They're very bad at magnifying their vision into any kind of product that is anything. They don't even have a real vision to try to technically represent in some way. **You see people who are obviously intelligent, who have seemingly radical underpinnings, and who want to get out there and rip the world up and oppose society . . . but they'll just do it in this lame way.** Like, why don't they go out and make "professional" films?*

♦ **JGB:** Have you ever seen *Eraserhead*? It was made a long time ago. That strikes me as an impressive movie. It reminded me, in a way, of *Last Year at Marienbad.* I don't know if you ever saw *that* "classic" movie, but that was probably *the* most boring film I've ever seen! *Eraserhead* was likewise quite boring, and yet cumulatively it left an impact that still lingers to this day. It was very powerfully formed, that film. I assume that if there's a mouse in your home, there's ten others running around somewhere. There must be ten other *Eraserheads* being shot right now—

♦ *MP: People are lazy—you'd think that, but don't count on it. People are bums in America and everywhere else. They need a tornado to stir them up!*

♦ **JGB:** Aren't there more intellectuals and artists in San Francisco

Photo: Ana Barrado

than there were in Paris in the 1920s? All the gays who have flocked to San Francisco . . . there must be one or two of them who are the Allen Ginsbergs of today—

♦ *MP: Afraid not. People aren't disciplined. You really have to know how to work, and very few people ever develop the skills to take their vision and be able to forge it into anything. Undisciplined minds don't produce, no matter how powerful they are. A car with no transmission makes a lot of noise, but it doesn't really get you anywhere.*

♦ **JGB:** I understand.

♦ *MP: I feel like I'm in a sort of cultural* On the Beach. *In almost every place, people have sort of ceded their will to the state. They haven't figured out how to operate without some kind of "scene" behind them. It's sad.*

♦ **JGB:** I understand, because **I'm a complete outsider.** I live out in this little suburb and have almost nothing to do with literary life in London. I don't go to conventions or conferences or literary gatherings of any kind, so I'm really the last person to ask, but my impression is that the same is true over here. There's almost nothing. You could almost stop reading [contemporary literature] and just read Burroughs and Genet, and that's enough.

One wonders whether one is now defining the *desert.* Maybe it's me; maybe it's my *maps* that are at fault. Here in England the novel has had a resurgence of popularity. It was almost dead on its feet at the end of the Seventies—if you looked at not just the Top Ten bestsellers but the Top 100 bestsellers in paperback and hardcover, they were mostly non-fiction. Then by the end of the Seventies the novel started to make a comeback.

I think that people started getting bored with television. Now the novel is enjoying a huge boom in the consolidated hardback bestseller list. Most of the titles are now novels, which was unthinkable ten or fifteen years ago. Sales of fiction overall are very strong, yet you look at all this stuff and it's so *bland.*

It's like . . . on British radio, we have afternoon plays which are sort of little half-hour or one-hour radio dramas designed for housewives. They listen to a drama about a bank manager who has an affair with a client; the housewives are preparing the pasta for the supper while waiting for the kids to come home from school. The novels are equivalents of these: studies of bourgeois life by and large, with very little real imagination. In fact, one feels that the *real* imagination has been filtered out. It's not true that most writers have more imagination than their readers—it's the other way around, probably.

I think there's a sort of *profound conformism* in the air today. I can only really speak firsthand of the situation here in England. Take rock music—popular music which is the main conduit for aggressive new talents. Well, let's take punk, which really got going here about 1975 or thereabouts. It became a powerful expression of all sorts of half-formed political ideas, ideas of a sort of, in the case of punk, *social vengeance* almost of a far more extreme kind than you would ever find in a novel, let's say.

Punk was rather like taking up bull-fighting in Spain. It was something for a working-class kid with no hope and nothing but his own sort of courage . . . It's his one way to make it to the *big time.* If you're a working-class kid from a rough council estate in the North, you just buy a guitar and you're ready to *go!* Whereas writing a novel requires a framework of literacy and a whole knowledge of fiction and literary culture in general. You can't just sit down and write a novel. Plus, there are the circumstances of getting published and all the rest of it. So all the creative vitality of today, I think, goes into popular music.

Yet I don't even have a—what do you call them now—I still call them gramophones, and I don't even have one! They're called record players. My impression, reading things like *NME* (*New Musical Express)* is that there are literally hundreds of small groups with powerful grudges against the life of the gentry. The impression is that they're pouring out a kind of healthy, vital, original critique—

♦ *MP: As a starting point, maybe. Music used to exist as a starting point for rebellion. Now it's a starting point that doesn't lead anybody to anywhere! People sort of figure, "That's all the work I have to do. I'll listen to this, wear the right kind of clothes, buy the right kind of things"—and that's* it! *It doesn't extend any deeper than that.*

♦ **JGB:** Hmm. What is **Graeme Revell** doing now? The last time I heard from him was about six months ago. He said he was about to go to Australia; I think his wife Sinan was having another baby. He was rather disenchanted with everything here. He's a marvelous character—

♦ *MP: Yeah, a great character.*

♦ **JGB:** I think—it's just that the crust of conformism has to solidify. It gets so thick that nobody beneath the crust can breathe, and then a few brave spirits break through to the air again. I've said many times recently that **the norms of bourgeois society have now conquered all.**

We are living in a totally bourgeois world, where the values of bourgeois society are now totally triumphant . . . even among the young—that's the frightening thing—I mean the 19- to 20-year-olds. If you look at a paper like *The Face,* which is supposed to be the chief organ for the talented young, in fact it's like *Vogue* but is full of interviews with young painters, designers, musicians—you name it. They're asked what their ambitions are and they come up with—sometimes they say it in just so many words—**they want fame and money. This is appalling! I mean, if that's all you want at the age of nineteen?!**

I think the values of bourgeois society by and large have triumphed. We're living in a world where people at the age of 22 and 23 are thinking about their *mortgages.* It is a fact, and there's nothing much one can do about it, except cultivate one's obsessions and one's own imagination—

♦ *MP: A lot of young people experiment with drugs—*

♦ **JGB:** But **the universal use of recreational drugs results in people's rebellious imagination being *tamed,* rather than the opposite.** Assuming there *are* authoritarian powers that run the West, well, if "they" wanted a device by which they could suppress any expression of the rebellious imagination, then the *one* way to do it—perhaps the most *efficient* way—is to make available, at a reasonable price, any form of recreational drug while maintaining that this is an "illicit activity." The *effect* of that is to dampen or smother any sort of possible rebellion!

Thereby you create a kind of **anesthetized generation**, don't you?

♦ *MP: It's like people got rid of the "middle man" in the control process and now everybody is glad to do it to themselves, with drugs. They're* happy *to do it, instead of coming up with* new idioms. *That's the crux of the problem: the youth aren't coming up with new idioms to express the contemporary world. Instead, it's all about nostalgia, and nowadays nostalgia can develop in just two years!*

Youth culture only looks backwards for its precedents. Imagine if more people with technical skills got angry, like a young microbiologist or an electronics expert—they could make things that are way beyond a Molotov cocktail. **Disenchanted youth with technical expertise and discipline could be a genuine source of real excitement in the world!**

♦ **JGB:** I think you're right, actually. I've often thought that the whole notion of the "avant-garde" has vanished. The nearest you get to that is **a sort of "designer" avant-garde offering a stylized rebelliousness** . . . a kind of *Perrier* avant-garde that's homogenized and made palatable for the weekend consumer.

It could be that the real rebels are . . . actually, if you want to be a rebel now you've got to join the real world! The biggest avant-garde artist, as it were—I wouldn't exactly call him an artist, but whatever you'd like to call him (a performance artist?) is that guy who shot Reagan—John Hinckley.

Today, if you want to be the equivalent of the pioneering artist of the 1880s—if you want to be a *Gauguin* of the present day, you might actually have to go and buy a gun and shoot Margaret Thatcher and Princess Di! **It's no longer enough to think in terms of changing the world through the arts anymore. The arts are a form of prurient entertainment.** What people are waiting for is someone like Hinckley but working at Livermore Laboratories. Someone like Hinckley working as a captain of a nuclear submarine.

♦ *MP: Well, they must be out there—*

♦ **JGB:** When that happens—when somebody like Hinckley is working in a lab that's manufacturing nerve gas—

◆ **MP:** *—or smallpox—*

◆ **JGB:** Then you may get a big surprise!

Right now things seem to be at a low water-mark. **To me, times are very reminiscent of the Fifties. There's the same triumph of bourgeois values and conservatism all around, there's the same sort of deadness in the air.** It may be that one needs this sort of slack water before the tide changes—

◆ **MP:** *Well, there's real bonuses to living right now. You can do anything you want now. You can get media attention—*

◆ **JGB:** That's true. You can be free now to go with your own obsessions—

◆ **MP:** *And the police can't even stop it. You can break all these laws and that sort of appeals to the police themselves because they see the glamour in it. Violence has been glamorized to such a great extent—*

◆ **JGB:** Whereas if you wanted to lead a march against whaling in San Francisco or London, or picket a nuclear airbase, the police would be out in force because they can *cope* with that. I agree with you. It *is* a good time to . . . as far as I'm concerned, I'm free to do what I want. I just sit here with my obsessions and I feel that one's free to pursue one's obsessions without having to worry what anyone else thinks—which is, in a way, rather a good thing.

Looking back just a decade or two, I can remember the history of *Rolling Stone* magazine—I can remember when it first came out. But it was nowhere near as original as *Search and Destroy*. Do you remember it from its earliest days?

◆ **MP:** *I was there. I lived in San Francisco when they first came out.*

◆ **JGB:** What struck me about it was, I'd been reading papers like that for fifteen or twenty years, but *Search and Destroy* was the first one you could actually *read*. You could spend four or five days actually reading original and interesting and well-researched articles and interviews. It was not something you sort of *skimmed* for a *frisson* of counter-culture excitement! Whereas *Rolling Stone*—I haven't seen one for five years—

◆ **MP:** *They didn't really adapt to anything new happening—*

◆ **JGB:** The last one I saw could have been read by your maiden aunt, practically.

J.G. Ballard on Astrology

♦ **JGB:** I remain terribly skeptical about all that sort of thing.
♦ *MP: Good. Smart move.*
♦ **JGB:** I have absolutely no feeling for the "psy" phenomena—the supernatural, telepathy. Completely skeptical about it all. It's all bunk, that stuff, you know. I'm constantly surprised by the degree to which extremely intelligent people have actually shown more than just a passing interest in these topics. It constantly astounds me.

On his R.A.F. training

♦ **JGB:** I remember when I was in the R.A.F. [Royal Air Force] in the early '50s. We were sent to Canada to do our basic flight training there at the R.C.A.F. [Royal Canadian Air Force] Flight Training School. When we arrived, we were put through, as a familiarization period, a curriculum on how to get to know what North America is like. So we spent about a month in London, Ontario at this base where we were supposedly acclimatized to the "North American way of life." This was great; we had a lot of fun. We spent a lot of time in bars.
♦ *MP: What year was this?*
♦ **JGB:** This was '54. Part of our acclimatization was seeing all these Canadian Air Force and Canadian military service instructional films. We were straight off the boat from England, and they made us sit in this viewing theater and watch movies. Among them were these *hygiene* films.

Now none of us had ever seen, at that time, a pornographic film, because they didn't exist in England except behind closed doors. And none of us, as far as I know, had ever been *behind* those closed doors. So there we sat in this darkened auditorium, hour after hour, watching this endless stream of films on sexual hygiene which were quite explicit.

A camera would show somebody washing his genitalia. We spent hour after hour watching these more-or-less identical films, many of which covered the exact same ground. These were films that were designed to warn us of the perils of promiscuous sex in a foreign country, and what to do about it. How to put on a sheath [condom], how to take off a sheath, how to wash your penis. It was strange; these films weren't in any way sexually stimulating. The neutrality and "instructional" element present had quite the opposite effect. The successive, repetitive imagery had a kind of deadening effect; it was a very peculiar experience—very, very strange. We also saw all kinds of other films, like: how to drive a truck.

♦ *MP: Speaking of driving, didn't you have a car crash? What did they do to you?*

♦ **JGB:** Well, there's no rehabilitation program for traffic offenders here—they just ban you from driving. Alcohol is a big problem here. There's a mandatory year's ban, which I've been through. The public transport system is okay for going to London by train—with a timetable you can just about cope. But going to the next town three miles away takes a whole day, just waiting for a bus there and then waiting for a bus back.

After a while I found that I never went anywhere—it was too much. I just shaped my life so I remained here—this was in 1972. After that crash, I would take walks to the horizon, which for a man of my height is roughly about half to three-quarters of a mile away. That was as far as I would be able to walk. So in effect, I was living on this planet about a mile wide, and never going anywhere. My whole universe just *shrank.*

Of course, by walking everywhere I became intensely aware whether so-and-so had washed her lace curtains today, and when somebody had gotten a new car, or cleaned their car. You can't help but pick these things out. Not having a car changes your life, because you cut down your contact with friends. How the hell do you get to North London to go out to dinner? You don't.

I never fully recovered from this, actually. I got a helluva lot of work

Photo: SM Gray

done during that period—that's the only thing I can say. Obviously, you don't drink and drive afterwards, because you only need two whiskeys to take you up to the limit. Two-thirds of a bottle of wine—that's almost impossible, if you drink socially. Even if you go to a party not intending to drink, you're going to drink more than the legal limit. So if you go to a party, you go intending to remain sober . . . it changes the whole *psychic economy* of these events. The place where you get drunk is at home.

When the breathalizer was introduced in the late Sixties, it caused a change in driving habits. Everyone commented on this. I used to come back from London at eleven o'clock at night, and it was quite apparent there had been a change in driving habits. Formerly, probably half the drivers on the road were drunk—you'd see a long line of cars weaving around the road. Now, people power along like they've got a newborn baby in the front seat. It did make a big change.

On *Empire of the Sun*

♦ **JGB:** I met Robert Shapiro, the Warner Bros producer, and Harold Becker, who had directed *The Onion Field,* which was quite a good film. They were both men about my age and I thought they were two extremely intelligent, refined and cultivated men, actually. I met them in London about a year ago and they took me out to dinner. They couldn't have been further removed from the stereotype of the cigar-chewing producer; they were extremely cultivated.

I said to them jokingly, "You'll forgive me for saying this, but when speaking to an American, one needs to be very careful about irony." They had wanted to do a very serious job and literally translate *Empire of the Sun* word-for-word onto the screen. I said, "No, no, a movie is something starring Charles Bronson or Steve McQueen. We need to get rid of this British schoolboy—he's a pain. What we want is a sixteen-year-old girl like Nastassia Kinski, and set it in Nicaragua. We can have gun fights, rapes . . ." We were sitting in this very formal English restaurant and they looked at each other wondering, "Who is this madman?" I said, "Relax—I'm just having a bit of fun." They may spend their time lying around swimming pools with starlets, but they didn't give that impression. They looked like senior corporation executives.

Harry Cohn of Columbia Pictures was the archetype of the loud-mouthed, cigar-smoking entrepreneur who had one hand on his cigar and the other up some starlet's skirt. He was responsible for some of the greatest films that Hollywood and Columbia Pictures produced. These two didn't strike me as being that type. They were like bankers, which is basically, I feel, what they are, actually.

♦ *MP: Right, and the kind of films they make reflect that. Bankers' films, unfortunately.*

♦ **JGB:** But I think there's been a move to make more exciting films. *The Hitcher* was well-received (for being a Hollywood film) by even the full range of critics. I think it's been proven that you can break the box office with a movie like that.

In the case of this "China" film of mine, I would say the precursor for it was *Gandhi,* which had just won the Oscar at the time Warner Bros. took up the option for my book. They think there's a "family" audience they can get, which includes middle-aged people who need something with a little more depth, maybe. Who knows?

♦ *MP: It's hard to say. They're experts at cutting* out *any type of imaginative material.* **Your average American doesn't like to be reminded they might remember their dreams**, *that they're haunted by . . . What sort of control do you retain in your contract?*

♦ **JGB:** None, nothing, nothing.

♦ *MP: Is there even a clause for them presenting the finished script to you for approval?*

♦ **JGB:** No. The Warners' contract is longer than my book—it's a huge document, which I had to get notarized by a vice-consul at the American Embassy. I went there with the publicity manager of my English publishing house—a young American woman, awfully intelligent and nice. This vice-consul was a big, solemn, serious-minded American who had me sign this and sign that. Then he looked at me and said, "Your name is J.G. Ballard?" "Yes." "Do you understand everything in these documents?" (meaning, "Am I *compos mentis?*")

and I said, "No."

This consul looked at me appalled, like, "Maybe I *won't* notarize this. Maybe this man is not of sound mind"—like, "He's signing away his inheritance or something." Then the publicity manager gave me a certain *look* and a nudge. So I said, "Oh yes, I *completely* understand it." I mean, this is a gigantic document—hundreds of yards long literally, full of legalistic stuff covering every conceivable eventuality. I didn't understand a word of it. I had this nightmare that they would make me go home and study it and then I'd be examined on it: "Do you understand Clause 75C: Distribution Rights in Mexico?"

On his house in Shepperton

♦ **JGB:** Everything's pretty dusty here. It needs a wash. That elderly English gay that was very wise—Quentin Crisp—lived in the same room for fifteen years in Chelsea. He said after three years it never gets any dirtier. That's true actually . . . I noticed that. You reach some sort of limit where the movement of air makes sure—

♦ *MP: I think that happens with people's body odors, too. **Bums that don't clean themselves almost start getting this self-cleansing action because the dirt starts flaking off after awhile, and the bacteria get so numerous they start killing each other.***

♦ **JGB:** I think that's true. I had a Golden Retriever for 12 years. Although he would go into the pond and paddle around now and then, he never had a bath, unlike the dogs I had in my own childhood. My mother was forever putting them in the bath and soaking them up. This retriever wouldn't allow that. I once tried it, and getting him in the bath took about half an hour. Then I turned on the tap and he would have *bit* me if I'd insisted! So he never once had a bath, yet his skin, if you reversed the hair (even on his stomach) was clean and white and had a lovely smell.

My son, when he was about nine years old, had a rabbit. Actually, he had a succession of rabbits, but I remember this particular rabbit called

"Whiskey." We bought him a brand-new big cage that cost about ten times as much as the rabbit. Within three weeks this rabbit, upon which my son lavished enormous love and care, caught some disease and was dead. My son buried it in the garden. He made a little head-stone out of cement, and when the cement was still wet he wrote on it, "Whiskey was a Dutch Rabbit, 1966-1966." He had seen this on gravestones: "1921-1958" or whatever. This rabbit had only lasted three weeks, yet this was so touching; I had all the parental guilt in the world. The tombstone's still out there. It struck me as being absurd.

My woman friend, Claire, has four cats, all of whom are about fifteen years old. They're brothers and sisters of the cat I had which died about four years ago at the age of ten or eleven. Her cats have spent their entire lives indoors in her flat. They've gone out onto a sort of roof in the back, but they've never gone out into the garden or roved the neighborhood. Recently a new neighbor released an aggressive black cat onto this roof and my girlfriend's cats were totally traumatized. It was a *culture shock* meeting this strange creature; they had never met any other cat. They were absolutely staggered . . .

♦ **MP:** *Are the Shepperton Film Studios still active?*

♦ **JGB:** They make commercials, but also a lot of features.

♦ **MP:** *They lease it to other countries to make features, too—*

♦ **JGB:** Yes, it's quite a big complex.

♦ **MP:** *I drove by it ten or twelve years ago.*

♦ **JGB:** It's very busy, actually. Part of the studios are owned by the rock group The Who. They do a lot of their own recording there and they [rent] out the recording facilities to other groups. It's quite a big media enclave, and feature films are made there—

♦ **MP:** *A media hive—*

♦ **JGB:** Yes, it is. But although we're close to the studios here, there's no spin-off in terms of—

♦ **MP:** *—no sense of this community being any different from any other?*

♦ **JGB:** None whatever; you wouldn't know otherwise. **I have nice, friendly relations with my neighbors**; otherwise it's a quiet life.

On Changing One's Life

♦ **JGB:** I keep thinking about how to do something different with my life—make a radical change . . . but it gets more and more difficult as you get older. At least it does for *me*. When my kids moved out, they left a huge vacuum behind. But one tends to fill that vacuum in small ways. When I was bringing them up I kept looking at the English rain sledding down, thinking, "Well, when they're all grown up and happily settled, I'll be able to take off for San Francisco or Tahiti or wherever." But when the opportunity came, television and a nice whiskey and soda in the evenings seemed to be what one's destined for.

You reach a stage in life where you need to remythologize yourself. You need a new set of dreams to live by, a new set of—

♦ *MP: Reinvent your wheel—*

♦ **JGB:** Right—you do actually, you do. Not because one's necessarily growing stale or repeating one's self or anything of that kind—which I don't feel I am. I still feel I've got plenty of original ideas, for what they're worth, but it's part of a larger sort of *need* to make the most of one's circumstances and one's chances.

♦ *MP: I think that's kind of a continual process; it's necessary to do that at any age. You have to be more conscious of that need to put more jags in the line from time to time.*

♦ **JGB:** It gets more difficult to do, because you tend, as you get older, to opt for the quiet life. There's a sort of need to turn down the thermostat (which I'm conscious of) just so I can *get on with my work*. I wouldn't say that the traffic noise bothers me more now than it did ten years ago, but I don't feel, curiously, that I need the input of foreign travel to do my best work. I may be wrong, but I don't feel I need to travel, so one just stays at home and works.

You work out of your own obsessions . . . that little universe inside of you. That's probably a bad thing. One no longer has the kind of instinctive need to move around the world and have new experi-

Photo: Ana Barrado

ences, that you had in your twenties and thirties. It's a problem, that, and god knows how to solve it.

I hate public appearances and public performances of any kind—I'm much too shy for that. Well, maybe I could pose as a dentist or something. I'm not talking about trips, because I *could* get on a plane and fly to New York for a week, make the rounds of the museums and the like. But I'm not thinking of that. I'm talking about a radical change of one's way of life. But that's almost impossible to do, actually . . . and it may not be necessary. I've always admired reading the life of somebody like Burroughs—he's no spring chicken, is he? He must be 70.

♦ **MP:** *He's 72, I think.*

♦ **JGB:** He's more or less retired now, isn't he? But he's still roving the world. When I first met him he was living in London in St. James which is a very strange place to live, actually, near Piccadilly Circus—

♦ **MP:** *In Piccadilly I saw a couple of plays by Tom Stoppard when I lived in London—*

♦ **JGB:** That's English club land, you know—and by "club" I mean gentlemen's clubs. Duke Street, St. James—curious place for an avant-garde writer to live.

♦ **MP:** *I love that, because he really does have a very conventional exterior.*

♦ **JGB:** Exactly. **Burroughs looks like a banker with a very courtly manner—always well-dressed. His flat in St. James, in central London, was very neat and tidy and clean.** He's very formal and courtly, really, but ever since his youngest days he has relentlessly traveled the world. Even when he was my present age he was still moving around.

I read that little book, *With William Burroughs in the Bunker* by Victor Bockris. He's the editor and organizer of this collection of interviews or recorded conversations with Burroughs and his cronies. They were done mostly at the Bunker, but also one or two other places. Fascinating, actually. I hadn't realized that it was actually a windowless apartment—

♦ **MP:** *John Giorno lives downstairs.*

♦ **JGB:** It's a curious place to choose to live, but fair enough. People said that about my house, too, but at least I've got windows—

♦ **MP:** —*and a fence.*

♦ **JGB:** But getting back to what I was saying, he seemed to have— I don't know if it had something to do with the gay world—this sort of transience, this relentless traveling: Tangier for two years, Paris for two years, London for two years, and then somewhere else, always shifting. As these people don't breed children, they don't have to put down roots anywhere—whether it's part of that, I don't know. I envy him that, actually. Just being realistic, I couldn't imagine myself going to live in Mexico City for two years for no particular reason.

I got a Christmas card from Burroughs, which was rather nice. In fact, the last book I reviewed for the *Guardian* was a book of his collected essays, many of which I had already read. It was called *The Adding Machine* and it included some fascinating autobiographical material. I loved the book. It was full of charm: Burroughs describing his early years when he was ten or twelve years old. Very difficult to imagine him at the age of ten or twelve!

Burroughs seems to be happy now. He's working away at quite an advanced age and he's pouring out the books. I was at a Christmas Party for his London publisher, John Calder. Calder was bemoaning the fact that after many years Burroughs has moved away from his London publisher (Calder) and gotten a five- or six-book deal with Picador—they recently brought out *Junky.* Calder said that this man James Grauerholz had taken over Burroughs' affairs and has "a bunch of new ideas." He was very critical, as you might have imagined, but I don't suppose Calder ever got much distribution for Burroughs—the sales must have been absolutely rock-bottom. Picador will sell lots of copies. It's a good thing; he'll be reaching a new audience.

You know, there aren't *that* many things that are interesting now. About eight years ago I was interviewed by a French magazine that was evolving from one medium to the next, like a fish climbing out of the primeval ocean. This was a monthly arts magazine published in France called *Faits Divers,* devoted to an avant-garde point of view. There were articles on architecture, computers, fiction and poetry as well. The publishers decided to turn *Faits Divers* into a video magazine and cease publishing as a traditional magazine.

They came to interview me for the first issue. It was very curious. They had a monitor set up, and I could see myself being interviewed. They had worked out the economics and could make a go of it with quite a small circulation—something like 5,000 copies. I can't remember the exact figure, but it struck me as a remarkably small figure, compared to the sort of circulation figures you would need for a reasonably successful monthly magazine.

In those days a one-hour videocassette cost something like $20. What does it cost now?

♦ *MP: In bulk, about $3 or less.*

♦ **JGB:** Back then, the annual subscription fee they wanted to charge (I think it was going to be a bi-monthly) seemed enormous; I thought, "Migod, you're never going to get 5,000 people to pay $200 or $300 a year." But of course, back then a blank tape cost $20.

Now I think there are more videos per person in Great Britain than anywhere else in the world. There's been a soft-porn video magazine for years here called *Electric Blue,* produced on the *Men Only* channel; it's like the *Playboy Channel.*

You know, of all the artists included in *Search and Destroy* and the *RE/Search* books, the only one whose presence surprised me was **Genesis P-Orridge**. He's completely dropped out of sight here; I dare say I haven't read any interviews for a while. He made his start here in the late Sixties doing performance art and was treated as a joke—he wasn't taken seriously by anybody. He used to do weird performances—vomiting on stage and stuff. Well, as I said, **the ultimate piece of performance art is shooting the Queen! ♦ ♦ ♦**

Photo: Ana Barrado

An Introduction to Lynne Fox
Interview by V. Vale

Lynne Fox was born Patricia Lynne Fox on April 27, 1949 at Chester (near Liverpool). She studied English and American literature at Kent University, and interviewed J.G. Ballard January 20, 1991 for her master's degree thesis. Now she teaches school to 9-10-year-olds. Her passion is taiko drumming; she said, "Frankly, I think it's amazing that at age 53 I can find a new passion like that!" Phone interview by V. Vale January 11, 2005.

VALE: *How did you get "turned on" to Science Fiction?*

LYNNE FOX: I don't know—probably a book cover. I probably saw a great illustration and thought, "Ooh—I want to go there!"

Actually, I had read Science Fiction since about age 12. I was reading Captain W.E. Johns who wrote the *Biggles* books—but he also wrote some Science Fiction, and I just got completely hooked when I was young. Biggles was this dreadful World War 1 pilot—frightfully "boys' magazine" writing, and an awfully nice chap. But W.E. Johns' Science Fiction books were about a space station orbiting the earth. I think that was the first time I realized I wanted to get *off* the planet!

V: *I don't meet many women into Science Fiction—*

LF: I think I'm also a "rivet counter"—I like *hard* Science Fiction; I like the "science" in Science Fiction. But you don't get much of that anymore. I admired Robert Forward; he's written a couple books about life on a neutron star. Larry Niven is another writer who has explored the implications of scientific fact.

I also read most of Roland Barthes' *Mythologies*. He does the same kind of analysis of our creative desires, or reading the latent meanings of real life, as it were. He's applying the same kind of logical analysis to the real world that Ballard is.

V: *And somehow you got led to J.G. Ballard?*

LF: I bought *Crash* [1973] and couldn't read it; I found it very shocking. Then I read other books by him; *Vermilion Sands* I particularly loved. Round about the time I came to do my M.A. at Kent University—

V: Oh, you got an M.A. in English and American literature—

LF: No, on Ballard!

V: Wait a minute; something's missing here—

LF: Okay. I left university and taught. I continued to read Science Fiction. I went back and tried to read *Crash* and I thought, "I have to understand this book," because—I don't know how you feel, but I really *trust* Ballard as a writer. And I knew he wasn't taking me anywhere terrible, but I was still scared. So I thought, "Well, I have to understand what's going on." And I went to the library to try and find some books about him, and there weren't any. So I thought, "Okay, well I'll try to do it myself then." So I got in touch with someone at my old university and said, "I need to do an M.A. on Ballard." And that's how my interview came about, as part of that.

V: You had to be the first woman to get a Masters degree (M.A.) on Ballard—

LF: Well, Lynn Barber is a big fan of Ballard. It was a strange experience: three years of most of my evenings, reading and thinking and writing about him. And I felt that I desperately needed to meet him, because it was like I had lived inside his head for so long. And he's such a nice guy. Interviewing him was a wonderful experience, because he's just so interested in talking about anything. I drove to Shepperton on a Sunday afternoon [January 20, 1991] and found him living in a very ordinary, semi-detached—it's startlingly *ordinary*. It didn't look like the house of someone who must have earned dollars over the years.

The interview took place in the back room—the one next to the garden with the big window. I brought him a bottle of whisky, because I didn't know what else to do to say Thank You. It was cold, and that's why the fan heater was turned on. I had a radio that was also a tape recorder, and I placed that on the floor next to the fan heater—not good. We just sat on the sofa and talked for about four hours.

V: Did you prepare for the interview?

LF: I went to see my M.A. advisor, and we tried to find an angle that hadn't yet been used to explore Ballard before. It was Surrealism. I didn't know much about Surrealist art before that. He had these huge Delvaux canvases just propped up against the walls.

V: Give me some of the reasons you like Ballard, and continue to like him, years later—

LF: I think Ballard is very poetic in the way he writes, and I love that. I think it's beautifully crafted writing. The thing above all I like is his honesty—his uncompromising honesty. He really challenges you as a reader, and makes you face up to very difficult things. I think he respects the intellect of other human beings, and doesn't make things easy or nice for you, because that's how it *usually* is. He challenges you.

I love the way he never takes the obvious route. In the interview we were talking about the Channel Tunnel, and he said, "But if they'd built a bridge—now that would have been something!" And you just think, "Oh, yeah!"

He was talking about 9-11, saying what an imaginative act it was. And it was! It's tragic and it's wrong, but it's also imaginative. He just has the courage to be honest about things. One of the things he said which I really use in my own life is, "Pursue your own obsessions." And that's what he does. He used the money from *Empire of the Sun* to have those Delvaux paintings recreated.

V: *I think he's an artist who uses the medium of words as his canvas. As a fiction writer he's the dialogue writer, the casting person, make-up person, interior set designer, landscape architect, cinematographer—*

LF: He's got a wonderfully visual imagination. When I talked to him about "character," he said that he's interested in them once they've kind of *transcended* the everyday; once they've moved on through some extraordinary experience to what they like, what they do, next.

I'm really enjoying that *J.G. Ballard Quotes* book because I keep coming across things and thinking, "Yes!" And even now, when I've read so much by him and about him, he still can surprise and amuse me. I just think he's a terrific bloke.

J.G. Ballard and Lynne Fox

♦ **LYNNE FOX:** *I know that you first became interested in the Surrealists when you were at school. What was the first point of contact?*

♦ **J.G. BALLARD:** I came to England in 1946 when I was 15, and up to that point I was totally unaware of the Surrealists. I'd never seen any reproductions of Surrealist paintings; there were no museums in Shanghai. I began to get interested in modern fiction—by which I mean modern classics, Kafka, Thomas Mann, Hemingway—and in psychoanalysis, so I was reading a great deal of Freud, and Surrealism abutted all those writers and thinkers. From the age of 16 or 17 I started see-ing reproductions of Surrealist paintings in books I was reading, and something just *leapt off the page.* There's no question about it.

The thing about the Surrealists is that there aren't many of them—only about seven or eight major painters—and it's easy to get a com-plete overview of the Surrealist movement in painting. I wasn't inter-ested in "literary" Surrealism at all; I've read some, but I'm primarily interested in the painters. In fact, the texts weren't available when I was still at school in England; unless you were a specialist, you would have had difficulty finding any of the classic Surrealist texts, writings by Breton and so on. It was only much later that I started coming into contact with Apollinaire, [Alfred] Jarry, [Boris] Vian. Much as I admire Breton as a commentator on the Surrealists, my interest is almost entirely confined to the painters, and since there are so few of them it was possible by digging around to rapidly cover the ground.

Many of the Surrealists were still exhibiting in London. I remem-ber going to exhibitions that ran completely new paintings by Magritte, Dali, Delvaux. De Chirico's career was over. Tanguy I only saw in museums, because he died fairly early on. There was a very big Max Ernst exhibition at the Tate Gallery in the mid-50's. So at school I began to discover the Surrealists for myself, and of course one thing that appealed to me was that they were beyond the critical pale.

The established critical view of the Surrealists was that they were unspeakable—lurid purveyors of sensation, vulgarity. They were regarded as an irrelevancy to the grand tradition of Modernism that began with the Post-Impressionists and ran on through Picasso and so on (even Picasso's Surrealist phase wasn't regarded with admiration). So the Surrealists were very unpopular, critically speaking. They were all regarded in the same way that Dali is regarded still. And this, of course, appealed to me enormously.

I disliked everything about England—English academia, Cambridge university when I became a student. And the fact that this group of painters who'd launched the greatest imaginative expedition of the 20th century were *unpopular:* that made them doubly attractive.

dichotomy, that contrast that the Surrealists required. Dali could paint soft watches, knowing that for everyone watches are hard objects; but, as I've said before, in the last 20 years if you stop somebody in the street and ask the time, you might look at a watch with Mickey Mouse on the dial—or Spiro Agnew watches, in Nixon's presidency. It cuts the ground from under classical Surrealism.

I don't say the Surrealist impulse has ended—it's been transformed. One has got to proceed on the assumption that there is no clear-cut division between reality and super-reality, or whatever you like to call it. **It would be very difficult to make the Dali/Buñuel films made at the end of the 1920s today, because the sight of people dragging dead donkeys through a drawing room would [seem to be] some sort of advertising stunt**—a beer commercial. The shock value has gone. The external world is so strange, so full of fantasy, that you can't use the classical Surrealist approach.

♦ **LF:** *I'm interested in the notion that **the Surrealists were trying to create a new mythology.** You have said that you were interested in mythologies of endings. I wasn't sure what you meant by that.*

♦ **JGB:** What I probably meant was that most of the classical mythologies describe beginnings of things, the creation of the world, how mankind fell, the birth of the gods. The body of myths underpinning the great religions—Genesis, other sacred books, the huge compendiums of mythology—represent myths about the creation of the world and of mankind and of the living order.

Also, there are myths about the first crises affecting man morally: the fall of man; the Garden of Eden in Jewish mythology, much of which has been taken over by Christianity; similar oral myths of crisis and redemption which we find in other religions. These are mythologies that grapple with the starting points of human experience, whereas I'm interested in the *other* end of the spectrum: with where all these events are leading us. It's a classic stand of Science Fiction: all these mythologies of ecological destruction, the end of the universe, great floods. And in my own fiction, if you think of novels like *The Drowned World*—that is concerned with ends rather than beginnings.

The crucial experiences in classical mythology tend to lie in the past;

they have already occurred when the myth begins to unfold itself, whereas **in my fiction the crises, the great critical experiences, lie in the future.** They are revealed in the driven obsessions of the characters of *The Crystal World*, where the character is assembling his own *escape from time*. This applies, I think, in the fiction I wrote in the '70s, books like *Crash* and *High-Rise*. The whole sequence of events that evolve in *High-Rise*, where the people living in this huge apartment building are reverting to barbarism, [is] heading towards the discovery of a new kind of psychological order which hasn't really fulfilled itself even by the last page.

So I'm concerned in most of my fiction with mythologies that draw a concluding line underneath the human experience. They represent end-points. I'm trying to suggest that **there's a new psychological order awaiting us**, which I'm as convinced of as an ordinary individual as I am as an imaginative writer. The twentieth century is a kind of cusp, a moving off from the old order into the new order that lies ahead. Of course, modern technology, modern communication systems, are creating this new order whether we like it or not. You try to anticipate this new order, but by and large **my fiction is littered with the debris of mythological end-points**: all these empty swimming pools, abandoned hotels, technological debris, silence, deserts — these are not the images of starting points; these are the mythologies of ends. **Ends are also the beginning of the next step forward.**

♦ *LF: There are critics who say that your books are doom-laden and despairing—*

♦ **JGB:** Pay no attention to them. As I've said many times, **most of my novels are stories of psychic fulfillment. That's the whole point; they'd be meaningless otherwise.** The characters do find psychological fulfilment, they accept the logic of events and pursue that logic to the end, and they find satisfaction there. It takes a long time to convince people. **So many of the things that I was writing about 20 or 30 years ago are starting to come true: global warming, desertification**, **a lot of my predictions about the media landscape,** plus all the things I wrote about in *The Atrocity*

Photo: SM Gray

Exhibition. I don't want to sound pompous, but there is a tendency that the more serious you are the more doom-laden you seem to be. You can't have it both ways!

♦ **LF:** *Do you think it's important to have a sense of a mythological dimension in life?*

♦ **JGB:** Absolutely. I think it's *the* most important thing other than one's own family, children and so on. **It's evident that people are constantly trying to place themselves within some sort of mythological framework, and if they don't they tend to be rather unhappy.** People need these sustaining dreams to live by. It's quite obviously the role that great religions play. Psychological cults like scientology, these all have a colossal hold on people's imaginations. Even the world of popular entertainment for young people to identify with—going back 20 years, the Rolling Stones, Elvis Presley, rock singers (now it would be somebody like Madonna). I think it's terribly important.

As you get older, you begin to accumulate enough from the great experiences in your life—marriage, having children—to begin to construct a personal mythology. You begin to discover yourself and the limits of your own abilities and character. You bring your dreams more down to earth. I think it's vitally important, and that's where the appeal of the Surrealists is—because in fact the Surrealists have maintained and *enlarged* their appeal over the last century.

Hardly anybody knew anything about the Surrealists in England in 1946; now they have been for the last 20 years probably the most instantly recognizable school of painters there is. **They've pervaded advertising, TV, stage design, department-store window displays, record sleeves. The impact of Surrealism has been colossal.** Some Surrealist images are now among the most famous icons of all time—some of Magritte's images: the man in the bowler hat, the eye (which I think is the logo of some airline) . . . It's interesting that the Surrealists have pervaded almost every aspect of imaginative life today, and that's because they illustrate the myth-making need of human beings.

♦ **LF:** *You have said that you are interested in the mystery and magic that underlies ordinary things. What's the nature of this magic?*

♦ **JGB:** I certainly didn't mean "magic" in the usual witchcraft sense; I'm totally uninterested in that. I meant it in the ordinary imaginative sense of the word. **I'm interested in the way any sudden revelation can transform experience.** It doesn't have to be anything terribly dramatic.

When you watch very young children, a toddler stumbling around in the garden and discovering some incredible thing like a lawnmower: What *is* this thing? Now that's the discovery of the magic of the commonplace. **Through the eyes of a very young child, we see a lawnmower as a bizarre, extraordinary machine—like something out of a Max Ernst landscape.** And perhaps the world of commonplace objects which we take for granted is actually full of all these magical things—*if only we could see them from a fresh angle.*

We take for granted a world full of cars all sliding around, washing machines, cookers. Then you go to a junkyard and see mountains of cars piled on top of each other, mountains of refrigerators, old washing machines, and they have a certain extraordinary hold on reality far greater than they had when they were in our own kitchens. These rusting hulks have been conjured into meaning by the accident of growing old, getting rusty and being cast aside. That really is a magical transformation. Now that sort of *revelation of the commonplace* is going on all the time.

That's why we take holiday snapshots, so that we can see what we were doing through a different lens. I think it's important, because reality perceived on a naturalistic level is rather boring. One longs for that sort of thing: *the transformation of things.*

♦ **LF:** *It's interesting to try and do it through language. Do you know Robert Graves at all?*

♦ **JGB:** Yes, I'm a great admirer of Robert Graves.

♦ **LF:** *The poem "The Cool Web": for children, because they have no language, every experience is like an acid trip.*

Photo: Ana Barrado

♦ **JGB:** That's what I've always tried to do. **In many ways, my novels and short stories are a series of described paintings. Had I had the technical ability, I would have become a painter.** I had just enough skill, draughtsmanship, as a boy to lead me to think that I could become a painter. [But] I never had the flair. I did have a certain flair for writing, so I became a writer. **I very much *see* my novels and short stories as I write.**

♦ *LF: Talking about images and taking them for granted, I decided that one aspect of the thesis I would do is to take the images from* Crash *and correlate them with photographic images and explore the techniques that were going on in both. I rang photo libraries asking for chic and elegant photos of crashed cars. Everyone found it very disturbing. I ended up taking my own photographs.*

♦ **JGB:** I know the feeling. About the time that I was writing *Crash,* I used to wander around car-breakers' yards and photograph crashed cars there. Normally nobody gives a damn if you wander around, certainly not 20 years ago, in car-breakers' yards. But the moment they see you with a camera, they suspect you're up to no good. At first I thought they thought I was an insurance company snooper, but no, it's just the *idea.*

A friend of mine, Eduardo Paolozzi, who's been making sculptures for years out of machine parts, said he's found exactly the same problem. Going to the big engineering waste tip he thought, "All this rusting junk . . . nobody gives a damn." But the moment you start taking an interest, they feel there's something afoot and this unsettles them. Because all these crashed cars have an immense amount of *latent* significance. How did this car get crashed; who was involved? Who were the people, and how did it shape their lives? What were their motives? What drove them into this nightmare? All these invisible dramas hover over each of these machines. There's an image that is *loaded* with frightening possibilities.

♦ *LF: I found* Crash *extremely difficult to read the first time.*

♦ **JGB:** It's still read, it's got through to people over the years. It challenges people across the entire spectrum of their received beliefs about things. I'm trying to prove that life equals death; death equals life, etc., or I appear to be doing so. I don't actually believe that car crashes are sexually liberating for mankind, but I *appear* to believe that, and this unsettles people endlessly. I was trying to provoke the reader on every page of the book, of course. That's the purpose: to test the reader.

♦ **LF:** *How do you imagine your readers?*

♦ **JGB:** Well, I never imagined that *you* might be one of my readers! Writers are unlike the painter who goes to a gallery, a playwright who can go to the theatre and see an audience watching one of his plays. A filmmaker can go to the cinema and watch people watching his movies; actors and composers, ballet dancers, choreographers, all can see their audiences and get a direct, clear impression of who their audiences are and how they react to their work. But a writer can't.

I've never seen anybody reading my books. Of course, you meet people at signings, people come to interview me, but one's view is so different. One can be read by teenage schoolgirls at one end of the spectrum, and old men in their late eighties at the other end. They have nothing in common except, in the case of my readers, some sort of shared response to the imaginative possibilities of life that my fiction touches.

♦ **LF:** *Do you want to mentally shake your readers?*

♦ **JGB:** No, I don't. *Crash* is not typical of my books as a whole. I don't set out in most of my fiction to deliberately provoke the reader, but just to offer my own hunches as to what experience may really mean, and the possibilities of the imagination.

♦ **LF:** *I was heartened to read* The Day of Creation *which I found so affirmative, particularly after* Crash *and* The Atrocity Exhibition.

♦ **JGB:** I'm glad. Yes, I think it is more affirmative. **I was interested there in the way in which the media landscape has now wrapped its umbrella around the world, and how it redefines reality as itself so that nothing can happen in the world without some TV crew arriving** on the spot and immediately becoming part of the unique experience which is unfolding.

The Day of Creation was in part about what creativity means today when the imagination is invaded by the watching camera which is using the experience for its own ends and then playing back some sort of sentimentalized version of the original at the same time as the original is unfolding. **Imagine Christ being born in his manger surrounded by all the TV networks buying exclusive rights as the baby opens its eyes to reality.**

◆ *LF: It's all going on now, isn't it?*

◆ **JGB:** In the Gulf. It's a classic case. We feel almost cheated because we don't have endless action. We want cameras everywhere; we want to see everything.

◆ *LF: And there's radio war now. A whole channel [of Radio Four] given over to the war.*

◆ **JGB:** That's bizarre. They're trying to do a radio version of CNN, which has been a big hit. You don't have cable? One of my daughters is a cable girl. She lives just south of Acton, and her street is cabled up, and she now has something like 30 channels. I saw her yesterday, and she has *CNN* broadcasting through the day as in America. I was in the States in 1987 and I had a free day—I think I was in Seattle—on October Black Monday when the world financial markets collapsed. I switched it on and I hardly stopped watching all day. It just went on and on—incredible coverage. I think Radio Four is trying to do the same thing. The trouble is, they don't have enough material.

◆ *LF: There's constant analysis, and reality keeps fracturing off to all the possibilities—*

◆ **JGB:** Which take on a life of their own, and then there's a jolt when reality refuses to conform to the fantasy. The stock market zoomed upwards after the first day [of the Gulf War], gained 50 points, because everybody believed the over-optimistic broadcasts, the coverage on radio and TV, which gave the impression that the war was practically over: 1,500 sorties, all these gung-ho pilots, missiles flying everywhere, total destruction raining down. The stock market went through the roof. Then suddenly reality has caught up, and people are saying, "Saddam's still got about 800 planes; we haven't knocked out any of them." People panic. It would be quite funny if it wasn't so serious. One

Photo: SM Gray

only hopes that the boys on the ground, who are actually having to do the fighting and dying, aren't watching too much TV.

♦ **LF:** *I'm sure all my relatives and friends are fed up with me saying that it's all in Ballard already—*

♦ **JGB:** Really! God bless you. The danger is that if there isn't enough direct footage, there's a tendency for the media to supply the deficiency itself, as you said, with all these invented possibilities which fracture off. **The whole thing becomes a continuous fictionalizing of a war experience which tends to float free of reality.** That's dangerous, because people have expectations that aren't fulfilled. This war could go on for months. I'm sure the ratings and newspaper sales have gone up enormously. I'm sure *CNN* is selling masses of advertising space.

♦ **LF:** *I suppose the test will be if we gets re-runs in a year or so.*

♦ **JGB:** Yes! The Falklands is a mini example of the way in which Thatcher's personality (whatever you think of Thatcher) completely fused with the leader of war. The two became one. In a way, one's grateful for this almost invisible Prime Minister we now have, who tends to downplay the whole thing. If Thatcher were in charge you can just imagine what would be going on.

Actually, I rather admired Thatcher, at least for the first six or seven years of her reign (as I suppose one has to call it), but I think she went off the rails towards the end. But if she were in charge now there's no question that it would be, "Margaret Thatcher Presents: Margaret vs. Saddam." It's extraordinary that a woman who was rather, how can I put this, *pre-TV* in many of her attitudes—rather an old-fashioned sort of person in her attitudes towards individual enterprise, personal morality, family values—should have lent herself so easily to the exploitative nature of the mass media. She had total grasp of the media, of the possibilities of the TV camera, remarkable in somebody of that generation—she would have been brought up in an era before TV.

♦ **LF:** *Yes, but I'm inclined to put it down to a not very pleasant understanding of the uses of power.*

♦ **JGB:** I think she could play on all sorts of half-conscious, unstated mythological strands running below the surface of people's lives and play them remarkably well. In a way that Reagan could too—but then you'd *expect* him to, because he had a professional actor's eye for all these things. She was a phenomenon. There's no question about it.

♦ **LF:** *Is she going to become another of the big myth-figures, like Marilyn Monroe?*

♦ **JGB:** I wonder about that. Not being American is a big handicap. **Most myth-figures of the twentieth century have tended to be American or have operated within the American sphere.** I suppose Princess Di could become another myth-figure; she's almost a completely manufactured figure anyway. But I'm not thinking so much of American film stars as people like, say, Jacqueline Kennedy. She was a genuine mythic figure, and still is to some extent. We haven't produced anybody quite like that, and it's difficult if you're not constantly being projected by the American media to take on those mythic overtones. Very few Europeans manage it.

Thatcher would be difficult to write about. People have said to me, "Why don't you do a follow-up to *The Atrocity Exhibition*, having a look at the myth-figures of the present day?" Thatcher intrigues me, and did even when she was in her heyday in the early '80s, because she was shaking up this country in an extraordinary way, challenging all sorts of judgments. Just about every assumption underpinning the post-war consensus was challenged head-on by Thatcher. Whether she succeeded in changing national character or not we'll have to wait and see. But she certainly challenged those assumptions for right or wrong. I used to think, "This is somebody I ought to be writing about," and yet, I never got a feel . . .

♦ **LF:** *Does it come, in a sense, too late? Are your heroes the ones you get when you're young, and then you're stuck with them?*

♦ **JGB:** I was nearly 40 when I wrote about Ronald Reagan. Most of the media people were created in the '60s, and that was a unique occasion. There was a major change in the way the mass media began to remake everyday reality. There was a collision between the private imagination that belonged to the individual and the media world that was peering from all horizons, and I think that this collision between the public and the private gave the '60s their special charge. That has ended now.

The mass media have swamped everything. The way that people perceived the great heroes of the '60s—Kennedy, Jackie, Marilyn Monroe, Lyndon Johnson, even events like the Space Race and the Vietnam war, all the great pop stars of the day—people generally felt that they were moving in and out of reality. One minute they were real figures, the Beatles laughing and joking and having a cigarette behind the bandstand, and the next they were mass-media figures playing their instruments on the TV screen. Rather like looking at a camouflaged ship at sea: one moment it fades completely into the background, the next moment you can see quite plainly that there is a ship there among all these waves. There was this sort of in-and-out feeling. That's gone now.

Look at Madonna and you're just seeing something that is *totally manufactured.* Or at least that is my impression—I'm probably showing my age. It's very difficult to imagine the "real" Madonna, if there is such a thing. That's where the role of dream and imagination has changed. That's why classical Surrealism doesn't work anymore, and why **the imaginative writer has to approach things in a rather more oblique way. He's got to get *behind* everything; somehow find a door out of the movie set and get behind it.**

♦ **LF:** *You've said you like lots of hard information. But most of us feel overloaded—*

♦ **JGB:** Well, most of us are not getting a very good grade of information. **We're tending to be given low-grade information about everything. We're not getting the hard facts, the hard news; the sort of things that really do feed the imagination**. We get the *Newzak* [!] all the time. It's been homogenized, trivialized, and there's too much filler added to smooth it down so that it comes out like paste from a tube. We're not getting the hard-edged material that I spent a lot of my time hunting down.

I won't say I do formal research, because I don't really, but **I tend to immerse myself in the year or two before writing a book in the hardest-edged imagery I can find, whatever the subject may be**. People, when they read non-fiction, prefer to get the absolute nitty-grit-

Photo: Tim Chapman

ty, whether it's the battle of Waterloo or the making of Hitchcock's *Psycho*. People want to get close to the truth.

When somebody tells you that half the archers at the Battle of Agincourt were suffering from dysentery, as I believe is true, and weren't even wearing their trousers as the French knights charged towards them into a hail of arrows, it gives a different impression of this battle and what's involved. And the same is true of almost anything. **The inside story is always much more interesting than the story we are first given**, and it touches our imaginations.

♦ *LF: The ways you use that kind of hard information in your novels. It's as if there's this extraordinary imaginative world, but the underpinnings are rock-solid. You can check back and see that it really is like this, which can be quite frightening.*

♦ **JGB:** A lot of people do find my stuff frightening, I'm well aware of that. I got a lot of new readers for *Empire of the Sun* who promptly left, I may say, once they'd finished that book.

There is a convention that war stories are allowed to be closer to the harsh truths about mankind than other forms of writing; and people tolerate the descriptions of violence and despair, humiliation and degradation in *Empire of the Sun*, that they wouldn't tolerate in my other fiction because the conventions don't exist.

There's no convention for the graphic, literal and utterly factual description of car crashes, so people say, "Ugh, please take that away." Whereas if you have the same levels of honesty in a war story, people say, "Oh yes, we know all about this; we've read it a hundred times and we're prepared for it."

It's not just the detailing of sexual and violent imagery that unsettles people, but even the unusual angles of quite ordinary and acceptable scenes unsettle people and they feel provoked. Most people like fiction that seamlessly emerges out of ordinary reality. They like TV sitcoms best of all. They like naturalistic fiction that accepts everything that they accept in their ordinary reality. They are unsettled by anything that challenges that cosy conspiracy. They resent it.

People would resent the Surrealists, even if there were no violent imagery in Surrealism. In some of the Surrealists there is none. Delvaux has a lot of sexual explicitness, but in Magritte there's very little sexual and violent imagery. But what you have is endless dislocation of reality, and people find this very unsettling. I can remember when Magritte was strongly disliked back in the '50s; people said, "What is he doing?" That applies to my stuff as well. One labors under these difficulties.

♦ *LF: When people have spent a long time carefully constructing their safe realities, the Surrealists, and your novels, are like* bombs. *They are dangerous things in people's lives—*

♦ **JGB:** I wish I'd known when I'd started out! I should have just written like E. M. Forster . . . I'm not sure how far my fiction would have been different had I not known anything about the Surrealists, or had Surrealism as a movement not existed. **I'm happy to admit that I've taken everything from the Surrealists, because I admire them all so much—but I think it's more that the Surrealists corroborated my sense of what I was doing.**

What I share with the Surrealists is a belief in the need to construct a dramatically coherent narrative space. The events that are going on inside a Delvaux or Dali painting may be bizarre and extraordinary, but they are presented as if they were actually taking place in a real world. It's rather like the "Alice" books . . . in *Alice in Wonderland,* let's say, the events are all fantastic but one is expected to accept that they are taking place in a coherent and objectively real world that the author has created. This is not a postmodernist joke-world where the reader's being nudged in the ribs all the time and being reminded that none of this is real. It's meant to be fantastic but *real,* and I share that with the Surrealists in particular.

♦ *LF: I'm curious about your landscapes, because they are always landscapes of the mind. Although they are described as real they are externalized states of mind. There's no nature in your novels, is there?*

♦ **JGB:** You mean this is a world where everything's been fed through the imagination and replayed onto the screen of reality? That's true of most imaginative fiction, painting, drama and so on, isn't it? As you move across the spectrum from absolute naturalism at one end towards the imaginative and the fantastic at the far extreme, there's a point where you are dealing entirely in dream-made worlds.

♦ *LF: There's also no counterbalance to man . . .*

♦ **JGB:** I have been accused of being solipsistic, the projection of a single ego. That of course is the drawback, the Achilles heel, or the great strength, of imaginative fiction. It is a wholly created world. But that's true of Edgar Allan Poe and Kafka and William Burroughs. It's true of Leonardo da Vinci, it's probably true of Shakespeare. It may be that at last **in *Empire of the Sun* I was able to strike a different balance between the imaginative and the realistic, write in a Surrealist vein but set it in naturalistic settings.**

♦ *LF: I thought that was interesting because it was showing the process of transformation of the external world into a thing manufactured by the inner. I feel that the other novels present it as a* fait accompli, *whereas* Empire of the Sun *is the process . . .*

♦ **JGB:** I think that's true. And one has to take account of the fact that I've been writing, professionally, for a long time, from a young man of 25 to the age of 60. One changes constantly in that time; experience impinges on the imagination and vice versa; one begins to see things from different perspectives.

♦ *LF: And yet the old preoccupations are still there.*

♦ **JGB**: Sure, that's true of all of us. We've probably all been shaking the same set of beads in the kaleidoscope . . . Well, no, it's more like an evolving garden: the basic contours, the flora and fauna of the garden, evolve over the years.

But I think also as one gets older one begins to apply the imagination in different ways. I've just finished a book [*The Kindness of Women*], nominally a sequel to *Empire of the Sun*, following the boy through the rest of his life, which bears roughly the same relationship to my real life as *Empire of the Sun* does to my real childhood. It is a fictionalized version that runs in parallel some of the time and at other times merges completely with it. It traces out the familiar events of my life, marriage, childbirth, etc. Reading this sequel, I was struck . . . it reads like a kind of hallucination, but in fact the events themselves are the commonplaces of all our lives. It's the angle through which one pho-tographs/sees them that gives that particular strangeness.

♦ *LF: Are there things that are omitted? I'm always aware of how much domesticity is omitted—*

♦ **JGB:** People have always criticized me for that. **My wife, when she was alive, would say, "Why are all these strange women in your stories?"** [!] I had a very happy marriage with her—all the stresses and strains of a couple who produce children and who don't have much money, but nothing unusual—and we were extremely close. Yet I produced all these odd women . . .

Oddly enough, in *The Kindness of Women*, I realized when I'd fin-ished that I'd presented about half a dozen women and that all of them, as far as I can see (and this has been confirmed by people who've read the book) are presented very sympathetically. Quite unlike all my previous books, which is very weird. The title is fully merited. It's difficult to explain that. I think it's that the conventions in certain fiction that I used to write—I'd almost say the conventions of imaginative fiction—do not allow warm personal relationships. The primus stove is pumped up to white heat, and the moment the narrative begins one's moved already into a realm where personal relationships have been left behind like another planet. Possibly a defect, but **there are no warm personal relationships in Kafka or Edgar Allan Poe, or damn few in Ernest Hemingway . . .**

♦ *LF: Do you still see yourself as writing Science Fiction?*

♦ **JGB:** No, I don't actually. That sounds as if I'm disowning my past, but I'm not. I was always proud to be a Science-Fiction writer. The trouble is that SF has changed so much. It's now completely commer-cial; it's all *Star Wars* and *Star Trek* and sword-and-sorcery. It's moved away from the kind of fiction that even the American writers of the 1950s were producing in the S-F magazines. If you think of the clas-sic American writers of SF—Ray Bradbury, Frederik Pohl, Kornbluth, Philip Dick, Sturgeon—they have almost nothing in common with present day SF.

♦ *LF: I wonder if the cutting edge is now with the women?*

♦ **JGB:** Women have moved in and changed it. Women may succeed in bringing Science Fiction back to reality. [But] I've got a feeling that the great achievements of SF—without going back to H. G. Wells and so on—if you think of the great years of the '40s and '50s, which of course built on the pioneers like Wells, the imaginative world created by those writers has diffused into the popular imagination at large.

There no longer needs to be something called Science Fiction, simply because of that diffusion of the imagery of SF. Intelligent SF has been diffused into popular novels, into film, into popular music—serious music, too. You see films which are not SF but have a kind of Science-Fiction feel to them. Since that diffusion has taken place, there is no need for a Science Fiction as such, and what we have left is Entertainment SF—a popular medium which thrives on glamour, excitement, sensation, as epitomized in *Star Wars*.

♦ *LF: I'm surprised that more of your books haven't been filmed.*

♦ **JGB:** So am I! It's disgusting! I've been handicapped by two things. One, there's been no British film industry, really, for about 20 years; and two, the special effects are very expensive. People have been interested in filming *The Drowned World* ever since it was published, but they look at the cost of building these sets and flooding them with water . . . The closest to actual fulfilment is probably *Crash*, [which] David Cronenberg is supposed to be filming. He's contracted to do it.

If you can film William Burroughs' *Naked Lunch*, you can film *Crash*! I've met him and spoken to him about his plans. It will be interesting to see what happens. Often, of course, what look like dead certs for a striking movie, like the *Vermilion Sands* stories, would require very elaborate filming and sets. They'd be expensive. A film based on *Vermilion Sands* would have to be done so exquisitely well, otherwise it would look awful. It would look like a third-rate Revlon ad.

♦ *LF: The technology's there to produce the film.*

♦ **JGB:** Oh, yes. **I wrote *The Unlimited Dream Company*, and the actor Richard Gere took an option on that, with a view to playing the hero himself.** It's fallen through, sadly. I said to him, "How are you going to manage all this flying through the air?" and he said,

"There's no problem." That can be done perfectly, as all these films like *Superman* show.

I'm a great film fan, [but] film is a tricky medium, isn't it? It's naturalistic, but it has huge built-in limitations. The scope of film seems to be limitless, allowing for the fact that it's completely externalized (you can't get inside a character as you can in a novel), but in fact there are vast areas of the imagination that film cannot cope with at all, that it's just shut out of for all sorts of reasons, some cultural, some built in to the nature of the medium.

American films never cope with war as a subject. They reduce war to a sort of entertainment—all these films like *Apocalypse Now*, *The Deer Hunter*, *Full Metal Jacket*, don't work on any level. **Film can't cope with something like war because it's too realistic. It purports to be realistic but it can't possibly show what really happens when a shell hits a tank or people are shot with rifle fire and are blown to pieces.** Film cannot show this; it can only show people with small dainty holes in their shoulders. A realistic medium, paradoxically, can't cope with something so realistic as the image of war.

And film can't really cope with fantasy—out-and-out fantasy, whether it's something like *A Midsummer Night's Dream*, which Hollywood actually attempted in the 1930s and which I remember seeing, or versions of *Alice in Wonderland*—the medium is too literal for fantasy.

The true domain of fantasy in film is probably in something like *film noir*, in those gangster thrillers. They're fantasy, though they purport to be highly realistic. It's a peculiar thing.

When I saw *Empire of the Sun*, which should be a fairly straightforward film, I was quite impressed by it, I thought Spielberg did a good job, [but] my first reaction was, "This has nothing to do with my book." This wasn't any failure on his part. It's just the nature of the medium; so remote from the medium of print.

It had a stand-up performance by the boy. He was tremendously good. How he managed it, I don't know. When I met him on the set he seemed much younger in ordinary life than on the screen. Amazing; I thought he was very sweet. **He came up to me and said, "Hello, I'm you." I thought, "Well, you're never going to be able to convey the character in this film," and yet he did—triumphantly. He held it together: it was one of the greatest performances by a child actor I've ever seen.** He managed to age himself (he was helped enormously by Spielberg). Right at the end, where he meets his parents, you really sense that death has passed him by and left a shadow on his face. I thought it was powerfully done.

♦ *LF: I felt very strongly reading that novel, and seeing the film, something that I felt about all the novels—that the central characters rarely express fear or apprehension about anything. They are too caught up in the excitement.*

♦ **JGB:** I think that's true. *Empire of the Sun* is fairly close to my own experiences. Although I was with my parents in my camp (I wasn't separated from them), I think the book is psychologically true in its *sense of estrangement.* The book is true to the atmosphere of those war years, and when you are caught up as a child, particularly if you are with your parents (even if you are not with your parents but with adults), until the reality of starvation or imminent death faces you I don't think you are frightened.

For short periods of time I was separated from my parents; I wasn't always with other adults. I did spend time wandering around on my own. I wasn't frightened; perhaps children don't feel fear in that sort of way. Girls tend to be more sensible, seeing ahead, saying, "Come on, watch out, something's coming." Boys are more stupid in some ways.

♦ *LF: But all the novels have this overwhelming faith that, whatever the apparent terrors of the transformation, you survive, and that there is this new life . . .*

♦ **JGB:** I'm glad you say that, because **I've always thought that my fiction on the whole presented a kind of optimistic message** that if you follow your obsessions to the end, rather like the classic heroes of myth, whatever the struggles and however many the disappointments, however many dark valleys and castles of despair, you will eventually, if you stay true your own obsessions, win through. I don't think any of my fiction has a message of out-and-out despair.

♦ **LF:** *Another thing which I think a number of critics miss is the humour. There's a very wry humour.*

♦ **JGB:** It's very nice of you to say that, but I think there's a slight lack of humour. There's not much humour in the Surrealists. The [greater] the imaginative pressure, the greater the degree of stylization which is inevitably part of it, the greater the potential achievement. At the same time there's a number of elements of humour and personal relationships, seamlessly merging with the ordinary world, that have to be left out.

The more stylized, the more extreme a work of the imagination is, the more by definition it has to leave out. I wish there were more humour in my stuff, because on the whole people who know me remark on how much more humour there is in my *life* than in my books. It's just that there isn't much room for humour in my . . .

What am I writing? Psychological romances, aren't they? They're not far removed from a modern Arthurian world, I sometimes think—full of emblematic figures. Not quite knights on horses riding through forests towards enchanted castles, but that sort of realm.

People have criticized me for my portrayal of women, but that's the price you pay for the sort of fiction I write. My women tend to be emblematic figures rather like damsels waving their chemises from the fairy towers. Or else they are enchantresses.

♦ **LF:** *I've always felt that was not the problem. Granted that there aren't many women, and they don't have very large parts to play, that is not what is being dealt with.*

♦ **JGB:** It's a bit late in the day, but in *The Kindness of Women* the women do dominate the book. **It's a mysterious business, inventing all these alternate worlds, some completely fictional, some quite close to the reality of one's life.** What is going on? At times the whole enterprise seems bizarre.

I look back on my life's work. I reached my 60th birthday in November [1990]. A very significant turning point. Curiously, I didn't feel 50 at all [when it happened]. Forty I didn't even notice, possibly because there were youngish children around. I was waiting for 50 to hit me between the eyes because it's such a famous date. But 60 came up and absolutely floored me. I still haven't recovered.

I look back and think, "What have I done? Written all these books." It's not the books, but this imagination churning away. Wouldn't it have been more sensible to build a bridge or something? One starts taking it for granted—all these castles in the air. Maybe that's why I'm starting to turn back to more naturalistic sorts of fiction. [But] old habits die hard.

In this novel I describe the birth of one of my children, at which I was present. As I wrote it I transcribed my memory of the actual experience. Yet when I read it, it seemed quite extraordinary: completely strange, weird, as if some bizarre event had taken place. It made me realize that **so many of the ordinary things that fill our lives are rather bizarre.**

♦ *LF: When you write or tell a story of something that's happened, does it make it more real, or less real?*

♦ **JGB:** One sees the super-reality that lies within, that we tend to be blind to. In order to lead our lives, to move around the rooms where we live, to boil water and make pots of tea, talk to our children, we've got to conventionalize, we've got to reduce the strangeness, to familiarize it all to ourselves, otherwise it would all be a ghost-train ride in a funfair. Every time somebody opened the door it would be like the shark on the Universal lot lifting out of the water and terrorizing the tourists. Life would be like that.

I've had experience of LSD, which I've taken once and had a very bad trip, years ago . . . Reality becomes like that. It's like getting very drunk when you're young, where walls are coming at you, striking you on the forehead, and furniture is revolving around you. Reality would be like that, so you have to familiarize it, damp it down, calm everything, like soothing a disturbed child. That applies to everything in life—not just to domestic interiors, but to one's relationships, to one's unfolding experience of existence over the years—you've damped it all down. Imaginative fiction, like Surrealism, tends to flick

Photo: SM Gray

off the dust covers and so we see the reality. It's a very strange place.

♦ *LF: You've written quite often in your novels about the importance of the angle of light. I have a sympathy with light, and to go where there is steep sunlight and not diffused light is wonderful.*

♦ **JGB:** Light here [in England] is very grey. Whenever I go south to Spain or Italy or Greece, even the South of France, suddenly the light does something to one. I was very struck, when I went to Florida a couple of years ago, by the light of the Caribbean, the reflectiveness of the beaches and the coral—quite unlike the Pacific.

The coast off Los Angeles was disappointing; the Pacific ocean there is very cold, the current comes down from Alaska and there's a lot of mist, and everything was very grey and dull. It brightens up as you move inland.

There *is* something about the light, particularly in Florida. Whereas New York, which is a remarkable city, was rather disappointing, I think partly because all those huge buildings are rather oppressive. They shut out the light, and it's always dark down at the bottom of those canyons. **I wouldn't dream of writing in New York, though half the writers in America seem to work there.**

♦ *LF: Somehow in your novels, whatever the setting, it is always desert light and an emptiness where each thing is significant.*

♦ **JGB:** Yes. I don't know why that is, because I've hardly ever seen the desert in reality. On the way back from China we stopped in Egypt for a while, going through the Suez Canal. I think there are landscapes of the mind that tap something deep in your central nervous system.

We obviously inherited through our genes a whole visual apparatus—grids and patterns are laid down in the brain. A human baby takes a long time to cope with its world, though recent research seems to suggest that babies of even a few hours are beginning to activate these pattern-recognition systems in their brains which are triggered off by everything—the mother's presence, a smell, a smile. They are beginning to assemble all the basic building-blocks of perception.

But I assume that the interest that deserts hold for a lot of people, is in some way connected with this inherited perceptual apparatus that assigns a certain special value to flat landscapes with isolated objects. Purely on the level of the nervous system—I'm not thinking of anything mystical. The brain, presumably as part of its pattern of recognition systems that are passed on through the genes, is waiting. It gives the baby a clear field of view, and it is instructed, as it were, through the wiring diagrams to notice especially some isolated object that comes into view. It's probably going to be your mother.

I imagine that the appeal of certain landscapes like deserts is in some way connected with the basic perception of objects in our primary recognition of the world around us. Something of that is being tapped when we respond strongly to certain kinds of landscape. We recognize that this is a moment of primary recognition. I don't know how I would fit abandoned swimming pools into that! But I think there's something related.

I'm a firm believer in the enduring quality of these pre-childhood experiences. It's not just the visual world, but the emotional world and our perception of our relationship with our mothers. These structures endure into adult life and are fed into our imaginations. You see them in dreams, don't you?

♦ *LF: As if our racial past were mediating?*

♦ **JGB:** I think so. We're equipped with an apparatus to see the world in certain ways, and these provide frameworks around experience which carry throughout our lives, and they re-emerge in our dreams and in our imaginations, too. Otherwise it's impossible to explain why certain kinds of landscapes which one has had no first-hand experience of (I didn't see a desert until I was 15) have such a hold. Why are people afraid of snakes and spiders? Most people have never seen a snake. Why are we so frightened of them unless we inherit the fear? I think one does inherit a set of operating formulae which we apply in dreams and the imagination decades after they first came into operation.

♦ *LF: There is a culture which actively cultivates its dreams, discussing them and encouraging children to go back into their dreams in an active way—*

♦ JGB: Dream manipulation is very difficult. There are people who claim to be able to control their dreams. I've never been able to do that. I think a lot about my dreams, and I can remember a large number of them. Sometimes I think that if I applied myself I could remember every dream I've ever had. I couldn't really, but I can remember dreams I had thirty years ago quite vividly. If something suddenly reminds me, I think, "God, yes, I remember that—I had that dream several years ago and I can play it in front of me." Then I forget it until something reminds me again.

I've read research about people who were learning to steer their dreams in certain directions. Sometimes there are images which you can control . . . you can see the imaginative power of the brain. I remember one instance: an ocean liner came into view and I started playing around mentally with the design: I sailed a succession of versions of the Queen Mary, but in different architectural styles so that I had (I remember this vividly) a classical Parthenon-like superstructure. Then I had a baroque Marienbad-palace superstructure with funnels with curlicues, and then I even had a half-timbered version of the Queen Mary. None of this was deliberate; I wasn't saying, "Let's try out a half-timbered version."

These extraordinary images, some of them rather witty in a bizarre way, were purely a result of a normal separation that the brain maintains between certain characteristics of things, e.g., ships and architectural styles. So that when you or I are sitting there thinking, "Shall we go on a cruise? What sort of ship shall we go on?," we don't immediately see half-timbered ships. We see sensible ships, otherwise life would be impossible.

The normal separation which the brain maintains in its good housekeeping had broken down, and it was just a conflation taking place on a basic neural level. But it's quite extraordinary: the apparent inventiveness. When I think of works of the imagination by the Surrealists, for example, they aren't all that extraordinary; [it's] simply that small crossovers are being made which appear much more significant and weird than they actually are. Even *Alice in Wonderland* is not so strange, perhaps. It's just a slight shifting of grids that's taking place.

Photo: Ana Barrado

But I've never been able to steer my dreams. I wish I could.

I slightly incline to the view where dreams don't really mean anything. They remind me of exercises when we were in school, and were told to make up a story involving a sea-captain, a penny, an umbrella and a parrot. You'd start thinking about this sea-captain walking in the rain one day, and the parrot was hungry so he bought some seed. Now anybody reading the story, treating the story as a dream, would ask, "What's the secret significance of all this?" A quest for food dominates this dream or story." But in fact it has nothing to do with a quest for food. It's just stringing together, in a plausible sort of way, these unrelated objects. **Presumably, inside one's head as one sleeps, it's not unrelated objects so much as unrelated *emotions.*** Say, a little memory of the first day at school touches consciousness, and then something else unrelated completely, and then something else, and then the brain, trying to make sense of all this, stitches a quick story out of it. But the story is meaningless.

♦ *LF: You know the feeling you have in dreams of being within the action and yet watching it? I feel that kind of double vision is in quite a lot of your novels.*

♦ **JGB:** I've forgotten so much of my early fiction, to be honest. I haven't read *The Drowned World* since I read the proof copy for the publisher in 1962. Occasionally I've looked at the odd page. There's something so strange, because one's evolved away from it. It's not the subject matter but the way of telling the story. It's like hearing a tape-recording of yourself from 30 years ago, or seeing a photograph of yourself at the age of 18. No, I never read any of my stuff.

♦ *LF: So who do you read—having said that **an hour spent not reading any modern novelist is an hour well spent**?*

♦ **JGB:** Did I say that? Oh God! I think it's true, though I hate to say it. Who do I read? Well, I don't read much fiction. I haven't read any English novels in recent years.

♦ *LF: Have you come across Iain Banks?*

♦ **JGB:** Oh! *The Wasp Factory*. I read that about three years ago and I never stopped talking about it to everybody, I was so impressed by it. It was wonderful, powerful, self-contained, and driven by its own obsessions.

♦ **LF:** *Have you read any others?*

♦ **JGB**: I read one about a bridge that was published soon after. I didn't think that was quite so good. I've met him a few times, and in fact he is a very prolific writer. **He suffers from the handicap of all prolific writers—their *success*.**

The six unpublished novels in the bottom of the drawer are all brought out into the light of day. There's this flood of rather second-rate S-F books, or so I'm told, which came out. But he wrote one, which I keep meaning to track down, about a concert pianist trapped in the Panama Canal—it sounds quite good. He's got a facility for writing a certain kind of Science Fiction, churning out these S-F novels, but are any of them any good?

I can't think who else. I did read a rather nice novel, *The History of Luminous Motion* [by Scott Bradfield, 1989]. If you spot it, grab it. I think if you like my stuff, you'll like that. It's told from the standpoint of a seven-year-old—wait a minute, don't wince—a seven-year-old who has the diction and vocabulary of an adult. But it's extremely well done; most unusual. That's good, because he and his feckless mother are wandering around motels in Texas. That was quite a powerful piece of work. But I don't know what all these young whiz kids are like: Julian Barnes and Martin Amis. What are they like?

♦ **LF:** *I don't know. There isn't time to read them all! One writer I haven't read that I'm curious about is Alain Robbe-Grillet.*

♦ **JGB:** I've only read *Jealousy*, a very long time ago when it first appeared, one of these "astounding new books": the *Nouveau Roman*. I don't know . . . I like a richer text. He's terribly flat—this diagrammatic approach to everything. But of course he's well regarded.

I'm a great fan of Burroughs. I never get tired of reading Burroughs.

♦ **LF:** *I find him very difficult.*

♦ **JGB:** Do you? Well, he's so anti-woman, isn't he? It's a masculine world. It's more than that; it's a very hardcore . . . and a homosexual world which I find very weird. I think *The Naked Lunch* is a remarkable book, as an apocalyptic world view. And it's got humour, you can't deny that. He's got a wonderful ear for dialogue.

Recently I re-read *Catch-22* for the first time in 30 years. I was terribly impressed by that. [But] most of the stuff I read is non-fiction.

♦ *LF: Do you like David Lynch's films?*

♦ **JGB:** Yes. I saw *Eraserhead* years ago. It certainly is an original work, no question of that, though it's got some odd things in it. There's a strange Science-Fiction undercurrent in it that I couldn't quite figure out, and some of it is childish. It had been on for a long while and finally I tracked it down to a tiny theatre near Baker Street tube, a little box of a cinema. It was almost empty, and I sat about three-quarters of the way up. The front three rows were occupied by a gang of skinheads. They were all lounging back with their feet on the seat in front of them. When anything took their fancy they shouted and kicked the seats. They were having a wonderful time. But of course all the things they laughed at, that got them really worked up, like a twitching chicken or whatever it was, I looked down my nose at. But the film was definitely pretty original . . .

Then **I saw *Blue Velvet*, which I thought was pretty impressive—a new kind of visual imagination is at work there. Frightening and extreme though that film is, it really does *create*. There are too few great originals at the cinema and he's one of them.** It's a very deranged film. He deconstructs, dismantles the ordinary reality of this middle-class suburban town and then reassembles it so that you feel everything is weird. Even the palings of the little white fences around suburban houses are weird—not obviously, but there's something odd about them. How he does it, I don't know. Then on top of that there's a strange story and a knock-out performance by Dennis Hopper as a psychopathic criminal. The relationship, where Hopper plays the gangster, with the girlfriend is very powerfully done. It's a very violent and brutal film, but there's no question of the original talent.

There was a follow-up film, *Wild at Heart,* about a man-chase across America. That was amusing but it wasn't quite so good. When *Twin Peaks* started I was rather disappointed with that. Maybe I didn't get into it, but now I find I can't watch it.

Did you see *Mad Max II*? *That's* a wonderful film, a genuinely apocalyptic movie. *Mad Max I* is not so good, and *Mad Max III* goes into SF of the worst kind. It must be seen in the cinema, not on video. Someone, knowing how much I admired *Mad Max II*, gave me the boxed set of the three films, and none of them worked on the small screen.

I love the movies and I watch a lot. I mostly rent them now—it's so much easier. If you get bored with it you can go away—go and have another gin-and-tonic and come back. What about Peter Greenaway's films? You don't like them?

♦ *LF: Not since I saw a program on TV titled "How to Make Your Own Peter Greenaway Film."*

♦ **JGB:** I'll tell you one that is good: ***The Belly of an Architect.* That's pretty impressive. In fact, I've rented that several times and it's unusual for me to rent anything more than once.** But I love that, for some reason. Maybe because the central character's an obsessive artist of a kind, and I identified with him. I loved Rome and the classical architecture. I saw that film in the cinema, and you really need to see that one on the big screen.

I enjoy American thrillers. I could watch those forever. Particularly the ones set in Los Angeles, and most of them are. Film is a very lively medium. I'm not sure the novel is a lively form. I feel the novel has become a very regional form; even a provincial form. It's distanced now from the main centres of importance—unlike the Victorians. One feels when reading a Victorian novel that it wasn't a regional or provincial form but almost international—it centered on the main events of the day in the most important way.

Now, that isn't true: the novel is regional in the sense that the novel of the American South means little to us, or the Jewish novel. American readers find our fiction very odd and mannered. How many French novels does one read, even allowing for the very few that are translated?

But also, there's the sense that **so many novelists who are working today have accepted that they are no longer concerned with the main issues of the world they live in and have gone off to live in the *provinces* of the imagination without facing the central challenges of the day.** That's the terrible fear: that it is a provincial form. I think it's primarily the naturalistic novel that this applies to. There's a sense in which one doesn't really need to read the novel any more—you're not really missing much. I think you are still missing something if you never see a film.

♦ *LF: Thinking of my three children, the eldest reads ferociously but the other two get their culture mostly from film, from TV.*

♦ **JGB:** Sure, I found that with my kids they hardly read anything even at school. They all went to university and I don't think they did any reading there either. One of them read English and I think she only read the set books. At the same age I was reading about 12 books a week. But I don't know whether that did me any good. In fact, I sometimes think *they* were more sensible: they were going to pop concerts and learning to cope with the opposite sex when I was wasting my time reading Dostoyevsky.

They did start to read once they'd left university in their mid- and late-20s. Possibly because everything is pushed back; maturity is pushed back—childhood lasts much longer—children and adolescents seem to be much more streetwise. But in many ways they are less mature than their counterparts 20 or 30 years ago. They're more reliant on parents and society at large. That's my guess, anyway.

If they start reading in their twenties, they've got the maturity to understand. I force-marched my way through Dostoyevsky at the age of about 16. Even though I'd been through a war, I didn't remotely have the maturity to cope with it. It was a terrible waste of time! ♦ ♦ ♦

J.G. Ballard and Maura Devereux

San Francisco writer Maura Devereux interviewed J.G. Ballard by telephone for *FAD* magazine on October 7, 1990. Google "Maura Devereux" for examples of her fiction and non-fiction, and also her biographical details. She may be contacted c/o RE/Search, or at *info@mauradevereux.com*.

♦ **J.G. BALLARD:** Can I ask who you are?

♦ *MAURA DEVEREUX: Yes, my name is Maura Devereux, and I'm with a magazine here called FAD.*

♦ **JGB:** Good. Sounds great.

♦ *MD: Well, my first question is regarding The* Atrocity Exhibition. *It seems—like* Crash, *both of these books focus strongly on the eroticism of the car crash, which seems to be an idea that is very specifically yours. I haven't seen that elsewhere, and I never would have thought of it. So what I want to know is: how did your fascination with this theme develop?*

♦ **JGB:** Where did I get the idea of the car crash? How did I become obsessed with it? I think it was just ordinary observation of people at the site of car crashes in real life, and also the sort of fascination people have looking at films of car crashes, whether they're newsreel film or feature films, where car crashes play—I don't *know* what role they play—but they seem to play an important role in people's imaginations, and say all sorts of things about our attitude towards technology.

So anyway, I put all of this together, and it seemed to me that there was a *special magic* surrounding the car crash that did not surround, say, bus crashes or airplane crashes . . . and for obvious reasons—I mean, the psychology is fairly straightforward because of our very close involvement with the motor car. And it all grew from there.

♦ *MD: It seems that you treat it almost like it's an esoteric sort of violence—like, is it different from a violence perpetrated on one human by* another?

♦ **JGB:** Yes, I think that's true. The thing is: as far as the car crash is concerned, in my mind, it's not the *car* that's the key thing, so much. The car wreck is a symbol of technology, and we're surrounded in our lives—our entire societies we inhabit, are the creations of technology. And we have rather mixed feelings about this . . . rather *ambivalent* feelings about the role technology plays.

At certain points in this technological world that we inhabit, there are *fracture lines* that somehow allow us to *see through* into the reality that lies beyond. And one of those fracture lines is represented by the car crash. It's a collapse in a technological system that has the same sort of revelatory power that, say, an earthquake in a major city has. Or even on a small level, something like an elevator failure forces us to—it *allows* us to—sort of *revalue* our relationship with the world of machines.

And the thing is, particularly, I feel that technology and eroticism are moving hand-in-hand, in a way—**there's a kind of *invisible conspiracy* between technology and human eroticism which we're largely unaware of most of the time.** You see it revealed in the car crash, or rather in our *image* of the car crash—which is really what all my stuff is about. So anyway, it's all pretty obvious, I think.

♦ *MD: I'll go on to another question, then. Another one of the common themes in* Atrocity Exhibition, Crash *and other works is the role of the media celebrities—primarily movie stars. It seems like the fascination in* Atrocity Exhibition *is basically: violence enacted upon these cultural icons—*

♦ **JGB:** Not altogether. Of course, I pick cultural icons who—many of the cultural icons I pick have themselves *been* the victims of horrific violence: the Kennedy family, Marilyn Monroe committing suicide. Reagan has been the subject of a violent attack, although of course he hadn't been when I wrote about him, and of course I don't subject him to any real violence in *Atrocity Exhibition.*

The other media figures at the end of the book were submitted to plastic surgery. I mean, in most cases somebody like Cher or Jane Fonda today—they've submitted themselves to more violence with the knife, the cosmetic surgeon's knife, without any encouragement from me! I mean, they've left scarcely anything to the imagination—for our imaginations to get to grips with.

♦ *MD: Yes, I find that very interesting, actually . . . . you're writing about these celebrities and their plastic surgeries more than twenty years ago, and now it seems like they* have *taken it on themselves—*

♦ **JGB: I think film stars have been having plastic surgery for a long, long time, haven't they?** I would think so. But in *Atrocity* I prophesied the Presidency of President Reagan a long time before he became President. But I don't know what that *proves.* Nancy and I were the only ones who believed in him!

♦ *MD: [laughs] When you wrote that piece, did you actually expect Ronald Reagan to become President? Or did you kind of consider this almost an absurd scenario?*

♦ **JGB:** At the time I wrote the piece in 1967, I think Reagan had just become the Governor of California. And it was obvious that—I felt that, for reasons I explain in the book in my marginal notes, he had his finger on the pulse of the American landscape in a way that would guarantee that he would be seen in the future possibly as a Presidential candidate and, you know, President.

I took him seriously from the word *go.* It seemed to me that he was responding to a deep need on the part of the American public—that was my impression. So I certainly took him seriously in 1967. It was more difficult to take him seriously when he *became* President.

I don't know how old you are, but I take it that you were probably not born in 1967—

♦ *MD: As a matter of fact I actually was. I was born in 1967.*

♦ **JGB:** How interesting! What I can tell you is that of course the Ronald Reagan I was writing about, as I say in my notes, was very different from the man who became President. You probably don't real-ize this . . . I don't suppose his old campaign speeches and commer-cials are run on American television very often, but the man in 1967 was a much harder, tougher, less attractive, far more aggressive and manipulative [figure] than the very amiable old man who entered the White House. You can see a character change, actually.

♦ **MD:** *As I understand, wasn't Mr. Reagan a registered Democrat? Then he switched, didn't he?*

♦ **JGB:** I think that was when he was active in the politics of the Actor's Guild and that sort of thing. I think he *was* a Democrat, but that was much earlier on in his career.

♦ **MD:** *Because he turned into such an almost right-wing, very,* very *con-servative Republican—*

♦ **JGB**: He certainly did in the 1960s, but there was an ugly strain to him, which had gone by the time he entered the White House. He was so much older by then. I mean, I wouldn't have written that piece about the man in the White House, because he was so amiable.

♦ **MD:** *How do you think that affected the way his Presidency ran? Do you think that was merely the image he was projecting, that made him more palatable to the American people? Or do you think that his politics as well became a lot more "toned down" than they might have been?*

♦ **JGB:** Well, I'm no expert on American politics; I'm a long way away. So I'd hesitate to offer a guess. But I take it for granted that in the mid-1960s Reagan, when he was campaigning to become Governor of California, caught a change in the public mood—a kind of hostility to excessive welfare spending, the inflated bureaucracies, and all that sort of thing. The same sort of mood that Margaret Thatcher, the British Prime Minister, caught ten years ago when she came to power. People had had enough of state interference and all that—high taxes, etc. I imagine Reagan caught that mood and began to play to it.

I think his amiability, when he reached the White House, is more a matter of his age. Also, he'd achieved what he wanted to achieve. I mean, once you get to the White House, I take it the only thing that interests you is getting re-elected. And I think he was able to soften his message by the time he got there.

But I've always regarded him as a sort of—as I said in one of my pieces about him, he's a *vacuum* in a way, an empty stage-set of a personality. But he's very interesting. His career is fascinating, of course. Because he is so completely a media construct, as I describe at length.

♦ *MD: What I find interesting about that, especially in light of George Bush's subsequent election, is that to me George Bush* lacks *the very qualities that made Reagan popular. And if Reagan was a media construct with almost an emptiness inside, then Bush is even* less *than that, because he doesn't have as strong a media construct around him—*

♦ **JGB**: I agree. I think Bush is a completely different kind of President. He's really a sort of throwback to a much earlier period. He's not an image maker, he's not an image projector. In the *Atrocity Exhibition* somewhere I say that Reagan belongs with what I call the mythographers, the mythmakers of politics—people like Roosevelt, Kennedy, Churchill, Thatcher. Reagan belongs with them. These are manipulators of images.

Bush belongs to the category of administrators, doesn't he? He could be running a large corporation. He doesn't project. There's no sort of media—I don't get the impression that he is in any way a manipulator of media images of himself. I don't think there *is* a media image of himself.

♦ *MD: No, there's not.*

♦ **JGB:** What you see is a rather serious, earnest man who could be president of some beleaguered university.

♦ *MD: But at the same time, he does get promoted a lot as the "American family man" and having the typical American values. He's projected as "Mr. Nice Guy," really—*

♦ **JGB:** That goes with the job, doesn't it? I mean, politicians like Roosevelt, Kennedy, Thatcher, Churchill were complete self-constructions: the image you get of them—what one had of the years of those politicians—is a complete fiction. You're looking at a character out of a *novel* or out of a *movie*. To be strict, what you're looking at, in the case of those politicians, is a character in a TV commercial who wants *you,* the viewer, to buy their product—*them.*

I don't feel that's the case with Bush, but I take it that Bush is an anomaly and that politics all over the world is moving in the Reagan direction. It will follow on. There's something inevitable about the media landscape that we all inhabit: that we respond most powerfully to media figures, to constructs (if you like), to fictional narratives, commercials, that engage our emotions. And somebody like Bush doesn't engage the emotions. But anyway—

♦ *MD: Okay. I wanted to get back to the plastic surgery stories and the recurrent theme of plastic surgery in your works, and of medical surgery, and of "medical" in general. You refer to this almost as a scientific pornography in that it's an obsessive pornography. How do you see this pornographic mind-set in terms of science, and of medicine?*

♦ **JGB:** I'm making the point which to some extent is made most clearly in the pieces immediately before the plastic surgery pieces—the pieces like "Plan For the Assassination of Jackie Kennedy," "Why I Want To Fuck Ronald Reagan," "Crash"—there are about five of those . . . which are couched in the form of imaginary scientific papers. It seemed to me that if you read a large number of scientific papers in scientific journals—particularly in journals of experimental psychology and so on—that **a lot of scientific work is moving closer to out-and-out pornography**, in a way. These plastic surgery pieces which are, of course, taken straight from a textbook of plastic surgery, with only the names changed, illustrate the process . . . sort of carry it to the nth point.

One could be reading in those pieces something very close to— one's almost reading pure pornography. They don't have any obvious sexual element, but apart from that they are as obsessive, and if you like, *flesh-obsessed* as any hardcore porn. And it seemed to me that science, generally speaking, has been moving away from taking its subject matter directly from nature—which it's always done in the past, to taking its subject matter from the obsessions of scientific researchers, particularly in the "soft sciences" like psychology and so on. They tend to set up experiments to test some hunch of theirs about how much pain can people take, say, and they set up an experiment in which they ask volunteers to inflict pain on each other. There have been some very famous cases, and *surprise surprise* they discover that people thoroughly *enjoy* inflicting pain on each other.

Now a lot of these experiments say more about the mind-sets of the experimenters than they do about the subjects being experimented on. **Science as a whole seems to be beginning to show the signs of sharing many of the sort of obsessive qualities of hardcore porn—even psychopathic strains that you get in real psychopathic pornography.** There's a very thin wall separating the two.

Those plastic surgery pieces represent an aspect of it, but you see the same tendency present in pieces like "Why I Want To Fuck Ronald Reagan," where imaginary experiments are being set up to test people's responses to various *manipulated images of the famous,* and what have you. Experiments like this have been going on for 20 or 30 years!

♦ *MD: When you said "pornography," it seems to me you're also implying an element of almost dehumanization, in that besides just the obsessive quality or whatnot—*

♦ **JGB:** Actually, I'd just like to say that I'm not opposed to pornography in any way—I think there should be *more* of the stuff! As long as the sexual acts portrayed are legal—I mean, I don't support kiddie porn or sadistic pornography. If criminal acts are being performed, I'm completely opposed to that. But as long as the sexual acts depicted are *legal,* I'm all for it. So no, **I don't take a hostile view towards pornography—quite the contrary. It's a powerful catalyst for social change, and for *imaginative* change, too.** I'm all for making it more easily available, particularly in this country, of course. I don't think you have a problem in the States.

♦ *MD: My question would be, then: just how are you defining "pornography"? Not just in the sense of the generally accepted term of pornography, but also, as you say, of the sort of scientific pornography that we were talking about earlier: if there is some sort of element of dehumanization in it that makes it—*

♦ **JGB:** There certainly is an element of dehumanization in a lot of sci-

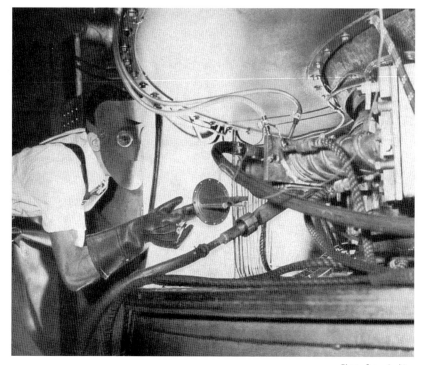

entific research—there's no question about that. Human subjects are being exploited in just the same way that, say, animal subjects are exploited in research laboratories testing the effects of cosmetics, and all the rest of it. I think there's an element of dehumanization in all pornography, but that's not *necessarily* a bad thing.

I mean, the feminist movement has made a very strong part of its case against pornography the fact that women are dehumanized by it. But I'm not so certain if that's true. Well, it certainly is true of certain kinds of pornography that fall within the "criminal" area. I think there's a sort of *close-focus* element in the *pornographic eye* that inevitably screens out human feeling, but then that is part of the sexual imagination. It *is* powerfully obsessive; **a lover may fix his or her gaze on the partner's ear and find all sorts of magic and mystery in the ear quite separately from any feelings of affection or what have you.** I mean, that's part of the way the human imagination *works.* So the *apparent* dehumanizing effects of the pornographic imagination don't worry me.

What *The Atrocity Exhibition* [and *Crash*] is in part devoted to, is **the quest to go beyond apparent dehumanization into a new realm where a wholly new sort of grammar and syntax, a new vocabulary, a new way of perceiving the world, will emerge.**

I mean, we already see traces of—we tolerate, for example, in our ordinary lives (and have done for donkey's years, since time immemorial) the infliction of pain, let's say, in contact sports like boxing or rugby/football or things like mountain climbing or motor racing or what have you. Very large elements of physical damage, pain and what have you are inflicted on the participants. But we've learned to take these in our stride, and look beyond them to the other elements that are present in, say, a football game or a motor race or a boxing match. In a boxing match we look beyond the pain and suffering of the boxers to the expressions of *courage and determination and physical valor.*

I feel that the same need to go *beyond* what appears to be this sort of dehumanized elements present in pornographic sex will lead to a richer world on *the other side*—which, incidentally, sexual perverts (and a large number of sexual perversions are completely legal) have already done this. I mean, people who enjoy tying themselves up go well beyond whatever pain is inflicted. The whole SM scene is an example of people going way beyond what appears to the outsider to be completely degrading and dehumanizing forms of behavior, into areas where presumably a new kind of transcendent *love* is present—or so I guess. I'm happy to say I have no first-hand experience.

♦ *MD: To just sort of tie it up then, in a larger sense, do you see that carrying through these "evolving themes" in terms of society and the future and all these different sorts of media landscapes and all the things that we've been talking about—do you see that focusing on* them *is going to bring us to another sort of* understanding, *where we have a whole other level of perceiving the world around us?*

♦ **JGB:** I take that for granted; right. I would assume so. I think it's a process that's already been in train for quite a long time. **That's the story of the 20th century, really:** *the harnessing of technology above all else in the service of a new kind of perception and a new kind of consciousness.* You know, the invention of the printing press, the camera, the cine film, television, video . . . all these devices are a means of extending consciousness and dismantling and then reassembling consciousness into completely new configurations—that's going on all the time. But I expect it to accelerate immensely in the next, say, 30, 40 years. Whether anything like Virtual Reality—these Virtual Reality systems—will become commonplace, I have no idea. But even if they don't, I think the transformation of the domestic home into a TV studio, where we are simultaneously actor-writer-director in our own limitless sitcoms, is going to arise within the next 20 or 30 years—if not sooner.

♦ *MD: Well, that says it all, then!*

♦ **JGB:** Do you know anything about the sales of the [*RE/Search #8/9: J.G. Ballard*] book?

♦ *MD: No, I don't. I haven't actually talked to Vale about that.*

♦ **JGB:** I just wondered how it was doing—

♦ *MD: I see it around in San Francisco everywhere; I assume it's doing quite well—*

♦ **JGB:** It's in shops?

♦ *MD: Oh yeah; definitely.*

♦ **JGB:** Good. [It's] a fantastic job, actually.

♦ *MD: Yes.*

♦ **JGB:** It's a brilliant, beautiful piece of publishing—no question about it. It's a beautifully designed and presented book. Marvelous books, those RE/Search books. ♦ ♦ ♦

David Pringle and V. Vale

David Pringle, who has been J.G. Ballard's archivist for over thirty years, was born March 1, 1950 in Selkirk, Scotland—in the same house as Andrew Lang (1844-1912, critic/fantasy author/compiler of *The Blue Fairy Book* and its sequels). David left Scotland when he was ten, was educated at various English grammar schools and at Sussex University, lived in Brighton for many years, and recently moved back to Scotland. He married Ann (née Quinn) in 1975 and they had one son, James Pringle. David has worked as a public librarian, Polytechnic administrator and editor, but now makes his living entirely as a freelance writer and editor.

He has edited various Science-Fiction anthologies and written several non-fiction books [google "David Pringle"], but is best-known as editor/publisher of *Interzone* (over 190 issues) and *Million: The Magazine About Popular Fiction*. He wrote *Earth is the Alien Planet: J.G. Ballard* (Borgo Press, San Bernardino, California, 1979) and *J.G. Ballard: A Primary and Secondary Bibliography* (2nd ed. in preparation; G.K. Hall & Co., 1984). David Pringle can be contacted at interzone@cix.co.uk.

♦ **DAVID PRINGLE:** What I *don't* see is a new Ballard coming along. One would hope that by now there would be a younger writer who's fully exciting—maybe there is, but I don't know who he or she is—

♦ *VALE: Or a new Burroughs. Burroughs and Ballard are my twin influences as far as writers go.*

♦ **DP:** They're very different in some ways, but both are uniquely original.

♦ **V:** *And they both don't shy away from telling you what they're really thinking. They're not always prevaricating, "Oh, I wouldn't want to offend your sensibilities"—no, they both speak their minds. They speak uncensored truth.*

Doing this quotations project, I came across a statement that's probably 30 years old: "In the future everyone will be living inside their own TV studio." Well, that's come true in a way; on the Internet there are many webcam sites where people have a video camera on 24 hours a day showing what's going on in their apartment—

♦ **DP:** Some of them are pornographic, but some of them are obviously not—they're just living a normal life. Although, **how *can* you be "normal" if you know there's a video camera always trained on you, broadcasting your life on the Internet?**

♦ **V:** *Right. These people have elected to let strangers intimately view their lives. To me that's not just strange, but Ballardian. It reminds me of his story "The Sixty Minute Zoom," in which a family never meets but lives their entire life through Virtual Reality technology—*

♦ **DP:** Yes. Recently I started re-reading all of Ballard's works from the very beginning again. **I was noting how beautiful the writing was—even when he's talking about downbeat and gloomy subjects, about the end of the human race or whatever** in a story like "Terminal Beach," it's striking how gorgeous the writing is. You get a kind of aesthetic thrill even when the subject is "depressing."

Some people find Ballard depressing but I never have, because he always gave me that *charge*—that sense of standing on a mountaintop. His writing and use of resonant words at times have almost a Shakespearean power—some of his images and phrases have a quality of writing that's dense and has such amazing style—a writing density that's missing in the new novels I pick up and browse through.

♦ **V:** *Well, my standard for* anything *cultural is: it has to have "deep meaning" both philosophically/poetically (you keep finding new meanings and implications, again and again), and it has to be "deeply beautiful" in that you can return over and over and keep discovering something new and aesthetically quickening. You find these both in a Hieronymus*

Bosch triptych and in Ballard's writing.

Recently I was doing something fun: comparing page-by-page the American edition of The Burning World *(1964) with* The Drought *(1965) which was published a year later in England. I noticed all these sometimes quite considerable changes and rewriting. Some involve several sentences being deleted or added.*

♦ **DP:** I think that's the only time he's done that with a novel. He revised some of the short stories when he collected them, but he made very small changes; he's not made any *substantial* changes.

♦ *V: Doing this project, I found there are basically two kinds of quotations: philosophical aphorisms/observations, like* **"In the future everyone will be living inside their own TV studio."** *Or, these striking passages which are really pure poetry, or prose poetry. So, they're either poetic ones or philo-sophical-aphoristic ones.*

♦ **DP:** J.G. Ballard reminds me of Bob Dylan. I was listening to an album called *Live at Budokan* (Japan) recorded about 1980. I listened to it carefully and you know, he changed the lyrics—he was singing *different* lyrics. There were variants, and some whole lines were new. And the new lines were *good.* He was doing this in a live concert—okay, it's been preserved on an LP. And I thought, that's the profligacy—that's the *carelessness of genius* . . . to be able to come up with variants on what you've done before, and do it so well . . . produce really good lines as almost throwaway improvisations. He wasn't just out of his head and forgetting; he was *recreating* the song as he went along. And that's exactly what Ballard does—he's got this capacity to go back over "old riffs" and at the same time make them new; renew them.

♦ *V: It shows an incredibly fertile, dynamic intelligence always at work, never satisfied with even a gorgeously-crafted phrase he might have come up with before. That happens when you have a* real *writer.*

♦ **DP:** I think Ballard will become part of the "Essential Corpus."

♦ *V: You've worked with J.G. Ballard for 32 years. Can you summarize his contributions and tell us why he's going to endure for at least a hundred years, if not more?*

For me personally, when I first discovered Ballard, **a key quotation** *was "Sex Times Technology Equals the Future"—that was around 1972. You can apply that quotation everywhere. For example, I've met a lot of Americans who lost their virginity in the automobile. And on the Internet, the first successful money-making usage was for sex—in fact, it's estimated that 70% of Internet traffic involves sexual content. And with cell phone cameras, people are sending each other "live" nude footage of themselves—way more than you might think. Every time there's a technological innovation, it gets steered toward sex, if possible. And that's just one example of a Ballard quotation.*

♦ **DP:** When I think about J.G. Ballard, the first thought that comes to mind is: *he's so wide-ranging.* Reading all these quotations you sent me, I was reminded of how much ground he covers: the sciences, visual arts, psychology—he's constantly citing papers about how the brain works. He's interested in the remote past and mentions prehistory a number of times, talking about instincts that were laid down hundreds of thousands of years ago—that kind of thing.

He's got this kind of Big View. **There's a quotation about how the writer today must take *everything* as his subject matter—the whole universe is his subject matter!** And I thought, "That's *you!*" (that's what Ballard does). The universe *is* his subject matter, in a sense. And that's a very big subject.

There's also the beauty of the language. I think this makes him "For the Ages." I think that in the classical sense, he's a very good writer indeed—instinctively it somehow comes out. He wrote a review of Norman Mailer's *A Fire On The Moon,* and there was one sentence in particular that's like poetry. [You could almost lay it out as blank verse:]

> "How many of us could say
> That these first flights through outer space,
> A dream as ancient as the sun-ships of the Pharaohs,
> Have substantially changed the real substance
> Of our lives, our private communion, however stuttered,
> With the unseen powers of the universe?"

Now *that's* Shakespearean language to me!

Ballard's talking about "God" and "prayer" there, but not in conventional religious terms. He's talking about Space and the Moon Flights and then puts in this back reference to the sun-ships of the Pharoahs, which is definitely poetic, but essentially he's talking about prayer and God but not in a religious way—in a kind of *non-religious* way. **"The unseen powers of the universe" doesn't mean any conventional idea of "God," but rather this sense of the *mystery of the universe*,** which he's very conscious of. It comes out in all kinds of ways in his quotations and in much of his writing: that *life is mysterious, and wonderful.*

♦ *V: I think Ballard produces poetic prose. I don't think poetry has to be broken up into versification to be poetry.*

♦ **DP:** He's a writer of power. He's got some kind of *mana* inside him that just comes out, even in brief newspaper quotes or soundbites. Yesterday somebody sent a new Ballard quotation to the Internet mailing list I'm on. It was a tribute to a writer called James Hamilton-Paterson, written by a travel writer named Ian Thompson. It turns out Ballard had read a couple of Hamilton-Paterson's books—he *likes* travel books. He came out with a one-liner probably casually done on the phone: "I love his elegant and intensely evocative style; strangeness lifts off his pages like a rare perfume." [laughs]

♦ *V: That's a perfect example. And these are like throwaway lines—effortlessly produced. Decades ago I was stunned by beautiful writing in* The Crystal World, The Drowned World—

♦ **DP:** —and in early short stories like "Prima Belladonna" (1956) onward.

♦ *V: He's an unacknowledged poet, really. Foundationally, he's like the best Surrealist poets. Yet what's amazing is how he has annexed cutting-edge science and technology into his writing. And **he's a philosopher—you find these stand-alone philosophical observations that rank with the best by Schopenhauer and Nietzsche.***

♦ **DP:** Everything about Ballard involves *paradox.* Now some people say, "He's not very good with character and dialogue; he doesn't have

Photo: Ana Barrado

the traditional virtues of a novelist like Jane Austen." Yet by being in some senses "limited" to following his own *obsessions,* at the same time he's immensely rich. He's not a scientific specialist, but he definitely has generous scientific knowledge, plus his knowledge in the arts.

I was reading Harold Bloom's *The Western Canon* on the topic of "What Makes the Great Writers Great?" (Shakespeare, etc.) Harold Bloom has this theory of the "Anxiety of Influence." **If you're a writer, you grapple with the great writers who have gone before and try to beat them at their game.** So James Joyce was in a kind of *agon* [dramatic contest] with Shakespeare, for example—in *Ulysses,* there's a chapter all about Shakespeare.

I was wondering, "How does this apply to Ballard?" Well, he's taken on a number of the writers of the past and tried to beat them at their own game. But I then thought, "He's done so much more!" Ballard's "Anxiety of Influence" extends not only to earlier writers (writers he has been influenced by, and reacted against, like Kafka and Hemingway), but to the whole of Western visual arts as well.

He's also taken on science—not to a great depth perhaps like a proper scientist, but the whole range of science, especially biology and to some extent physics and so on. Of course **he takes on psychology and the "soft" sciences; he regularly subscribes to a journal on the topic of the brain.**

I'm impressed by Ballard's ability to absorb, over his lifetime of writing (50 years), so many different dimensions, and play it back to us, transformed. You can't really make a distinction between his fiction and his non-fiction pronouncements and interviews—it's kind of all *one big continuum.*

♦ *V: And you haven't mentioned all his experiments with form itself, like the advertisements he designed and placed in a magazine. I think he also took some of the photographs, like the one of his girlfriend—*

♦ **DP:** I hope so, because she was naked.

♦ *V: To get back to his innovation in all the forms that words can cloak themselves in—I love his "Wish You Were Here" story which is just postcards sent from some futuristic beach resort.*

♦ **DP: He's done quite a few innovations. "The Index" was a story told just by the index. There's one story that's all footnotes to one sentence.**

♦ *V: One of my favorite early books consisted of stories grouped together under the title* Vermilion Sands. *To me it just seemed like a movie of the future, with houses that respond to your emotional state, clothing that changes colors, and sculpture/sound installations that change depending on what you do around them. Some of that is coming true, of course.*

♦ **DP:** There was a short story by Ballard that made its debut in *Japanese.* Takayuki Tatsumi was the first to publish a Ballard short story that was set on a Caribbean island, "Dream Cargoes." That was initially published in Japan [*Shincho,* 9/90], and only later appeared in *War Fever.*

♦ *V: Ballard was amazingly generous with his short stories, often just giving them to friends such as Emma Tennant, the publisher of* Bananas, *and Martin Bax, who published* Ambit. *Then there's that other side of Ballard—the painting side. Apparently he was friends with Francis Bacon as well as Eduardo Paolozzi—*

♦ **DP:** Paolozzi is still alive [died April 22, 2005], but is not very well; he had a stroke and I think he's been house-bound since then. There was a special exhibition on him in his hometown of Edinburgh for his eightieth birthday this year. I don't know if Ballard actually was friends with Francis Bacon—he died some time ago—but he admired his work. He also struck up an acquaintance with Helmut Newton, late in the day. Newton died recently—

♦ *V: —in a car crash directly into a wall.*

♦ **DP:** A lot of Americans drive automatic transmissions, don't they? My brother is an ambulance paramedic, and he tells me this is quite a common accident for old people. Quite often they put their foot on the accelerator—there's no clutch to help control the car—and ram into something.

♦ *V: **Ballard is one of the most forward-thinking social theorists about the darker implications of technological innovation**, yet he* *himself still writes in longhand or just uses a typewriter—*

♦ **DP:** Well, in recent years he's employed a sort of secretary to turn out his final manuscripts—when he's doing a novel, anyway; I don't think he writes short stories anymore, unfortunately—hasn't written one for years. **Since about the time of *Empire of the Sun* he has preferred to write in longhand and then take it to this woman who lives up the street. She word-processes it for him**, gives it back, and he marks up the manuscript and makes changes and gives it back to her and she makes the final copy.

♦ *V: Well, at least he has a tiny bit of a social life—*

♦ **DP:** I think he has quite a bit of a social life. He keeps in touch with a lot of people by phone or letter or postcard, and he goes up to London at least once a week and stays overnight with Claire, I think. Shepperton's about an hour's train ride west of London; about as far as you can go and still be in the Greater London area—beyond that, you're in the countryside. He lives very close to a railway station, which is probably why he bought that house. He was commuting to London every day to work on *Chemistry and Industry* magazine in the Sixties.

♦ *V: What's the story behind Ballard commissioning the re-painting of the two lost Paul Delvaux canvases which were destroyed during WWII?*

♦ **DP:** There was something on the Internet Ballard mailing list about that. Tim Chapman wrote, "[The paintings were reproductions] by the artist Brigid Marlin." Here's a quote by Ballard: "While going through a collection of Delvaux reproductions, I noticed several black-and-white photographs of paintings that had been destroyed during the Second World War. When I met **Brigid Marlin** at her gallery, I omitted to ask for the prices of her own works and tactlessly suggested that she accept a commission from me to recreate two of the lost Paul Delvaux paintings. She gracefully accepted, and on my visit to her studio in Hemel Hempstead I got to know this remarkable American woman, saw many more of her paintings, and learned a great deal about her unique visionary imagination. Later still, **she painted my portrait, which is now part of the National Portrait Gallery collection in London.**"

On Brigid Marlin's website there's also a statement describing how she did her portrait of Ballard: "One of my problems was that he was a very reluctant sitter . . . soon he was ensconced in my studio grumbling that he would rather be at the dentist! He had the most extraordinary face. In it one could see a darkness which made one remember that he had been in a Japanese prisoner-of-war camp as a young child. In his face there was also humor, a formidable intelligence, and an odd, almost motherly quality; caused by his having to bring up three small children by himself after his wife had died."

♦ *V: Is there anything else you can say about Ballard, to give us a larger appreciation of him? He seems to be the most universal writer of our day, who's both a poet and a novelist—*

♦ **DP:** I think he's the most universal writer of our day—that's a good phrase. As I said earlier, he grapples with so much subject matter. Yet ironically this is not widely recognized—that he's universal—because he has this label of being a Science-Fiction writer. Personally I'm proud he is, because I like Science Fiction, or at least the best of it. But to a lot of people that's kind of belittling or damning. If anything that's part of his great breadth—his great ability to: a) absorb a lot of subject matter and replay it in his fiction; and b) to reach audiences.

Ballard may not be a mass seller in the United States up there with Stephen King, but he's got all these groups of audiences around the world that really appreciate him. They come from many different directions. Many people in the art world admire him and are fans of his. The British sculptor **Tacita Dean** is sort of a younger British version of Robert Smithson, and just as Smithson was a Ballard fan, she's a Ballard fan. **Rachel Whiteread**, another woman artist in Britain whose subject matter is the interiors of hollowed-out houses after the houses have been demolished and are left standing—whenever she's interviewed, she mentions "I'm very inspired by J.G. Ballard." So he's got a big following in the contemporary art world—

♦ *V: Not to mention musicians like **Ian Curtis** of Joy Division who wrote "The Atrocity Exhibition," and **Daniel Miller** [aka The Normal] whose hit "Warm Leatherette" was inspired by* Crash—

♦ **DP:** In that post-punk era of the *Search & Destroy* world, quite a few bands named themselves after his work. Remember Gary Numan? He's a Ballard fan, apparently. So, Ballard has audiences—including a lot of artists and musicians—that don't link in any other way except through his fiction. And that's rather impressive.

Film is another art that Ballard is very knowledgeable about. He watches a lot of films—

♦ *V: Yes, he's an amazing film critic. So how much more universal can you be? He takes on practically all of the Seven Arts, plus science and "The Future"—*

♦ **DP:** And human psychology—he wanted to be a psychiatrist at one point, and that's really his main subject, in a way.

♦ *V: Those tools from **psychiatry, that training, gave him a way to decode what's going on very quickly and get right to the heart of the matter.** It's rapid psychoanalytic decoding of phenomena and technological innovations—*

♦ **DP:** A certain understanding or knowledge of Freud is definitely helpful in understanding Ballard, because I think **he was deeply, deeply influenced by Freud. He talks about Freud being a great novelist**, which may not be literally true, but symbolically—! I think he was very smitten by Freudian theory when he was about nineteen. It underpins a great deal of his thinking and approach—

♦ *V: If one were trying to become a "Ballardian writer," that might be a key—**maybe Ballard should have his own university. Partly under Ballard's influence (and that of the Surrealists) I read Freud, especially** The Interpretation of Dreams*, The Psychopathology of Everyday Life, *and* Civilization and Its Discontents *which was practically Marxist. That reminds me—Ballard seems to be kind of Marxist, but never mentions Karl Marx—*

♦ **DP:** You know, in a recent interview he was asked about this [*Independent on Sunday,* September 14, 2003]. It's the most interesting of the ones he gave to promote *Millennium People.* It was titled "The Dog Beneath the Skin"—why, I don't know.

John Walsh is asking Ballard about politics: "Are you now, or have you ever been, a Marxist? Did you go through a Marxist phase when

Photo: Ana Barrado

you were young?" Ballard replies, "No, John, I went through a Marxist phase when I was *older!* Actually, **I've just read *The Communist Manifesto* for the first time. A very powerful piece of work—I'd recommend it to anybody. Very sharp—written about 150 years ago and feels like it could have been written yesterday.**"

John Walsh asks him, "Did you believe in a *Revolution* as an inevitable thing, in which the working class would take over?" Ballard says, "When I was young, I did. When I was a student." "Did you study politics at university?" "No, I read medicine. And like most students, I was left-wing." So, he may have read *The Communist Manifesto* for the first time recently, but I don't think he's going to turn into a firebrand Marxist.

♦ *V: He's beyond that—in fact, Marxists ought to be beyond that themselves, what with the consumerizing effects of this global corporate media inundation—*

♦ **DP:** So Ballard didn't go through that ultra left-wing phase; he was moderately left-wing but never had a Marxist phase. He's read a lot of Freud but never read Marx. So then he can be refreshingly different—all these bloody academics and post-Marxist theorists these days have their grounding in Marx, don't they?

♦ *V: The only "theorist" Ballard seems to like is Baudrillard—*

♦ **DP:** That may be because Baudrillard likes *him*—he wrote an essay on *Crash* and that was brought to Ballard's attention. Of course Baudrillard's *America* would appeal to Ballard—he obviously acquired a copy, read it, and liked it. But I don't think he's really into those French theorists. Back in the Fifties he was keen on people like Sartre and Camus when he was young—he was quite into things French and French literature then. But I don't think he's kept up with it, apart from becoming acquainted with Baudrillard in recent years.

♦ *V: Ballard seems to be the very opposite of a pack rat—he throws out letters, etc. Is that true?*

♦ **DP:** We were talking earlier about his almost "casual genius" in throwing out gems just in a newspaper interview or phone conversation. Maybe that goes with the territory. Can you imagine somebody

capable of producing so much also having a pack-rat mentality?! I
don't think so—the two don't go together.

If you can casually come up with a new gem every time you speak,
every time you open your mouth, then why would you want to hoard
old manuscripts or whatever? Well, he knows that people like you and
me exist to help if he needs to put together something like the *User's
Guide to the Millennium.* Maybe it's part of his mentality that **somebody like him can't afford to be too much of a hoarder and pack
rat, because he's doing something new every day, imaginatively.**

♦ **V:** *I'm sure you've kept every scrap you've ever gotten from Ballard—*

♦ **DP:** I've got two 3-ring-binder files of them now. It's not that he's
written to me that often, but over thirty years things do build up. I
suppose you have letters too—

♦ **V:** *They're kept in a 3-ring binder, too.*

♦ **DP:** That's another project for the future: *The Letters of J.G. Ballard.*
He tends to write short letters, although I've got one about eight pages
long in which he was quite angry about something—not with me, but
with somebody else. I won't tell you what it was; I'm pledged not to!
He was having an argument with another writer. I've got things like
that, although he normally writes very short letters or postcards. But
I've got some, you've got some, other people have some—basically,
what's important is making sure that none of this gets destroyed.
Again, it's an example of the "prolific casualness of the genius."

♦ **V:** *Not to mention all the little radio and TV interviews he's done—*

♦ **DP:** Not his main forte, appearing on TV, but he has done some
interesting things.

♦ **V:** *I'm sure I'll be reading Ballard til I'm dead, and that he will remain
relevant. I doubt the world will change that much—*

♦ **DP:** It's kind of hard to imagine. He may not produce a book every
year, but there seems to be a quote from him in the newspaper every
month. Journalists in this country know that "If you want a good
quote, phone Ballard!" And he's quite happy to be phoned up and
asked for a quote. Sometimes he says no; when people deluged him

after Princess Diana died in 1997, I think he said, "No, I'm not saying anything."

♦ **V:** *Who has Ballard been friends with?*

♦ **DP:** Well, he's known Paolozzi a long time—in fact, I met Paolozzi at one of Ballard's parties. Ballard had a launch party in 1984 for *Empire of the Sun.* Angela Carter was at this party, and Eduardo Paolozzi and Emma Tennant and Kingsley Amis and Martin Amis.

I remember Kingsley Amis arriving. I was talking to the literary editor of the *Guardian* newspaper—he didn't know who the hell I was. We were standing by the stairs, he was looking over my shoulder and his eyes suddenly widened—coming up the stairs was Kingsley Amis. He was puffing a bit; he was getting on in years and was a bit fat. Behind him a small young figure was trotting—literally *trotting*—behind him, and it was his son Martin—I hadn't seen him before. He was a tiny little man. And Martin Bax was there—

♦ **V:** *Is Bax still alive today?*

♦ **DP:** Oh yes; he's around Ballard's age. And Michael Moorcock. I talked to quite a few people there. This was in 1984, 20 years ago.

There was also a launch party a few years later for the next book, which was *Day of Creation* (1987). But after that Ballard and his publisher stopped having launch parties—I don't know why. The 1987 event was quite fun as well; Kingsley Amis was there again, but not Paolozzi. **Kathy Acker was there—another small person; she had a kind of topknot with her hair sticking up.** She looked rather girlish.

♦ **V:** *Right; she died November 29, 1997. I just cut an ad out of the* New York Times Book Review *quoting Ballard as saying, "Is Alex Garland the new Graham Greene?"*

♦ **DP:** He wrote a book called *The Beach* that was turned into a movie starring Leonardo Di Caprio a few years ago. What happens is, quite a few younger writers have grown up reading Ballard, and they like him and are influenced by him, so they contact him and befriend him. And he's genuine; he probably *does* admire some of these writers' work—he isn't *just* being nice to them. You see quite a few Ballard endorsements on books and often they're personal acquaintances.

There's Jeremy Reed, kind of a free spirit, who wrote a book called *Diamond Nebula* which actually features Ballard as the character—it's not a very *recognizable* character, but a character called "Ballard" is all through the book. There's Will Self, William Boyd who's written quite a few novels, and Iain Sinclair, of course. And Ballard used to be quite friendly with Martin Amis.

Ballard *likes* to be nice to people. It may be that he genuinely sees merit in some of these writers. He's very generous—he talked his own neighbor into becoming a novelist! There was a story in a Welsh paper from Cardiff about this guy with a Welsh name—Vernon Hopkins, the man who discovered Tom Jones, the singer. He's an ex-rock musician who was never very successful; he was dropped from Tom Jones's backing band in the Sixties.

Anyway, he was telling Ballard over the garden fence about his background in rock music in the Sixties, and Ballard said, "You should write a book!" And he did. A couple years later he gave this novel based on his rock music background to Ballard and he read it, and then wrote a nice endorsement for it. Don't know if it's actually been published or not, but it's all been described in this newspaper story from South Wales: "Local boy makes good; happens to live next door to world-famous writer. And world-famous writer tells him to write a book, and here it is!"

Fancy being Ballard's next-door neighbor and chatting over the garden fence with him?!

♦ *V: Let's discuss how J.G. Ballard has predicted the future. Wasn't he the first to predict Ronald Reagan would become President of the United States?*

♦ **DP:** But that was in 1967 when Reagan was Governor of California and he wasn't the only one to predict that; another Science-Fiction writer—John Sladek?—also did. What's more important is the absolutely eerily prophetic quality of Ballard's fiction in general terms rather than specifics. You can look at everything Ballard has written or said for the past forty years and it's pretty hard to go, "Ah, he got *that* wrong, didn't he?!" If you try turning it around and putting it negatively like that, it would be a *challenge* to find something where he was completely wrong.

Now it may be that the terminology he used will sound quaint after thirty or forty years—for example, now that we're in the so-called "Digital Age" the terms "cassette" and "videocassette" already sound out of the Stone Age—

♦ *V: Yes, global corporations have replaced them with "CDs" and "DVDs," but ten years from now they'll introduce some other acronyms to outdate those, so they can make everybody buy the same movies again in yet another "advanced" format. They keep recycling old content that way, just to make their obscene profits.*

♦ **DP:** So sometimes, the technical terms may sound old-fashioned, but the real, essential *content* of what Ballard is saying is very rarely outdated.

♦ *V: The corporations launch campaigns to "obsolete" certain words; make them repugnantly passé overnight so that you feel you must buy the newest format. We just saw* The Corporation, *which many people think is the biggest enemy we face today. Can we relate the ascendancy of the global corporation, which buys and sells politicians and countries, to Ballard?*

♦ **DP:** Immediately I think of the cyberpunks of the mid-eighties like William Gibson and Bruce Sterling, who were attacking big corporations, brand names, etc. You don't quite get that quasi-Marxist stress and language in Ballard, although he does make statements like "The future may be a nightmare marriage between Microsoft and Disney."

Ballard, being a good Freudian, is much more interested in the individual's—yours and mine—collusion with what's going on, our secret wishes, than in the idea of conspiracy—that there are conspiratorial entities out there trying to "get us." That's more of a William Burroughs concept. **Ballard asks, "What are you out to do to yourself? What are your *own* darkest wishes? What are we *all* doing to ourselves, collectively?"**

♦ *V: Especially if it's unacknowledged or left unconscious.*

♦ **DP:** Precisely. So there's a bit less of that standard "projection" onto evil corporations or evil entities of any kind out there. It's more a constant probing of what we're all doing; what we human beings are up to collectively and individually, rather than pointing the finger. . .

♦ *V: What other predictions by Ballard might have come true?*

♦ **DP: I think Ballard was best known, starting in the Sixties, for his prediction that the Space Age was over.** He provoked so much reaction: "What do you mean—there are astronauts going up there all the time!" But in a longer-term sense, again he was absolutely right. Now it might be, as Ballard has conceded in interviews when prodded deeply enough, that human beings will go into space in a big way and land on Mars and even go further. But it's not going to happen in his lifetime, and quite likely not in ours.

All that's happening now is we're getting the occasional astronaut blown up in a junky old shuttle that needs to be replaced. In a very real sense the Space Age has not taken off since 1957 (Sputnik) or 1969 (the moon landing)—it's withered away. Remember all those optimists who were predicting, "We'll be on *Mars* by 2001!"?

♦ *V: When I saw the moon landing on television in 1969, I immediately felt a sense of disappointment. I also thought, "This looks like a* Twilight Zone *episode that was filmed in some television studio."*

♦ **DP: Ballard is good for paranoids, in the way that William Burroughs was. But he does it without being paranoid!** You don't have to believe in a crazy conspiracy theory to find Ballard right on, or correct. Ballard's not the kind of person to spin a yarn about who *really* killed Kennedy, or, "Didn't those astronauts really land on some desert in California rather than the moon?"

However, a great many people *are* drawn to paranoid theories these days. And Ballard's imagination almost meshes with that, without actually *participating* in that.

♦ *V: But it's amazing how often paranoid theories are eventually revealed to be true. And history shows that when America went to war, the pretexts were often contrived and misleading, if not preventable: the explosion of the Maine, America's invasion of the Philippines, the sinking of the Lusitania, Pearl Harbor, the Gulf of Tonkin, Grenada, 9-11—*

had been made of Tennessee Williams plays, like *Suddenly Last Summer* which has Elizabeth Taylor in it. She claimed to find that very Ballardian! Now **I don't think Ballard's ever been much of a theatre-goer**—probably most of his knowledge of theater comes from film. But he's seen *A Streetcar Named Desire* and the later Tennessee Williams plays that were turned into films. To this day Ballard still keeps up with films—he watches a lot of the new movies on video.

♦ *V: Of course, I'm very interested in knowing everything that influenced Ballard—*

♦ **DP:** I did try to reconstruct what it was that Ballard read as a boy or young man up to the age of 25, when he published "Prima Belladonna" [1956] and started his own career. It ranges from *Winnie-the-Pooh* up to Sigmund Freud. The interesting thing is, once you make up the list, you realize there are omissions. And one thing I realized missing was Charles Dickens. I was reading an interview with one of his daughters and she said, "My father once admitted to me that he'd never read a Dickens book."

I suppose the American equivalent of the Dickens "hole" would be Mark Twain. It's not to say that Ballard hasn't read him, but he doesn't mention him anywhere, although as a boy he must have read *Tom Sawyer* at the very least. But it's pretty clear that **he read an immense amount of literature, especially in his teens and early twenties, while at the same time reading all of Freud and all of Jung, plus the sciences, too.** In one interview Ballard claimed that when he was at Cambridge, he and his classmates had a kind of dare: "I could read all the Shakespeare plays in a week!" He claims he did, and won the bet. So he hasn't just dipped into the plays like most of us have; he claims to have read every one of the plays. He does make allusions to Shakespeare frequently—and that fits with an interest in Freud.

Harold Bloom's *The Western Canon,* which besides including the expected chapters on Dante, Dickens and Tolstoy also includes a chapter on Freud—he makes the case that Freud is a *literary* figure (as does Ballard). He claims that Freud was completely obsessed with Shakespeare, while at the same time having this curious resistance to him. Bloom reckons that Freud got his *notion* of the "Oedipus complex" from reading *Hamlet,* but not wanting to acknowledge Shakespeare went to the classical Greeks and named it the "Oedipus complex." Anyway, the point is: if Ballard was soaking up a lot of Freud, it's logical he would also soak up a lot of Shakespeare—the two go together.

Now Ballard doesn't write plays, and he doesn't create characters like Hamlet, but in his use of language and his understanding of human psychology—well, one of the reasons Harold Bloom said Freud owed so much to Shakespeare was that Shakespeare saw so deeply into human psychology, getting inside the heads of Hamlet and King Lear and every character. He shows the different movements of the mind from the *inside,* without theorizing it. In a sense, Freud came along and theorized it later. I think that analogously, not exactly like either Shakespeare or Freud, **Ballard *does* get inside the psychology of the modern mind of the last fifty years and shows us the *modern mind from within*—from unusual angles.**

♦ *V: I think you've nailed it. That's why Ballard is so relevant. I don't think any other writer is doing this as accurately and truthfully, and is as* uncensored. *Everyone else has too many hidden agendas, like, to please critics or friends—*

♦ **DP:** Right. Maybe we shouldn't be so harsh; we're all less than perfect. But I get the feeling that most writers are out there to impress, in all the accepted ways of high culture. Ballard never had any aspirations to be published in the *New Yorker;* he's quite content to be published in Science-Fiction magazines. And yet he's made his way through to the position he's in now in his old age: as a grand old man of writing whom a great many people look up to. He's kept true to his view of the world and what he wanted to say.

♦ *V: Ballard wrote an illuminating obituary of Burroughs in which the final line is, "Now we are left with the* career *novelists."*

♦ **DP:** There are only a few writers who have a particular take on the world, a particular view—you get inside their heads when you read them. There's just no replacement for that one individual—when they're gone, they're gone. The same is absolutely true of Shakespeare or Ballard—they're unique talents with unique voices. Yet **most of** the time it's the *lesser fry* who are publishing the books and getting the acclaim and reviews and all that.

♦ *V: That's for sure. It's amusing to look at best-seller lists from 50 years ago and note how virtually none of these once-lionized and ubiquitous "writers" have survived.*

♦ **DP: The greatest writers have to stretch themselves. And the only way to stretch yourself as a writer is against the best writers in history—for example, William Blake or Tolstoy.** The great writers take on the writers of the past, right back to Homer. Consider a story like Ballard's "The Drowned Giant." You get the sense that here Ballard's taking on Jonathan Swift—his story of Gulliver and the people of Lilliput, with the twist that this Gulliver is washed up *dead.* The giant lying on the beach may symbolize a great wreck of Western civilization and culture, disintegrated by the Lilliputian-type figures who take him apart.

♦ *V: Now that's a goal: pitting yourself against the* greatest *writers of the past.*

♦ **DP: There are two writers Ballard has often been compared to: Herman Melville (*Moby Dick*) and Joseph Conrad (*Heart of Darkness*).** I was looking for Ballard's comments on these writers, and in both cases Ballard is a bit ambivalent. He said, "Yes, I think Herman Melville's *Moby Dick* is a great novel of the sea. . . but of course I've never finished it!" Now I don't know if this is true or not, but he seems to have this need to: a) praise it; b) say he never finished it.

When Ballard's *Drowned World* came out in 1962, people like Kingsley Amis said, "It's very Conradian." Ballard retorted, "But I've never read a word of Conrad!" But more recently I heard a radio interview with him and he admitted having read Conrad as a boy. I was trying to figure out this contradiction—perhaps he just read a few sea stories by Conrad as a boy, and then later on was told Conrad was one of the "great writers." Maybe he *hadn't* read *Heart of Darkness.*

The point I'm trying to make is: if you accept Harold Bloom's theory of the "Anxiety of Influence," *the writers who you're perhaps most influenced by are the ones you also most reject.*

Ballard apparently read all of Dostoyevsky's novels when he was in his teens; he'll mention *The Brothers Karamazov* and *Crime and Punishment* quite happily, without any sort of qualification—perhaps because Dostoyevsky's a more *distant* sort of influence. No critics have said, "What a Dostoyevskian novel Mr Ballard has written!"

♦ *V: Also, there's the argument that Ballard was more influenced by Surrealism and certain painters than by writers. One thing for sure, he's not influenced by radical political realists like B. Traven or Sinclair Lewis—*

♦ **DP:** Personally, I'm rather opposed to the idea that anyone with a strong political agenda can be a great writer. There may be great works of art that are also great propaganda works, but what are they?

♦ *V: It's hard to say. Are the* Communist Manifesto *and Mao's* Little Red Book *"great" works of the written word? They once inspired millions. Are Diego Rivera's political murals great art? Well, on a real-life level, I personally avoid political groups, no matter how much I may sympathize with their so-called ideals—*

♦ **DP: Ballard has never been much of a "joiner."** He turned down the offer of membership in the Royal Society of Literature, which is the highest conventional honor a writer can get in England. This is a club which you cannot join voluntarily; you have to be *asked.* And he turned it down—he didn't want to join anything with the word "Royal" in it. **He was also offered a "Commander of the British Empire" (CBE) medal and he turned it down.** Whereas Mick Jagger and members of the Beatles have gladly accepted a Knighthood and all the rest of it.

♦ *V: That was an ethical decision—to turn down a CBE. Well, a few thinking artists like David Bowie and Graham Greene have also turned it down as well—*

♦ **DP:** Yes, Ballard has definitely maintained his stance (although it's less obvious *visually)* as a rebel. In a real sense he has maintained a rebellious Outsider persona. Well, he *is* an Outsider—he didn't grow up in England.

♦ *V: Did you tell me that Ballard renounced his first novel,* The Wind From Nowhere?

♦ **DP:** He didn't "renounce" it in a big way; he just quietly let it go out of print in the late Sixties. When he's been asked, he's said no. It's obviously of great interest to us Ballard fans, because it's by him and it's his first novel. Now **his very first short story was the one he won a student prize for at Cambridge in 1951, "The Violent Noon," published in a student newspaper called *The Varsity.*** But that's never been reprinted, not even in the *Complete Short Stories.*

♦ *V: I got an email from an artist named Scott Alexander claiming that six stories in* Billenium *and other places didn't make it into the* Complete Short Stories—

♦ **DP:** Some stories have changed titles over the years. "The Concentration City" was originally called "Build-Up" in its original magazine appearance and in the Berkley books paperback called *Billenium.* He revised the story slightly, but the main thing is that he changed the title.

In the early days, magazine editors often changed the title of stories. As *Interzone* editor *I* did that too! Ballard sent me a story called "The Visible Man"—a play on H.G. Wells's title, *The Invisible Man.* The trouble is, Gardner Dozois had already published a story called "The Visible Man" which won a Nebula award. Ballard considered retitling his story "The Enormous Room," but that was an existing title by e.e. cummings! So I said, "Why not call it 'The Enormous Space'?" And it's been called that ever since, reprinted in *War Fever* and other places.

When Ballard collected all the stories for the British edition of *Vermilion Sands,* he revised them. He tends to cut out adjectives and adverbs and rather over-flowery writing, and sometimes I regret that—I'll go back to the original version and I'll quite enjoy the more flowery writing. First there was a paperback original in 1971 published by Berkley Books (U.S.) which contained the unrevised magazine texts of eight stories. He then did an official version in Britain in 1973, in which he revised the stories and added a ninth. The later Carroll & Graf U.S. edition which may still be in print follows the U.K. edition.

Mind you, the changes are not major—Ballard has revised things over the years but not actually made wholesale changes that mattered terribly. Even with *The Burning World* (U.S., 1964) which became *The Drought* (U.K., 1965), the changes weren't *that* big. More majorly, in *The Drought* he broke the book up from 15 long chapters to 42 short chapters. He also changed the name of the town from Larchmont to Hamilton, which sounds more bland and universal. I think he was trying to get more of a placeless feel; it's not clear where the book is set—Canada, the U.S., even Australia? It's his only novel which is placeless.

Maybe that's a reason for Ballard's international appeal; he has set his books in widely spaced locations around the globe. His best-known book, *Empire of the Sun,* is set in China. *The Drowned World* is set in London. *The Crystal World* and *Day of Creation* are set in Africa. *Hello America* is set in the United States. *Rushing to Paradise* was set on a South Sea Island, *Cocaine Nights* was set in the South of Spain, next door to the British possession of Gibraltar, and *Super-Cannes* was set in the South of France. *Millennium People* is set back home in London, for the first time since quite a few books.

On the other hand, while his novels may be set in international locations, the hero is almost always British (although arguably Ransom, in *The Drought,* is American). In the short story "Dream Cargoes," the central character comes from a poor district in the Bahamas and in my opinion is Black. Ballard has the capacity to be a kind of universal writer who can be read widely—he's popular in Italy, France, Spain and Japan, for example—but at the same time he remains British.

In Britain, the Science-Fiction world thought Ballard's "best" early novel was *The Drowned World,* while in America it was always *The Crystal World.* Most American S-F fans haven't read any Ballard since the Sixties, but they often say, "Yeah—I read Ballard back then; *Crystal World*—great book!" But it didn't make that much of an impact on a wider public outside of the S-F field. His books gradually lapsed out of favor in the Seventies, and then there was another attempt to boost him into favor with *Empire of the Sun* (1984), which had been a best-selling novel in Britain. It wasn't until Spielberg's *Empire of the Sun* came out [1987] that the U.S. sales took off; about half a million copies of the American paperback movie-tie-in were sold in the States. That's the biggest sale any of his books have had anywhere. But that's purely riding on the back of Spielberg, probably.

♦ **V:** *You mentioned earlier that the Ballard short story "Dream Cargoes" appeared first in Japanese. Did anything like that happen again?*

♦ **DP:** A short story titled "The Secret Autobiography of J.G.B." first appeared in French in 1981, and was not published in English until 1984, in *Ambit*. That's because the French translator never returned the manuscript, and Ballard hadn't bothered to keep a copy! So Ballard had to back-translate it from the French text which was published in a French magazine. Luckily, Ballard can read and write French well enough to do this. As a schoolboy Ballard had had Latin rammed down his throat; at one point he said that he and his schoolmates were good enough to do *conversational* Latin! But I doubt Ballard learned conversational Chinese or German or Spanish or anything else.

When I went to grammar school in the early Sixties, every kid studied Latin for at least three years—then they studied French as their second living language. Nobody does that anymore. You can see this kind of classical British education coming out in Ballard's books. Ballard attended the Leys School in Cambridge, which had been set up in the 19th century by non-conformist, dissenting Protestant industrialists from the North of England to educate their children *away* from the influence of the Church of England. He comes from that kind of family—Northern mill owners from Lancashire and other parts of Northern England, who were an important stratum of Victorian society.

Ballard had a good education insofar as it gave him a grounding in a lot of the classics, in the Latin language, and in literature. A lot of the tone of his writing comes from that educational background. But America seemed to give up that grounding in Latin and the classics earlier than Britain—

♦ **V:** *I think Burroughs had that kind of education in America in the Thirties. He certainly knew his Shakespeare—*

♦ **DP: Back in the days when Burroughs and T.S. Eliot went to Harvard, the education there wasn't much different from what was offered in England.** The whole roots of Western culture lie in "Latin Christendom" as it was called. If you look at the history of Western science up to the 18th century (Isaac Newton's time), most of the great scientists wrote in Latin because it was the *lingua franca*—the international language—of educated people in Western Europe.

Of course Thomas Aquinas wrote in Latin, and scientists after him like Galileo and Kepler automatically wrote in Latin. The Reformation in the sixteenth century didn't change this, either. So Latin's important not just for the history of words, but for anyone who wants to delve into the history of science—or for that matter, the history of *any* intellectual endeavor before the 18th century. I'm not saying we all have to go out and learn it, just that there's a historical *reason* why education up to the middle of the 20th century was so Latin-based. **A knowledge of Latin gives a pipeline back to thousands of years of Western history and culture, which people lacking Latin may be more cut off from than they realize.**

♦ **V:** *It seems we've devolved, and that's not necessarily good . . . **Even though Ballard is not exactly "religious" and may even consider himself "anti-religious," nevertheless in his writing he expresses a great deal of religious concerns—***

♦ **DP:** He does. More than once in interviews, when asked if he believes in God, he says, "No, I'm an atheist." So there's not much doubt about that. At the same time he has a very atheistical interest in religion! There's a number of references to things both numinous and perhaps religious in a sense—

♦ **V:** *But anybody who tries to be a thinker will always be concerned with questions about the purpose and meaning of life—*

♦ **DP:** Absolutely; Ballard's always concerned with the larger picture. He'll talk about a scientific view of the universe *but* he'll quite often couch it in religious-sounding terms. So his writing opens up a sense of mystery—giving a sense of mystery to the matter-of-fact.

I'm looking at a Ballard quote: "**A thousand images of childhood, forgotten for nearly forty years, filled his mind, recalling the paradisal world when everything seemed illuminated by that prismatic light** described so exactly by Wordsworth in his recollections of childhood." That's a reference to Wordsworth's "Ode on Intimations of Immortality," and a quote from *The Crystal World.*

I like the cadences of Ballard's sentences. There is something a bit Latinate about it—people who are brought up on more colloquial modern literature might find that old-fashioned, too formal, sentences too long, too many subordinate clauses . . .

If you look at any average modern novel, just glancing at the structure of a page without actually reading it, there's a great fashion for very short paragraphs and very short sentences—often verb-less, having only three or four words standing alone as a paragraph. The actual way the prose is structured tends to be pretty chopped-up and often quite ungrammatical. Sometimes this is deliberate, but often you get the feeling the writer's just ignorant—they couldn't write a well-structured sentence if they tried hard!

People have written books about the "dumbing down of America" and I think it *is* going on—not just in America, but over here as well. Partly, I think education has been damaged by too many attempts to reform it and make it "relevant." So much of the past has been ditched, including the teaching of Latin. And along with ditching much of the past, one of the things we've ditched is a respect for good writing—

♦ **V:** *But there's nothing more important than being able to recognize and love truly great writing. Otherwise, how can you evolve? I still believe in the notion of "evolving." But there is one concept I disagree with: the notion of "progress" which Modernism embodies—*

♦ **DP:** Well, this is a big subject. You have to beware that you're not throwing out babies with the bathwater all the time. We like to think that the world progresses and that society progresses somehow, but if you destroy something that has worked for centuries and what you've put in its place is not working as well, then you've made a mistake. I

Photo: Charles Gatewood

think **education has been damaged by too much attention to "relevance"**—

♦ *V: As well as by* fads, *which exist in academia too. It's ludicrous that Freud is completely out of fashion now amongst all these "hipster" academics, many of whom have never even read him*—

♦ **DP:** Looking as an outsider dipping occasionally into academic books, you see the tides of fashion moving through them. They're all quoting the same people, like Foucault or Derrida or whoever—it's *fashion;* they have to go with the flow of who's "in" at the moment or the past decade. *If* everybody's dumping on Freud, a whole other bunch come along and dump on Freud, too.

♦ *V: How successful has Ballard been? Didn't he have the most sales with* Empire of the Sun?

♦ **DP:** Very definitely. But I think it took him by surprise when the book was such a financial success. The interesting thing is: it's not changed his life. In one interview he was asked, "What do you do with all your money—you must have made half a million pounds from *Empire of the Sun?*" His reply was, "I gave half of it to the tax man and half of it to my three children." Certainly his outward life has not altered; he still lives in the same house in the same condition and with the same unpretentious lifestyle.

♦ *V: Well, I can think of two places where some money might have gone: a) to pay the woman down the street to word-process his novels, and b) pay for those two lost Delvaux canvases to be re-created large-scale.*

♦ **DP:** He doesn't live a rich lifestyle—far from it. Interviewers often comment, **"Such a famous writer—why is he still living in an ordinary shabby house?"** I think interviewers from major newspapers either expect a famous writer to live in rural bliss, or have a great penthouse apartment in the city. That's something that's been admirable: his refusal to change his circumstances *one jot,* despite his fame and whatever money's come his way.

♦ *V: And Burroughs was the same way—I visited him just before he died, and he lived in a small wooden-frame house in Kansas. Whereas* **Warhol—after he was shot, he seemed to associate mainly with rich** *people and celebrities.*

♦ **DP:** Most people when they become "celebrities"—a horrible word in itself, isn't it?—seem to totally cease mixing with the ordinary human race. In his quiet way, Ballard has gone on being himself and not changed—which is rather nice for us who have known him slightly over the years. It's kind of reassuring that you know he'll always be at that same house in Shepperton, and nothing will have changed!

♦ *V: Right. . . Did you know Ballard's children?*

♦ **DP:** I only met the two daughters very briefly in the Seventies when they were still teenagers. I went to interview Ballard once and they were there in the house. But that's the only time. I've not met them since they've been grown up, and never met his son. Ballard now has four grandchildren, I think. . .

Having children grounds you in reality—it attaches you to the rest of the human race! **You can drift off too much if you don't have children.** I think the classical way for people who didn't have children was to go into education—all those monks and nuns used to become teachers. In Ballard's case, he's got such an extreme imaginative faculty, such a strange mind—he was so out on a limb compared to everybody else. After his wife died so young—they were both in their early thirties—he made the decision to bring up the three children himself, rather than do what is traditional and pass them on to female relatives to raise.

♦ *V: It must be shocking to have your wife die so young—*

♦ **DP:** Yes, and it became part of the subject matter of *The Kindness of Women.* He had to become a kind of *mother-cum-father* figure.

♦ *V: What do you think inspired Ballard's* Millennium People?

♦ **DP:** It was started well before 9-11-2001. In 1999 there was a guy called the "Nail Bomber" who set off three terrorist bombs in London within a couple of weeks, and he turned out to be a lone nut. The bombings were obviously racially motivated and anti-homosexual—one of them exploded in a gay bar, killing two and badly injuring several others. The other two didn't kill anybody, but they injured a number of people. This guy was captured and is now in prison.

There was also an incident where **a TV presenter called Jill Dando was killed on her doorstep by a stalker who had an obsession with her—a total stranger.** Ballard has obviously worked both those incidents into *Millennium People.* Unfortunately, he became ill— he got a bad virus which might have been a hangover from his childhood, he claimed. This was in 2001, and for the better part of a year he didn't do any writing.

I wonder if the events of 9-11 which happened during the middle of the writing of the book might have knocked him back a bit as well. . . it may be that was a factor in the delay of the book. There's a different conception now of what people mean by "terrorism," compared to what they meant before 9-11. Three thousand people killed as opposed to three, and foreign conspiracies being involved—that's a much bigger scale of things. . .

♦ *V: Well, international, country-vs.-country terrorism is not the same topic as a middle-class insurrection in London. To me,* Millennium People *is about "Revolution": people rebelling against a smothering, over-corporatized cultural environment—*

♦ **DP:** It seems to form part of a trilogy along with *Cocaine Nights* and *Super-Cannes,* and it's absolutely stuffed full of good lines. It was also more obviously comedic, making me think of *Hello America*—which was also described as a comedy. So I was thinking, "This is his *Hello Britannia."* [laughs]

But the combination of it being clobbered by history right in the middle of the writing of the book, and it being a comedy, was perhaps unfortunate in that some of the reviewers didn't like it as much as *Cocaine Nights* and *Super-Cannes.*

♦ *V: I think the fault lies with their expectations, not the book itself. Did they expect a Ballardian retelling of 9-11? Well, what do you think is on the agenda for Ballard?*

♦ **DP:** As to what he's going to do next, I haven't the faintest idea. I wrote to him a few days ago and got a two-page reply instantly—he's obviously in good form. I happened to ask him, "Oh, by the way, are you working on a new novel?" And he didn't answer that, so. . .

♦ *V: Burroughs was writing in his eighties, up to the very end.*

♦ **DP:** One of the things I'm confident of is: he'll write until he drops. I'm pretty confident he'll carry on for however many years he has left. Graham Greene was still writing in his eighties. Let's hope Ballard is, too! ♦ ♦ ♦

Helen Mary Ballard

♦ *V: Wasn't J.G. Ballard's first wife named MARY, not Helen? Or was it something like 'Mary Helen Ballard'?*

♦ **DP:** Her maiden name was Helen Mary Matthews. Ballard has a brother-in-law, an architect by profession, called Matthews, who has at least two daughters—so there are a couple of Matthews nieces knocking around, as well as the two Ballard daughters and JGB's unofficial "stepdaughter," Claire's girl. He's always been surrounded by young women!

I suppose Helen was JGB's wife's official first name, on her birth certificate and on documents such as her passport, etc., but she was generally known as Mary. Proof of this can be seen in Mike Moorcock's dedication of an anthology he edited, *The Traps of Time:* "To Mary Ballard."

A while ago, I started doing a little study of the usage of names in Ballard's fiction:

Names in J.G. Ballard's Books

Charles

Charles Foster Nelson in "The Waiting Grounds" (1959); Dr Charles Gregory in "The Insane Ones" (1962); Charles Renthall in "The Watch-Towers" (1962); Charles [narrator] in "The Lost Leonardo"

(1964); Charles Sherrington in "The Reptile Enclosure" (1963); Charles Kandinski in "The Venus Hunters" (1963); Charles Van Stratten in "The Screen Game" (1963); Charles Foster Marquand in "The Illuminated Man" (1964); Charles Gifford in "The Delta at Sunset" (1964); Charles Vandervell in "The Volcano Dances" (1964); Dr Charles Ransom in *The Drought* (1964); Charles Van Eyck in "The Cloud-Sculptors of Coral D" (1967); Charles Rademaeker in "Cry Hope, Cry Fury!" (1967); Charles Whitehead in "The Comsat Angels" (1968); Charles Remington [deceased] in *Crash* (1973); Charles Manson (r.n.) in *Hello America* (1981); Charles Ogilvy in *Running Wild* (1988); Charles Rice in *Rushing to Paradise* (1994); Charles Prentice in *Cocaine Nights* (1996); this adds up to 19 occurrences of the forename Charles in JGB's fiction, two of them the protagonists of the novels in which they appear (*The Drought* and *Cocaine Nights*); clearly, this is the most frequent forename to be found in his fiction; the name's popularity in Western Europe derives from the Frankish leader Charles Martel, via his grandson Charles the Great (Charlemagne), and long lines of kings and princes of various nationalities since (including the present heir to the English throne); the twice-occurring combination "Charles Foster" (in Charles Foster Nelson and Charles Foster Marquand, above) probably derives from the character Charles Foster Kane in Orson Welles's 1941 film *Citizen Kane.*

Helen

Helen Bartley in "Escapement" (1956); Helen Waring in "Billennium" (1961); Helen Clement in "Journey Across a Crater" (1970); Dr Helen Remington in *Crash* (1973); Dr Helen Fairfax in *Concrete Island* (1974); Helen Winthrop in "My Dream of Flying to Wake Island" (1974); Helen Wilder in *High-Rise* (1975); Helen in "The 60 Minute Zoom" (1976); Helen Garfield in *Running Wild* (1988); JGB's wife's maiden name was Helen Mary Matthews.

Judy/Judith

Judith in "Billennium" (1961); Judith Franklin in "The Subliminal

Man" (1963); Judith Elliot in "The Sudden Afternoon" (1963); Judith [deceased] in "The Terminal Beach" (1964); Judith Maitland in "The Gioconda of the Twilight Noon" (1964); Judith Ransom in The Drought (1965); Judith Glanville in "Tomorrow is a Million Years" (1966); Judith Groves in "The Dead Astronaut" (1968); Judy Walsh in "The Comsat Angels" (1968); Judith Forrester in "Low-Flying Aircraft" (1975); Judith Loughlin in "Notes Towards a Mental Breakdown" (1976); with 11 occurrences, Judith is probably the most frequently-used female name in JGB's fiction. Like Miriam, it's a Hebrew-derived name, originally meaning "woman from Judea"; I know of no particular family associations for JGB; just possibly, he was inclined to use the name frequently because of his friendship with Judith Merril, Science-Fiction writer and anthologist, who was the first to reprint JGB's stories in America.

Matthews

Dr James Matthews in "The Impossible Man" (1966); Reverend Matthews in *Empire of the Sun* (1984); the Dr Matthews who occurs in "The Impossible Man," a story about the acceptance of death, is very much a wise elder (and that piece is likely to have been the first new short story JGB wrote after his wife's death in 1964); JGB's wife's maiden name was Helen Mary Matthews; he has a brother-in-law (an architect) named Matthews, and at least two nieces who were probably born with that surname.

Miriam

Miriam Mason in "Now Wakes the Sea" (1963); Dr Miriam St Cloud in The Unlimited Dream Company (1979); Dr Miriam Reade in *Running Wild* (1988); Miriam in *The Kindness of Women* (1991); JGB's wife's maiden name was Helen Mary Matthews, but she was generally known as Mary rather than as Helen; he has never used the forename Mary, nor its variants, Marie or Maria, in his fiction, but seems to utilize Miriam (which is the Hebrew root-name from which Maria, Marie and Mary derive) as a substitute.

Richard

Richard Mason in "Now Wakes the Sea" (1963); Richard Lowry in "The Delta at Sunset" (1964); Richard Foster Lomax in *The Drought* (1965); Richard Maitland in "The Gioconda of the Twilight Noon" (1964); Dr Richard Mallory in "The Day of Forever" (1966); Richard Wilder in *High-Rise* (1975); Richard Forrester in "Low-Flying Aircraft" (1975); Richard Northrop in "Notes Towards a Mental Breakdown" (1976); Richard in "Having a Wonderful Time" (1978); Richard Foster in "One Afternoon at Utah Beach" (1978); Richard Pearce in *Empire of the Sun* (1984); Dr Richard Greville in "The Object of the Attack" (1984) and *Running Wild* (1988); Richard Winterton, also in *Running Wild* (1988); Richard Sterling, also in *Running Wild* (1988); Dr Richard Sutherland in *The Kindness of Women* (1991); Richard Maxted in *Super-Cannes* (2000); Dr Richard Gould in *Millennium People* (2003); with at least 17 occurrences, Richard is the second most

frequent male forename in JGB's fiction; like Charles and another JGB favourite, Robert, it is a Frankish/Norman name, introduced into England after the Norman Conquest of 1066; and like those names it still carries certain heroic/aristocratic associations.

Robert

Robert Powers in "The Voices of Time" (1960); Robert Maitland in "Storm-Wind" (1961); Robert Kerans in *The Drowned World* (1962); Dr Robert Franklin in "The Subliminal Man" (1963); Robert Melville in "Cry Hope, Cry Fury!" (1967); Robert Hamilton in "The Dead Astronaut" (1968); Dr Robert Vaughan in *Crash* (1973); Robert Maitland in *Concrete Island* (1974); Dr Robert Laing in *High-Rise* (1975); Dr Robert Loughlin in "Notes Towards a Mental Breakdown" (1976); Dr Robert Franklin in "News from the Sun" (1981); Robert Joubert in *The Kindness of Women* (1991); Robert Fontaine in *Super-Cannes* (2000); note: the Robert Maitland who appears in the serial "Storm-Wind" had his name changed to Donald Maitland for the book version, *The Wind from Nowhere* (1962); note also: the two occurrences of Dr Robert Franklin in the above list (in "The Subliminal Man" and "News from the Sun") are not intended to be the same character; with 13 occurrences, Robert is probably the third most frequent male forename in JGB's fiction; like Charles and another JGB favourite, Richard, it is a Frankish/Norman name, introduced into England after the Norman Conquest of 1066; and like those names it still carries certain heroic/aristocratic associations.

Tony

Tony Harcourt in "Passport to Eternity" (1955, 1962); Tony Miles in "Prima Belladonna" (1956); Tony Sapphire in "Studio 5, The Stars" (1961) and "The Screen Game" (1963); Tony Johnson in "Having a Wonderful Time" (1977); a personable but "light" young man-on-the-make, the name probably inspired by Jack Vance's use of a similar character called Tony LeGrand in his story "Meet Miss Universe" (1955)—a usage possibly also reinforced by the types of parts played by the Hollywood actor Tony Randall in the 1950s, e.g. in the comedy movie *The Seven-Year Itch* (1955); c.f. JGB's description of the politician Tony Blair as resembling "a hotel greeter" (quoted in the *Sunday Times,* 14 May 2001).

◆ ◆ ◆

J.G. Ballard & V. Vale, August 29, 1983

This August 29, 1983 telephone conversation was not included in *RE/Search #8/9: J.G. Ballard,* which was published in 1984. What follows is a nuts-and-bolts "process" interview illuminating the interactions between the writer and the publisher, V. Vale. Here J.G. Ballard reveals his generosity and unflagging sense of humor ...

♦ *VALE: Hello, this is Vale—*
♦ **J.G BALLARD:** Hello, Vale. How are things in San Francisco?
♦ *V: The weather has been great. I need to get your permission to use some of your writings—*
♦ **JGB:** Insofar as you need *my* permission, you can have it . . . when you need my permission *alone,* you can have it. But when you need to ask permission from other people, e.g. other publishers, I'll have to leave that to you, because I can't speak for them. I left you a little message on a tape—
♦ *V: I played it over and over; that was amazing! We're trying to give the widest perspective of you, not just as a "Sci-Fi" writer, but as a total cultural thinker, philosopher, etc. So with that in mind, let me go over what we're using. Obviously, our long interview, and the one that Graeme Revell just did with you, and the David Pringle interview—he gave us his permission. And from the fiction, we want to reproduce the handout given at the Republican convention, "Why I Want to Fuck Ronald Reagan" with the Republican National Party letterhead over it.*
♦ **JGB:** That was not my design; you realize I had nothing to do with it. What they did was take my piece from *The Atrocity Exhibition,* "Why I

Want to Fuck Ronald Reagan," and use it—

♦ *V: The person was obviously trying to create an act of subversion—*

♦ **JGB:** It was very witty! I liked it.

♦ *V: I remember a long time ago when I read the piece, "The Atrocity Exhibition." It really affected me, so I'd like to use that—*

♦ **JGB:** Yes. You don't have to ask permission from Grove Press to use that story by itself.

♦ *V: The book has been out-of-print for a long time—*

♦ **JGB:** Then you can use it.

♦ *V: Okay. Incidentally, tell me if there's something you'd like to add, to enlarge the scope of the project—*

♦ **JGB:** I'm glad you're using some of my stuff; I'm very pleased.

♦ *V: Believe me, it hasn't "dated" a second. "Plan for the Assassination of Jacqueline Kennedy"—*

♦ **JGB:** Fine.

♦ *V: We'd like to use the story, "Myths of the Near Future." A photographer, Ana Barrado, volunteered to go stay with her parents and photograph Cape Kennedy, to illustrate that story.*

♦ **JGB:** Fine, you're welcome to use it! You're acting as an anthologizer, so I won't give you "exclusive, unique" rights to it, but . . . I think your friend taking photographs is excellent. It'd be very interesting to see how Cape Kennedy matches up to my vision of it. I'd like to see the photos. I like the sound of what you're doing, by the way.

♦ *V: The next pieces are "Notes Towards a Mental Breakdown," from* Bananas—

♦ **JGB:** That's a story. You've got the copy, haven't you? You're welcome to use it.

♦ *V: "The Index"—*

♦ **JGB:** That's one of my favorites. You'll have to worry, when typesetting it, to get the numbers right!

♦ *V: Don't worry! We're correcting constantly.*

♦ **JGB:** I love the idea of using that; that's good.

♦ *V: We like "The Air Disaster" from* Bananas—

♦ JGB: You can use that—

♦ V: *Good. And we'd like to use "The Sixty-Minute Zoom" from* The Venus Hunters—

♦ JGB: Oh, that's about a murder, isn't it?

♦ V: *That's the closest marriage between watching a video and the solitary process of reading a work of fiction that I've ever seen—*

♦ JGB: Well, you're welcome to use that—go ahead, if you like the story. It's not one of my favorites, but I leave it to you.

♦ V: *Well, it's because of the approach. It's so memorable.*

♦ JGB: Well, you're welcome to use all this stuff. Listen, about "The Air Disaster"—*not* that one.

♦ V: *Okay.*

♦ JGB: I hope one day to have another anthology to follow one from my previous collections. "Myths of the Near Future" was first published in *Fantasy and Science Fiction,* the American S-F magazine. You're welcome to use it. I think it's a good advertisement for a large range of my fiction that is *not* covered by "The Atrocity Exhibition" style of story.

♦ V: *Exactly.*

♦ JGB: It's the more imaginative, fantastical side of my stuff. As for the others, you're welcome to use "The Index," the "Notes Towards a Mental Breakdown." When we're getting to "The Air Disaster," well, that would be the fourth story if I had another collection—and I hope your book would help me towards that aim—so perhaps if you *don't* use that . . . do you see what I'm driving at? A New York publisher would *not* want to use "The Index"—most unlikely. He might not want to use "Notes Toward a Mental Breakdown" because it's not conventional enough. He might not even like "The Sixty Minute Zoom," so you're welcome to use that one. But leave out "The Air Disaster," because that *is* one he would like.

♦ V: *Okay; that's fine.*

♦ JGB: Is that all right with you?

♦ V: *Yes, of course—we're trying to please you.*

♦ JGB: But I want to cooperate with *you.* However, I don't want to find that I've cut the ground from under my own feet—

Photo: Ana Barrado

♦ *V: That's perfectly understandable. It's still going to be a very compre-hensive project, anyway. Now there's two things I'm going to ask you about.* **David Pringle told us that when Crash was printed, there was a fair amount that was cut out and not used.** *Is there any way to get an unused excerpt that was never allowed into print by the editors?*

♦ **JGB:** That wasn't the reason. Vale, what happened was: I did it and the book was too long. My London publisher was very impressed by the book but he said, "It's a bit too long." I read it, and after an interval of about a month I read it and he was right. So I cut about a third of it. I don't think the material exists! It was my own choice; there was certain repetition.

♦ *V: Gee.*

♦ **JGB:** It doesn't exist.

♦ *V: You don't even have the original manuscript?*

♦ **JGB:** No, I don't.

♦ *V: Oh, my goodness.*

♦ **JGB:** I don't know if the original is with the publisher of ten years ago. But there were no solid pieces, you see. I just went through delet-ing two or three lines each page.

♦ *V: So there were no chapters deleted, for example?*

♦ **JGB:** I don't really remember. There might have been one or two, but they would be very repetitive. I do know that everything I cut I didn't like. Everything I liked I left in!

♦ *V: Although . . . you* did *like it all when you first submitted it—*

♦ **JGB:** That's true, but maybe I hadn't thought about it enough. I'm not sure there's anything there. It's not as if I cut a substantial chunk which you could print. That would be a wonderful idea if that were the case.

♦ *V: Or even something, shall we say, for the fanatics?*

♦ **JGB:** Listen, I'll have a look around. I don't even think I have a man-uscript. I don't keep any of that stuff, you see.

♦ *V: Well, David Pringle didn't have it. He suggested that I at least ask you—*

♦ **JGB:** If I can find anything I'll let you have it, but I don't think any-thing's left. I don't think I liked what I did cut. I think it was repetitive.

♦ **V:** *Well, since you can't find anything, can I use that first stunning chapter from* Crash?

♦ **JGB:** Yes, go ahead! You're welcome to it. And, if I can find anything, I'll send it to you. But I've got a feeling that it doesn't even exist anymore. And there wasn't any sort of *chunk* of stuff, anyway.

♦ **V:** *Well, it sure sounds like a lot was deleted—*

♦ **JGB:** Maybe a quarter. I don't really remember.

♦ **V:** *Now, can I have any excerpt from the novel you're writing on your days in Shanghai?*

♦ **JGB:** Uhm—that's a difficult one, because I'm still working on it. Let me think about that. What sort of deadline?

♦ **V:** *Well, everything I'm going to read off has already been typeset.*

♦ **JGB:** About the new novel: I'm still typing it up. It's rather difficult, because I'd have to type out a chunk of it *again*. It would break my rhythm, and I haven't even done the final read-through, you see. And I'll have to make changes, inevitably.

♦ **V:** *We could also give a prefatory note that it's an early draft, but anyway I'll leave it up to you.*

♦ **JGB:** It would be a good idea, but I'm not sure about it.

♦ **V:** *Bear in mind that it's possible to xerox, not retype—*

♦ **JGB:** Right.

♦ **V:** *Now, in the Non-Fiction Section, we'd like to use these things: "The Coming of the Unconscious," "Time, Memory and Inner Space," the review of the film* La Jetée, *"Alphabets of Unreason," the piece on William Burroughs titled "Mythmaker of the Twentieth Century," and that wonderful piece, "Things I Wish I'd Known at Eighteen." Also, the introduction to the French edition of* Crash *which you wrote, "Fictions of Every Kind," (that's on Science Fiction), and the review of the book on Elvis Presley, the book review on Gary Gilmore, and we'd like to excerpt some things from the Sam Scoggins screenplay—the questionnaire is fantastic, as well as your responses. He gave us permission to use it.*

♦ **JGB:** You're welcome to use all of that. Apart from Sam Scoggins, you don't need to ask permission from anybody. I own the rights to all that material, so you have my permission. Don't bother to write to anyone else.

♦ *V: Now, wrestling with the problem of your biography, we'd like to use the entire "From Shanghai to Shepperton." And David Pringle said it was fine to use it.*

♦ **JGB:** That would be a good picture of my life, if you could use it at length. You're welcome to use it.

♦ *V: We're going to use some bibliographical and quotations material David Pringle supplied, as well as an abridged version of his essay, "The Fourfold Symbolism of J.G. Ballard."*

♦ **JGB:** Sounds like a good idea.

♦ *V: And from your various printed interviews, we want to use a whole section of quotes called "J.G. Ballard's World View," or "The Wit and Wisdom of J.G. Ballard," or something like that. You have a number of incredible short quotations that we thought could stand alone—fantastic ways of stating certain observations, etc.*

♦ **JGB:** You're welcome to do that, if you can find anything.

♦ *V: Yes, there's plenty there. And we're printing a condensed bibliography of your fiction, non-fiction, foreign-language editions, etc.*

♦ **JGB:** Good idea. More of my stuff is available in foreign countries than it is here!

♦ *V: Well, America is the most shameful example—it's an outrage. **There's only one book listed in** Books In Print **now,** The Crystal World. But I think you have an appeal to radical young people—*

♦ **JGB:** Vale, I think I have an appeal to *you,* and seven of your friends, sadly. Of course, being realistic, I can't blame the New York publishers. *The Atrocity Exhibition, Crash*—they were published in America. Farrar Straus is a good firm, by all accounts.

♦ *V: I think they should have been brought out in cheap paperbacks, which are what my friends and I tend to buy, rather than in expensive hardbacks. We almost never even look at the hardback sections of new bookstores; we automatically know we can't afford to pay the price.*

♦ **JGB:** Yes, I agree about that. That is true, and it's true in this country, too—the hardbacks are too expensive. They basically just provide a library edition. The readership of young kids and younger people wait for the paperback. But my books came out in paperback in America and they didn't do well in paperback, either!

♦ *V: Well, there's also the problem of the store ordering—if they've never heard of you, they don't order, and if they don't order, nobody will ever find out. It's a circle.*

♦ **JGB:** Yes. Back in the Sixties, when my first books came out, they did reasonably well. Berkley used to publish them. Oddly enough, I think it was *The Atrocity Exhibition* and *Crash* which just nailed the lid down on my coffin!

♦ *V: Anyway, our goal is to give the biggest possible picture/introduction to you, because your purview includes different, books, films, Surrealism, Gary Gilmore—it's a wide scope. But please suggest anything that would make the project better.*

♦ **JGB:** Well, I think you've covered the ground enormously. I can't think of anything; nothing stands out. Bearing in mind that it's not feasible to publish a whole novel; it's not possible to give anybody an idea of my novels. That's something one can't do anyway, anymore than you could have published the whole of *Naked Lunch* or something. An extract from a novel is often off-putting, in a peculiar way.

Anyway, I think you've covered the full range of my short fiction extremely well. If you include "Myths of the Near Future" and "The Atrocity Exhibition" and "The Index" and "Why I Want to Fuck Ronald Reagan," you're covering the whole spectrum of my stuff, aren't you, of short fiction? I think you're doing a very good job there. I think it sounds staggering, actually. I'm very impressed. I'm extremely grateful to you.

♦ *V: There's also a whole visual side to this project which you won't be able to see until it comes out—*

♦ **JGB:** I have absolute confidence in you. But **I don't have any photographs of myself sort of standing around stroking a gun, or anything. I'm rather a bourgeois character**—there's no photographs of me molesting a child, or climbing out of the wreckage of a Cadillac. [laughs] Which is sad.

I can't think of anything else. Listen; just a thought. You know that Burroughs wrote an introduction to the Grove Press edition of *The Atrocity Exhibition* when it was called *Love and Napalm: Export USA.*

♦ *V: I was actually going to ask William if we could use it.*

♦ **JGB:** I'd be delighted if you did. I would be very pleased to be associated with The Great Man in any way.

♦ *V: Wonderful.*

♦ **JGB:** I can't think of anything else. I think you picked a very good selection of my short fiction. Very, very good. I wish I could give you more help, but I don't have an archive of material.

♦ *V: Now, you mentioned a photo of yourself on a horse—we'd love to have that. We could pay for a copy to be made—*

♦ **JGB:** Right. **I'm not a great collector of personal memorabilia—in fact, my whole cast of mind (and I'm not making excuses here) is that of a man who dislikes collecting mental and other luggage. I junk everything: manuscripts, everything. I can't *stand* all that stuff.** I'll have a look to see if I've got everything.

♦ *V: Here's another priority: photos of you with your three children—*

♦ **JGB:** I have plenty of small colored snaps. I'll have a look around.

♦ *V: Now, I already asked you for the photo of the woman aviator that's on your desk, but we don't need it now. We were told that we couldn't get permission to use it—*

♦ **JGB:** That is by a commercial firm.

♦ *V: Besides, we got somebody to do a painting of a woman aviator.*

♦ **JGB:** Right, *any* woman aviator will do! Just pose some woman in 1950's aviator gear . . .

Now, in the course of all this typesetting you do, you will find that there are a lot of errors that crept into all the printed text of these stories and book reviews—particularly in the *Guardian* newspaper, which is famous for typo's. Do correct them! The Jonathan Cape material is well-edited; I think it was pretty good. But the *Guardian* newspaper was very erratic—that's the book reviews.

I'm very impressed and very grateful. I've got a terrible fear you're going to be left with hundreds of copies—

♦ *V: We don't care if that happens; eventually they'll find astute readers—*

♦ **JGB:** Well, it's sweet of you to be encouraging; I appreciate it.

♦ *V: Anyway, that's pretty much it.*

♦ **JGB:** I'll have a look around. I could possibly find some black-and-white photographs from my early twenties, which I'll let you have. After all, a large part of the material you are using was written quite a while ago, so you might as well see the author at the age he was writing the stuff, rather than now.

♦ *V: That would be wonderful.*

♦ **JGB:** Of course, many of these would be just ordinary photographs; they won't be very good.

♦ *V: No, they're* better *if they look like that; they look more authentic! Anyway, I'll send you in writing a list of the proposed table of contents we've talked about today. We're doing the best we can to make your interviews as presentable as possible—*

♦ **JGB:** Great. Let me know if you have any other problems. You've obviously typeset about 100,000 words—well, it must be a lot.

♦ *V: Yes. Well, I'm sure I'll call you again—*

♦ **JGB**: Right, do. I'm always here. Okay Vale, cheers for now! Bye!♦♦♦

Photo of J. G. Ballard's mantel: V. Vale

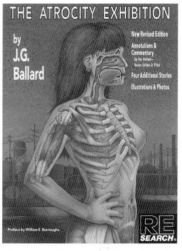

THE ATROCITY EXHIBITION
New Revised Edition
by
J.G.
Ballard
Annotations & Commentary
by the Author—
Never before in Print
Four Additional Stories
Illustrations & Photos
Preface by William S. Burroughs
RE SEARCH

What follows is a 1990 telephone conversation between J.G. Ballard and V. Vale "ironing out" discrepancies in different editions of The Atrocity Exhibition, *which RE/Search subsequently published in an expanded, illustrated edition. Again, J.G. Ballard reveals his generosity, charm and sense of humor . . .*

♦ *VALE: You know, there are little differences between the Grove Press [U.S.] hardback,* Love and Napalm: Export USA, *and the Panther [U.K.] paperback titled* The Atrocity Exhibition. *For example, in the Grove edition a character is called Catherine Austen, but in the Panther edition her name is changed to Claire Austin.*

♦**J.G. BALLARD:** Well, I think I was trying for consistency—in which case the Panther edition is probably "correct." It doesn't matter, though! Let me explain. You've got to remember that the individual pieces that make up *The Atrocity Exhibition* were written independently—virtually as short stories—and published independently, all of them in various magazines. So a certain element of inconsistency crept in. These were first published by Jonathan Cape in the U.K. The Grove press hardback is a photograph of the hardback Jonathan Cape edition. So what obviously happened, though I don't remember it, was when Panther released their paperback edition titled *The Atrocity Exhibition,* I updated it slightly (I can only assume that that was the case).

I had a very strange sensation, actually: when I recently wrote the annotations to *The Atrocity Exhibition,* I suddenly for the first time—after an interval of 25 years—felt I understood what *The Atrocity Exhibition* was about. It was like understanding a dream. It was a very peculiar sensation.

♦ *V: Catherine Reuther is supervising all the proofreading. Actually, we all proofread—*

♦ **JGB:** By the way, Catherine is a stunning young woman, isn't she?

♦ *V: Oh, thanks—I'll tell her you said that.*

♦ **JGB:** I was immensely struck by her, you know—beauty and intelligence. I am terribly embarrassed that I appeared to criticize her driving—

♦ *V: Oh, no—*

♦ **JGB**: I've been feeling very guilty about that. I've spent so many years criticizing my daughters' driving, and it was just a sort of reflex. And I regret it.

♦ *V: Oh, no—that's nothing.*

♦ **JGB:** She's a beautiful young woman.

J. G. Ballard with Catherine Reuther. Photo: V. Vale

♦ *V: Well, thanks! She's sort of supervising all the proofing, because we have several copies that have to be integrated into one final proofing, if you know what I mean—*

♦ **JGB:** Sure! Well, you've done a wonderful job in the past. I loved your introduction to my previous book, and all the introductions to the other wonderful books you've made. Incidentally, your last publication, *Modern Primitives,* was extraordinary. That was an amazing book—that was a genuine work of modern urban anthropology. It was incredible. You could have been Margaret Mead going to Samoa—it was the equivalent of that. And it was never voyeuristic. It was an

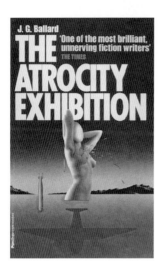 

extraordinary book, beautifully conceived and researched in such depth. That's what's so wonderful about all your publications: the depth of them—they just go on and on. Where most books end, yours are just about beginning. I mean they really are very, very impressive. You've produced really amazing books; there's no question about that. By the way, what future projects do you have on the board?

♦ *V:* Incredibly Strange Music, *which frankly I consider, philosophically, to be a much less important project. It's kind of the musical equivalent of our* Incredibly Strange Films *book—*

♦ **JGB:** Of course. Marvelous book.

♦ *V: There's a corresponding musical territory to that film book, which has never been mapped in a book. There are many people who have now mostly been forgotten, but they produced some really quite imaginative records which are now out-of-print. Because they were not rock or jazz or opera or in a discrete genre with its own niche publications and academic scholars, these border-crossing, wild-card recordings have escaped commemoration or celebration—which means they're in danger of total extinction. Yet some of these recordings are triumphs of the unfettered imagination, and it would be a shame if they just vanished into oblivion.*

However, in terms of, shall we say, the advancement of our personal consciousness—if I have any extra time at all, I'd rather read, or watch a

Buñuel movie, than listen to music—

♦ **JGB:** I understand.

♦ *V: Reading gives access to a far richer information system—*

♦ **JGB:** Exactly. You know, I've always thought that one subject which you ought to tackle, though I don't know *how* you would tackle it, is the subject of pornography. I don't mean producing a book which looks at the varieties of pornography, but conceivably you might do interviews with pornographers and people who take part in pornography and are interested in the sort of *psychology* of it, if you see what I'm driving at.

The problem is that so many of these people are on the fringes of crime, aren't they? They might be very reluctant to talk. Actually, a lot of them probably *would* talk, I think. Particularly the people who make porno movies of various kinds, and people in porno publishing, and people who take part—the women in particular—and the men who take part in these porno movies. It could be great.

♦ *V: Well, I'm definitely interested in a succinct history of censorship involving* Ulysses, Lady Chatterly's Lover, Howl, The Love Book *and so forth. One could include key quotations and easy-to-read summaries.*

♦ **JGB:** That sounds good—

♦ *V: Something that would clearly indict this "bluenose" mentality that keeps recurring in every generation—the kind of people* who can't mind their own business, *and who want to censor everything they can—*

♦ **JGB:** Here, people want to censor the *news* on TV. We have this "negative body count" obsession going on: you've got to get the body counts down. You know, **some Boeing 707 flies into a mountain in Spain with 180 British tourists on board, and you're not allowed to show the bodies—which makes the whole thing into a sort of *demolition derby*** or whatever you call it in America. So TV viewers think that it's *fun* to fly into a mountainside, because nobody gets hurt. That's the unconscious message

Anyway, that pornography project is just an idea. Try to get the people who make the stuff to open up, if you see what I'm getting at.

I'm drawing an analogy with your *Incredibly Strange Films,* but it could be very difficult.

♦ *V: We'll give it some thought—*

♦ **JGB:** Ignore it, ignore it, ignore it! Vale, listen, it's great talking to you! Give my regards to Catherine. Look after yourself! ♦ ♦ ♦

J.G. Ballard, April 25, 1990

What follows is a second telephone conversation between J.G. Ballard and V. Vale on the final preparation of the expanded, illustrated RE/Search edition of The Atrocity Exhibition . . .

♦ *VALE: Hi, J.G. Ballard—this is Vale from San Francisco—*

♦ **J.G. BALLARD:** Hi Vale. How's everything going?

♦ *V: Well, pretty good. I'm just calling about a few things—*

♦ **JGB:** Did you get my letter about the Fonda—

♦ *V: Thank you very much for that sweet letter. Of course, we're going to go ahead and publish the Jane Fonda piece; we're not going to destroy the integrity of this thing.*

♦ **JGB:** Okay. All right. Good for you. Don't hate me if it all goes wrong! Of course, the curious thing is, I think Fonda actually has *had* a breast-lift. (I know: what else will I prophesy?!) And I'm sure Princess Margaret *will* have a facelift! If you wanted to change "Fonda" to "Cher," you'd have no problem—I mean, she *admits* she's had all the plastic jobs done.

♦ *V: No, of course not. There were just a couple things I wanted to get your opinion on.*

♦ **JGB:** Sure.

♦ *V: Chapter 8. "Koster" in the British paperback of* The Atrocity Exhibition *was spelled "Koester" in the hardback. I thought maybe we'd change it to what it was before.*

♦ **JGB:** You can change it, by all means. This is the first I remember it.

It's a long time ago. To be honest, I didn't realize that I had made changes between the hardcover and the Panther paperback. I completely forgot there were changes—that surprises me—but by all means standardize on the Panther edition (or whatever you prefer to do).

♦ **V:** *Okay, that's "Koester" with an "e."*

Now Chapter 9. There are a couple references to "Elizabeth Austen" (Dr Austen), but how about going back to "Catherine Austen"?

♦ **JGB:** I think go back to "Catherine." That must be in the Panther, but not in the Cape. Why I changed that I have no idea!

♦ **V:** *We don't own the Cape edition. I'd love to get one—*

♦ **JGB:** The Cape is the same as—

♦ **V:** *That's right; it was photocopied to be the Grove hardback edition.*

♦ **JGB:** It's exactly the same: same pagination, same text—it's basically the same book.

♦ **V:** *Anyway, today, finally, we have things proofread enough to send you a copy. If you see something, please let us know* right away, *because we have several weeks to make changes.*

♦ **JGB:** What, in fact, will you be sending?

♦ **V:** *We'll send you a xerox of the real book exactly as it's going to appear. Obviously, the illustrations will look lousy, because they're xeroxes.*

♦ **JGB:** But you'll have the *main* text—

♦ **V:** *You'll have all the text with the annotations to the side. I think you'll like the design; it's very clear what is annotation and what is text—*

♦ **JGB:** That's great. Don't worry—listen, I 100% trust your judgments on all things—

♦ **V:** *Yes, but please, if you see something—don't hesitate to let us know right away, when you get the xerox. I have to ask you about one other thing. The four plastic surgery pieces and "World War III"—we're calling that an "appendix" in the back, so people will know they are additional pieces. Those have no annotations on them whatsoever, so I wrote an editor's note, because I thought we should have something there in the annotations column. We started out with "Princess Margaret's Facelift."*

♦ **JGB:** When you're talking about "World War III," you mean the

Reagan story? I never realized you were going to use that.

♦ **V:** *Oh yes,* you *sent it to us: "The Secret History of World War III."*

♦ **JGB:** You're happy to use that?

♦ **V:** *Oh yes! Now, I wrote these editor's notes which are actually based on a letter from you, but I want to get your approval, because I can rewrite them very quickly and easily. We have this appendix, and I'll read my "annotation" on the phone and hear your comment on it:*

[Editor's Note: Our presentation of *The Atrocity Exhibition* includes five additional works not in the original edition. The first four are recently written plastic surgery pieces, about which Ballard writes, "I feel myself that they do belong in the book as they are themselves examples of the sort of imaginative crossovers that the book describes. All of them consist of straight transcriptions from a text-book of plastic surgery in which all I have done is change 'the patient' to 'Princess Margaret,' 'Mae West,' etc. The effect was very curious . . ."]

♦ **JGB:** That sounds fine to me. Would you like me to write slightly more extensive notes?

♦ **V:** *Yes! Of course.*

♦ **JGB:** I have no idea why I stopped when I did stop. Maybe I thought I'd burdened you enough—

♦ **V:** *It's no burden—are you kidding? We'd* love *to have more!*

♦ **JGB:** What I will do is: I'll do an annotation. You can use your intro—the one you just read out loud—that's fine. And then I can have a little space and I'll write about 500 words or so—I'll happily do that. I can do a piece for "World War III" rounding out Reagan. Incidentally, the "World War III" piece is going into a new collection of stories of mine, which will be published not in the States but over here in December. It's going to be called *War Fever,* after another of the stories.

Can I at the same time send you a few corrections to the "World War III" piece. For example, somewhere in the story I say, "In the first *uncontested* presidential election in the history of the United States." Now, I don't know my American history and whether that's, strictly speaking, true. Was there ever an *uncontested* presidential election? I

Photo: Ana Barrado

doubt it. So I just *eliminated* that, because I wasn't sure of the facts.

Anyway, I'll send you a few little corrections—I think I have the Reagans retiring to Santa Barbara, when in fact they retired to Bel Air. Little things like that.

I'll do those extra introductions and I'll send you the small corrections to the "World War III" piece. And I'll try to let you have the new notes—actually, it's difficult to write 500 words about Mae West! What the hell do I say?

♦ *V: You can write whatever you want—*

♦**JGB:** It's easy to write about the Queen and Princess Margaret—actually, Princess Margaret's a bit of a bore—she's not the figure she was when I wrote that piece, of course.

♦ *V: I've seen little pieces on her in the American press, so she's not completely unknown over here—*

♦**JGB:** I don't mind switching, say, Princess Margaret to somebody else.

♦ *V: No, let's leave it.*

♦**JGB:** You believe in *integrity,* Vale! [laughs] Actually, the whole point of these Pop Art pieces, which these things are, is that you can just switch from X to Y to Zed—they're all interchangeable! I'm still wondering if we shouldn't take advantage of that principle and update all these names! Vale, is it possible that Jane Fonda is a little bit passé?!

♦ *V: No, not at all. In fact, I just saw her picture in the paper yesterday, because they're showing her movie* Klute *on TV, and there was a picture of her.*

♦**JGB:** That was a long time ago—nearly twenty years ago.

♦ *V: She still looks great.*

♦**JGB:** Oh, she's still a terrific woman—oh, she's a remarkable woman.

♦ *V: She definitely is; her and Patty Hearst.*

♦**JGB:** Yes. Well, I'm thrilled about all this.

♦ *V: Me, too. We're on the home stretch.*

♦**JGB:** How much time have I got?

♦ *V: Whatever it takes.*

♦**JGB:** When do you need to receive them by?

♦ *V: Just do them as soon as you comfortably can. Believe me, we will wait.*

♦**JGB:** Good. I'll write them within the next three or four days, so you should get them within a fortnight.

♦ *V: And I'll send you today a xerox of the manuscript.*

♦**JGB:** Incidentally, when will you have copies available?

♦ *V: After we send it to the press, we should have advance airmail copies in about a month to six weeks. I'll send you an advance copy immediately—*

♦**JGB:** I only mention this because last September, a New York journalist called Luc Santé—a very intelligent and likable guy—came to interview me for the *New York Times.* Now, nothing happened—the profile never came out. But about three days ago the *New York Times* called, saying that they would be running this profile and would I agree to be photographed? The photographer is coming tomorrow.

They say they will probably publish this profile in about two months' time. Now, I talked at great length to Santé about the RE/Search firm and its wonderful books and how you are doing *The Atrocity Exhibition.* It seems to me this is an opportunity to make certain that the *New York Times* piece refers to your publications. What I'll do is, the photographer who's coming to see me tomorrow has a copy of the actual article. I'll read it and—let's put it like this: if he *doesn't* mention RE/Search adequately, I will let you know. I suggest you give the *New York Times* a ring and say that "the new Ballard book, the update of *The Atrocity Exhibition,* is coming out, and how about giving us a good mention?" And I will do the same. Because it's mutual publicity.

♦ *V: That would help a great deal.*

♦**JGB:** Anyway, we'll see. Okay, Vale, it's all good stuff. I'll send you the five new annotations.

♦ *V: Oh, and of course, if you find something you want changed, regardless of what it is, don't hesitate to let me know.*

♦**JGB:** Okay, Vale, I'm looking forward to it tremendously. You'll get my stuff in about a fortnight. Give my best to Catherine—

♦ *V: Will do. Okay, cheers for now! Bye!* ♦ ♦ ♦

hero taps this feeling of emptiness that the central character, my young doctor, has felt all his life. And he becomes obsessed with this great river which he really believes is flowing from his own bloodstream . . . to the extent he believes that he cannot drown.

Anyway, he resolves to sail the river to the source, and in the company of a young African girl who attaches herself rather mysteriously, and with whom he rapidly becomes infatuated. He steals a car ferry which happens to have lashed to its deck the secondhand Mercedes of the local police chief. This crew sets sail for the source of the river, named after the central character. And this chapter is called "Out of the Night and into the Dream." It describes the scene just after they've stolen the ferry and escaped from the forces . . . [reads chapter]

So they sail upwards towards the source of the river as the landscape becomes increasingly surreal, as if the released imagination of this very repressed and disappointed man, the doctor, is at last beginning to flower like the arid sand which the river is irrigating. Delusions of grandeur begin to set in, and he feels an intense rivalry with the river, as if it challenges him in some way. And, without giving away the ending (and I hope *some of you* go on to read the book), he finds a resolution in himself in terms of this huge channel of possibility that seems to flow from his mind, and which has provoked him with its ambiguous nature, and which he finally betrays, but *wins,* I think, in the end. And right at the end he finds a kind of peace. But I hope you go on to read it, and meanwhile . . .

I'm happy to answer any questions you might ask.

♦ *Q: If the people in your Japanese prison camp in Shanghai were suffering from borderline scurvy, why not eat some of the local plants?*

♦ **JGB:** In my camp there weren't any local plants. Two thousand people were living in an area about the size of—well, there were *some* plants. The inmates grew a certain amount of what they ate. I remember my father and I—because I was unlike the boy in the book, which I'd like to make quite abundantly clear—**I was interned in the camp with my parents, and I remember my father and I growing a few tomatoes. But the soil was destitute, and the tomatoes looked like children's marbles.**

I think the people in the camp were pretty resourceful, in their ways: 2,000 people in a comparatively small area. The ground was beaten flat by their feet.

♦ *Q: Are you familiar with David Cronenberg's film,* Videodrome?

♦ **JGB:** Sadly, I haven't seen any of his movies, but I did see a full-scale documentary shown on British TV about a year ago. It made his movies look absolutely amazing . . . they're not shown on our censored television . . . Unfortunately I've not seen any of his films, but they look like genuine works of Surrealism.

♦ *Q: What were your feelings about Steven Spielberg's movie version of* Empire of the Sun?

♦ **JGB:** I was very impressed by it. I thought it a very powerful and moving film. It was remarkably faithful to the spirit of my novel, and I don't necessarily think that is a particular recommendation either way. Film *is* a different medium, but in fact it was extremely faithful to my book.

I had a number of long conversations with Spielberg during the making of the film and I was impressed by his commitment to the book—he wanted to film *the book,* not just an idea in his own head that the book generated, which as far as I can tell is the way these things work in the film business *most* of the time.

I think the film is very dark . . . quite somber. It's quite a subtle movie; it's really an art film disguised to look like an epic. That's quite a tricky mix! (And I think possibly a tricky mix for the audience, too.) It reminds me, in some respects—I said this to him, and I don't mind saying that he took everything I said with a large dose of salt—but I said that it reminded me of *Gone With the Wind!* It sounds silly, but in fact *Gone With the Wind* is another art film disguised to look like an epic. I saw it for the first time in 1945 or 1946 after the war.

Gone With the Wind is regarded as *the* quintessential epic, but in fact when you see the film it's only an epic in its opening half-hour. In fact, the film is a rather dark and downbeat study of this very determined woman's desperate fight for survival. It's downbeat in its ending. In many respects Spielberg's film of my book follows the shape of

Gone With the Wind—there are remarkable comparisons between the two, which suggests to me that perhaps it's very easy to misinterpret the Spielberg movie. I thought *Empire of the Sun* was surprisingly hard-edged.

The one thing I didn't like was the music—all those heavenly choirs! However, I recently saw *Gone with the Wind* and the first thing that struck me was the celestial choirs! And Spielberg loves those. Well, I'd love to see a black-and-white version of *Empire of the Sun*—actually, I can do this with my own TV set—and tune out the music.

So I thought *Empire of the Sun* was pretty impressive as a dark movie. It did modestly in the States, I gather, which is a shame because I think Spielberg deserves more. The film has done extremely well in Britain and Europe, possibly because people there have firsthand experience of war occupation and all that follows.

♦ *Q: Are there plans to make any of your other books into movies?*

♦ **JGB:** There are a lot of lunches going on! . . . The trouble is, enthusiasms in the film world tend to last about as long as a lunch! But I keep my fingers crossed. There's a '70s novel of mine called *Crash* which has been optioned a lot of times. This seems to be getting somewhere near pre-production (or whatever you call it). There's a young American director called Mark Romanek who made a film that some people say is good, *Static.* I don't know if anyone's seen it—I haven't, but he apparently is an upcoming talent and he seems to be interested in *Crash.* But again, I have no idea if anything will happen.

♦ *Q: Are you going to appear in that one, too?*

♦ **JGB:** Well, I'd like to drive the *car!* [laughter]

♦ *Q: What's the difference between fiction and Science Fiction?*

♦ **JGB: The difference between writing Science Fiction and more traditional fiction? Publishing labels stick, and are almost impossible to take off.** I began writing Science Fiction back in the late '50s and '60s, but really *since* the late '60s I've written very little straight SF—almost none. My '70s novels like *Crash,* **High-Rise** and so forth are not SF—you really have to stretch the definition of "Science Fiction" to call something like *Crash* an SF novel! But I don't *mind* if a book like that is thought of as Science Fiction.

I think of myself as an imaginative writer who's interested in the world around him. I've always been intensely interested in the elements of change in the everyday landscape, and these elements of change are brought about by science and technology. **It seems we almost live inside of an enormous novel, thanks to the media landscape which has now locked itself around our planet.**

In many respects that novel we live inside is a Science-Fiction novel. And it's very difficult to write truthfully about the present day without including elements that are thought of as belonging to the realm of Science Fiction. And it's interesting that many so-called mainstream writers today have written straight Science-Fiction novels—Anthony Burgess, Doris Lessing . . .

Awhile ago I was in conversation with the literary editor of the *Sunday Times* newspaper in England, and I said to her that **Doris Lessing has written more Science-Fiction novels than I have.** She thought I was joking. But Lessing has written something like seven of them, which is more than I can say. Lessing, Burgess . . . **Thomas Pynchon has always included large elements of the scientific imagination in his writing.** There are also other writers—Calvino, even Borges—some of his short stories seem very close to the sort of imagination you find in speculative SF.

There's almost the beginnings of a new mainstream emerging which is non-realist. I think realist fiction has shot its bolt—it just doesn't describe the world we live in anymore. We're not living in a world where you can make a clear separation (as you could, say, during the heyday of the 19th-century realist novel) between the external world of work, commerce, industry, and a fixed set of values, and the internal world of hopes, dreams and ambitions. It's the other way around—**the external world is a fantasy nowadays. It's a media landscape generated by advertising, and politics conducted as a branch of advertising.** [laughter]

There's an envelope of fantasy that is just *pouring* out of the air all the time, shaping all of our most ordinary perceptions: friendships, the way we furnish our homes, what we think of as the "right" way to live and go on holiday, and so on. I mean, our impressions, say, of what the medical profession is about . . . Speaking as somebody who studied medicine for a couple of years and who remains friendly with numerous doctors of my own age, the public's perception of the medical profession (I can't speak for America, but it's certainly true of Britain) is a complete *fiction* created in part by the profession itself, and partly by our own needs which the mass media work for on our behalf.

Fiction surrounds us—it's more than fiction, it's fantasy of a very peculiar kind that creates our environment. And to describe it, you've got to get away from pure realism. Yet the bourgeois novel survives and of course it's immensely popular—which is a bit of a *problem.* [laughter] The realist tradition survives in the popular novel . . . well, fair enough.

♦ *Q: Have you continued to do more experimental writings like* The Atrocity Exhibition *and "Notes Towards a Nervous Breakdown"? Also, in* High Rise, Crash, *and* Myths Of The Near Future *there seems to be a protagonist, an antagonist and a couple of women in fairly passive roles to be fought over (or not fought over), against a background of a natural or very unnatural disaster. Can you comment on this observation? Do you think it's valid or not?*

♦ **JGB:** Sounds like an interesting writer you're talking about! [laughter] Yeah, I think what you are saying is pretty accurate. I don't know whether you could say *Crash, High Rise,* and *Myths of the Near Future* are really the same story told over and over again. *Crash* is a pretty— I don't know if it's any good or not—it's a *one-off.* [laughter] I haven't read it since I wrote it, and looking back, I take for granted that it's a deeply perverted and psychopathic work! I mean that seriously. I also think it's my best book! Solve that paradox how you will, but I don't think I've *repeated* myself . . .

♦ *Q: I didn't mean to imply—*

♦ **JGB:** If you mean the fictional formulas I used, you could say that about almost any writer you care to name. Far greater writers than me have used rather limited formulas.

♦ *Q: I didn't mean that in a negative way. I found the repetition being used in the same way as minimalism is being used in music. In other words, these forms are repeated over and over again and they are familiar, but then you change things slightly—*

♦ **JGB:** Yes, that's true—I do that. I pursue my own obsessions and obviously I'm limited by the gamut of my own obsessions. I mean, there are large numbers of things I'm *not* interested in. I am not a Balzac. I'm not interested in everything that the local butcher, baker and candlestick-maker get up to. I know; it's a weakness. I accept that I write a special type of fiction, but I do my best within *that category.* I do rework—it's not so much that I rework my obsessions, because they're constantly changing, but I follow them with as much loyalty as I can muster. And if a particular obsession begins to emerge in my mind, I *follow* it wherever it leads me.

If I seem to use the same narrative formulas—I'm not sure if I *do,* actually! It may be that my vision of the world is largely fixed—*that* I *do* see. **I accept the Surrealist formula: the need to place the logic of the visible at the service of the invisible, to remake the world around us by the power of one's imagination, which after all is all we've got.** I mean, **the central nervous system is faced with a world of Marriott hotels and ex-actors turned world leaders**, [laughter] dangerous medicines and you name it. The individual central nervous system can only attempt to make sense of this. So I follow the limits of my own abilities.

♦ *Q: Didn't you write* Hello America *without ever having been here?*

♦ **JGB:** That's not true—that's a myth! I've never been in San Francisco before, but I visited the States when I was 8 or 9 years old, before the Second World War with my parents. I spent about a year in Canada in the mid-fifties, and made a number of visits across the border. What I'd never done until last December was—thanks to Steven Spielberg—visit either Los Angeles or New York, which in their different ways are regarded as the only cities worth going to. So the myth grew that I'd never been to the States because I hadn't visited *those* cities. But I had been here before. I hope that answers your question—

♦ *Q: As a New Yorker, I think you're right!*

♦ **JGB:** I can see that. My impression is that compared with Los

Photo: SM Gray

Angeles, New York is a European city. There's a more serious point: America has been so successful, in broadcasting to the world for the last 60, 70, 80 years, an image of itself that is largely accurate, so that when you come to the States for the first time, you're not surprised by it. It's not like your first visit to, say, France, which is after all only 25 miles from the south coast of Britain, and yet is a *genuinely* strange country. [laughter] **I've been going to France almost every year for the past 40 years and I continue to find it strange.**

I went to Los Angeles for the very first time in December of last year. I had never been there before. I was picked up at the airport by a driver in a stretch limo who said, "Hi! I'm Sam!" So we're cruising down Santa Monica boulevard and he said, "What are you doing here?" I said, "I'm involved with this Spielberg," and he said, "Oh, I've written a lot of movie scripts. I do a bit of investment counseling, and I'm a karate instructor." [laughter] And I thought, "That's wonderful! This can only be Los Angeles." It could only be America, perhaps.

I looked around and saw this city which was one of the great mythic cities of the 20th century, and the fount of—**most of the 20th century's dreams had emerged from the landscape around me** as I was going down this big avenue from the airport. And nothing about it was unfamiliar. It was 1000 episodes of the *Rockford Files,* and so on. Hundreds of feature films had identified it with absolute exactness. There was only one thing that was wrong—just one thing—and that was: suddenly I saw this huge billboard the size of a tennis court with "Steven Spielberg's *EMPIRE OF THE SUN"* with *my* name, and I thought, "This shouldn't be happening!" I drove on a bit more and there was *another* one of these things. Anyway, I got to the hotel, switched on the TV and out came this high-powered commercial for the movie. I opened up the newspaper: full-page ads.

I looked up in the Beverly Hilton hotel and it was like a Science-Fiction film from the '50s: A monster has gotten out of control from this mad doctor's mind and it's crawling across the rooftops of L.A. The ironies of all this weren't lost on me, I can assure you. By and large the States have presented its image more accurately. I mean, when you think of the certain image that Britain, for example, purveyed to the world, which is, you know, beef and toast, the Tower of London guides, and I don't know what the image is . . . broken-down Jags by the wayside or whatever? I mean, the image is ludicrously out-of-kilter with reality. But not in the case of the States.

♦ *Q: Describe your first encounter with Surrealism—*

♦ **JGB:** First encounter with Surrealism? I came to England in 1946 when I was sixteen. At that point I knew nothing about the Surrealists. Within about two years (this is just after the Second World War) I became intensely interested in them—I must have seen illustrations. I don't know; it's very difficult to remember how I did. In England—I can't speak for the States, but in England, until really the late '60s, the Surrealists were completely—I wouldn't say out of fashion—but they were looked down upon as bizarre purveyors of the lurid and perverse. **No reputable art critic would even *go* to an exhibition of Surrealist paintings.**

Even in the '60s I used to go to exhibitions held in London in sort of second-rate galleries, of works by Delvaux, Ernst, even Dali. I remember new Magrittes selling for about 500-600 pounds—about a thousand dollars each—paintings which are now sold for two to three hundred thousand dollars. The only place in the late '40s and '50s where you were likely to see a reproduction of a Surrealist painting was in the popular tabloid newspapers, where the latest Dali outrage would be illustrated.

Something clicked. I think the Surrealist formula tapped something within my own experiences in Shanghai and China before and during the Second World War, when Shanghai itself was a kind of Surrealist landscape in which all of the malevolent elements of the unconscious were made manifest in this bizarre city. When I came to England, I set about as a Science-Fiction writer using the techniques of Surrealism to remake contemporary Western Europe (and the United States, by proxy) into something consonant with the landscapes of wartime Shanghai. I assume that explains everything!

♦ *Q: What's your own internal perception of your obsessions, after you write about them (as opposed to before)? Is it therapeutic in any way?*

♦ **JGB:** Do I feel better for it? I know that if I don't write—a lot of writers will say this and it's true . . . **if I don't write for a couple weeks, say, while I'm on holiday, I begin to feel edgy in a way that people are supposed to feel if they're not allowed to *dream*.** I've always assumed that for the imaginative writer, the exercise of the imagination is a sort of necessary part of the way the central nervous system functions. This separates the imaginative writer from the realistic, naturalistic writer in a very important sense.

It's rather like—we've all met *actors* who seem to need to act all the time—that is, every little gesture: drinking a glass of water, picking up a book, is sort of stressed and exaggerated in some curious way—even if nobody's present, they do it! It's as if their sense of themselves is not fulfilled until they have done everything twice.

I think the imaginative writer is doing exactly the same thing. It seems as if the imaginative writer's nervous system needs to run a continuous series of *updates* on the perception of reality. And just sort of *living* **isn't enough—one feels one needs to *remake* reality in order for it to be meaningful.**

Long before I've finished a novel, I've lost interest in it and I'm already thinking about the next one . . . because the main work is probably done before the book is even started, before the first word is written. A certain amount of *hard work* goes into writing a book: one has to invent the situation, the characters, the narrative, the story. One has to *embody* the sort of half-formed obsessions, images, whatever you want to call them . . . one has to *dramatize* all this material. **I think the difference between the serious successful writer and the unsuccessful writer lies just in *the ability to dramatize*—**to put flesh on the bones. But *I* don't feel any better for it! [laughter]

♦ ***Q:*** *About* High-Rise: *by having the women rise to the rooftop . . . was that a token attempt to be "feminist"?*

♦ **JGB:** Nobody's accused me! All the women I've known regard me as "totally unreconstructed"! When I begin to write a novel, I have a *general idea*—as in this new novel: a man invents a river and then sails up it. This would apply to *High-Rise:* I had a vague feeling for the overall formula. Individual episodes like the women on the roof—

♦ *Q: The wife was counting on making her appearance at the end, on the top of the roof—*

♦ **JGB:** Well, that seemed like justice. It seemed to be just, fair—imaginatively speaking—that this woman who had been downtrodden should assert herself at the end. Because, as we all know, women have immense resources of courage, cruelty, [laughter] justice . . .

♦ *Q: What do you think of AIDS and "the new model of sexuality based upon non-exchange of fluids"? For instance, I saw this magazine from Brazil and it showed this Aryan-looking couple wrapped in plastic bags, supposedly having sex together. Another time I was in a video booth and there was anal sex between two men—they wore rubbers. This was safe sex; whatever. Do you think there's a new model of sexuality operating here? [laughter]*

Photo: Tim Chapman

♦ **JGB:** Please read my next book! **AIDS is fearsome—let's not joke about it. It's almost like a kind of Science-Fiction disease.** It's like a disease invented by a malevolent deity who's read too much Science Fiction! As for me, at my age I don't know *what's* going on these days. I drink whiskey-and-soda and watch TV. I mean, *you* tell me what's happening!

♦ *Q: I can't; it's too close to me.*

♦ *Q: Have any of your works been adapted to the stage? Do you have any interest in seeing them made into operas?*

♦ **JGB:** Operas?! Oddly enough, there have been one or two musicians who said they would be interested in adapting a book of my short stories set in a kind of imaginary desert resort: *Vermilion Sands,* in which there are a lot of avant-garde experimental art forms—sculptures that sing; this sort of thing. This must have set the imaginations of these musicians working, but nothing has ever come of it.

What we call the stage theater in this country doesn't hold much appeal to me. It sounds like a bad pun, but it's too "stagey" for me! I'm a product of a movie-going generation. I reached adolescence during the heyday of the movies. All those movies this generation rhapsodizes about: all the so-called *film noirs;* all the great Bogeys and Cagneys—I saw when they first came out, and *they* are what shaped my young imagination.

The theater is something I came to in England and it seemed to be full of people with weird British accents—like *mine,* now [laughter]—over-acting all the time! If you subtract the works of Shakespeare (who's the greatest literary genius who has ever been), the world canon of great plays, certainly in the English language—what is there? I could name you a hundred great English and American novels from the last three centuries. But what plays could I name? Wilde's *The Importance Of Being Earnest,* and precious little else! I think the conventions of the stage drama are too limiting: they're just people talking all the time! I'm a philistine, by the way. [applause] ♦ ♦ ♦

JGB, V Vale & Catherine Reuther

V. Vale and J. G. Ballard, RE/Search headquarters, May 6, 1988

♦ **J.G. BALLARD:** [talking, while in V. Vale's Volkswagen Beetle] My daughter's VW was about ten years old when she bought one, and it lasted another six or seven years.

♦ *CATHERINE REUTHER: Well, Vale's car is a '59!*

♦ **JGB:** Drive safely!

♦ *VALE: Wow, so you've already visited three cities: New York, Miami, and Chicago—*

♦ **JGB:** Yeah. Miami is a major intellectual center, I'm telling you. I did a book reading there and it was like tonight [full crowd]. I thought it would be nothing but retired Long Island dentists, but there were a lot of hip young people who knew my stuff. I was amazed!

I was out-of-print throughout the '70s until Vale sort of reinvented me for America. I'm staggered!

♦ *V: Whoever reissued those English editions did a nice design job on the covers. They're striking!*

♦ **JGB:** As a format that designer came up with an original idea.

♦ *V: All the reissues are linked together by the design.*

♦ **JGB:** How's **Mark Pauline**? He came to see me about a year ago. Somebody came to see me who said she was a friend of yours—or maybe she made it up. It was only about ten days ago. A young sculptress called Barbara Chestnut. She wrote to me about a year ago, and then came and saw me in Shepperton. She seemed very sweet.

It's been an amazing tour. I discovered Miami beach. It's just incredible—it's my spiritual home! All those Art Deco hotels in ice cream colors, all those condominiums with gangsters—it's paradise! You just need one of those private airstrips. Los Angeles is a teeny bit on the tacky side. It's really quite a tacky town. I think Los Angeles is the capital of the Third World. **Miami Beach is my idea of what Hollywood *ought* to be like.**

♦ *V: It's too bad you didn't get to go north and see the Space Center—*

♦ **JGB**: I didn't get that far north. I did a reading at a place called Coral Gables. It wasn't a town but a district of South Miami. Very nice. On the way we passed hundreds of Banyan trees. Have you ever seen a Banyan tree? These are vast, with multiple trunks. I've seen them in Southeast Asia a long time ago. They're 20 or 30 feet wide; they're like great elephants by the side of the road.

Chicago was nice. **Quite a tough town, Chicago. Fanatical fans hopped up on speed or acid or something—one fan shook my hand so fiercely that it bled!** Somebody came next and said, "Could you sign this copy of *Crash?*" My hand was bleeding; I said, "Should I do it in my own blood?" So I did.

♦ *V: That's Ballardian, almost.*

♦ **JGB:** He squeezed my hand so fiercely that this finger squirted blood. He was highly agitated. When I left afterwards he was screaming from the side of the road, "Mr Ballard!" The woman who was chaperoning me around got me rapidly into the car and locked the door. But what next? If somebody who *likes* you shakes your hand and draws blood, what happens in Chicago if they *don't* like you?! I wouldn't like to live there. San Francisco, however, is really nice.

How is *Pranks* doing? It's a wonderful, marvelous book. It's much more than a book about practical jokes—it's *profoundly* subversive, because it's a whole new way of looking at reality. It's amazing. The guy who did the "Cathouse for Dogs"—

♦ *V: Oh yes, Joey Skaggs*—

♦ **JGB:** That man is a conceptual genius! The idea of taking all these hippies to Long Island and to these bourgeois upper-class parties—he drove these Long Island residents crazy. It's so brilliant. It's a wonderful book, beautifully designed.

♦ *V: We saw an interview with your daughter*—

♦ **JGB:** The one in the *Sunday Times?* That was sweet of her, very loving. How did you come across that?

♦ *V: It was sent to me. I'd love to catch up on all your interviews. You mentioned a movie I'd never heard of, which you singled out along with* Blue Velvet *and* Blood Simple. *It was called* Raising Arizona—

♦ **JGB:** That was made by the Coen brothers, who made *Blood Simple.* They made *Raising Arizona* which was shown in England about 7 or 8 months ago. It was their follow-up film to *Blood Simple*—no question about that—because they were interviewed in England about it.

♦ *V: Everyone we know likes* Blue Velvet. *I love those little film reviews you wrote for* American Film *magazine.* **We had a fantasy of having you do a reading, and then showing** When Dinosaurs Walked the Earth*, which you wrote the screenplay for*—

♦ **JGB: Oh, I *hate* that film!**

♦ *V: Then I'm glad we didn't do it! We haven't seen it yet*—

♦ **JGB:** Oh, don't ever! Maybe I'll buy up the only surviving print! That was a terrible film—it's the worst film ever made. I really think that.

♦ *V: It would be nice if you could go see Mark Pauline's shop if you have a chance. It's an original experience*—

♦ *CR: Things are really hopping there right now, too. This is a good time to swing by.*

♦ **JGB:** It looks like a kind of converted factory or something, doesn't it? This girl Barbara Chestnut who came to see me a couple weeks ago said that it was very, very strange. She said Mark spent his time hammering nails into bottles of gasoline or something—

♦ **CR:** *He makes these incredible machines. They are really genius engineering feats, besides being so imaginative—*

♦ **JGB:** It sounds like he's about to break through into real success.

♦ **CR: *He's going to do a show in New York on the theme of what "paradise" means to people.*** *I have a print shop and he asked me to make 14,000 pieces of $100, $50, and $20 bills to put into bombs. The bombs will be detonated and then money will explode all over the audience—*

♦ **JGB:** It sounds wonderful!

♦ **V:** *Yeah, but those bombs can be dangerously real—*

♦ **JGB:** Did he hurt his hand?

♦ **CR:** *He definitely blew off his hand.*

♦ **JGB:** I'm sorry about that. There's some wonderful surgery that they've done; he's got the use of a kind of thumb, hasn't he?

♦ **V:** *Yes. You* should *see his place. He has this absolutely enormous portrait of you right above his bed—it's one that I had made. In 1984 at Fort Mason, when our* RE/Search #8/9: J.G. Ballard *issue came out, we had this show in honor of you, called "The Crash! Show." And we had these huge photo blow-ups made, including a photograph of you.*

You know, I heard traffic was all blocked today because someone tried to jump off the bridge—

♦ **JGB:** What bridge are we on?

♦ **V:** *This is the Bay Bridge.*

♦ **CR:** *This isn't the bridge people traditionally jump off. On the Golden Gate Bridge, people jump off all the time and there's never a traffic jam—*

♦ **V:** *They don't even notice. On this bridge, you have to* drive *to commit suicide—*

♦ **CR:** *There was this horrible story I remember reading about a Doberman pinscher that got stuck on this bridge. It was so terrified by the traffic that it finally just jumped off.*

♦ **JGB:** Is it a long way down?

♦ **CR:** *Yes.*

♦ **V:** *That was such a brilliant idea when you had those Delvaux paintings*

recreated—

♦ **JGB:** I wish he had destroyed *more* paintings! . . . so I could have them reproduced. Actually, there are about six that were destroyed during the Second World War, but the others are not very good.

♦ *CR: I wish you were here longer*—

♦ **JGB:** So do I!

♦ *CR: We know a lot of interesting places to take you to*—

♦ **JGB: One has the illusion you've seen a place in fact when you haven't seen it at all. All you've seen are the airports and the hotels**—

♦ *CR: And a lot of books to sign!*

♦ **JGB:** I don't mind doing that; it's okay. They're the audience. It's a wonderful crowd. I've never seen such a crowd.

♦ *V: We're coming to Fremont Street, an exciting exit. You're going 50mph and all of a sudden you have to go 10mph to survive. You make a complete circle here.*

♦ *CR: He's used to British driving. You have to be an expert driver to survive in England. I love it, though—everybody understands the rules*—

♦ **JGB:** There *are* no rules!

♦ *CR: People are good drivers there. My mother's English and I spent a lot of time there and I'm really impressed.*

♦ **JGB:** I disagree 100 percent. I rented a car in Los Angeles. I'd never driven in America before, and I spent a whole day driving. I thought American drivers in Los Angeles were very leisurely, sensible, mature, adult. It was the easiest place for a visitor to drive in—no *harum-scarum* driving! By comparison, Italy, France and England are madhouses.

♦ *CR: But England—I love it. You're on the motorway and nobody is in the fast lane unless they are going much faster than anybody else*—

♦ **JGB:** In that way they're okay. But ordinary roads are dangerous there. It took me awhile to work out in L.A. why everybody was so sort of *relaxed*. The reason, of course, is that all the cars have automatic transmissions. The average English driver with a stick shift is sitting there with the engine revving fast, his foot slipping off the clutch. The lights just change from red to amber and *vroom!* The thing about an automatic transmission, with those heavy cars, the automatic transmission stops you from misbehaving. Everyone pulls away slowly like great *tugboats*...

Italy is ridiculous; that's a fiendish place. **I'll tell you the most dangerous place of all: Greece. *Never* go driving in Greece!** Greece is the only place where I have actually seen accidents occurring: cars actually crashing into each other, like sort of dodge-em tracks. What do you call those here?

♦ ***V/CR:*** *Bumper Cars!*

♦ **JGB:** Cars crash but nobody gets out and complains. They just carry on.

♦ ***CR:*** *But in Spain they do get out and complain; they start pounding on windows. People are always rolling up windows as soon as they bash into somebody.*

♦ **JGB:** I was once near the American Express offices in Athens, going very slowly. At an intersection I saw this teenage boy looking at me, and I knew exactly what he was going to do. And **I actually *stopped* my car and I was stationary, and he came up and threw himself against my car. He *wanted* to make a collision!** It was quite weird.

♦ ***V:*** *Wow!*

♦ **JGB:** They're crazy there. L.A. drivers, I think, are cool, relaxed and mature.

♦ ***CR:*** *They have to be—they spend half their day driving.*

♦ **JGB:** Everything is so spaced out. They have to drive safely.

♦ ***CR:*** *That's their life. Driving is a way of life there.*

♦ **JGB:** It's a very strange city. I've got a soft spot for mysterious long highways reaching out forever. It's unique in that the casual visitor has no sense of the city's topography—a sense of the terrain which you get in most cities after a couple of days. Los Angeles seems infinite, and it's open-ended.

♦ ***CR:*** *Are you still a pilot?*

♦ **JGB:** No. Drop me off at a nearby point. You don't need to go to the hotel as long as I can see where it is.

There's no tricky one-way systems here? London is fiendish; once you get into a one-way system with no right turns, no left turns, you could go on forever. Very irritating. **I think it's a device to prevent people moving their cars around in the event of *civil insurrection*. They prevent people from the East End of London, where they're poor, coming west! I think it's designed to thwart revolution.**

Oh goodness, this is sweet of you. [J.G. Ballard exits car.]♦ ♦ ♦

J.G. Ballard after Dark Carnival

V Vale and RE/Search Assistant Editor Catherine Reuther gave J.G. Ballard a ride to RE/Search headquarters in San Francisco after the Dark Carnival book signing Sunday noon, Berkeley, May 8, 1988.

♦ **JGB: After signing dozens of books at a book signing, you start having to work hard at remembering *who you are.*** Just try, experimentally, writing a word—*any* word—over and over and over. Deterioration sets in.

♦ *V: How was yesterday?*

♦ **JGB:** I did a reading in Palo Alto at Printer's Ink, and then at Books Inc. in San Jose, at a big shopping mall. The reading at Black Oak Friday night—there must have been two hundred people there; there were a hundred people in the *overflow.* Well, I think I owe Vale—your RE/Search Publications may have saved my life . . . You and Steven Spielberg!

♦ *V: I noticed that the publicity for* Empire of the Sun *featured* you. *A lot of times the authors are barely mentioned—*

♦ **JGB:** That was a deliberate decision by Spielberg. He wanted to identify the film as an autobiographic statement. Warners pitched the whole publicity campaign, in large part, around that fact. Spielberg doesn't like giving interviews, and there were no big stars in the film. They only had the 13-year-old boy, and there was me.

There was a promotional film made on the making of *Empire of the Sun*. They showed photographs taken in Shanghai, 1939-1940, of Japanese soldiers, and then showed these photos merging into exactly the same scenes in the film—it sprang to life.

♦ *V: I can't wait until* Empire of the Sun *comes out on video, so I can watch it and get rid of the music—*

♦ **JGB:** The music was terrible.

♦ *V: It introduces a sentimentality that you never have in your work.*

♦ **JGB:** It's a shame about the music.

♦ *V: We rented* Raising Arizona *which you recommended. It's very cinematic, following those Doberman pinschers along those grocery store aisles . . . the tracking shots were great. Such an unlikely premise for a film.*

We're looking for Silent Running, *another one you recommended—*

♦ **JGB:** With Bruce Dern. That's quite a moving film.

♦ *V: It's strange: we read that some people dug up these 8,000-year-old corpses that have been preserved in a Florida peat bog and their DNA is still alive!*

♦ **JGB:** I saw that in the paper.

♦ *V: You'd think they'd be able to clone someone from that someday.*

♦ **JGB:** They probably will one day—that's the amazing thing. That'll happen probably long after I'm gone, but maybe you people will see it. I'm certain that will happen.

♦ *CR: They patented a new life form in a laboratory—I suppose you read about that.*

♦ **JGB: Somebody has patented a new kind of laboratory rat. It's amazing: you can get a patent on this *living creature!*** Maybe you can patent a certain kind of young man—Neiman-Marcus will be able to supply you with a certain kind of "toy boy" for only $200,000! Or, Playboy Industries will supply you with a certain kind of playmate—

♦ *V: A Neiman-Marcus catalog was selling for $5,000 a special breed of cat they had invented, which simulated a wild cat—"only available from*

Neiman-Marcus"!

♦ **JGB:** That's wonderful.

♦ *CR: They're working on humans; it's just not legal yet.*

♦ **JGB:** It'll happen. You'll get designer human beings. They'll begin by eradicating tendencies toward hemophilia or sickle cell anemia—they'll eliminate those, and that will be a very good thing. Then they'll move on, upgrading intelligence, and then certain physical attributes like desirable big breasts. This will come in by the back door, because first they'll get wider-hipped women to minimize birth problems. This will produce nice big bottoms, and they'll have to have nice big breasts to go with them. And the rationale will be, of course: better milk production—natural feeding for children, right? Then they'll move on to psychological qualities—tinker with the DNA, with certain segments of genes, and you'll tend to get better mothers—warmer and more caring mothers. Before they know it, they'll have a new kind of human being moving around on the planet, and it'll all be done for the most enlightened reasons, because that's the future.

The crimes of the future will be done for the most enlightened reasons—that's the really frightening thing. As long as the crimes of this planet were committed by people whom everyone recognized to be beyond the moral pale, we were safe. But **when the crimes are committed by the most high-minded people for the best reasons, you have no defense, have you? That's the *real* threat. And that will come.**

♦ *V: We just saw an old '60s episode of* Star Trek *where everybody's dressed in Nazi uniforms. You have Spock saying, "This* was *the most interesting social experiment of the twentieth century."*

♦ *CR: He even used the word "utopian."*

♦ *V: And in a certain sense it was. It was the Nazis who invented the Volkswagen—they wanted everyone to have an affordable, durable, easily repairable car.*

♦ **JGB:** Porsche designed the Volkswagen for Hitler in something like 1933 or 1934. The first VW was produced before WWII.

♦ *V: **We recently met the person who founded the Church of Satan*** *in San Francisco in 1966. He has an amazing library.*

♦ **CR:** *He's a musician, knows a lot about films, animals—he was in the circus. He was working on a script with Marilyn Monroe back in the early Fifties. He was a crime photographer—*

♦ **V:** *He has thousands of negatives from those days. He said the whole of San Francisco is like an invisible grid for him, where all these murders took place that he photographed.*

♦ **JGB** Is that the Golden Gate Bridge?

♦ **V:** *Yes, the suicide bridge.*

Photo: Charles Gatewood

♦ **JGB:** Do people swim in there?

♦ *CR: Yes, people swim in the Bay and swim to Alcatraz. But the problem is, the currents are very, very strong—it's very dangerous.*

♦ **JGB:** There are sharks?

♦ *CR: Well, they don't usually come into the Bay. They say that **underneath the Golden Gate Bridge the currents are so strong that it's possible to get broken bones** just from that. Surfers go there.*

♦ **JGB:** This is nothing like Los Angeles.

♦ *V: San Francisco is more like a real city; you don't necessarily need a car to get around. North Beach is where the Beat Generation started, and my building is where Odetta, the black folk singer, and the black actor Paul Robeson lived—he was in* The Emperor Jones. *The rents are now twenty times what they were in the Beatnik days. We interviewed someone who used to live here during the Fifties. His North Beach apartment used to be $35 a month, and now it's $750.*

♦ **JGB:** That's happening all over. Every area that artists live in becomes expensive: Chelsea in London, and the Left Bank in Paris.

♦ *V: How about where you live, in Shepperton?*

♦ **JGB:** Ah, that's a different kettle of fish—that's a small town. Property costs are gigantic. My little house—I live in a tiny little house in a classic old lower-middle-class housing tract built in the 1930s, and it originally sold for about 750 pounds—a thousand dollars. Now they are selling for—well, mine is a bit rundown—but the houses to the side are selling for 100,000 pounds. [JGB takes photo]

I have to bring back some photos for my girlfriend.

♦ *V: You've had a long-term relationship—*

♦ **JGB:** Yes, well, she's in your book, in one of the first of my ads. I've known her over 22 years. Oh, there's **City Lights Books—that's a nice-looking shop. It's the most famous bookshop in America as far as Europe is concerned. It's the only bookstore anyone in Europe or Britain has ever heard of**—City Lights, because of Ginsberg and Co. The Counterculture began there. [JGB takes photo]

This is a nice area. I can see the boutiques moving in and the rents going up. It's nice around here.

♦ *V: This area used to be swarming with "Beatniks."*

♦ *CR: It was very Italian and now it's more Chinese-influenced.*

♦ **JGB:** It looks nice. Did they shoot the car chase in *Bullitt* here, or was that somewhere else?

♦ *V: They shot footage on Union Street over to the left. They started out trying to shoot the film in Los Angeles, but it didn't work. Here's the RE/Search typesetting office. I want to take a photo of you outside our window.*

♦ **JGB: Let me get a photo of you here. Say "Whiskey"!** [various photos are taken] This is a historic moment. My girlfriend will be thrilled. I'm proud to be here. I do believe Vale turned a corner for me—nobody knew about me in America. This is quite a chic set-up.

♦ *V: A friend, Peter McCandless, painted the place for free. But because of the rise of desktop publishing on the small personal computer, I think the days of typesetting are numbered—*

♦ **JGB:** It looks very, very successful. My girlfriend works for a company that's associated with Lloyds Underwriting Insurance Firm. It's a very big firm; it employs 3,000 people. They have a huge volume of printing, and it's all done internally now, with desktop printing. They no longer send work out to be printed. She's senior press officer/publicity manager, so she's responsible for a large segment of their commercial work, and it's all done in-house now. [Everyone gets into the VW and drives to the parking lot on Romolo Place.] ♦ ♦ ♦

May 8, 1988

J.G. Ballard relaxes at RE/Search headquarters in San Francisco before his book signing at City Lights Bookstore on Sunday, May 8, 1988 at 4pm. Present were V. Vale and Catherine Reuther. Here J.G. Ballard reveals his love for cats.

♦ **J.G. BALLARD:** I'm practically a zombie—can I take off my jacket?

♦ *VALE: Catherine brought this whiskey for you—*

♦ **JGB:** That looks like a rare single malt, isn't it? It would be a pity to put water in *that.*

♦ ***CATHERINE REUTHER:*** *Drink this—this is on me, okay? This is for you!*

♦ **JGB:** If you don't mind me drinking this with water in it—give me a *big* glass! Some people are so bloody fussy—*that's* more like it! I'll be so drunk when I get to City Lights! Joyce, the very nice young woman who's been chaperoning me around, is terrified I'm going to start running around getting drunk or—

♦ *CR: She's the wife of the guy who owns Cody's. She was embarrassed that they don't carry our* RE/Search #8/9: J.G. Ballard—*she said she'd make sure it's always in stock.*

♦ **JGB:** This trip has been wonderful, but it's a real strain. It's been an amazing trip. So compressed. This is the fourth city, and tonight it's Seattle. Back to New York on Wednesday, and then London. It's been incredible—Miami, and Chicago. The first 5 days I had flights on all but one. Sunday, Tuesday, Wednesday, Thursday—they were all flights. Readings, signings, and handshakes—it's been terrific. *Instant America,* you know! Miami, I thought, was terrific—I loved it. I mean, *this* is a civilized place—not compared with Miami, because Miami's quite civilized, but compared with L.A.

Los Angeles is the capital of the Third World, I've decided. It's a real frontier town, psychologically and literally. My theory is that the U.S./Mexico border roughly follows Wilshire Boulevard. Once you go south of there, it's where they say, "Keep your buttons down and wind your windows up."

How's Mark Pauline? Ready to start blowing up the world? Good for him. My theory is: when he gets to Eastern Europe to do a performance (or close to there), he's going to start World War III! All those Russians dozing by their tanks on the Eastern border will suddenly spring into life and start rolling westward. He's an amazing character. I liked him very, very much. I thought he was a terrific character.

[Ballard tries, with difficulty, to photograph the resident Korat cats—

he forgot to remove the lens cap, the flash doesn't work, the batteries seem dead, etc.] These are interesting cats. What's their temperament like? Like Siamese or Abyssinians? One of my girlfriends—one of my girlfriend's *cats* [laughs] . . . you see, the batteries aren't working anymore, the lights aren't coming on, I'm forgetting to wind the . . . one of my cats is a tabby which is actually half Abyssinian—it's incredibly sensitive; it's like a dog.

That is a lovely Scotch . . .

For this new book of mine [*The Day of Creation*] I did a mini-Canadian tour, but in fact it wasn't that "mini." I did five days in Toronto, a couple days in Vancouver . . . a two-city tour, but it was hectic. That was in October. Then in December I did Los Angeles and New York for the movie [*Empire of the Sun*]. Now, I'm on this tour.

I thought the movie of *Empire of the Sun* was terrific. It didn't do all that well in the States. But it has done tremendously well in Britain and in Europe—I think they *forgive* Spielberg for being a success! But my impression is . . . when I was in Los Angeles doing quite a lot of interviews there, I was quite surprised by the hostility that the L.A. critics felt toward him—it was quite open. The people who came to interview me, two or three days before the premiere, from the leading L.A. papers, were quite openly hostile to him. Some of them hadn't *seen* the film, but they were writing it off as "this is not a book for him"—as if he shouldn't be allowed to "grow up." For them, he must *always* make his sentimental Disney kids' movies, and shouldn't be given the chance to make an adult film.

I thought the film was great, actually. Oh, I've got reservations about it . . . I thought the music was over-the-top. The celestial choirs drive me frantic. And there's a slight . . . I mean, Spielberg's style is a little *sweet*. **It's as if everything is an advertisement for itself**, if you know what I mean. There's a slight sweet tendency there. But not withstanding that, I thought it was a pretty good movie—pretty hard-edged and quite dark towards the end. I liked it. I thought it was good.

♦ **V:** *Wow, this is your third publicity tour in the past six months—*

♦ **JGB: I've stopped being a writer—I'm in the PR business**

now! I can reach more people this way than by *writing* the stuff—*why bother?!* I have a direct input into their central nervous system; I can dispense with all this "writing fiction." No, it's been a terrific boost. It's brought a lot of my books here back into print, and a whole mystified new readership is discovering the delights of books like *Crash.* I get all these strange letters: "I read *Empire of the Sun* and I was very moved by it, and I've just been reading *Crash.* Can you please explain, Mr Ballard, what you were trying to *DO* in this novel?" I have to say things like, "Actually, it's a *deeply moral statement.*"

Do you remember Dean Swift's "A Modest Proposal"? Swift wrote this brilliantly clever piece suggesting that during the Irish famine, when hundreds of thousands of Irish were starving to death under the British heel, the Irish should be encouraged to eat their own babies— from the *nutritional* point of view. It's a brilliantly clever piece, ahead of its time. Of course, it's the perfect "get-off": "Oh yes, just like *A Modest Proposal,* I don't *really* want people to die in car crashes!"

All the *earnest middlebrows* have started reading my stuff and

Photo: Charles Gatewood

can't quite figure it out. They'll all leave me in due course, and I shall go back to depending on you for my readership . . .

I told Robin Straus, my agent in New York, that I'm absolutely happy with you publishing *The Atrocity Exhibition.* If you'd like to include one or two pieces that I've done—the "operations" pieces, "Mae West's Reduction Mammoplasty," and "Princess Margaret's Facelift"—they're just one-page things that I take from textbooks on plastic surgery.

I've got a classic textbook on plastic surgery in which various operations are described in detail, and where the author (who is a plastic surgeon) writes "the patient" I slot in "Princess Margaret" or "Jane Fonda" or whatever it may be in the piece. There are four of them, and I've got a new one coming out in the *Semiotext(e) Science Fiction* special number that should be out in a couple of months.

I *hardly* "write" them; I just copy them out and slot in "Jane Fonda." Where the text reads "the patient was worried about the large size of her breasts" I put in "Mae West was worried about the large size of her breasts" (or whatever it may be). They're pop art, or *pop-in* work. I thought you could add them. They're only six pages, and they could give the book a little more freshness. One was in *Tri-Quarterly,* two have been in *Ambit,* and the fourth is in the *Semiotext(e)* coming out. Also, you could add in the "Zodiac 2000" piece. Then you could say "New Complete Edition with Previously Unpublished Material." That brings this book up-to-date, in a way, because it was first published in 1971.

♦ *V: Catherine and I were comparing an early edition of* **Vermilion Sands** *with a later one, and the stories had been considerably modified. It was really exciting to see the differences—*

♦ **JGB:** Yes, I touched up those stories a teeny bit, because they were written originally for S-F magazines back in the '50s and '60s. I was writing in such a hurry that I became quite sloppy, really, at times. I tightened them up a teeny bit. But generally speaking, **I never reread my stuff—***the mistakes come off the page at you!*

I've signed a helluva lot of RE/Search books in New York, Miami,

Chicago, and in my trips around here—I've signed *hundreds* of the
RE/Search volumes. So if you've got any piled up in the garage, get 'em
out! It's a pleasure. [autographs a few copies]

My impression is that the RE/Search series, particularly the later
ones—*Pranks* and *Incredibly Strange Films*—are being recognized for
what they are, as brilliantly original. I think you're going to be profiled
in the *New York Times,* wait and see—and then you'll be seduced into
producing *The Jane Fonda Cookbook!* [laughs] Stick to your guns, don't
sell out—not that you ever would, but you know what I mean . . .

In Toronto last October, I was preceded by another writer on a book
tour who said to the Canadian publisher's public relations woman,
"You know, you *do* realize that Ballard is a *heavy drinker.* You've got to
watch this." I didn't know this, and I am not, contrary to what you may
imagine, a heavy drinker anymore. When I arrived, I had my suitcase
and a duty-free bag from Heathrow with a bottle of *Teacher's* in it, and
I saw her eyes light up. When I got to the hotel, I was exhausted after a
long flight across the Atlantic. I'm sitting in a strange city and I pour a
Scotch. We had some function that evening and I got back late, by
myself, and of course I had a Scotch.

The next morning she came to the hotel to start the day's interviews,
and I said something about "I slept well; I only needed one Scotch." She
said, "I *know;* I looked at the bottle in the bathroom." And I thought,
"She's keeping an eye on the bottle, at the *level.* Next time I'm going to
have *two* bottles!" The level on the "official" bottle will go down slowly, and then there'll be the secret bottle!

Last night Joyce said, "There's a nightclub on the top of your hotel."
I said, "Oh . . . maybe there's a *scene* going on there!" She said, "You've
got to be careful; there are these *diseases* these days"— as if I were going
to spend the night sort of *whoring away* with the hostesses!

♦ **V:** *At the recent reading, somebody did ask about AIDS, and—*

♦ **CR:** *I thought your response was really funny: "Read my next book."*

♦ **JGB:** Some strange character said something about—he was all gar-
bled up, and was in a real tangle—

♦ **V:** *He was using a real post-*Semiotext(e) *vocabulary—*

♦ **JGB:** He said something about he'd seen a picture or a film—I can't remember which—of two males, each totally enclosed in a plastic envelope, having anal intercourse, and what did I think of *this?* (What did I think of it, for heaven's sake?!) [laughs] **Give me something *simple* to answer, like, What do I think is the meaning of the universe?!**

In Chicago there was a *bizarre* character; you do come across some really spaced-out people around. I've had very intelligent, sympathetic audiences, but there was a young man in Chicago in a crowded audience who was so excited . . . this agitated character. And when the questions were called for, he was the first; he just burst out with this *torrent* of weird stuff—very sympathetic, but incomprehensible. Then when I tried to sign a book for him, he shook my hand so fiercely that he drew blood from one of my fingers (he was obviously on amphetamines or something). I noticed that as I was signing, there was blood pouring from my fingers. Somebody said, "Please sign *Crash*," and I said, "I'll do it in my own blood!" It was crazy. He was so violent—it must have been amphetamines; maybe it was cocaine—he was so hyped up, half-crazy with excitement.

Nobody's tried to crash his car into me yet, so it's been a terrific trip! Pussy, are you pregnant? I like cats . . . One of my daughters, Bea, was here recently producing a film for British television on the 49ers, a local football team. She came here twice, first on a reconnaissance trip with the director, and then with the presenter who was fronting the whole thing. They did a lot of interviews.

One of these footballers turned out to be a keen private pilot, and on some airstrip not far from here he's got a World War II British single-engine fighter, which is the fastest single-engine propeller-driven plane ever built. He's a very lucid and intelligent man; **many of these footballers *are* very bright. I know—it's only the bright ones that get interviewed!** Some of them are real thicko's—all that banging of heads together can't do your brain cells any good. But this particular one was very sympathetic and intelligent. So Bea was here twice. They filmed the big match, whatever the big match is—the big finale of the American football season.

♦ **V:** *It's called the Super-Bowl.*

♦ **JGB:** San Francisco being a big port city, is there a traditional red-light district going back to the 19th century?

♦ **V:** *It* was *here in North Beach, around Pacific Avenue.*

♦ **JGB:** Does that mean the main dockyard area was somewhere close to here?

♦ **V:** *It used to be. It died twenty or more years ago, what with this mayor named Alioto who diverted it to Oakland, allegedly enriching himself in the process.*

♦ **JGB:** All that's ended, just like in London. London was a major port, but today the great dockyard areas of London are no longer used—ships no longer ply up the Thames. **Now the great London docks are being given over to the condominiums-and-BMW set. Many of these warehouses have been demolished**, and these very expensive 500,000-pounds-and-upwards big apartments and townhouses are being built for the yuppies who work in the city of London, which just happens to be half a mile down the road.

♦ **CR:** *Very much like here.*

♦ **JGB:** So this was the "red light area"?

♦ **V:** *Yes, and in the Sixties it became famous for topless dancing.*

♦ **CR:** *It was called "The Barbary Coast" in the Gold Rush days.*

♦ **JGB:** Close to my hotel, the St. Francis, there's a theater marquee proclaiming "All Male Nude Live Show." So what exactly are they doing? Don't tell me; I don't want to know! "Live" in Europe means penetrative sex is going on onstage, but I take it *that* isn't going on here—

♦ **CR:** *Carol Doda was the most famous local stripper, known for her huge siliconic breasts, but she retired and became a nightclub vocalist. There's another area here called the Tenderloin—*

♦ **V:** *Where a few surviving prostitutes are still trying to earn a living despite AIDS—*

♦ **JGB:** —broadcasting AIDS to the world. AIDS isn't as big in London as it is over here, of course. But because of the long lead time—the incubation period is so long—everybody predicts there will be a continuous rise in the figures. But it doesn't seem to have got into the heterosexual community, yet.

Well, shared needles—for some reason there's a lot of drug abuse and sharing of needles in Scotland. The poor working-class districts are full of heroin users who are sharing needles, and AIDS is rampant among both men and women in these groups. In Glasgow and Edinburgh there are great areas of poverty. Just because of our lavish social security system, they've got people who live at home with their parents—they get about 40 pounds a week, or sixty-seventy dollars a week, so they've got enough money to cultivate a small habit. The girls go on "the game"; a woman can go on "the game" and have enough to support herself and her boyfriend. So a lot of sharing of needles goes on, and this is spreading AIDS.

In Britain, almost all the women sufferers from AIDS are either hemophiliacs who've had contaminated blood, or needle sharers. Very few heterosexual women share AIDS by normal intercourse. It's still basically a homosexual disease. There has been massive, terrifying government propaganda—these sort of *horror films* shown on TV. They've let their imaginations rip—you see these *giant icebergs* collapsing—like those Hollywood movies of the Fifties where on [billboards] you had architectural letters: "KING OF KINGS" with *crumbling letters.* There's one that shows "AIDS" crumbling, as if a cliff face ten miles high were falling on the human race. What is going on here? But they won't spout out a message. So it's not clear what the meaning is, unless you're "tuned in." [cats circle around J.G. Ballard]

♦ *CR: I have two Korat cats at my place and you can't keep them away from you.*

♦ **JGB:** They're nice cats, sleek and very handsome. You know, I'd love to see an [**SRL**] show. I've only a hazy idea—I mean I've read these various articles, but I've only got a hazy idea of what his work actually involves.

♦ *V: I could give you a videotape—*

♦ **JGB**: I think it's an incompatible standard. And I don't have a VCR! But I'm watching everything anyway on television, though we have so few channels compared with yours; we only have four channels in our nannyfied, bureaucratically-run world. But my *girlfriend* has a VCR.

♦ *V: What did you think of Los Angeles?*

♦ **JGB:** Everywhere in Los Angeles (all the hotel receptions, newspaper offices, and in New York going around to the radio and TV stations) it was just stretch limo's *all the way.* I never rode in anything else.

On the first trip my girlfriend came with me and we had to take a cab somewhere—I think we went to Rodeo Drive. There was this cab break outside the Beverly Hilton, and we got into this yellow cab which was a ten-year-old Oldsmobile with a Black driver. And everything in this car was broken: the ashtrays, the doors; the vinyl upholstery was torn and spotted with alcohol, blood—you name the bodily fluid and it was in recent occupation of the interior of this car. My girlfriend—she'd just been limo'd everywhere—said, "What *is* this?" I said, "Relax, dear; this is a cab." There was no suspension. "This is what people normally drive around in; not everybody has a stretch limo service at their beck

Photo: Tim Chapman

and call, with a social secretary pouring drinks. Keep reminding yourself of that."

The great thing about having four channels is that you know what's coming up. If you had 37 channels, you could easily miss something. Watching TV in Los Angeles and New York and now in this trip around the States, it's very difficult. Obviously if you live here in one location, you get the hang of what there is to watch. But it's just a blur, because there's so many ads, and there's no sort of *shape*. But it's a wonderful array.

I like the public access channels which I saw in New York. There was this small group of two or three people in a very modest set who were explaining how wine should be served. They knew all about it, and how certain wines should be kept at certain temperatures, and how you should pour wine *this* way. I thought it was rather sweet. I don't know how they got on TV.

In Chicago I was interviewed by a group of youngsters who were going to put this interview on some public access channel. But who decides what goes on? What about cranky stuff, like "I can tell the future for you" . . . "I can cure your cancer for you"?

♦ **V:** *Most of it gets shown.*

♦ **JGB:** I think that's wonderful, actually—I think that's *real freedom.* In New York City, Channel 23 seems to put on what is very close to hardcore movies in a *Blue Velvet* type of set—in a sort of sleazy, tenth-rate hotel. By habit I watch TV with the sound off. And this woman was talking to the camera while slowly opening her legs; I thought: *"What's going on here? This is amazing!"* And then an ad for a dating service came on.

We watched this mesmerized because it was sort of *nothing*—so reductive in its basic elements. These were paid commercials, I assume, for these dating agencies. Obviously, all you had were the basic elements of *imagination and desire:* a room, a woman, a telephone number and a brief message. There was a whole series, end-to-end, of these women speaking to the camera in an apparently erotic way as a come-on for the potential customer: this minimal, reductive presentation of themselves. They were like a whole series of mini-*Blue Velvets.*

It was wonderful. I thought, "This is amazing!" because this is everything reduced down to its *absolute elementals:* the blue-y color, the tacky little bedrooms, the cheapo costumes. It's as if somebody said to you, "You've got thirty seconds just to present yourself, to save your life," and you've got to "come on" in a sort of clichéd way that some guy with a gun is going to appreciate.

It's an absolutely iconic, minimal, reductive representation of human desire and imagination. And one after another of these things were going on into the night, mixed up with slightly longer, sort of *semi-softcore* movies. But I thought the women's ads, whatever they were—escort agency ads, basically—were extraordinary in their . . . it was their *cheapness* that was so interesting.

There were one or two dating agencies that obviously had more money. There was one (what the hell was it called?) that sounded like a perfume—the "Oasis Dating Service"? There was this very glossy presentation that looked like a perfume ad, with stretch limos and wealthy women photographed by skilled photographers, stepping out of stretch limos and doormen are raising their hands as they go into the apartment building, and everything was like an ad for *Tiffanys* and had no sexual interest *whatever,* because these women were too *stylish.*

Whereas **these really crude commercials had *the force*—they get right to the point: she just opens her legs and you knew what was going on.** But that reductiveness was so fascinating. Like I said, they were mini-*Blue Velvets*—I half-expected to see Dennis Hopper looking around a door, or Burroughs on the next bed!

It's like any suburban house or flat where the husband and wife have had a few drinks, and the wife starts putting on a little act for the husband. And the husband sort of doesn't know if he's really interested or a bit bored; the wife's a bit bored—they say, "Let's take a polaroid photo of this." At least there's *authenticity* there.

I thought it was fascinating. Our impression was that these things are on every night. And they must have some influence on the sexual imaginations of the next generation of filmmakers. If you're watching this stuff all the time (and presumably teenage kids are watching), it's bound to circulate into the imaginations of young filmmakers who will start shaping their own imaginations in terms of—not the glamorous images of yesterday, but these *tacky* images.

♦ **V:** *I saw a magazine article describing the search and seizure of a Mafia home in which a huge collection of books and videotapes on the Mafia was found. The final comment of the article was,* **"They're looking to the movies to learn how to act."**

♦ **JGB:** Right; the actual Mafia gangsters are watching the movies to learn how to get "in style." It's terribly funny, that. In England we've had American imports for years and years, but now, thanks to the common market, we're getting French and German mini-series on TV.

Recently I saw a fascinating West German crime series that was filmed in New York, but with German-speaking actors. It was about a heist that took place at the Lufthansa terminal at Kennedy airport. The film was shown in German, with subtitles, on British TV. And to begin with, we see Lufthansa employees speaking German, setting up this heist and all the rest of it. Then we move away from Kennedy into Manhattan. And in a very peculiar way, suddenly all the cops are speaking German, the call girls are speaking German, and the Blacks in the sleazy nightclubs are speaking German. But the ultimate is when the Mafia (of course) muscle in on this heist—these heavy-set *Italo* types are also speaking German! [laughs] Because German is sort of a *strong* language.

Watching this, I was thinking, "What *is* this? It's as if Hitler had won the war!" Absolutely bizarre.

If there's more of this coming, everybody's going to be totally scrambled, because nobody's going to know—we're going to see the Japanese version of this thing: an all-Japanese language Mafia movie. Or an all-Hindi version of a Mafia movie set in Manhattan. **We'll have a sophisticated sex comedy set in Paris, spoken in Swahili** or something. I mean, it's just *weird.* The psychological *profiles* or definitions we take for granted are completely *subverted.* It's absolutely weird—very, very odd. All sorts of bizarre things are going on now.

In England, I support Margaret Thatcher immensely . . . for *sexual reasons*. I admire her for mythological and sexual reasons. When I say this, people are totally fazed—they can't understand what I'm talking about. But her economic liberalism *has* led to the regeneration of British industry—there's no doubt about that. But the *nanny* aspect of the thing has led to a philistine approach to everything: **money is *all* that counts. Young artists don't *care* that they've got no ideas. They think that if they're ambitious enough, they can *work the system* and become terrific successes by the time they're 27.** That's all they want to do. They don't care about whether they're going to be *this* kind of photographer or *that* kind of photographer—what counts is *just* being rich and famous.

The economic "Thatcher miracle" has brought terrific economic prosperity, simply because all the bureaucratic restraints have been lifted. But it's been bought at a price, because the bureaucratic restraints have been placed on mass entertainment. In our restricted TV world, these people are obsessed with what they think is the flooding of British television by images of sex and violence. These people are talking about censoring all images of violence out of TV, and now they include the *news!*

♦ *CR: But it was British TV that produced a Mafia documentary called* Crime, Inc. *America would never do something like that, ever.*

♦ **JGB:** I saw that series. Yes, that was a good one; I agree with you.

♦ *V: They showed an angry red-haired man whom the Mafia had targeted, and then later they show his blown-off arm lying in the parking lot of a shopping mall.*

♦ **JGB:** That was rare, though. That's pretty rare on our TV. They no longer show films like *The Wild Bunch* that they showed in the Seventies. And now they heavily edit classic gangster movies to get the images of violence out.

That's a real nasty strain or tendency, actually. There's even talk about bringing in a new "Obscene Publications Act" which would cover books and newspapers.

♦ *CR: That has happened in America. Recently a law was passed whereby each individual community can decide what is "pornographic."*

♦ **JGB:** But you've got more built-in freedoms here, haven't you? Like "Freedom of Expression." You've got a resistance built in to central government that we don't have. The European nations have been so long established that there's immense built-in authority and respect for the central institutions of government which you don't have here; states' rights are guarded jealously here.

They've recently shown in British magazines the interiors, apparently never seen before, of Warhol's house on the Upper East Side not far from where I was staying in New York; it was in a posh area. There was all this classical French furniture. **He obviously came back from the Factory and all these spaced-out people to this *Louis Quinze* interior with these *objets d'art*,** Fabergé ornaments and the like. Quite bizarre.

What's your next project?

♦ ***V:*** Modern Primitives. *We try to be concerned with individuals and how they elaborate their obsessions. So you do have some—at best—extraordinary rationales. Maybe as children they read old* National Geographics *and instead of being repulsed by seeing rings through a nose, they wanted to try it, and when they got older they were able to.*

♦ **JGB:** Body modifications, including tattooing—

♦ ***V:*** *More elaborate, very personalized tattoos.*

♦ **JGB:** Plus self-mutilation of some kind? There were performance artists in the Sixties; one famous one, a German, was cutting bits of himself off—

♦ ***V:*** *Rudolf Schwarzkogler.*

♦ ***CR:*** *There's this one man they've interviewed heavily named Fakir Musafar who has been doing these body modifications since he was fourteen—and he's done* everything. *He's done these really extreme acts. Yet he's also an ad executive; he's comfortable in all these worlds.*

♦ **JGB:** I'm sure that's the pattern of future things, isn't it? I was interested to see in the newspaper recently that a leading surgeon, who was making half a million dollars a year (you can assume that he's reasonably successful)—he and his ex-stripper girlfriend were making porno films in which he was the star. Their best friend was a gay professional stripper who also appeared in these films. But they were charged with procuring, or whatever the word is here, an underage girl to perform in these films,

He's just been acquitted. It was decided that the girl, although she was fourteen, looked seventeen, and was sexually very experienced—therefore this surgeon couldn't be accused of "corrupting the morals of a minor." But he has decided to move to the Virgin Islands or somewhere and give up his practice (I think it was in Chicago) because of the ignominy brought upon him. But—I thought this was very interesting—his patients had all rallied around him.

He made something like thirteen porno films. He said, "This was just my hobby. I *liked* making them." I thought, "He's on the cusp, the edge, of real change." In the future patients won't mind *what* a doctor does. If your surgeon likes to collect stamps or whatever, making porno films is no worse, as long as you're not corrupting six-year-old kids or underage kids—fair enough. You're using adults; why not? I thought it was very interesting that his patients had rallied around him. But he didn't quite have the courage of his convictions.

♦ *V: Well, you included a precocious 12-year-old playing a central role in your latest book,* The Day of Creation—

♦ **JGB:** Too old—I should have made her a 10-year-old! [laughs] Things are getting more advanced, aren't they? No, I had to have somebody who had reached puberty.

Miami was wonderful—I loved Miami. I had the equivalent of Joyce showing me around; a very enthusiastic, charming woman—I loved her dearly. She's in her second marriage; she's produced five kids of her own—three from her first husband whom she married at sixteen; divorced him at the age of 21; he went on to a life of crime and ended up in jail—she told me all this. She then married her second husband and had two more kids. In between marrying two husbands she worked as a bunny girl, and she now runs her own PR company.

She's a passionate admirer of Miami, and she drove me around Miami and Coral Gables, which has all those wonderful banyan trees growing out of the roads. These banyan trees are as wide as this room. They're vast. They put down these creepers that turn into roots—they're like great herds of elephants along the roads there. It's quite impressive. This is south of Miami. Then she took me through Miami Beach and we drove past all these art deco hotels that have been lovingly restored in ice cream colors. The city itself is ultra-modern, with all these automated monorails linking the business quarter with the hotel district. It's an amazing place!

Now, **I thought Los Angeles was quite a scary place, actually.** There's something very mysterious about that city. We were there for five days. One of the days was Sunday and there were no interviews to do—everyone was heading for the beach or whatever they head for there. They assumed we would just stay by the swimming pool at the Beverly Hilton and loaf around.

But I noticed the Avis office at the Hilton, and said, "Let's rent a car"—Sunday is a good day to drive, you see. So we clocked just over a hundred road miles in greater L.A., which means quite a lot of driving. Having almost no idea where to go, we went to Malibu and then down to Venice where the Sixties are alive and kicking, which was sweet. **My girlfriend loved Venice because it was her youth still playing to an appreciative audience.**

Then we set out across the central heartland of L.A., from Culver City toward Silverlake where the Amok Bookshop is. And of course we got hopelessly lost, driving around. I remember thinking, "*Hey*—we haven't seen a white face on the streets for miles." Even the drivers—everybody had a black face. Now I didn't give a damn about that, but I thought, "Hmm; curious."

The next morning, Monday morning, all these Warners people turned up, bright-eyed and bushy-tailed from Sunday spent lounging around their pools watching their porno films or whatever they do there. I said, "We spent yesterday driving around." They all sat up: *Ohmigod—this crazy Englishman, renting a car!* "Where did you go?" I told them and they went, "My god—thank god you're alive!"

I thought L.A. was a strange place. It's a frontier town, and *there's*

the Third World. Wilshire Boulevard is the real U.S./Mexico border—
cross Wilshire and you move into what *they* (the people in Beverly
Hills) refer to as "the ghetto." Of course, it's Beverly Hills which is the
real ghetto. **The L.A. which they think of as "the ghetto"—the
Black and Hispanic area—covers an area about the size of
Belgium! Nine-tenths of L.A. is this Third World city.**

There's something very odd about the landscape of unstated possibilities there which is curious, because it's not a self-defining city,
which most are. Most cities have a central core and then an outer area,
and municipal buildings tend to be in certain areas and the entertainment quarter and financial section in another, as in San Francisco. But
in L.A. it's undefined, with these *vast* boulevards—the only thing that
defines Los Angeles are the *roads.* Unlike New York, where you feel the
roads and the avenues and so forth are merely separating these vast
urban masses of buildings that are the only reality. In a sense, the
avenues and streets in New York are an irrelevance.

**Most of the landscape in L.A. is ticky-tacky—I mean it's paint-
ed glue. The only reality is provided by these highways**, and these
highways are sort of abstract entities that go on *forever.* It's very, very
strange, I thought.

There's a sort of Third World feel to L.A. We drove around all these
places: Hollywood Boulevard, Sunset Boulevard, Santa Monica
Boulevard. East of Hollywood, you drive down these world-famous
boulevards and you see street life starting as you do in a Third World
country. I wouldn't say people are cooking out on the streets, but damn
nearly—they've got their electrical appliances out on the street, they're
watching TV out on the street—that kind of thing. It's weird; it's very,
very strange.

You get that Third World sense that this could be Beirut—not Beirut,
because then people would be shooting at you! But you feel a different
psychology of "today": just, *you live for today.* You scratch together
enough to rent a video or whatever life requires—get a bottle from the
liquor store; nothing else matters. It's a very, very strange place. I
thought it was fascinating, actually. Fascinating.

Then there are the Hollywood Hills, and Westwood, and Beverly

Hills—all these rich people in these incredible houses looking down on this Third World advancing towards them. You talk to these senior Hollywood Warners producers as I did, and they're unaware of what's going on! It's very strange. L.A. is a mysterious city. Whereas San Francisco appears to be a "normal" sort of Western city, doesn't it?

♦ *V: And American cities are more violent than Europe's—*

♦ **JGB: Violent crime of any kind is actually quite rare in England.** We have something like 250 homicides a year in England, of which, like homicides everywhere, something like 2/3 are family feuding. So the number of homicides committed in pursuance of violent crime is terribly low. Whereas in L.A. alone it's something like 2,000 a year. In England a lot of publicity is given to rapes, quite rightly, but the number committed is terribly small.

♦ *CR: Whereas here, I personally know several girls who've been raped.*

♦ **JGB:** Really? By men breaking into apartments and the like, or—? It's not young women dragged off bicycles on remote country lanes, is it? Having two daughters, one of whom now lives alone in her own house—the other lives with her boyfriend, but he often goes away—one can't help but worry for them. These men who break into apartments, often in pursuit of burglary loot—they're all hopped up on drugs or something and they see this vulnerable young woman, and it taps the *need to humiliate* and all the rest of it. Then you have these nightmare scenarios unfolding which are absolutely *grim . . .*

Well, you've got a great security door out here—that wire door. Nothing could get through that! **Most of the people who buy handguns in the States have no weapons training** because you don't have military service anymore. In the armed forces, the RAF, I went through basic infantry training in the handling of the Smith & Wesson revolver, etc. In my basic training in the submachine gun, the rifle, and the handgun, we were warned that, even under the closely supervised regime of an Air Force or Army weapons training center, accidents are immensely frequent. People pick up a handgun and the damn thing goes off and shoots them in the foot. And this happens on a military base. Why half the owners of handguns in the States haven't had an accident and shot themselves, I don't know! Americans must have a gene that predisposes them to the sane handling of firearms . . .

As for indiscriminate killers, we had one in England six months ago: the Hungerford killer, Michael Ryan. He had a Kalashnikov and some handguns and he just started going around shooting people in this archetypal English village. Then he killed his own mother and set fire to the house. He went into a classroom in his own school and there he was cornered by the police and he shot himself.

♦ **CR:** *That's what they usually do; they end up killing themselves—*

♦ **JGB:** It's a logic that's inescapable; most of them do. There have been a few "final shootouts." The British police have more access to firearms than people realize, and they turn up heavily armed and start blazing away indiscriminately! **There have been tragic cases of armed men who have seized passersby and the passersby have been shot down by the British police blasting away.** Tragic endings!

Of course, the Michael Ryan-Hungerford thing played into the hands of the moral majority: the "Ban all violence from TV, ban Starsky and Hutch, etc" brigade. And the British tabloid press, which is a huge fantasy industry, carried stories about how Michael Ryan had no friends and spent all his time in his mother's house, where he lived, watching violent videos. Supposedly he was obsessed with violent crime, reading crime magazines of various kinds. There was this huge exposé of "the psychology of Michael Ryan."

But there was an interesting documentary on British television which only just got shown, because the authorities wanted to suppress it. Very interestingly, it showed that **the British tabloid exposé of Michael Ryan's behavior patterns was completely phony! This man never rented violent videos—he didn't even have a video player** or access to one! All he spent his time doing was reading books. The papers had said, "Rambo Killer Stalks British Village . . . Ryan was wearing a U.S. combat jacket and had on a Rambo headband as he moved around the streets with his M-15, blazing away." It turned out that he didn't wear a headband, he didn't have a combat jacket, and he did not watch violent videos. He lay on his bed in his mother's house reading books. And I thought, "That's interesting."

[looking at the book *Killing for Company,* Ballard remarks:] That *is* an amazing book, isn't it? It's very disturbing; profoundly unsettling and weird. Very, very strange. **He killed these people so he could have company for watching TV.** Every so often when he got bored he'd open the four walls and watch TV with them. How weird. Yeah, he was really crazy; very, very strange. An ex-policeman.

♦ *CR: We recently got this book featuring several Death Row murderers suffering from these fatal diseases. Yet the authorities have gone to all this trouble to keep them alive for their execution date!*

♦ **JGB:** Yes, yes, yes. Strange. It's a real treat to come here. Keep in touch. When the time comes I'll track down these extra elements, and even possibly write another story so that you've got a bit more original material [for *The Atrocity Exhibition*], so you can update the whole thing—give it an extra dimension.

They're lovely cats, aren't they? Yes, he's so sweet. [takes photo of cat] Bye bye, pusses. ♦ ♦ ♦

Photo: Charles Gatewood

J.G. Ballard, V. Vale, Graeme Revell

IN the spring of 1985 V. Vale visited J.G. Ballard in England with the intention of filming 30 minutes of conversation in Super-8mm; sadly, the cameraman did not capture the sound! Also present were Graeme Revell, his wife Sinan and their infant son Robert—who received lavish attention from Ballard, himself a parent of three. Topics included fame, literary piracy, William S. Burroughs, guns, Weegee and Diane Arbus, drug addiction and AIDS, censorship and corporate media, and tourism ...

♦ **GRAEME REVELL:** *Has the success of* Empire of the Sun *changed your life very much?*

♦ **J.G. BALLARD:** Look around—the same old dust and dirt's everywhere. Nothing has changed—why change it?!

♦ **VALE:** *Except, there's been some pruning in your garden—*

♦ **JGB:** That's because it's winter. Nothing has changed. Everybody's expecting this *change.* I'm supposed to buy a nightclub, or something!

♦ **GR:** *I was just wondering, What exactly does happen when recognition comes in the literary world? Nothing much, I suppose—*

♦ **JGB:** I don't know what recognition *means.* Writers are pretty isolated. I avoid public appearances. Once you have even a modest success, a vast number of invitations come in, and if you took them up it would be a *secondary career*—you'd never have the time to do any work.

Of course there *are* writers who do that—they're going all over the

Photo of J.G. Ballard: V. Vale

place, to this bookstore and that festival—well, I avoid all that. I don't do any of that. I turn down the dinner invitations—I don't mean from friends, but for these public appearances. You've got a lovely baby, Graeme. What can we give him to play with? Maybe a very expensive camera! [laughs] Or his own personal Super-8mm system?

How was your flight? Ronald Reagan was given a special diet ["The Jetlag Diet"] when he flew to Europe—he was given masses of a high-calorie pasta beforehand. I was worried: "Suppose this diet doesn't work? He's going to blow up the world!"

If you'd come a fortnight ago, god it was freezing—it was incredibly cold. Here in Shepperton we're on the same parallel as Moosejaw, Saskatchewan—I say that having spent a lot of time in Moosejaw. We're roughly just above the 49th parallel. New York City is quite well south of the 49th parallel. This whole area was covered in snow for a fortnight.

These days I consider England to be a Third World country. I said this to a *Newsweek* reporter and she said, "Two-and-a-half!"
♦ *GR: It's already got one of the lowest standards of living in Europe. London gives a very false impression of what the rest of Britain is like. The minute you get out of the stockbroker belt, things get really desperate. It's amazing for us, because comparatively, Australia is very wealthy like America is. The contrast is enormous.* [Graeme, Sinan and baby leave to get lunch.]

♦ **JGB:** The *RE/Search #8/9: J.G. Ballard* book is an incredibly impressive effort; everybody here says so, too. Very impressive layout-wise; it's beautifully designed. My reaction to it was, "This writer sounds interesting; who is he?" [!]

♦ *V: I noticed my American edition of* Empire of the Sun *didn't include the map of Shanghai that's in the U.K. hardback. But I was just in Hong Kong and I picked up a paperback of* Empire of the Sun, *which had the map—*

♦ **JGB:** You got the anti-pirate edition, the one with the red cover. These pirate publishers, who are mostly based in India, bring out paperback editions of a hardback book long before the authorized paperback—perhaps a year before. So, my publisher printed a special anti-pirate paperback edition about the same time as the hardcover, which goes out only to the Far East: Singapore, Hong Kong, India. These Indian pirate publishers have semi-formal links with people regularly doing the London-India run, like airline personnel, who pick out the brand-new titles at the airport bookstore. If a certain title is a success, the pirates can have them out on the streets within about a week!

Did you know that I met Brion Gysin? The *Guardian* newspaper holds an annual party. I went to it last year and he was there. We chatted in a friendly way. We agreed that the RE/Search book on Gysin was a gem; that was the first time I saw how well-designed the RE/Search books are—this was before you went to the large format. He seemed very well; very chipper. A very nice guy!

♦ *V: Have you ever seen his paintings?*

♦ **JGB:** Only reproduced. Of course, his main fame is as the inventor of

the Cut-Up Method, plus his friendship with Burroughs. **I haven't seen Burroughs in the flesh for a long time**; I'm glad he's still moving along strong. He's had a big sort of boom lately. Well, he was enormously famous in the Sixties, but by the mid-Seventies he seemed to be in a bit of a trough. I don't know why that was, but now he's come back with a huge surge. That's good. He's still producing books, and that's pretty impressive, because he must be in his seventies [age 72].

♦ *V: He's settled down in Lawrence, Kansas.*

♦ **JGB:** I reviewed his most recent novel for the *Guardian;* I've reviewed quite a few of his books. About the same week as his novel came out, the American nuclear disaster TV special [*The Day After*] came out—the one that was set in Lawrence, Kansas. You could just imagine Burroughs in that crowd ambling up to the director and saying, "Listen, I've got a few ideas of my own toward improving this picture." [!] You see, much was made of the fact that the extras used were the townspeople of Lawrence, Kansas—among whom was William Burroughs. That's a nice irony, for those interested. Seems a strange place to settle. But he is a Midwesterner; that's something to bear in mind. He's a remarkable man, all right.

♦ *V: Nothing makes Burroughs happier than the newest model of firearm; the state of the art—*

♦ **JGB:** That's not something that people in England respond to. They get rather snooty about people who are interested in guns. Even though we were in a world war and have had military involvements all around the world as part of the colonial process, nevertheless most people in this country have never handled a gun. The uniformed police in this country—the average bobby—don't carry weapons, except on very special assignments . . . let's say, a gunman is known to be hiding out somewhere.

Most people in England have never seen a handgun, let alone touched one. The only gun the average citizen will have seen will be a rifle or shotgun, and that only in country areas. You have to go to a police station to get a license. And you can't just go buy a shotgun and start roving around the land firing at anything on four legs or anything that flies, because all the land is owned, and is either farmed or is part of people's domestic property. So the average person has not even seen a shotgun, unless he lives in a rural area or is a farmer himself. The only weapon that most people in this country will ever have seen, eye to eye (as opposed to on television, or in movies) will be a rifle carried on parade, and that's at a long distance.

When I was in the RAF doing my basic weapons training, most people had never handled a Smith & Wesson .38, although they'd been watching all these movies since they were nine years old. But to actually hold this revolver and fire it at a target was a shambling experience. When we fired the Sten submachine gun, for most people it was totally unnerving—what with the noise and everything else.

Myself, I'd seen a lot of weapons growing up in the Far East. Although I'd never fired a weapon as a teenage boy, I'd certainly handled a lot of weapons given to me by British soldiers to clean or mess around with, or by Americans after World War II. I'd never fired a submachine gun and certainly wasn't prepared for the experience. **We only fired a submachine gun on two separate occasions, because the problem is, the consumption of ammunition is so vast**, and they're just sort of scatter-guns, anyway. I don't think you can *train* somebody to use something like a Sten gun, because it's just a close-range sort of *blunderbuss* weapon.

We did all the hard rifle-range training with the old British Lee-Enfield bolt-action rifle—we did a lot of that, and got used to that. And that was *deafening*—after an hour on the rifle range, you couldn't hear for three days, because we didn't wear muffs [ear protection]. But, most people here have never seen a weapon. So anybody who comes on, like Burroughs, as being interested in guns, and is photographed fondling a Colt .45 or something, is regarded *suspiciously*—like the next thing to molesting a child!

That whole American tradition of being able to go out and shoot, is absent here. Now in New York City, I think if you want to actually legally own a handgun, it's much more difficult than people think, rather like over here, for the same sort of reasons: everybody's too close together. The murder rate is very low in this country compared to the United States, and I think the availability of handguns is what makes the difference.

If I wanted a gun, a pistol—say I just wanted to kill myself, I would have quite a job to get one. The average person wouldn't know how to go about it. *I* wouldn't know.

♦ *V: Whereas in New York City alone, there's an estimated one million illegal firearms—so I've read. And in all of America there's enough guns to arm every man, woman and child—and then some.*

Yesterday I visited the London Dungeon. It seemed quite extreme. Some of the displays were very animated, with wax people swinging from ropes. You heard the howls of the tortured, and the victims sometimes had intestines coming out, or a hatchet in their head—

♦ **JGB:** The British have always had a keen interest in bloody murder—Jack the Ripper and all the rest of it. That's a kind of theme park!

♦ *V: I was in Foyles bookstore afterward and got a book by Weegee—*

♦ **JGB: Weegee was living in New York. He had a police radio in his own car; he got to the scene of the crime before the cops did. He was the tough street New York photographer**, producing classic police-style photos. He was faintly in the sort of **Diane Arbus** area, but not so arty. From what I remember he didn't consider himself an "artist," just a working photographer. But his own police photos have a wonderful quality. I don't know the technicalities of it, but presumably it's the harsh front lighting; the backgrounds are kind of dark. They're wonderful old-style photos shot at the bottom of stairwells—that kind of thing. Didn't Diane Arbus use the same technique of using flash in the same way?

♦ *V: I think so. Weegee and Diane Arbus seem somehow related. They both made a kind of celebrity out of non-celebrities, like Arbus did with Eddie the Jewish Giant. How do you relate to "the press"?*

♦ **JGB:** This peculiar thing happens when you get suckered into this sort of "mediaphile" stuff: **you begin to play the roles that are assigned to you. Without being aware of it, you become other people's idea of yourself—without realizing that's going on.** It's a very peculiar thing. I certainly don't like it, being actually extremely shy. It's a great relief that it's over.

♦ *V: When I called you, I was amazed you actually answered your phone. I thought, "By now he must have an answering machine."*

♦ **JGB:** I'm pretty "low-tech" around here!

♦ *V: I feel sorry that you've had to answer hundreds of phone calls, with people coming over—*

♦ **JGB:** That's in the past now, thank god. What are you doing in Paris?

♦ *V: We're meeting Brion Gysin.*

♦ **JGB:** Well, do give him my very best wishes, and tell him what a pleasure it was meeting him. Is he still working?

♦ *V: Yes. I'm trying to photograph all his paintings.*

♦ **JGB:** The few I've seen were very impressive. Vale, you're a one-man Renaissance! You're playing the role, to the late twentieth-century avant-garde, of what Pope John *whatever-it-was* played to fifteenth-century Rome, maybe producing the electronic version of the Sistine Chapel! It's pretty impressive: any sort of avant-garde or publishing activity that runs against the mainstream and commercial art and publishing world—it's a miracle that it takes place at all. Those currents are so strong. You're up against things like distribution. In this country, the Smiths newsagency/bookshop chain is so important, and if you've not got access to that, you may as well not exist.

It's a peculiar thing: **modern technology, which is supposed to be so liberating, often has the opposite effect.** Computer-controlled distribution is supposed to bring more diversity, but instead you get *less* diversity. In England we have Smiths, a big bookshop chain that's everywhere around the country—in railway stations, airports. I think *Empire of the Sun* is probably the first novel of mine that's ever been carried by them. They have this central buying office where each publisher has about 15 minutes to make a presentation of all their books released for the next six months. These three people sit behind a desk and make a judgment then and there as to what they'll take. So if it's Science Fiction, they'll go, "Well, we've got three Science-Fiction titles already; we've got Arthur C. Clarke and Isaac Asimov and Frank Herbert—we don't need anymore." So you don't stand a chance! It's a big problem, but one has to live with it.

♦ *V:* Empire of the Sun *isn't Science Fiction—*

♦ **JGB:** In fact **I haven't written a Science-Fiction book since the Sixties. But of course, labels stick, and people in the book trade love labels.** In England, *Empire of the Sun* has outsold all my 8 previous novels put together. I've got a whole new readership for the first

Photo: Ana Barrado

time. So people are going off to the library looking for "Ballard" and they get things like *Crash!* They can't believe their eyes. **People send me letters asking, "Did you *actually* write *Crash?*" Or, "I came across this book *The Atrocity Exhibition;* did *YOU* write it?"**

You're on your way to Paris; do you speak French?

♦ *V: No, and the French are merciless if you don't speak French. But I can sort of read it—*

♦ **JGB:** Me, too. I can't speak it, but I go there every summer. Fortunately, my girlfriend speaks quite good French, so I don't have to open my mouth at all. I get into such a state on holiday; if we bump into some English or American people in France, I don't speak to them *either,* and she sort of digs me in the ribs, saying, "They're Americans—they speak English!" and then I go, "Yes, hello. Hi!" Because I've sort of practiced not saying a word, in case I'm going to make myself look like a fool in front of some Frenchman.

♦ *V: Where do you go?*

♦ **JGB:** Well, this summer we went to a town near Antibes, a beach resort. We rented an apartment by a swimming pool in one of those holiday complexes—very nice place. Slumming about, sunbathing, trips up into the hills and all that kind of stuff. It was very pleasant.

♦ *V: Do you go to Spain often?*

♦ **JGB:** Yes, I have been to Spain a lot over the years, particularly with my kids, because it's cheaper than anywhere else.

♦ *V: I'm making my first trip there, particularly because I'm a big Gaudi fan—*

♦ **JGB: There's a lot of Gaudi in Barcelona, what with the big church [the Sagrada Familia] and the Parc Guell.**

♦ *V: You stayed at the Hotel Colón—*

♦ **JGB:** Right. It overlooks a nice Gothic cathedral—not Gaudi's—and has a nice view. If you're interested in Gaudi, Barcelona is definitely the place to spend quite some time. From there you can drive up to Port Lligat near Figueras where Dali's house is. Then there's the Dali Museum in Figueras which is quite close to Port Lligat; a half hour drive. Barcelona to Figueras is about ten miles; it's Dali's birthplace, and where his museum is. That's a two-hour drive. You can go up to Figueras for the Dali Museum, which is well worth doing. Then another half hour will take you to Cadaqués, which is a quite fashionable resort town. **Port Lligat is kind of a suburb of Cadaqués; it's worth the trip. The rocks there are quite something.**

♦ *V: Where's Benidorm?*

♦ **JGB:** That's like Coney Island, if you know what I mean. It's sort of a British package—don't go there, you *won't* like it; take my word for it. It's just high-rise hotels. There are plenty of lovely towns along the coast. I haven't been to Ibiza but I'm told that it's very nice. You can fly directly there. There's an island south, Formentera, which is a sort of artist's colony and which is supposed to be really nice. I think you get there by boat, in a motor launch.

Then, of course, there's the whole of Spain: Grenada, Seville, Madrid, and so on. There's an awful lot to see there.

I rather like the South of France, myself. Although, the whole of the French Riviera is now nothing but eight-lane motorways with apartment complexes—it's just concrete. But it still retains great charm with its lush gardens and palm trees, which give it a certain style that's very pleasant.

I remember one afternoon in Grasse, a small city about 15 miles inland, which is a perfume center. We drove away from the coast, away from all the concrete and motorways and huge supermarkets, back into old Provence, up into the hills. You half expected Cézanne to appear around the first corner, way back in traditional France. So we climbed up into Grasse. My girlfriend looked in the *Michelin* guide and saw there was a famous scenic view about a thousand feet above Grasse. So we drove along endless roads, around and around, with the odd little villa here and there hidden behind high walls.

We found this beautiful spot, got out of the car, walked to the edge and looked out over, and what had seemed to be old Provence, with all sorts of terra-cotta and ochre, had suddenly changed. Looking down, all we could see was hundreds of blue rectangles—swimming pools. Quite amazing. Grasse is quite a rich place; the whole Côte d'Azur is rich, and people have all these villas up in the hills. But as you drive up, you can't *see* any of them.

But when you get to the top and look down, you see hundreds of these swimming pools. It's bizarre. You suddenly realize that far from being old Provence, this is ultra-new Provence, with the perfume manufacturers and their expensive villas with their pools. It was quite an extraordinary sight.

I suddenly thought, "My god, these things are sort of cut into the mountainside with reinforced steel and concrete pools. They're going to last 100,000 years—long after all these people are gone from the Riviera, these pools are *still* going to be there!" Just imagine a race coming from another galaxy, wondering, "What are these damn concrete rectangles for? What did people *do* with them? It's so inexplicable. **Were they waiting for some sort of marine deity to fall out of the sky to catch one? What are they—time machines or time traps?"** Quite strange. Because they're really part of the landscape now—talk about a Cubist landscape! They actually do reshape the landscape in a direct way. Ah, it's strange.

It's very nice actually, inland. It's very, very pleasant. If I were a millionaire, I'd have a place there. But god knows what I would *do* in the evenings, having the TV in French? That's always a problem there.

♦ *V: Right; TV watching is one of your principal evening recreations—*

♦ **JGB:** It's terribly important to me, you see. **I always get a bit flummoxed in Spain or France when I end up watching *Hawaii Five-O* in French or Spanish! It's not quite the same.** The *Rockford Files* dubbed into Greek or Italian?!

I keep meaning to go back to China. One or two people have suggested paying my fare to speak to a university class on the state of the modern novel or something. [laughs] In fact, it wouldn't matter what one said—they wouldn't have a clue. You could invent a lot of totally fictitious writers; do anything.

Also, in China you have those organized tours from morning til night: 9 a.m. the factory tour; 10 a.m. the nursing home, etc. I like *real freedom* to look around, and I'm not sure how easy it would be in a very big city like Shanghai—not speaking a word of Chinese. It's a terrible thing to think about going back after forty years; it's really like getting into a time machine—like **one of those Ray Bradbury stories where you suddenly go back to the hometown you grew up in and everything looks a bit sinister.** It could be a very odd experience. I have mixed feelings about it, but I might do it.

♦ *V: It's only 24 hours away, at most—*

♦ **JGB:** It's a helluva flight. The journey puts me off. I think you'd have to go by ship and take three weeks to sort of mentally cope with that. Twenty-four or thirty-six hours in airplanes, airports, with swelling feet—that I can't take. The last really long flight I took was to Rio de Janeiro. We were flown first class and were given little slippers to put on. When the plane landed I felt fantastic: "Let's get out of this steel hearse!" But I found I couldn't put on my shoes—it was a ludicrous state of affairs; I was sitting there with these shoes in my hands. I finally managed to force them on. I felt shaky for days.

When you don't move around, the blood pools in your legs or something. You're sitting in the damn seat for hours. When they stop at airports now they don't allow you off the plane—they just refuel and you're on your way.

During the big hijacking scares, my mother, in her seventies, flew to China—this was about four or five years ago. In places like Rome you weren't allowed off the plane when they flew on to Persia or some Saudi Arabian area for refueling. You didn't get off the plane until you were somewhere like Karachi. Anyhow, I'll see it in the newsreels!

I don't know if you ever heard that story about the English couple going to Australia who stopped off somewhere in China. They had this little dog traveling with them—this is a true story, apparently. They went into a restaurant and told the waiter they wanted the dog to be taken to the back and given something to eat. The waiter said, "Sure," and took the dog away. They ordered dinner and some delicious thing came, looking like duck. **They ate this delicious meal and then at the end asked, "Where's Fido?" "Huh? You've eaten it!"** The woman had a nervous breakdown and had to be sent back to England. The English are such dog fanatics. I've seen this story so many times I think it's probably true! Dog is quite a delicacy in China.

♦ *V: I saw a documentary on sausage-making, and there was a huge tray of eyeballs next to a tray of thoraxes—*

♦ **JGB: The food processing industry has raised to a high art the maximum usage of almost everything in the animal carcass. It's quite incredible what they will do, stripping every last bit of protein from the bone.** Particularly in these pig processing plants where pigs go in one end and pork pies and sausages come out the other, and there's nothing left—even the bones have been crushed—crushed bone meal is a constituent of a lot of animal pet foods. I think in this country 5% of crushed bone meal is allowed in sausages.

There was a famous kidnapping-murder case about ten years ago in which two Pakistani immigrants kidnapped what they thought was the wife of Rupert Murdoch, the Australian newspaper tycoon who owns the *Times,* the *Sun*—huge-circulation Fleet Street newspapers over here. These two brothers successfully kidnapped this woman who was in fact the wife of the Chief Executive of Murdoch's newspapers—a middle-aged woman whom they held by mistake. She was never found—just vanished off the face of the earth. The brothers were caught and they're now serving long sentences.

At one point in the kidnapping, they held this woman in a farmhouse they had rented. Next door—literally fifty yards—was a big pig-processing plant one of them was a manager for. **The police have always assumed that after they killed her, they just put her "on the line" and she ended up in somebody's pork pies!** Because no trace of her body has ever been found. It's the perfect way to get rid of somebody—before you know what's happened, they're coming out in some kind of Doggie Mix with a printed label wrapped around them!

Recently I read about these people who conducted some experiments. They started out in Central London at a train station in Piccadilly Circus or West End (or somewhere). They would pick somebody at random and follow them all day. They never *did* anything or tried to steal from them—they just trailed them.

They would follow somebody, a middle-aged man or youngish woman (there was nothing unpleasant about it, it was just a game of "Play the Sleuth") into a department store, out into the street, get on

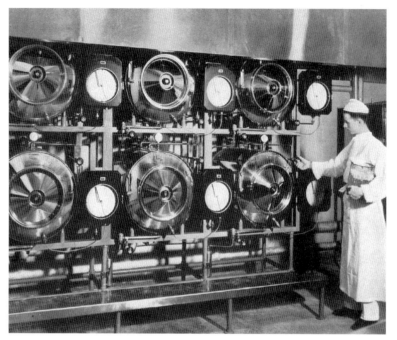

the tube, go to a lawyer's office, then go maybe all the way onto the Northern line, or take the subway system to some remote suburb like this [Shepperton]. They'd see the person go into their front door and that would be the end of it.

They did this many, many times and they said that nobody (even though they were following people around, say, Harrod's in quite close quarters) recognized them or realized they were being followed. Even those people who clearly said, "Didn't I see you in Harrod's with me two hours ago?"

On one occasion they actually shared a taxi! They saw their quarry get into a cab, and there were no other cabs around so they charged up and said, "Could we come with you? This is an emergency!" and the person said, "Oh yes, by all means!" and gave them a lift. And when their quarry said, "Oh, I'm getting out here," *they* got out too. And the quarry *still* didn't realize.

It's obvious that contrary to the impression you get in movies where people become immediately aware that they're being trailed—most people are not aware; they're not expecting to be followed. And if they become aware, they rationalize it away: "Oh, it's just coincidence." They won't believe it.

What do you do for recreation? I imagine that everyone in California is sniffing coke all day long, or has needles hanging out of their arms—

♦ *V: Graeme was saying that there's a heroin problem in London and that it's very cheap.*

♦ **JGB:** It's so cheap. These kids are living in these rundown housing estates, parents out of work and on the dole. It's a habit. How they do it I don't know—

♦ *V: They prostitute themselves or steal—*

♦ **JGB:** The world price of heroin has really dived. When the stuff's expensive, it's just high society, but when it reaches the schoolkid on the street, then it becomes a problem. I've never understood the drug's tie-in with AIDS. Is dirty needles the only reason? I wonder whether the prolonged use of things like heroin and cocaine, which are powerful pain-killers—well, they suppress appetite, and I suppose you don't look after yourself quite as much—you sit in cold drafts; all that kind of thing. Your nerve endings have dulled in every respect. I suppose personal hygiene starts to get neglected, and all the rest of it.

Over here we're constantly told that if you're a heavy drug user and a homosexual, you're doubly at risk. Is that just because of needles? I don't know. **My impression is that the old style addict in a public lavatory with a needle up his arm belongs in the past.** These new-style heroin users—these kids—are smoking it, aren't they? They're not injecting it. I don't know. I'm an outsider.

The AIDS thing is a real scare—it's most frightening, because you never know. You can't trust anybody in this world, not even your nearest and dearest. And that's not just paranoia . . .

♦ *V: AIDS can also be transmitted through blood transfusions—*

♦ **JGB:** Then the thing to do is to build up your own blood bank! There was an article a few years ago in the *Guinness Book of Records* about the rarest blood groups in the world. There are some very rare blood groups, and the rarest of all is RGH17 (or something like that), and there are only three known people with this. One is a guy living in New Jersey, another is a Yugoslav barrister, and the third is somebody in Canton, China. The first two have been building up their own personal blood banks for years, in case they ever need it for an operative procedure. But **the idea of having your own personal blood bank is rather nice!**

♦ *V: How does a rare blood type evolve?*

♦ **JGB:** I think that by very rare coincidence, two recessive genes give rise to these rare blood groups by coming to meet at conception.

♦ *V: Have you ever had an operation?*

♦ **JGB:** Not for about 35 years! And I'm not looking forward to the next time, either.

♦ *V: Well, if you're going to avoid AIDS—*

♦ **JGB:** You'd better go to somewhere in the Bible Belt! Where is the most god-fearing heterosexual zone in America? Go and have your operation there, where you know the blood is going to be okay! You read about this AIDS scare, and every time you go to an Italian restaurant you think, "My god, is one of these waiters going to give me a dose?"—you know, as he's serving the cannelloni. Has it changed gay life in San Francisco?

♦ *V: It's reduced the promiscuous lifestyle more towards monogamy and respectability—*

♦ **JGB:** My god! Bourgeois life reaches down—you can't resist it! They'll get you in the end, even if they have to think of some weird disease! I think AIDS has always been around (probably at some low level) but not to this extent. If homosexuality is this key vector for the transmission of AIDS, one *has* to assume that it's always been around. Until comparatively recently, homosexuals were spread over the population as a whole. They didn't get concentrated in enclaves.

Smallpox is supposed to have been eradicated totally. I read somewhere that malaria is coming back—strains resistant to Quinine. Of course, the hospital systems of the world are the greatest repositories and breeders of new strains of disease. So **keep out of hospitals at all cost!** There they've got the most virulent strains.

All the heteros will have to go to some boring place like New Zealand where homosexuality is unknown. That's sort of The End, you know. Opt for a dull, bourgeois life—it's the only way of *staying alive.* Early to bed, early to rise, you know . . . monogamy!

Aren't you tired from jetlag?

♦ *V: No, I think the Jetlag Diet must really work. I slept on the plane, too.*

♦ **JGB:** I've *never* been able to sleep on a plane, or a train, or a bus. Trains are impossible. My girlfriend and I drove down to the South of France, but couldn't face the drive back—it takes two or three days to cross France by car; it's quite a big country. There's a train/car ferry system running from Nice to Calais on the Channel; the train leaves Nice at about 7 p.m. and pulls into Calais about 7 o'clock the next morning. We had a little two-bunk cabin.

It was very nice. We drove the car onto the train and then we could sit back and have dinner. We watched the last of the sunlight going down on the Riviera while the train was chugging along, stopping at one or two places like Cannes or Marseilles to pick up more people and more cars.

Then night fell and we turned North. The train was only going about 50 or 60 miles an hour. **I had just gotten into my bunk and suddenly this damn train accelerated to about 120 mph! It was like being in a great iron hotel on roller skates.** I just lay rocking in this bunk all night long. It was like being inside a washing machine. And the noise! This train is leaping through the darkness—*whoosh!*

At 6 o'clock in the morning we pulled into some Northern French town. I was still lying in my bunk in this town—Amiens or somewhere—about 30 miles from the coast. I was exhausted. I gazed out at this bleak railway station, just clanking and banging and hissing as we were taking on more diesel fuel. Suddenly, going past my window came this section of rail-cars, and on one of these I saw MY car heading the other direction! I thought, "My god—they've made a mistake; they're sending it all the way back to Nice!"

I nearly had a nervous breakdown, being mentally displaced by no sleep and all that rocking noise. In fact, what happened was: half the train went off to Belgium, and the other half went to Calais—they were just moving some cars around. But I never recovered from that. I never recommend anybody to try to sleep on a train—impossible!

Even when I traveled across Canada in '54, it was much quieter being on a North American train. Although it wasn't *that* easy to sleep—those trains travel too fast. I remember when they only went 50, 60 miles an hour—you could sleep. But these trains go over 100 mph—it's just impossible, not to mention the noise of the rails screaming. I think I'd rather travel by daylight.

♦ *V: Right; then you can see the country. I heard about this new crime on the Paris-Madrid train. These people creep through sleeping cars and when they hear you snoring, they spray something on you that knocks you out, and then they take your valuables—*

♦ **JGB:** I daresay I believe it. I wish somebody like that would come into my cabin on the train and I could be knocked out for a few hours. I'd have spent all my money and there would be nothing left!

The real worry recently has been tourists mugging tourists. There've been quite a lot of British tourists killed by muggers in places like Benidorm and so on—handbag snatchers who jump out of cars. They all carry knives and they don't mind using them. London's peaceful by comparison!

♦ *V: Do you like the outdoors?*

♦ **JGB:** I like *some* landscapes. Meadows and pastures are great for *cows,* but **I love the landscapes of Spain, for example—they're much closer to a state of mind: red rocks** . . . Their landscapes seem to say something. I also like the landscape of the French Riviera. Rolling English meadows are not for me. [John] Constable country—not for me. What's the landscape around San Francisco like? Basically what? Mountains? What's the natural cover—pine-covered hills?

♦ *V: Bushes, shrubs, some trees.*

♦ **JGB:** Is there a lot of market gardening around there or is that further south in California? Commercial cauliflowers and cucumbers and tomatoes?

♦ *V: That's further south.*

♦ **JGB:** You've got vines, of course—there are all those wineries, which means it's fairly arid because vines like arid conditions. The coast is spectacular around there in Northern California, judging by what I see in newsreels and movies and from what I've heard. Friends of mine have told me that the Northern California coast takes some beating.

♦ *V: In London yesterday I passed a travel agency which advertised a round-trip ticket from London-Paris for 32 pounds—*

♦ **JGB:** That's amazing; I don't know how they do it. Here's the peculiar thing: **Travel, in the old-fashioned sense, has more or less ceased to exist. What we have now is *tourism.*** Point-to-point travel anywhere in the world is probably cheaper than it's ever been in history. If you want to go from London to Tahiti—if that's your one ambition, you could probably do it very cheaply. With a hotel thrown in, it would probably cost you 1000 pounds, or 1500 pounds at the most. Likewise, if you wanted to go to Rio de Janeiro for a week on a package holiday you could do it, or Miami, or what have you.

But traveling in the true sense, in the way that, say, Hemingway traveled in the 1930s, or Evelyn Waugh or Graham Greene in the '30s or '40s—that is out of the question now. If I said, "I've had enough of England; my book's been a success. I've always wanted to go to South America. I'll spend six months there, using scheduled airlines, staying at hotels, asking taxi drivers to take me to hot spots and airports"—I mean, that would cost a fortune. An absolute fortune.

Everywhere, they're catering to commercial and business travelers, diplomats, academics. They know most people who travel aren't paying for it out of their own pockets—"the firm" is paying. Prices have gone up accordingly.

♦ *V: **When I went to China, there were two economies: one for the tourists, and one for the people who live there.** I had great meals that people would make for me on the street, and those cost 40 cents. Yet my hotel*

Photo: Tim Chapman

room, which I was forced to stay in, cost $27 a night—

♦ **JGB:** A glass of water probably cost you ten dollars!

♦ *V: I think that if I were Chinese, I could have found a cheaper hotel, but I couldn't figure that out. It seemed as if Chinese people who* live *there don't travel—maybe they stay with their relatives, but they don't patronize the hotels where Westerners are. The few hotels there seem to be just for tourists. And I could buy gloves and a hat there for 60 or 80 cents—it was very cold, with snow everywhere.*

I went to this movie and there was no heat in the theater—it was partially open-air. I paid 15 cents to see this '70s American feature which had been dubbed into Chinese. Everyone in the theater was wearing huge overcoats. In the open-air lobby there was this roaring fire blazing out of a steel barrel. It almost seemed medieval—

♦ **JGB:** It probably was! Things probably haven't changed much since the Ming dynasty.

It'll be fascinating to see how far liberalization really goes in China. **If a thousand million Chinese decide to, say, move into the electronics field, they'll be able to produce a video-recorder for a tenth of the price of the Japanese product. Hundreds of millions of busy fingers will take over the world.** They're tremendously industrious; they're a really hard-working people. And they plow everything back into their business.

If you take a small businessman in England, say a guy running a garage, if it's been a success he opens another garage. Then his wife wants a bigger house and a fur coat. He wants a Jaguar, so the business remains static. Now, a Chinese doing the same thing may open a restaurant. His family and the grandmother will all live in two rooms above the restaurant. And if the restaurant's a success, he'll open another restaurant, but they'll all go on living in the two rooms above the restaurant. Even when they've got *six* restaurants, they'll still be living in those two rooms, plowing it all back. Nobody will ever have any holiday; there'll be no damn mink coats or Jaguar cars.

♦ *V: In San Francisco, I see a number of Chinese running little sweatshops. You don't see Blacks operating sweatshops—*

♦ **JGB:** That's true: Blacks don't exploit other Blacks in the sweatshop method. Practically every other race and nationality exploits its own kind, given half a chance, but Blacks don't do that. I don't know about, say, the South. Do you have Black landowners who use stoop labor, paying tiny wages to other Blacks? I doubt it.

Here in London there's a big Indian immigrant population and they work all hours of the day and night in small businesses. They own the little grocery stores. Also, there are a lot in the rag trade. There are an awful lot of little businesses owned by Indians, staffed entirely by middle-aged women with families of their own they see for a few hours a day. And they spend all day churning out little piece goods for the clothing trade, being paid minute wages—equivalent to $2 a day or something—something tiny, working 12 hours a day. Ruthless exploitation by their own kind.

♦ *V: There have been articles in the local press about the Japanese mafia moving into California, which seemed far-fetched to me. I also read about them moving into the Philippines, running sex clubs—that also seemed exaggerated. But, the Japanese mafia do exist in Tokyo—*

♦ **JGB:** The Yakuza, or whatever you call them. Some wonderful photos surfaced in the press over here on TV. There was some big gang dispute about the succession to the leadership of one of the big Japanese crime syndicates. They showed these Yakuza at a funeral; there seemed to be thousands of these big men in blue suits. Apparently all of them were gangsters. It was quite bizarre.

♦ *V: I'm supposed to meet a couple Yakuza who are coming to San Francisco to show off their tattoos at a forthcoming tattoo convention.*

♦ **JGB:** Running a business like yours, do you get any attempts at extortion?

♦ *V: Book publishing? No.*

♦ **JGB:** It's only in the restaurant business, liquor stores—that sort of thing. Anything with a high cash turnover on the retail side.

♦ *V: You're referring to the "protection" racket, as they call it in the States. I think it may happen in San Francisco's Chinatown, but I never hear about it*—

♦ **JGB:** Yes. There was a report published here by some government-sponsored group about the Chinese community in England, which is very long-standing—there's been a Chinese community here since the turn of the century. And in the past twenty or thirty years there's been a huge influx of people from Hong Kong, Singapore and so on. But the amount of integration that's taken place is apparently very, very low. Something like half the Chinese population in England cannot speak English. Even kids attending school—you'd think they'd learn English despite themselves, but many of them, after completing school, go back into Chinese communities and stay there and start to lose their English. They don't report cases of crime against themselves to the police. But also, in areas of, say, women's medical complaints not necessarily gynecological at all, a Chinese woman will hesitate to go to an English doctor—the cross-cultural thing is too great. It was an extraordinary portrait, actually.

One's superficial impression is: they're all integrating marvelously, because when you go into a Chinese restaurant or take-away place you're always greeted by somebody who goes, "Hi, guys!" You think they're all like that. But behind that front person, that Chinese teenage girl who takes down your chop suey order, there are six people stir-frying who can't speak a word of English.

I imagine that until, say, the 1950s, there were probably substantial Italian and German communities in the New York area who didn't speak English—the older generations. I know that when I went to Canada in 1954, I spent a little time in Quebec, which is admittedly a French-speaking part of Canada, but I met a number of young Quebeçois who didn't speak any English. I think they just lived in French-speaking communities and never felt any need to learn to speak English.

But you'd think that in the age of TV, movies, radio, magazines, advertising—everything—that you couldn't *help* but learn the language of commerce and trade in the consumer goods society. But it doesn't seem to be the case—it's very strange. What the hell do you do when you buy a new car and can't read what all the knobs are supposed to be? Or even traffic signs, for that matter.

♦ *V: Or names. One thing I like about English pubs is the quaint names that people have dreamed up. "Elephant and Castle" is one.*

♦ **JGB:** Of course, there are changing fashions in those. A lot of the traditional ones: The Jolly Gardener, The Swan and the Crown—those names are now being replaced by a whole lot of more upscale names that make the pubs sound as if they're boutiques (Earl's) or fashionable *baths*. The big breweries who own all the pubs are refurbishing them constantly—you go into a pub one day and it's traditional Elizabethan England. The next week it's been redone up as a *Passage to India* Bombay-style Hotel. The next week it's something else. And the names change along with them. There are still some very nice old-style pubs. In the Bloomsbury area near the British Museum there should be some good ones.

♦ *V: Do you ever go to pubs, like the Crossroads down the road?*

♦ **JGB:** Not very often. I meet people at pubs around the river. Well, when my kids were here I used to sort of slip out for a pint, just for a change of scene. But **I'm not a beer drinker, so there's not much point in going to an English pub unless you're a beer drinker.** I do sometimes go to pubs when I'm in London and have half an hour to kill. But in the summer, there are pubs down by the river, and you can sit on the riverbank—it's very pleasant. I go to these around here.

♦ *V: I must admit I never go to a bar unless it's to keep someone company.*

♦ **JGB:** What does one measure of whiskey cost?

♦ *V: If you call the brand, $2.50 to $3.00.*

♦ **JGB:** That's quite expensive, by English standards. Here a shot of whiskey costs less than a pound; about 80p which would be about 75 cents. A pint of beer costs a pound. Pubs these days are really for younger people, with music, video games or *Space Invader*-type things, pool, and god knows what else—even striptease in some London pubs. [Graeme, Sinan, and baby Robert return from eating at Kew Gardens]

♦ **JGB:** Haven't you got a lot of electronic equipment?

♦ *GR: I've got tons of that.*

♦ **JGB:** Will you move that around with you, or do you sell it and buy more at the other end?

♦ *GR: It's really annoying—it becomes obsolete within about three months after them inventing it.*

♦ **JGB:** [admiring baby Robert] He's gorgeous, isn't he? He really is a Super Baby, I must say. Isn't he lovely?

♦ *GR: What are your plans, Jim? Working on something new?*

♦ **JGB:** I was just saying that I've done nothing for a year. Last week I wrote a short story and put it in the mail, but it's the first piece of writing I've done for about a year. I've been so wrapped up in the promotion of the book. It was only about a month ago that I was able to calm down—the phone was going all the time. It was actually wearing me out. I'd just had enough. I finally started turning things down; *enough is enough.* Publishers expect you to do everything—well I *did,* more or less. Were you here in September, October, November?

♦ *GR: We were here until about a month after the prize.*

♦ **JGB:** Well, that prize was only a marginal aspect of the total—it didn't actually affect me very much. But doing all the radio broadcasts and newspaper and TV interviews was terribly exhausting—going up to town. Actually, **it's finding somewhere to *park* that's a nightmare!**

♦ *GR: The new editions of your books look nice; a big improvement—*

♦ **JGB:** Yes, they are. I'm very pleased . . . That's a fine baby!

♦ *GR: Have you ever read anything by Jim Thompson?*

♦ **JGB:** No, I haven't, actually. Isn't that one of those reprinted "classic thrillers"?

♦ *V: He wrote* The Killer Inside Me, *written from the standpoint of the psychopath. It's very convincing.*

Sinan Leong Revell, Graeme Revell. Photo: Yoshitsugu Yubai

♦ **JGB:** When are you going to annex [Robert] into [SPK]? What was the youngest Osmond called?

♦ *GR: Jimmy. He joined the group at age two or three.*

♦ **JGB:** Well, there you are: Baby Rock, or something. We had a fiendish program over here, the little Muppets thing: Mini-Pops. That was incredible.

♦ *GR: A pederast's delight, really.*

♦ **JGB:** Right; a sort of pedophile's dream.

♦ *GR: It featured all these kids made up to the hilt, playing all these adult roles—*

♦ **JGB:** Vamping. These little five-year-old girls were glammed up with adult make-up, vamping to cutie-pie roles. I kept doing double-takes. Four-year-olds sexily flirting with three-year-old boys. It was quite bizarre. To this beat of rock music, pop music. It was a half-hour TV program with huge viewing figures.

♦ *GR: The kids were talented.*

♦ **JGB:** Lovely children. Gorgeous children.

♦ *GR: They were really playing all these adult sex roles together, at the age of about five.*

♦ **JGB:** It was quite something, actually. It was one of those programs that accidentally gets on the air before anybody realizes what's actually happening

♦ *GR: There was an American film,* Pretty Baby, *that starred a very young girl growing up in a New Orleans whorehouse . . . There's one thing I wanted to ask. The scene in* Empire of the Sun *where the coffins are going in and out on the tide: is that an imaginative one or is that a real one?*

♦ **JGB:** Yes, it's real.

♦ *GR: They actually set them afloat by the docks?*

♦ **JGB:** Yes; they were just taken for granted. **There were great *regattas* of corpses sailing out with the tide and floating back.** It wasn't maybe quite as *gymnastic* as I made it sound in the book, but it was a pretty brutal place, actually, during the war.

♦ *GR: Life would have been cheap—*

♦ **JGB:** Yes. [looking at infant Robert] **Having a child does change your perspective on time and your place in the universe. I got this terrible sense of the finiteness of time: my life was over, and this new generation had arrived to take over.**

♦ *GR: I think the only sense that I have is a feeling of how disgustingly* banal *the world is, and how the poor child's going to have to put up with fourscore and ten years of it! . . . We're going to go have dinner with Chris Bonn, one of the writers for the* NME. *He's quite a nice guy.*

♦ **JGB:** Have you met Charles Shaar Murray?

♦ *GR: He did quite a good article on you.*

♦ **JGB:** He's a nice guy. He rang me a few days ago to ask me if I'd write something for *NME,* which I'd been promising to do for years, but really never know what to write. They'd say, "Something like your *Why I Want to Fuck Ronald Reagan* piece." But if I actually wrote something like that, I wonder if they'd really publish it? I don't think they would, somehow. I think there might be a sort of *sudden faltering of the nerves.* Because *NME* is produced by the *Daily Mirror* or something; there must be a little overview.

♦ *GR: I don't read it much myself, but I think from memory if they do use "fuck" they have to print "f**k."*

♦ **JGB:** You've got to remember that in underground and independent publications you get four-letter words in the business. But those that are produced by big Fleet Street organizations tend to observe the "rules." Do you get "fuck" printed out in, say, the *New York Times?* No. And you don't see it in *Newsweek* or *Time* magazine, do you?

I haven't seen it for a long time, but Norman Mailer's ***The Naked and the Dead***—have the recent editions gotten away from "fug"? I remember that **when it was first published in 1950 or so, what was most shocking was that it had this word "fug" all through it.** Fug was shocking, for some peculiar reason!

♦ *GR: Fug is actually an English word as well. It's an old Anglo-Saxon word meaning "musty."*

♦ **JGB:** All of a sudden, "You fugging—"

♦ *GR: "You musty varlet!" You know, this guy we're going to see, Chris*

Bonn, is a potentially interesting guy. He's sort of given up his journalistic career to write travel books of the kind that people used to write at the turn of the century when it was really like a voyage of discovery. He's trying, anyway. I gave him Elias Canetti's Voices of Marrakesh.

♦ **JGB:** I give you full marks for this child—I think this is an amazing achievement. He's really lovely.

♦ *V: In America, having babies has gotten really "chic" in the last year, because who can afford to have them?*

♦ **JGB:** Yes, **it's a status symbol now, to be able to afford a child!**

♦ *GR: Speaking of bad language, in a magazine recently I saw a sex survey that was quite intriguing. They actually printed out the results. 44% of the readership, which is about the age of 19, have had anal sex, etc. Rather odd to read in a teenage girl's magazine!*

♦ **JGB:** Yes, I saw that survey, and it was rather baffling. To me, a lot of legs were being pulled! Maybe not.

I think Baby wants to go home. Walking all around Kew Gardens is exhausting, isn't it?

♦ *GR: It's a classic situation. We had to wait in a queue half an hour for a cup of tea in the kiosk, and when we got to the counter they had sold everything. All that was left were pre-packaged biscuits! That's typical, actually.*

♦ **JGB:** I watch the TV and saw your band [SPK] recently. You were on more times than you realize—

♦ *GR: About three times.*

♦ **JGB:** They used clips from a bigger appearance.

♦ *GR: We did a video recently which had 20 seconds shown on* The Old Grey Whistle Test. *The reason they wouldn't show any more of it was because we had a percussion track with all these machine gun or shotgun sounds—things like that.* **They wouldn't show the video because it showed a dummy going through a car windshield.**

♦ **JGB:** Ridiculous!

♦ *GR: But if you turn to other channels, there are all these American car crash shows.*

♦ **JGB:** Not only that, but you see dummies going through windshields in documentaries all the time.

♦ **GR:** *But the hypocrisy is that you can't show that in a medium which is supposedly for entertainment purposes only.*

♦ **V:** *They don't want you to confuse entertainment with education!*

♦ **JGB:** Right, right. Have you made a full-scale commercial video?

♦ **GR:** *Yes, a short one. We're supposed to be doing another one soon, but whether it will be really shown, we don't know. But to us that's the only point of working in a trivial medium right now: is just to try and* test it *a little bit.*

Tonight we're taking Vale to Skin Two, one of the few serious fetish clubs in London, where they're whipping each other out back in the toilets and so on. Sixty-year-old guys turn up in full wetsuit gear. Very strange. I can't relate to it at all, personally.

♦ **V:** *Jim, thanks very much for everything.*

♦ **JGB:** It's been a real treat seeing you. Best of luck for the future. The next time I see that little chap he'll probably be about this high [gestures shoulder-level]. Sadly, they grow so fast, don't they? ♦ ♦ ♦

Photo: Charles Gatewood

J. G. BALLARD: QUOTES
Does the Future Have a Future?

Amazing, provocative quotes from J. G. Ballard illuminating the human condition, arranged by topic. Edited by V. Vale with Mike Ryan. Dozens of gorgeous photos by Ana Barrado, Charles Gatewood and others. 416 pages, index, 5¼ x7", $19.99. Limited Autographed Flexibind Edition of only 250 copies, $60. Library Flexibind Edition (not signed; only 100 printed) $35.

NEW! FALL 2005

J.G. BALLARD CONVERSATIONS

The British visionary writer J.G. Ballard converses with V. Vale, Mark Pauline, Graeme Revell, Lynne Fox, and others. Plus an interview with Ballard's long-time archivist, David Pringle. Introduction by Joe Donohoe, taxicab driver. Stunning photos by Ana Barrado, Charles Gatewood and others. 360 pages, index, JGB recommended booklist, 5¼x7", $19.99.

Other Ballardiana:

- ✔ *RE/Search #8/9: J.G. Ballard.* Essential Interviews, History. $19.99
- ✔ Signed, Limited *Atrocity Exhibition* hardback, ed. 400. $50.00
- ✔ *Search & Destroy #10:* JGB interview (W.S. Burroughs intv, too!) $6
- ✔ JGB "Zodiac 2000" 11x17" *art centerfold!* in *R/S #1*—3 tabloids, $20

J.G. BALLARD

RE/Search 8/9: J.G. Ballard J.G. Ballard has predicted the future better than anyone else! His classic, *CRASH* (made into a movie by David Cronenberg) was the first book to investigate the psychopathological implications of the car crash, uncovering our darkest sexual crevices. He accurately predicted our media-saturated, information-overloaded environment where our most intimate fantasies and dreams involve pop stars and other public figures. Also contains a wide selection of quotations. "Highly recommended as both an introduction and a tribute to this remarkable writer."—*Washington Post* "The most detailed, probing and comprehensive study of Ballard on the market."—*Boston Phoenix.* "Open it up anywhere and you'll find inspiration."—Eric, *Show Cave* 8½x11″, 176 pp, illus. PB. **$19.99**

Atrocity Exhibition A dangerous imaginary work; as William Burroughs put it, "This book stirs sexual depths untouched by the hardest-core illustrated porn." Amazingly perverse medical illustrations by Phoebe Gloeckner, and haunting "Ruins of the Space Age" photos by Ana Barrado. Our most beautiful book, now used in many "Futurology" college classes. 8½x11″, 136 pp, illus. PB **$17.50. LIMITED EDITION OF SIGNED HARDBACKS with Dust Jacket, only $50**

HUMOR

RE/Search GUIDE TO BODILY FLUIDS by Paul Spinrad. Everything you ever wanted to know about: Mucus, Menstruation, Saliva, Sweat, Vomit, Urine, Flatus, Feces, Earwax & more. Topics include: constipation (such as its relationship to cornflakes and graham crackers!); history and evolution of toilet paper; farting; smegma and more! Ideal bathroom reading! A perfect gift for that difficult-to-shop-for person! A scientific text; educational, yet fun. 8½x11″, 148 pp., PB only. Almost out-of-print. **$15.99**

RE/Search 11: PRANKS! A prank is a "trick, a mischievous act, a ludicrous act." Although not regarded as poetic or artistic acts, pranks constitute an art form and genre in themselves. Here pranksters such as Timothy Leary, Abbie Hoffman, Monte Cazazza, Jello Biafra, Earth First!, Joe Coleman, Karen Finley, John Waters, Henry Rollins and more challenge the sovereign authority of words, images and behavioral convention. This iconoclastic compendium will dazzle and delight all lovers of humor, satire and irony. *Pranks!* is a classic of the *rebel literature canon.* The definitive treatment of the subject, offering extensive interviews with 36 contemporary tricksters . . . from the Underground's answer to Studs Terkel."—*Washington Post* "Pranks comes off as a statement of avant-garde philosophy—as a kind of wake-up call from an extended underground of Surrealist artists."—*S.F. Chronicle.* 8½x11″, 240 pp, 164 photos & illustrations, PB, **$19.99**

PUNK & D.I.Y.

PUNK '77: an inside look at the San Francisco rock n' roll scene, 1977 by James Stark

Covers the beginnings of the S.F. Punk Rock scene through the Sex Pistols' concert at Winterland in Jan., 1978, in interviews and photographs by James Stark. James was among the many artists involved in early punk. His photos were published in *New York Rocker, Search & Destroy* and *Slash*, among others. His posters for Crime are classics and highly prized collectors' items. Over 100 photos, including many behind-the-scenes looks at the bands who made things happen: Nuns,

Avengers, Crime, Screamers, Negative Trend, Dils, Germs, UXA, etc. Interviews with the bands and people early on the scene give intimate, often darkly humorous glimpses of events in a *Please Kill Me* (Legs McNeil) style. "The photos themselves, a generous 115 of them, are richly satisfying. They're the kind of photos one wants to see..."—*Puncture*. "I would recommend this book not only for old-timers looking for nostalgia, but especially to young Punks who have no idea how this all got off the ground, who take today's Punk for granted, to see how precarious it was at birth, what a fluke it was, and to perhaps be able to get a fresh perspective on today's scene needs . . ."—*Maximum Rock'n'Roll* 7½x10¼", 98 pp, 100+ photos, on archival paper. Only a few copies left. **$19.99.**

ZINES! Vol. One & ZINES! Vol. 2: Incendiary Interviews with Independent Publishers

Making Zines [self-publications] is part of the Punk Tradition of Do-It-Yourself. Following the imperative: "Destroy the society that seeks to destroy you!", *ZINES!* #1 & 2 show how easy it is to express yourself, and thus change your world. Fascinating conversations reveal a host of inspiring ideas for empowering your personal creativity and firing up your imagination and righteous indignation. Vol.1: *Beer Frame, Crap Hound, Fat Girl, Thrift SCORE, Bunny Hop, Housewife Turned Assassin, Meat Hook, X-Ray &* more! Vol. 2: *Murder Can Be Fun, 8-Track Mind, McJob, Dishwasher, Temp Slave,* Bruno Richard. EACH: 8½x11", quotations, excerpts, zine directory, historical essay, index. Vol.1: 184 pp. PB, **$18.99;** Vol.2: 148 pp. PB, **$14.99.**

RE/SEARCH #1, #2, #3—the *shocking tabloid issues.* **Deep into the heart of the Control Process; Creativity & Survival, past, present & future.** ◆ **#1:** J.G. Ballard, Cabaret Voltaire, Julio Cortazar, Octavio Paz, Sun Ra, The Slits, Conspiracies, Throbbing Gristle. **#2:** DNA, James Blood Ulmer, Z'ev, Aboriginal Music, Surveillance, SRL, Monte Cazazza, Diane Di Prima, German Electronic Music Chart. **#3:** Fela, New Brain Research, The Rattlesnake Man, Sordide Sentimental, New Guinea, Kathy Acker, Pat Califia, Joe Dante,

Johanna Went, SPK, Flipper, Physical Modification of Women. 11x17", Heavily illus. **$8 ea, all for $20** (Rare, not at stores, direct order only)

PUNK & D.I.Y.

SEARCH & DESTROY: The Complete Reprint (PUNK ROCK)

(in 2 big 10x15" PB volumes)
"The best punk publication ever"—Jello Biafra Facsimile editions (at 90% size) include all the interviews, articles, ads, illustrations and photos. Captures the enduring revolutionary spirit of punk rock, 1977-1979. Vol. 1 contains an abrasive intro-interview with Jello Biafra on the history and future of punk rock. Published by V. Vale before his

RE/Search series, *Search & Destroy* is a definitive, first-hand documentation of the punk rock cultural revolution, printed as it happened! Patti Smith, Iggy Pop, Ramones, Sex Pistols, Clash, DEVO, Avengers, Mutants, Crime, Dead Kennedys, William S. Burroughs, J.G. Ballard, John Waters, Russ Meyer, David Lynch, etc. EACH 10x15" PB book, 148pp,
Vol. 1: $30 new; $20 used. Vol. 2: $20. (extra shipping charge overseas)
Also available: SEARCH & DESTROY TABLOIDS #1-11, complete set only $40

REAL CONVERSATIONS: Henry Rollins, Jello Biafra, Lawrence Ferlinghetti & Billy Childish
New Edition!

V. Vale interviews four counterculture stalwarts, each with a proven track record of integrity and commitment, despite the perils of celebrity. Fascinating conversations on the effects of the Internet, Global Corporatism, the population bomb, mind control, branding and advertising. Other topics: Beat history, literary censorship and the fascist mentality; sex and relationships; rare record collecting. Full of lists of recommended books, films, websites. "Like most RE/Search books, *Real Conversations #1* flies by."—*Maximum Rock'n'Roll.* "*Real Conversations* will stir something in the reader, be it creative juices or righteous indignation."—*Weekly Planet.* "Thought-provoking ideas and good stories"—*Activist Guide.* 5x7", 240pp, 30 photos. **$14.99**

LOUDER FASTER SHORTER punk video by

Mindaugis Bagdon San Francisco, March 21, 1978. In the intense, original punk rock scene at the Mabuhay Gardens (the only club in town which would allow it), the AVENGERS, DILS, MUTANTS, SLEEPERS and UXA played a benefit for striking Kentucky coal miners ("Punks Against Oppression!"). One of the only surviving 16mm color documents of this short-lived era, *LOUDER FASTER SHORTER* captured the spirit and excitement of "punk rock" before revolt became style. Filmmaker Mindaugis Bagdon was a member of *Search & Destroy*, the publication which chronicled and catalyzed the Punk Rock Cultural Revolution of the '70s. "Exceptionally fine color photography, graphic design and editing."—*S.F. International Film Festival review,* 1980. 20 minute video in US NTSC VHS only. **$15.**

RE/SEARCH CATALOG

MUSIC: Read & Listen!

RE/Search #14 & 15: *Incredibly Strange Music* Vol. 1 & 2—BOOKS

These are the two books that launched the mad record-collecting fad of the '90s, inspiring publications like *Cool & Strange Music*. DJs, vinyl collectors and music lovers will greatly benefit by these illuminating books. Focus: "Easy listening," "exotica," and "celebrity" as well as recordings by (singing) cops and (polka-playing) priests, religious ventriloquists, astronauts, opera-singing parrots, and gospel by blind teenage girls with bouffant hairdos. EACH 8½x11″, 220 pp, over 200 photos, PB. Vol. 1: **$17.99**, Vol. 2, only a few copies left: **$25**

Incredibly Strange Music

Incredibly Strange Music, Vol. 1 An amazing anthology of outstanding, hard-to-find musical/spoken word gems from LPs that are as scarce as hens' teeth. These tracks must be heard to be believed! Cassette with original artwork packaging, sealed, only **$12**.

Incredibly Strange Music, Vol. 2 Lucia Pamela's barnyard frenzy "Walking on the Moon"; "How to Speak Hip" by Del Close & John Brent; "Join the Gospel Express" by singing ventriloquist doll Little Marcy, and many more musical gems. Full liner notes. **CD $16**

Ken Nordine COLORS A kaleidoscope of riotous sound and imagery. The pioneer of "Word Jazz" delivers "good lines" which are as smooth as water, inviting the listener to embark upon a musical fantasy. Contains extra tracks not on original vinyl record. **CD $16**

The Essential Perrey & Kingsley Two fantastic, classic LPs (*In Sound from Way Out* and *Kaleidoscopic Vibrations*) combined on one hard-to-find CD. Contains all the tracks recorded by the Perrey-Kingsley duo. Sounds as fresh as tomorrow! **CD $16**

Jean-Jacques Perrey CIRCUS OF LIFE The latest from French electronic music pioneer Jean-Jacques Perrey. Entertaining, danceable, and FUN! **CD $16**

CDs: **$16** each, cassette **$12**. (Special: ALL 4 CDs + 1 cassette: **$55 plus shipping.**)

SWING! The New Retro Renaissance Rockabilly, swing, lounge and Vegas Show Acts PLUS MORE. Fads can come and go, but the music of Lavay Smith, Big Sandy, and Sam Butera will remain with us! Learn about *the life:* vintage clothes, hairdos, shoes, cars, books, movies. Photos of bands, aerial dancers, classic cars, hairstyles, clothes, shoes, ties, accessories, and interiors of homes. 8½x11″, 224 pp, with hundreds of photographs; lists of recommended books, records and films; informative essays; movie reviews; index. PB. **$17.99**.

BODY MODIFICATION and S&M

RE/Search 12: MODERN PRIMITIVES [part of our S&M Library]The *New York Times* called this "the Bible of the underground tattooing and body piercing movement." *Modern Primitives* launched an entire '90s subculture. Crammed with illustrations & information, it's now considered a classic. The best texts on ancient human decoration practices such as tattooing, piercing, scarification and more. 279 eye-opening photos and graphics; 22 in-depth interviews with some of the most colorful people on the planet. "Dispassionate ethnography that lets people put their behavior in its own context."—*Voice Literary*
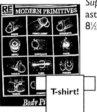 *Supplement* "The photographs and illustrations are both explicit and astounding . . . provides fascinating food for thought." —*Iron Horse* 8½x11", 212 pp, 279 photos and illustrations. PB **$19.50**

> **SPECIAL OFFER: *Modern Primitives* book & T-shirt gift-pack—only $25**

Modern Primitives T-shirt, beautiful design! **Multi-pastel colors on black 100% cotton T-shirt** Illustrations of 12 erotic piercings and implants. **Xtra Large only. Black, Purple, Red, Blue. $20.**

MODERN PAGANS: A Sequel to MODERN PRIMITIVES. Modern Primitives restored  to readers the right to symbolically decorate one's own body in accord with thousands of years of tradition. *Modern Pagans* restores the experience of poetic, Nature-based ritual celebration, especially important in child-raising. Children love the original "Easter" egg hunt and the Maypole. Charles Gatewood, Starhawk, Thorn Coyle, Isaac Bonewits, Oberon & Morning Glory, Sam Webster, and many others eloquently offer a vision of living counter to our bankrupt Western society which has lost its mythology and purpose. Densely informative about all aspects of Pagan cosmology, creativity, child-rearing, history, activism, ritual, ceremony, aesthetics, and sex magic. 8x10", 212 pp., many photos, lists, guides, etc. **$19.95.**

BOB FLANAGAN: SUPERMASOCHIST [part of our S&M Library] Bob Flanagan grew up with Cystic Fibrosis. His childhood suffering was principally alleviated by masturbation, wherein pain and pleasure became linked, resulting in his lifelong practice of extreme masochism, branding, piercing, whipping, bondage and endurance trials. ". . . an eloquent tour through the psychic terrain of SM, discussing the most severe sexual diversions with the humorous detachment of a shy, clean living nerd. I came away from the book wanting to know this man."—*Details Magazine.* 8½x11", 128 pp, 125 photos & illustrations. PB. **$19.99.**

The Torture Garden by Octave Mirbeau This book was once described as the "most sickening work of art of the nineteenth century!" Long out of print, Octave Mirbeau's macabre classic (1899) features a corrupt Frenchman and an insatiably cruel Englishwoman who meet and then frequent a fantastic 19th century Chinese garden where torture is practiced as an art form. The fascinating, horrific narrative slithers deep into the human spirit, uncovering murderous proclivities and demented desires. "Hot with the fever of ecstatic, prohibited joys, as cruel as a thumbscrew and as luxuriant as an Oriental tapestry. Exotic, perverse . . . hailed by the critics."—Charles Hanson Towne 8½x11″, 120 pp, 21 mesmerizing photos. **Hardcover only** (edition of just 100 copies, with beautiful dust jacket) **$40 ... A few paperbacks left for $25.**

MASOCHISM, FEMINISM

Confessions of Wanda von Sacher-Masoch Married for 10 years to Leopold von Sacher-Masoch (author: *Venus in Furs* & many other novels) whose whip-and-fur bedroom games spawned the term "masochism," Wanda's story is a feminist classic from 100 years ago. She was forced to play "sadistic" roles in Leopold's fantasies to ensure the survival of herself & their 3 children–games which called into question who was the Master and who the Slave. Besides being a compelling story of a woman's search for her own identity, strength and, ultimate-  ly, complete independence, this is a true-life adventure story–an odyssey through many lands peopled by amazing characters. Here is a woman's consistent unblinking investigation of the limits of morality and the deepest meanings of love. "Extravagantly designed in an illustrated, oversized edition that is a pleasure to hold. It is also exquisitely written, engaging and literary and turns our preconceptions upside down."—*L.A. Reader* 8½x11″, 136 pp, illustrated, PB. Only a few copies left: $19.99

RE/Search 13: Angry Women 16 cutting-edge performance artists discuss critical questions such as: How can revolutionary feminism encompass wild sex, humor, beauty, spirituality *plus* radical politics? How can a powerful movement for social change be *inclusionary?* Wide range of topics discussed *passionately*. **Included:** Karen Finley, Annie Sprinkle, bell hooks, Diamanda Galas, Kathy Acker, Susie Bright, Sapphire. Armed with contempt for dogma, stereotype & cliché, these visionaries probe into our social foundation of taboos, beliefs & totalitarian linguistic contradictions from whence spring (as well as thwart) theories, imaginings, behavior & dreams. "The view here is largely pro-sex, pro-porn, and pro-choice."—*Village Voice* "This book is a Bible—it hails the dawn of a new era–the era of an inclusive, fun, sexy feminism. Every interview contains brilliant moments of wisdom." *Am. Bk Review* 8½x11″, 240 pp, 135 illus. PB. RE/Search edition out-of-print, only a few copies left: **$18.99**

www.researchpubs.com • (415) 362-1465 • info@researchpubs.com

TWO BY DANIEL P. MANNIX

MEMOIRS OF A SWORD SWALLOWER Not for the faint-of-heart, this book will delight all lovers of sideshows & carnivals. "I probably never would have become America's leading fire-eater if Flamo the Great hadn't happened to explode that night . . ." So begins this true story of life with a traveling carnival, peopled by amazing characters—the Human Ostrich, the Human Salamander, Jolly Daisy, etc.—who commit outrageous feats of wizardry. This is one of the only *authentic* narratives revealing the "tricks" (or rather, painful skills) involved in a sideshow, .and is invaluable to anyone aspiring to this profession. OVER 50 RARE PHOTOS taken by Mannix in the 1930s and never before seen! Sideshow aficionados will delight in finally being able to see some of their favorite "stars" captured in candid moments. Rugged Individualist *Americana* history at its best.
8½x11", 128 pp, 50+ photos, index, PB, **$15.99**
Rare, autographed (in 1997) copies of paperback available for only $30

FREAKS: We Who Are Not As Others

Amazing Photos! A fascinating, classic book, based on Mannix's personal acquaintance with sideshow stars such as the Alligator Man and the Monkey Woman. Read all about the notorious love affairs of midgets; the amazing story of the Elephant Boy; the unusual amours of Jolly Daisy, the fat woman; hermaphrodite love; the bulb-eating Human Ostrich, etc. 8½x11", 124 pp, 88 wonderful, nostalgic yet shocking photos. PB. **$15.95** Author died in 1997. **Autographed hardbounds (a few left) $50**

OUT-OF-PRINT

Wild Wives A classic of hard-boiled fiction, Willeford's *Wild Wives* is amoral, sexy, and brutal. Written in a sleazy San Francisco hotel in the early '50s while on leave from the Army, Willeford creates a tale of deception featuring the crooked detective Jacob C. Blake and his nemesis—a beautiful, insane young woman. Set in 50's San Francisco! 5x7", 108 pp. PB. **$10.99**
ME & BIG JOE by Mike Bloomfield with Scott Summerville. Classic coming-of-age story with young Bloomfield meeting Chicago blues musicians, most scarily Big Joe Williams. Out-of-print, 5x7", PB. **$8.**
BOB FLANAGAN: SUPER-MASOCHIST. Made into a movie. RE/Search's most hardcore-illustrated book, yet surprisingly engaging. A few copies left, 8.5x11." **$19.99**
SEARCH & DESTROY Tabloids #1-11 full set. 1977-1979. Classic punk. **only $40**
KATHY ACKER: GREAT EXPECTATIONS. RE/Search edition fabulously rare, PB **$50**
INCREDIBLY STRANGE MUSIC #1 CD, long out-of-print. Mint/sealed. **$30**
W. S. BURROUGHS & J.G. BALLARD interviews in Search & Destroy #10 $6
SRL piece by **Mark Pauline** in **RE/Search #2 tabloid** (mint, from 1981) **only $8**
JOHN WATERS interview in *Search & Destroy #7* (from 1978!; mint) **$6**
HERE TO GO extremely rare R/S hardback by Brion Gysin, Burroughs (ed. 100) **$100**
RE/SEARCH GUIDE TO BODILY FLUIDS. Funny! Almost out-of-print. **$15.99**

353

W.S.Burroughs, I.S.Films, Industrial

R/S 4/5: WS Burroughs, Brion Gysin, Throbbing Gristle A great, unknown Burroughs-Gysin treasure trove of radical ideas! Compilation of interviews, scarce fiction, essays: this is a manual of incendiary insights. Strikingly designed; filled with radical references. **Topics discussed**: biological warfare, utopias, con men, lost inventions, the JFK killing, Hassan I Sabbah, cloning, the cut-up theory, Moroccan trance music, the Dream Machine, Manson, the media control process, prostitution, and more. Includes part of *Revised Boy Scout Manual.* 8½x11″, 100 pp, 58 photos & illus. PB, **$15.99** Order Direct!

William S. Burroughs T-shirt! Black & red design on white, 100% cotton T-shirt.
"We intend to destroy all dogmatic verbal systems."—*WSB*. Original design hand-screened on 100% heavyweight cotton T-Shirt. **$20** XL only.

RE/Search 6/7: Industrial Culture Handbook

This book provided a radical education for many of the most subversive artists practicing today. The rich ideas of the *Industrial Culture* movement's performance artists and musicians are nakedly exposed: *Survival Research Laboratories, Throbbing Gristle, Cabaret Voltaire, SPK, Non, Monte Cazazza, Johanna Went, Sordide Sentimental, R&N, & Z'ev.* **Topics include:** brain research, forbidden medical texts & films, creative crime & *interesting* criminals, modern warfare & weaponry, neglected gore films & their directors, psychotic lyrics in past pop songs, and *art brut.* Many book lists, film lists, and record lists. 8½x11″, 140 pp, 179 photos & illust. PB, **$25**

RE/Search 10: INCREDIBLY STRANGE FILMS

First to champion Herschell Gordon Lewis, Russ Meyer, Larry Cohen, Ray Dennis Steckler, Ted V. Mikels, Doris Wishman & others who had been critically consigned to the ghettos of gore & sexploitation films, this book allowed artists to rationally explain how they made gripping dramas with zero budgets and overflowing imaginations. 13 interviews, A-Z of film personalities, "Favorite Films" list, quotations, bibliography, filmography, film synopses, & index. "Flicks like these are subversive alternatives to the mind control propagated by the mainstream media."—*Iron Horse* "The interviews are intelligent, enthusiastic and articulate."—*Small Press.* Has been used as textbook at UC Berkeley, etc. 8½x11″, 224 pp, 157 photos & illus. PB, last of this printing: **$17.99**

LIBRARIES & PACKAGES

Package deal: RE/Search #1-16 (no #6/7,#15; save $50!)

Offer includes *RE/Search #1, 2 & 3* tabloids, *#4/5: Burroughs/Gysin/ Throbbing Gristle, #8/9: J.G. Ballard, #10: Incredibly Strange Films, #11: Pranks!, #12: Modern Primitives, #13: Angry Women, #14: Incredibly Strange Music, Vol. 1,* and *#16: RE/Search Guide to Bodily Fluids.* $175 worth of books for **$125** (plus shipping). RE/Search founder V. Vale will autograph **upon request.**

The Other Package deal: 8 books for $80

Offer includes *Freaks: We Who Are Not As Others, Memoirs of a Sword Swallower, The Confessions of Wanda von Sacher-Masoch, Wild Wives, Swing, Zines Vol. One, Zines Vol. Two, and Me and Big Joe.* **$80.** This is a "good deal" for people who wish to complete their collection, and who also like to give hard-to-find gifts.

Our rare, limited edition, autographed hardbounds

The Atrocity Exhibition autographed by J.G. Ballard, ed. 400. Dust jacket. $60
Freaks autographed by Daniel P. Mannix, only a few left. Dust jacket. $60
Torture Garden autographed by publisher V. Vale, ed. 100! Dust jacket. $40
J.G. Ballard QUOTES Flexibind, edition of 250 signed & numbered. $60.

Incredibly Strange Music Packages

1) Incredibly Strange Music Vol. One BOOK and companion cassette. **$25.**
2) Incredibly Strange Music CDS & cassette: *ISM Vol.1* cassette, *ISM Vol.2, Best of Perrey & Kingsley, Ken Nordine's COLORS,* and Jean-Jacques Perrey's *Circus of Life.* $76 value; 5 items for **$55.**

RE/SEARCH PUBLICATIONS - V. Vale, founder, 1977
20 ROMOLO #B
SAN FRANCISCO, CA 94133
tel (415) 362-1465 fax (415) 362-0742
EMAIL: *info@researchpubs.com*

www.researchpubs.com
Phone, fax, mail or email orders
Please contact us for
Wholesale Information

SHIPPING USA: $4 for first item, $1 per additional item. (Add $2/item Priority Mail USA) Note: extra ship. costs for *Search & Destroy* books
Overseas Global Air: $11 per item. Please call or email for an economy overseas shipping quote
Call us for a catalog! (Our best catalog is at *www.researchpubs.com*)

INDEX

France 324-326,332-333
Freud, Sigmund 22,53,110,230-231
Game Theory 9,11-12,
gated community 31,70-73,117
Genet, Jean 142
genetic engineering 291-292
Gere, Richard 184-185
Gibson, William 226
Gingrich, Newt 22
Ginsberg, Allen 142
Giorno, John 157
Godard, Jean-Luc 44
Gone With the Wind 271-272
Grauerholz, James 157
Graves, Robert 170
Greene, Graham 233,243
guns 313-314,319-320
Gysin, Brion 318,322

H I J

Hamilton-Paterson, James 214
Hearst, Patty 266
Hemingway, Ernest 162,183,216
heroin 92,330
Hinckley, John 145
Hirst, Damien 120
Hitchcock, Alfred 228
Hitler 9-10,19-20,53,74,80,100,128,307
Hopper, Dennis 306
Huntington, Samuel 13,97
Hughes, Robert 55
Hussein, Saddam 10,51,87,105,176
imagination 119
Incredibly Strange Films 260,262,300
Incredibly Strange Music 260-261
Independence Day 15
infantilization 28,68-70,73,75
Inquisition, The 55
Internet 34,39-41,58-59,62-64,67,70,
    78-79,90-91,109-110,115-116
"Islam" 96-99
Jarry, Alfred 163
Johns, Capt. W.E. 160
Jung, Carl 230

K L M

Kahle, Brewster 39
Kafka 162,182-183,216
Kennedy, J.F. 12,85-88,178,201,204,227
Kennedy, Jacqueline 177-178,205
Khadafi 10,127-128
Kinski, Nastassia 150

Kornbluth, C.M. 183
Kurzweil, Ray 64
Lakoff, George 22
Last Year at Marienbad 82,140
Las Vegas 43-44,71-72,113
LaVey, Anton 292-293
Le Pen, Jean 50
Lessing, Doris 274
Lewin, Albert 228
Lewinsky, Monica 88-89
London Dungeon 321
Los Angeles 304-305,311-313
LSD 188
Lynch, David 113,196
MacLean, Paul (3-brain theory) 23
Mad Max, Mad Max 2 11,197
Madonna 178
Mafia 307-308
Magritte, Rene 181,279
Mailer, Norman 213,342
Mann, Thomas 162
Marlin, Brigid 218-219
Marx, Karl 220-222
Matrix, The 65
Matta, Roberto 93
McCarthy era 80
Mead, Margaret 259
Melville, Herman 232
Merril, Judith 245
Millennium People 12,242
Miller, Daniel 219
Modern Pagans 17
Modern Primitives 259-260,309
Monroe, Marilyn 178,201
Moorcock, Michael 224
Moore, Michael 34,74
Mori, Mariko 121
Moses and Monotheism 22
music & instruments 65,117-119
"Muslims" 13,16-19,96-99
mythologies 160,166-167,169

N O P

Naked and the Dead, The 342
NASA 93-94
Nazism 19,24,53,74,99-101
New Dark Age 24-25,38-39
Newton, Helmut 217
Nixon 106,134,166
Numan, Gary 220
On the Beach (by Nevil Shute) 142
operas 121

J.G. BALLARD READING LIST

Annotated Alice, The
Apollinaire
Aulier, Dan ed.
 Hitchcock's Secret
 Notebooks
Baudrillard, Jean
 America; The Gulf
 War Did Not Take
 Place
Berkoff, Steven Tough
 Acts
Biskind, Peter Easy
 Riders, Raging Bulls
Borges, Jorge Luis
Bowles, Paul The
 Sheltering Sky, etc
Bradbury, Ray
Brown, Andrew
 Darwin Wars
Breton, André
Bruce, Lenny
Burleigh, Michael The
 Third Reich: A New
 History
Burroughs, William
Cain, James M.
Campbell, Joseph
 Hero w/1,000 Faces
Camus, Albert The
 Stranger
Capote, Truman
Carey, John ed. Faber
 Book of Utopias
Carpenter,
 Humphrey Geniuses
 Together
Carroll, Lewis
Catch-22 (Jos. Heller)
Celine
Cervantes, Miguel
Chandler, Raymond
Cloetta, Yvonne In
 Search of a
 Beginning
Connolly, Cyril The
 Unquiet Grave
Coleridge, Samuel T.
Conrad, Joseph
Crosland, Margaret
 The Enigma of

Giorgio de Chirico
David, Elizabeth
Davis, Mike City of
 Quartz; Dead Cities
Dawkins, Richard The
 Selfish Gene
de Chazal, Malcolm
De Sade, D.A.F. The
 120 Days of Sodom
Defoe, Daniel
Demuth, Charles
Dick, Philip K.
Dostoyevsky, Fyodor
Durrell, Lawrence
Evans, Robert The
 Kid Stays in the
 Picture
Fitzgerald, F. Scott
Fraser-Cavassoni,
 Natasha Sam
 Spiegel
Frayling, Christopher
 Sergio Leone
Freud, Sigmund The
 Interpretation of
 Dreams, et al
Genet, Jean
Goethe
Golding, William Lord
 of the Flies
Goncourt Brothers
 Journal
Graves, Robert:
 Goodbye to All That;
 White Goddess
Gray, John Straw Dogs
Gray's Anatomy
Greene, Graham
Hamilton-Paterson,
 James
Heilbroner, Robert
Hemingway, Ernest
 Col. Short Stories
Henry, O.
Hitler, Adolf Mein
 Kampf
Hoeg, Peter Smilla's
 Sense of Snow
Hughes, Robert
Huxley, Aldous Brave

New World
Huysmans, J.K.
Irvine, Lucy Castaway
Jarry. Alfred
Kafka, Franz
Keats, John
Kerouac, Jack On the
 Road
Lautréamont Song of
 Maldoror
Leiber, Fritz
Lewis, Wyndham
 Blast
Lindsay, David A
 Voyage to Arcturus
Little Nemo in
 Slumberland
Los Angeles Yellow
 Pages
Lowe, John Edward
 James
Lynas, Mark High
 Tide: News From a
 Warming World
MacPherson, Mal.
 The Black Box
Matheson, Richard
McManus, Chris Right
 Hand, Left Hand
Melville, Herman
Miller, Henry Tropic
 of Cancer
Morris, James Venice
Orwell, George 1984
Overy, Richard
 Interrogations: The
 Nazi Elite in Allied
 Hands
Pettifer, Julian and
 Turner, Nigel eds.
 Automania
Pinker, Steven The
 Blank Slate
Plato
Poe, Edgar Allan
Purser, Philip Where
 Is He Now?
Pohl, Frederick
Rime of the Ancient
 Mariner

Rimbaud, Arthur
Secret Life of Salvador
 Dali, The
Shakespeare, William
Sheckley, Robert
Shelley, Mary
 Frankenstein
Simmons, Sylvie A
 Fistful of Gitanes
Sinclair, Iain London
 Orbital
Southern, Terry
Spencer, Stanley
Story of O, The
Surrealists, The
Swift, Jonathan A
 Modest Proposal
Thomson, Ian
 Bonjour Blanc
Thomson, David A
 Biographical
 Dictionary of Film
Toussaint-Samat,
 Maguelonne: A
 History of Food
Trevor-Roper, Patrick
 The World Through
 Blunted Sight
Vasari Lives
Warhol, Andy
Waugh, Evelyn The
 Loved One
Wells, H. G.
West, Nathanael Day
 of the Locust, etc
Wilson, Andrew
 Beautiful Shadow: A
 Life of Patricia
 Highsmith
Wolfe, Bernard
 Limbo aka Limbo 90
Woolf, Virginia Mrs.
 Dalloway
Wordsworth
Wright, Robert The
 Moral Animal
Young, Gavin In
 Search of Conrad
LIST COMPILED BY
 VERMILION SANDS